# CRAVE

## A NOVEL of the FALLEN ANGELS

## J.R. WARD

| Bi 10/10 | HC 2/14 | | |
|---|---|---|---|
| | | | |

piatkus

PIATKUS

First published in the United States in 2010 by New American Library,
A Division of Penguin group (USA) Inc, New York
First published in Great Britain as a paperback original in 2010 by Piatkus

A CIP catalogue record for this book
is available from the British Library.

ISBN 978-0-349-40019-8

Typeset in Times by Palimpsest Book Production Limited,
Falkirk, Stirlingshire
Printed in the UK by
CPI Mackays, Chatham ME5 8TD

Papers used by Piatkus are natural, renewable and recyclable
products sourced from well-managed forests and certified
in accordance with the rules of the Forest Stewardship Council.

Piatkus
An imprint of
Little, Brown Book Group
100 Victoria Embankment
London EC4Y 0DY

An Hachette UK Company
www.hachette.co.uk

www.piatkus.co.uk

For Judith Peoples, PhD,
and all her good works—
she is proof positive that angels can have GREAT shoes
while their feet touch the ground.

# ACKNOWLEDGMENTS

To Kara Welsh, for everything!
And with thanks to Leslie Gelbman and Claire Zion
and everyone at NAL who are so amazing.

Thank you to Steve Axelrod, my voice of reason.

With huge props and thanks to Team Waud: D, LeElla,
and Nath, without whom none of this would be possible—
what would I do without you? And with a shout-out to Jac
(and his Gabe!): My kitchen is your kitchen. No, really.
Please. Don't make me beg.

Thank you also to Ann, Lu, and Opal—the most
incredible line tamers I've ever seen! And Ken—
I'm trainable, see? I really am—you can send back
the Gorilla Glue. Also to Cheryle, who I take
orders from because I'm no fool.

With big hugs to all the mods on the boards—
I'm so grateful for everything you do out
of the kindness of your hearts.

Tremendous thanks to my C.P., Jessica Andersen,
who has been endlessly supportive and smart and
lovely and brilliantly funny for all these years.
I still wish I were in your top five. *sigh*

And, of course, with thanks to Mother Sue (Grafton).

As always with love to my mother and my husband and
my family and the better half of WriterDog.

# CRAVE

# Prologue

*The desert, far from Caldwell, NY, or
Boston, MA, or . . . sanity.*

*Some two years after the fact, when Jim Heron was no
longer in special ops, he would reflect that Isaac Rothe,
Matthias the Fucker, and he, himself, had all changed their
lives the night that bomb went off in the sand.*

*Of course, at the time, none of them knew what it all
meant, or where it was all going. But that was life: Nobody
got a guided tour to their own theme park. You had to hop
on the rides as they presented themselves, never knowing
whether you would like the one you were in line for . . . or if
the bastard was going to make you throw up your corn dog
and your cotton candy all over the place.*

*Maybe that was a good thing, though. As if back then he
would have believed he'd end up duking it out with a demon,
trying to save the world from damnation?*

*Come on.*

*But that night, in the dry cold that washed in the sec-
ond the sun went down over the dunes, he and his boss had
walked into a minefield . . . and only one had walked out.*

*The other? Not so much . . .*

*     *     *

"This is it," Matthias said as they came up to an abandoned village that was the color of the caramel on a Friendly's sundae.

They were fifteen miles northwest from where they were staying in a barracks full of army boys. Being that he and his boss were XOps, they were outside the stream of defined corps, which worked to their benefit: Soldiers like them carried IDs from all branches of the service and used them whenever it suited.

The "village" was more like four crumbling stone structures and a bunch of wood-and-tarp huts. As they approached, Jim's balls went tight when his green night-vision goggles picked up movement all over the place. He hated those fucking tarps—they flapped in the wind, their shadows darting around like fast-footed people who had guns. And grenades. And all kinds of sharp and shiny.

Or in this case, grungy and gritty.

He hated desert assignments; better to kill in civilization. Although a proper urban or even suburban assignment carried more exposure, at least you had a shot at knowing what was coming at you. Out here, people had resources he was unfamiliar with and that always made him twitchy as fuck.

Plus he didn't trust the man he was with. Yeah, Matthias was the head of the organization with a direct line to God. Yeah, Jim had trained with the guy way back when. Yeah, he'd been under him for the last decade.

But all of that just made him more certain he didn't want to be alone with the big man—and yet here they were, at a "village" in the fine township of Nowhere-anyone-could-find-a-body-ville.

A gust of wind went Nike across the flat landscape, sprinting over the sand, picking up those tiny little particles, and carrying all of them right smack into the collar of his digital-fatigues. Beneath his black, lace-up boots, the ground was constantly shifting, as if he were an ant walking across the back of a giant and irritating the piss out of the bastard.

You began to feel that at any minute, a great palm could come down out of the sky and flatten you.

This trek to the east had been Matthias's idea. Something that couldn't be discussed anywhere else. So naturally, Jim had worn a Kevlar vest and about forty pounds of weapons. Along with water. MREs.

He was a pack animal for real.

"Over here," Matthias said, ducking into the doorless entry of one of the stone structures.

Jim paused and looked around. Nothing but tarps doing the cabbage patch, as far as he knew.

He got out both his guns before going inside. Bottom line? This was the perfect locale for a forcible inquisition. He had no idea what he'd done or what he'd learned to warrant an interrogation, but one thing he was clear on — there was no reason to run. If that was the "because" he'd been brought here for, he was going to go in and find another two or three XOps guys in there to work him over while Matthias asked the questions. If he bolted? They'd just hunt him down all over the globe, even if it took weeks.

Could explain why Isaac Rothe had shown up this afternoon with Matthias's protégé and second in command. That pair were straight-up killers, a couple of pit bulls ready to go for anyone's throat.

Yup, this made sense and he should have figured it out sooner — although even if he had, there was no escape from a reckoning. Nobody got out of XOps alive. Not the operatives, not the fringe-playing intel guys, not the bosses, either. Die with your boots on was the way you lived — not that you knew that going in.

And the thing was, he had been thinking of ways to get out. Killing people for a living was all he knew how to do, but it was starting to fuck with his head. Maybe Matthias had somehow tweaked to that.

Time to the face the music, Jim thought as he stepped through the doorway.

Might as well give 'em a fight—

Just Matthias. No one else.

Jim slowly lowered his guns and scanned the cramped space again. According to his night goggles, there was only the other man. With a flick of a switch, he changed to heat-seeking mode. Nothing but Matthias. Still.

"What's going on?" Jim demanded.

Matthias was over in the far corner, about ten feet away. When the man's hands came up from his sides, Jim flipped his SIGs back into firing position . . . but all his boss did was shake his head and loosen his gun belt. A quick toss and it was in the sand.

And then he took a step forward, opening his mouth and saying something quietly—

Light. Sound. Blast of energy.

Then . . . nothing but the soft rain of sand and debris.

Jim came back to consciousness sometime later. The explosion had thrown him against the stone wall, knocking him cold, and going by how stiff he was, he could have been out for a while.

After a couple minutes of what-the-fuck, he sat up cautiously, wondering if anything was broken—

Across the way, there was a pile of rags where Matthias had once been.

"Jesus Christ . . ." Jim repositioned his night goggles and retrieved his weapons, then crawled through the sand to his boss.

"Matthias . . . oh, fucking A . . ."

The man's lower leg looked like a root that had been torn up out of the ground, the limb nothing but a ragged stump that was shredded at the end. And there were patches of darkness on his fatigues that had to be blood.

Jim checked the pulse at the neck. There was one, but it was faint and uneven.

Unbuckling and shucking his belt, he cranked the leather around Matthias's upper calf and pulled hard, torniqueting the limb. Then he quickly searched for other inj—

Shit. When Matthias had been tossed back, he'd fallen onto a wooden spike. The damn thing went right through him, the toothpick to his pig in a blanket.

Jim pretzeled up and tried to see whether it could stay in place to get Matthias out of here. . . .

It appeared to be freestanding. Good.

". . . Dan . . . ny . . . boy . . ."

Jim frowned and looked at his boss. "What?"

Matthias's eyes opened like his lids were steel shutters he could barely raise. "Leave . . . me."

"You're blown to shit—"

"Leave me—"

"Fuck that." Jim reached for his transistor and prayed that Isaac, not that freak second in command, answered. "Come on . . . come on. . . ."

"What y'all needin'?" The soft Southern drawl coming over his earpiece was good news.

Thank God for Isaac. "Matthias is down. Bomb. Make sure we're not target practice as we come into camp."

"How bad?"

"Bad."

"Where y'all at? I'll get a Land Rover and pick you up."

"We're forty-six degrees n—"

The gun went off across the way, a bullet slicing through the air right next to Jim's ear—to the point where he assumed he'd been hit in the head and the pain had yet to register. As he braced himself on one palm, Matthias let his SIG fall to the side . . . but what do you know, Jim did not fall over thanks to some kind of cranial wound. Warning shot, evidently.

His boss's one working eye shone with unholy light. "Get yourself . . . out . . . alive."

Before Jim could tell Matthias to shut the fuck up, he became aware that something was biting into the hand he'd put out. Lifting the thing up, he found . . . part of the bomb's detonator.

Turning it over and over, at first he didn't understand what he was looking at.

And then he knew all too well what it was.

Narrowing his eyes on Matthias, he put the fragment in his front pocket and crawled over to his boss.

"You're not playing me like this," Jim said grimly. "No fucking way."

Matthias started to babble just as squawking curses came through the earpiece.

"I'm okay," Jim said to Isaac. "Misfire. I'm starting back for camp. Make sure we're not shot as we approach."

The Southerner's voice became instantly strong and steady, just like the guy's killing hand. "Where you at. I'll just get a—"

"No. Stay put. Find a medic on the QT and make sure they can keep their mouth shut. And we're going to need a chopper. He's going to have to be airlifted—discreetly. No one can know about this."

The last thing he needed was Isaac out in the middle of the night looking for them. The guy was the only thing standing between Jim and an accusation that he'd murdered the head of the deadliest shadow organization in the U.S. government.

He'd never live that one down. Literally.

But at least the hush-hush was not going to be a news-flash. Keeping quiet about shit was the MO in XOps—no one knew exactly how many operatives there were or where they went or what they did or whether they went by their own name or an alias.

"Do you hear me, Isaac," he demanded. "Get me what I need. Or he's a dead man."

"Roger that," came the reply over the earpiece. "Over and out."

After confiscating the gun that had been put to use, Jim picked up his boss, settled the dead, dripping weight on his shoulders, and started hoofing it.

Out of the stone shack. Out into the blustering, frigid night. Across the sand dunes.

His compass kept him on the right track, true north orientating him and leading him on through the darkness. Without the point of reference, he would have been utterly lost as the desert was a mirrored landscape, nothing but a reflection of itself in all directions.

Fucking Matthias.

God damn him.

Then again, assuming the guy lived, he'd just given Jim his ticket out of XOps . . . so in a way, he owed the guy his life: The bomb was one of their own and Matthias had known precisely where to put his foot in the sand. And that only happened if you wanted to blow your damned self up.

Guess Jim wasn't the only one who wanted to be free.

Surprise, surprise.

# CHAPTER

## 1

*South Boston, present day*

"Hey! Wait a— Save that shit for the ring!"

Isaac Rothe shoved the advertising flyer across the car hood, ready to slam the damn thing down again if he had to. "What's my picture doing on this?"

The fight promoter seemed more interested in the damage to his Mustang, so Isaac reached out and grabbed the guy by the front of the jacket. "I said, what's my face doing on here?"

"Relax, will ya—"

Isaac brought the two of them close as sandwich bread and got a whiff of the pot the SOB smoked. "I told you. No pictures of me. *Ever.*"

The promoter's hands lifted in the conversational equiv of a tap-out. "I'm sorry . . . I'm really . . . Look, you're my best fighter—you get me the crowds. You're like the star of my—"

Isaac curled his fist tighter to cut off the ego stroking. "No pictures. Or no fighting. We clear?"

The promoter swallowed hard and squeaked, "Yeah. Sorry."

Isaac released his hold and ignored the wheezing as he crumpled the image of his face into a litter ball. Looking around the abandoned warehouse's parking lot, he cursed himself. Stupid. Fucking stupid of him to have trusted the smarmy bastard.

The thing was, names were not all that important. Anybody could type up a Tom, Dick, or Harry on an ID card or a birth certificate or a passport. All you needed was the right typeface and a laminating machine that could do holograms. But your mug shot, your face, your puss, your piehole . . . unless you had the funds and the contacts to plastic-surgery your ass, that was the one true identifier you had.

And his had just gotten a workout at Kinko's. God only knew how many people had seen it.

Or who had zeroed in on his whereabouts.

"Look, I was just doing you a favor." The promoter smiled, flashing a gold grille. "The bigger the crowd, the more money you make —"

Isaac shoved his forefinger up the guy's stovepipe. "You need to shut the fuck up right now. And remember what I said."

"Yeah. Okay. Sure."

There were a number of all-rights, no-problems, and anything-you-likes that followed, but Isaac turned his back on the babble, babble.

All around, grown men were getting out of cars and shoving at each other like fifteen-year-olds, the bunch of juiced-up, armchair quarterbacks ready to peanut-gallery it up: The closest they were going to get to the octagon was standing on the outside of the chicken wire looking in.

The fact that Isaac was almost done with this underground MMA moneymaker was irrelevant. The people who were looking for him didn't need any help, and that happy little close-up along with the telephone number in the 617 area code was precisely the exposure he didn't need.

Last thing he needed was an operative or ... God forbid, Matthias's second in command ... showing up here.

Besides, it was just too fucking dumb of the promoter. Unregulated bare-knuckle fighting coupled with illegal gambling was not something you advertised, and anyway, given the size of the crowds that showed up, the audience clearly had enough mouth.

The guy in charge, however, was a greedy moron.

And the question was now, did Isaac fight or not? The flyers had just been made, according to the man who'd shown it to him ... and as he mentally counted the money he'd salted away, he could sure as hell use the extra thousand or two he'd earn tonight.

He glanced around and knew he had to get in the octagon. Shit ... once more to pad his wallet and then he was gone.

Just one last time.

Striding over to the warehouse's rear entrance, he ignored the *Holy-shit's* and the pointing and the *That's-him's*. The crowd had been watching him beat the shit out of random guys for the last month, and evidently this made him a hero in their eyes.

Which was a whacked value system, as far as he was concerned. He was about as far from hero as you could get.

The bouncers at the back door both stepped aside to let him pass and he nodded at them. This was the first fight at this particular "facility," but really, the locations were all the same. In and around Boston, there were plenty of abandoned walk-ups, warehouses, and whatevers where fifty guys who wished they were Chuck Liddell could watch half a dozen who were definitely not flap around in circles in a makeshift fighting cage. And that uninspiring math added up to why the promoter had repro'd Isaac's head. Unlike the other bare-knucklers, he knew what he was doing.

Although considering how much money the U.S. government had put into training him, he'd have to be a total tool not to crack skulls like eggs by now.

And weren't all those skills, as well as so many others, going to help him stay AWOL.

God willing, that was, he thought as he stepped into the building.

Tonight's poor-man's MGM Grand was about sixty thousand square feet of cold air anchored by a concrete floor and four walls' worth of dirty windows. The "octagon" was set up in the far corner, the eight-sided ring bolted in and surprisingly sturdy.

Then again, there were a lot of construction guys who were into this shit.

Isaac went past the pair of thick-necks who were handling the gambling and even they paid him respect, asking if he needed anything to drink or eat or whatever. Shaking his head, he went to the corner behind the ring and settled in, his back to the juncture of the walls. He was always the last to fight because he was the draw, but there was no telling when he'd be up. Most of the "fighters" didn't last long, but every once in a while you got a pair of stayers who pawed at each other like two old grizzlies until even he was ready to yell, *Enough, already*.

There were no refs and things got stopped only when there was a heaving, red faced, walleyed idiot who was flat on his back with the winning urban warrior Weeble-wobbling next to him on sweaty feet. You could go for anything, liver and family jewels included, and dirty tricks were encouraged. The one restriction was that you had to fight with whatever the good Lord gave you at birth: You couldn't bring brass knuckles, chains, knives, sand, or any of that crap inside the wire.

When the first match got rolling, Isaac panned the faces in the crowd instead of what was doing in the ring. He was searching for the out-of-place, for the eyes that were on him, for the face he knew from the past five years instead of the five weeks since he'd been gone.

Man, he knew he shouldn't have used his real name. When he'd gone for the fake ID, he should have chosen another. Sure, the social security wasn't his own, but the name ...

It had seemed important, however. A way to piss on the territory he was in, mark this fresh start as his own.

And maybe it had been a little bit of a taunt. A come-and-find-me-if-you-dare.

Now, though, he was kicking himself. Principles and scruples and all that ideology bullshit were not nearly as valuable as a viable heartbeat.

And he thought the promoter was a schmuck?

About forty-five minutes later, Kinko's number one customer got up on the chicken wire and cupped his hands to yell over the crowd. The promoter was trying to be all Dana White, but Vanna was more like it in Isaac's opinion.

"And now for our main attraction ..."

While the mob on the floor went wild, Isaac took off his sweatshirt and hung it on the outside of the octagon. He always fought in a muscle shirt, loose track pants, and the requisite bare feet—but then again, that was his whole wardrobe.

As he went in through the octagon's gate, he kept his back to the corner of the warehouse and waited calmly to see what tonight's entrée was going to be.

Ah, yes. Another Mr. Tough Guy with delusions of the glandular variety: The instant the opponent ducked in, he started bouncing around like he had a pogo stick for a colon, and he capped off his pregame show by ripping his T-shirt in half and punching himself in the face.

Fucker kept it up and Isaac wasn't going to have to do anything but blow on him to put his ass on the ground.

At the sound of the air horn, Isaac stepped forward, raising his fists to chest level, but keeping them tight to his torso. For a good minute or so, he let his opponent show off and throw air punches that snapped out with all the aim of a blind guy with a garden hose.

Piece of cake.

Except as the crowd pressed in, Isaac thought about how many copies a Xerox machine could make in sixty seconds and decided to get serious. Snapping out a left jab, he nailed the guy in the sternum, temporarily freezing the heart that beat behind that bone. Follow-up was a right hook that caught Pogo under the chin, clapping the man's teeth together and knocking his head back on his spine.

Cue the tap-dancing: Mr. Tough Guy went Ginger Rogers and twinkle-toed it backward into the chicken wire. While the roar from the kibitzers filled the open space and echoed around, Isaac closed in and worked the poor bastard out so that he was Pogo no mo', nothing but a staggering drunk whose head was spinning too fast to organize his body. And just when it looked as if there was a whole lot of dead faint coming on, Isaac backed off and let the man recover his breath.

To get an extra grand, he had to make sure they lasted more than three minutes.

Walking around, he counted in his head to five. Then he came back at—

The knife swung in a fat circle and sliced across Isaac's forehead, catching him just at the hairline. Blood streamed out and effectively clouded his vision—the kind of thing he would have called strategic if the guy had had a clue what he was doing. Given the way those punches went, however, it was obviously just a lucky strike.

As the crowd booed, Isaac flipped into business mode. An idiot with a blade was almost as dangerous as somebody who actually knew what he was doing with one, and he wasn't about to get a nip and tuck from this motherfucker.

"How'd that feel?" his opponent hollered. Actually, it came out more like, "Hof thath fill?" given his fat lip.

Last three words the guy said in the ring.

As Isaac spun a kick into the air, his own blood splashed the crowd and the impact blasted the weapon from the guy's grip. Then it was a case of one, two . . . three punches to the head and all that swagger went down harder than a side of beef at a packing plant—

Which was precisely when the fine men and women of the Boston Police Department swarmed into the warehouse.

Instant. Chaos.

And, of course, Isaac was locked into the octagon.

Jumping over his dead-fished opponent, he clawed up the six-foot-high side of the ring and vaulted over the top. As he landed on both feet, he froze.

Everybody was in full scramble except for one man who stood just off to the side, his familiar face and tattooed neck speckled with Isaac's blood.

Matthias's second in command was still tall and built and deadly . . . and the fucker was smiling like he'd found the golden egg on Easter morning.

Oh, shit, Isaac thought. Speak of the devil. . . .

"You're under arrest." The cop's hi-how're-ya came from behind him, and less than a heartbeat later, he was in cuffs. "Anything you say can and will be used against you in a . . ."

Isaac spared the officer a glance and then searched out the other soldier. But XOps' number two was gone as if he'd never been.

Son of a bitch. His old boss knew where he was now.

Which meant the fact that a Boston PD unit was all over his ass was the least of his problems.

# CHAPTER
## 2

*Caldwell, New York*

As Jim Heron stood on the front lawn of the McCready Funeral Home in Caldwell, he could picture the inside sure as if he'd already been in the brick two-story: Orientals on the floors, paintings of foggy flower arrangements on the walls, bunches of rooms with double doors and lots of floor space.

From his limited experience with them, funeral homes were like fast-food restaurants—they all kind of looked the same. Then again, he guessed that made sense. Just like there were only so many ways to doctor up a burger, he imagined dead bodies were likewise.

Shit ... he couldn't believe he was going in to see his own corpse.

Had he really died just two days ago? Was this now his life?

With the way things were going, he felt like some godforsaken frat boy who'd woken up in a strange bed going, *Are these my clothes? Did I have a good time last night?*

At least he could answer those: The leather jacket and combat boots he had on were his, and he had *not* had a good time the night before. He was responsible for battling a demon over the souls of seven people, and although he'd won the first contest, he was gearing up for the next one without knowing who the target was. And he was still learning the tricks to the angel trade. And, hello, he now had wings.

*Wings.*

Although maybe bitching about that was a lie, as his pair of magical feathered flappers had gotten his ass here from Boston, Massachusetts, in lickety-split time.

Bottom line? As far as he was concerned, the world he once knew was gone and the new one in its place made his years as an assassin in XOps seem like a desk job.

"Man, this rocks. I love the creepy shit."

Jim looked over his shoulder. Adrian, last name Vogel, was precisely the kind of whack job who'd be into a bunch of stiffs having a lie-down in refrigerator units: Pierced, leathered, tattooed, Ad was into the dark side—and given what their nemesis had done to the angel the night before last, it was a two-way street: The dark side was into him as well.

Poor bastard.

Jim rubbed his eyes and glanced at the saner of his two backups. "Thanks for the assist. This won't take long."

Eddie Blackhawk nodded. "No problem."

Standing in the stiff April wind, Eddie was his usual biker-ass self, that thick braid of hair running down the back of his leather jacket. With his square jaw, and his tanned skin, and his red eyes, he reminded Jim of an Incan war god—fucker had fists the size of most men's heads, and shoulders you could easily land an airplane on.

And what do you know, he wasn't exactly a Boy Scout, even though he had a heart of gold.

"Okay, let's do this," Jim muttered, knowing that the infiltration was outside the scope of his "employment" so they'd better shake a leg. But at least his new CO hadn't had a problem with it: Nigel, the tight-ass English archangel, had given permission for this morbid diversion, but there was no reason to take advantage of the leeway.

As Jim and his boys dematerialized through the brick walls and took form in . . . yup, yup, a big open foyer with a chandelier and a bunch of dour rugs and enough space for a cocktail party . . . he looked around, wondering where the hell the bodies were kept.

And just standing in the place reaffirmed the fact that this was a diversion he simply had to make. He might be in the business of saving souls, but right now a man's life was on the line: Isaac Rothe had bolted from the XOps fold, and Jim was supposed to kill him for it.

File that under Fuck No.

Except here was the problem: The way Matthias the Fucker worked, if Jim didn't off the AWOL soldier, someone else was going to do it . . . and then an operative would come for Jim.

Little late on that one, boys—he was already dead.

His immediate goal? Fake out his former boss and find Isaac. Then he was going to get that soldier out of the country and safe . . . before returning to his day job of going head-to-head with Devina.

He hated the delay because no doubt that demon was already gearing up for their next battle. But stepping out of one life and into another was never simple and never cut-and-dried. Inevitably, there were tendrils of what had gone before that you had to snip and cast off, and that took time.

The truth of it was: He owed Rothe. Back in the desert two years ago, when Jim had needed help, the man had been there for him, and that was a debt you didn't walk away from.

It was also probably why Matthias had given Jim the assignment. The fucker was well aware of their connection and of what had transpired that night on the other side of the globe: At the time, their boss might have been in and out of consciousness, but he'd tracked enough during those dark hours of transport and flight and medical intervention to know who was around and what was doing.

Right. Focus. Where were the stiffs?

"Downstairs," he said to his boys as he strode over to an Exit sign.

On the way to the stairwell, the three of them walked past all manner of motion detectors without setting the things off, and then they ghosted through a closed door one by one.

Bringing Adrian and Eddie on this little excursion was safer, because God knew Devina could be anywhere at any moment—plus Jim was still learning all the tricks that came with being a fallen angel, and Eddie was the master at them. Spells, potions, magic—that wizard and wand shit was Blackhawk's forte.

He'd clearly gotten his PhD in Abracadabra and didn't that make the SOB handy.

Down on the cellar level, everything was stark and clean, the cement floor and walls painted gray. The sweet smell of embalming fluid drew Jim to the right, and as he strode along, he felt like he'd jumped back in time. Fucking weird. This sneaking-around routine was exactly what he'd excelled at for all those years with Matthias—and precisely what he'd been determined to get away from.

Yeah, well, all the best-laid plans of mice and men, yada, yada, yada . . .

In his first battle with Devina, he'd required some information—and Matthias the Fucker had been the only place to go for it. Naturally, when it came to that bastard, things were strictly quid pro quo, so if you wanted something, you had to give something and the "quo" had been killing Isaac. After all, there were no pink slips for the fired or gold Rolexes for the retired in XOps—you got a bullet in the head and, if you were lucky, maybe a coffin for your corpse.

And yet he was curiously grateful: Being assigned to

assassinate the guy was the only way to help him; otherwise there would have been no way to know that Isaac had taken off and was now a hunted man: Jim was the only one who'd been let out free and clear.

But then his situation had put the "by your short hairs" in Matthias's "extenuating circumstances."

He stopped in front of a pair of stainless-steel doors marked STAFF ONLY and looked over his shoulder. "Keep your hands to yourself, Adrian."

God knew the angel seemed willing to fuck anything that moved—which made you wonder if not moving would be a rate-limiting step for him.

With a curse, Adrian went all holier-than-thou. "I only touch if they ask."

"What a relief."

"But you know, reanimation is possible."

"Not tonight it isn't. And certainly not in this place."

"Man, you could suck the fun out of a strip club."

"Pass."

Ghosting into the large, clinical room, it was damn obvious why horror movies used morgues for settings. Between the green security lighting, the rolling gurneys, and the drains in the floor, the place was the perfect backdrop for a case of the heebs.

Even though he'd died and gone to heaven and all that crap, his adrenal glands still waved its flag well enough. Then again, the twitches were probably less about the other dead guys and more about the fact that he was going to look his own corpse in the face.

As he headed for the massive refrigerator unit, with its rows of cold flats, he knew exactly what he was doing. When he didn't kill Isaac on schedule, two things were going to happen: Someone else would and somebody would be sent out looking for Jim.

And that was the reason they were here. His old boss was going to want to make sure Jim had bought the farm, so to speak: Matthias didn't believe in death certificates, autopsy reports, or photographs because he knew all too well how easy it was to fake that kind of documentation. He also didn't trust funerals, burial sites, or weeping widows and mothers, because he'd substituted too many bodies one for another over the years. Face-to-face verification was the only way to be sure in his book.

Usually Matthias sent his second in command to do the double-check, but Jim was going to make certain the big man himself was the one to do it in this case. The bastard was hard to flush out of hiding, and Jim needed his own face time with the guy.

The only way to make that happen was to use his own frozen ass as a lure.

And a little of Eddie's magic.

Checking the nameplates set into the holders on the front of the doors, he found himself between D'Arterio, Agnes, and Rutherford, James.

Flipping the latch, he opened the three-foot-by-two-foot door ... and pulled his dead body out of the refrigerator. There was a sheet covering him from head to foot, and his arms had been neatly tucked in by his sides. The air that wafted out of his hole was cold and dry and smelled like antifreeze.

Man, as many stiffs as he'd seen over his violent and bloody life, this skeeved him out.

"Give me my marching orders," he said to Eddie grimly.

"Do you have the summoning object?" the angel asked, coming to stand on the other side.

Jim reached into his pocket and took out a small piece of wood that had been carved many, many years before in the tropics on the far side of the planet. He and Matthias had not always been at odds and Matthias hadn't always been the boss.

And back when they'd both been grunts on the floor level of XOps, Jim had taught the guy how to whittle.

The miniature horse was done with surprising competence, considering it had been the first and only thing Matthias had carved. If memory served, it had taken about two hours—which was why it was being used: Apparently, inanimate objects did more than just collect dust. They were sponges for the essence of whoever owned or made or used them, and what lingered in the space between the molecules was very useful if you knew what to do with it.

Jim held the horse up. "Now what."

Eddie whipped the sheet off Jim's gray, mottled face. For a moment, it was hard to concentrate on anything but what he looked like forty-eight hours dead. Holy hell, the Grim Reaper was no makeup artist; that was for sure. Even Goths had better complexions.

"Hey, don't be harshing on my peeps," Adrian cut in. "I'd do one of us way before some SoCal bimbo with plastic melons and a spray tan."

"Stop reading my mind, motherfucker. And you'd do the bimbo anyway."

Adrian grinned and flexed his heavy arms. "Yeah. I would. And her sister."

Yup, that angel appeared to be over whatever the demon Devina had done to him the night of Jim's official "death." Either that or all the self-medicating with living, breathing Barbies had exhausted any introspection right out of him.

Eddie took a metal file from his pocket and presented it handle first. "Grate some of that carving onto the body. Anywhere is fine."

Jim chose the flat pads of his chest, and the scraping sounds were soft in the tiled cavern of the cold room.

Eddie took the tool back. "Where's your knife?"

Jim took out the hunting blade that had been given to him way back when he'd first joined the armed services. Matthias had gotten an identical weapon at the same time—had used it to carve the horse, matter of fact.

"Slice your palm and hold the object hard. As you do,

picture the person you want to come here clearly in your mind. Remember the sound of his voice. See him in memories that are specific. Watch how he moves, the gestures he makes, the clothes he wears, the smell of his cologne if he uses it."

Forcing his head to focus, Jim tried to call up something, anything, about Matthias the Fucker. . . .

The image that dove into his frontal lobe was stunningly clear: He was back in the desert on that night, with the chemical stink of the explosive in his nose and the ringing sound of time-to-get-a-move-on banging in his ears. Matthias had no lower leg, his left eye was nearly gone from the socket, and his digital fatigues were covered with pale dirt and bright red blood.

". . . Dan . . . ny . . . boy . . . my Danny boy . . ." he was saying.

Jim put the blade to the center of his palm and dragged it through his skin, letting out a hiss as the steel bit deep and clean.

Eddie's voice cut through the memory and the icy pain. "Now take your palm and rub it on the wood shavings. Then get out your lighter and fire it up. Lifting your hand, blow across it into the flame and onto the body, keeping that picture in your mind."

Jim did as he was told . . . and was amazed to see a blue glow coalesce on the far side of his Bic, like the thing had magically turned into a blowtorch. And the hey-check-its didn't end there. The flare settled around the body, blanketing it in a shimmer.

"You're done," Eddie said.

Jim flicked his Bic off and just stared down at himself, wondering what Matthias was going to think.

There had been a time, long ago, when he and the guy had been tight. But as the years had passed, the bastard had gone one way, Jim another. And that was before the whole being-dead, fallen-angel thing.

But this wasn't about him and Matthias.

Jim pulled the sheet back into place, covering his own face and wondering how long it was going to take for the spell to call Matthias here and for Jim to see the guy again.

He slid the table into the refrigerator and shut the door, cutting that phosphorescent blue glow off. "Let's blow this joint."

He was quiet on the way out, lost to the bad memories of what he'd done and who he'd killed while in XOps. And what do you know. In addition to his adrenal glands, it seemed like his personal demons had also survived his death. In fact, he had a feeling his regrets were eternal luggage: The not-so-hot part about being immortal was that there was no endgame to be had, no prospect for getting off the ride that you could hold on to when things got rough and overwhelming . . . and you despised yourself.

As he and his comrades reemerged onto the funeral home's side lawn, it was back to the hunt for Isaac Rothe.

"I've got to find that man," he said grimly. Although it wasn't likely they'd forgotten what they were doing.

Closing his eyes, he summoned that which would carry him over the miles between Caldwell and where Isaac had been seen last. . . .

Jim's massive wings unfurled on his back, the span of iridescent feathers stretching out and flexing like limbs that had been cramped. When his lids lifted, Eddie and Adrian were sporting theirs as well, the two fallen angels magnificent and otherworldly in the light of the streetlamps.

As a car drove by on the street, it didn't screech to a halt or get derailed from its lane. The wings, like him and Eddie and Adrian, were neither there nor not there, real nor unreal, tangible nor intangible.

They just were.

"You ready," Eddie asked.

Jim glanced back at where his earthly form was now not only frozen stiff but a beacon for a man he'd come to hate.

Even though he'd saved the fucker's life.

"Yeah, let's do this."

Up, up, and away, and all that shit: In the blink of an eye, they were flying through the dark heavens and the sparkling stars on the strong, steady wings of Angel Airlines, as he called it.

Aloft and alive, he resumed his hunt for a hunted man . . . and headed off for Boston with all proverbial guns blazing.

# CHAPTER
## 3

The demon Devina was as close to all-powerful as you could get without being the one who had created the Earth and the heavens: She could assume all manner of visages and bodies, becoming anyone at any time in any place. She could imprison souls for an eternity. She commanded an army of the undead.

And if you crossed her, she could make life a living hell for you. Literally.

But she had one little problem.

"I'm sorry I'm late," she said as she rushed into the cozy red office. "I had a meeting that ran longer than I'd thought."

Her therapist smiled from her arm chair. "Not to worry. Would you like a minute to collect yourself?"

Devina was indeed frazzled, and as she sat down, she put her Prada bag to the side. Taking a deep breath, she patted the corporeal illusion of brunette hair that the human woman saw, and pushed at the lizard-print leather pants that actually existed.

"Work has been hell," she said, glancing down to double-check that her bag was zipped up. There were bloodstains on the sweatshirt inside, and the last thing she needed was to have to explain them. "Absolute hell."

"I was glad you called for the extra night session. After last week, I've been thinking about you and what happened. How are you doing?"

Devina downshifted out of the chaos she'd just come from and focused on herself. Which was not a happy thing. Instantly, tears sprang to her eyes. "I'm . . ."

Not okay.

She forced herself to say something. "The movers got everything into my new place, and most of it is still in boxes. I spent the afternoon trying to unpack, but there's so much, and I have to make sure it's ordered correctly. I need to check that my—"

"Devina, stop talking about the things." The therapist made a little note in her black book. "We can get to planning toward the end of the session. I want to know how *you* are. Talk to me about how you *feel*."

Devina looked across the needlepoint rug and wondered, not for the first time, what the woman would think if she knew she was treating a demon. Ever since Devina had been in Caldwell, she'd been coming to see the psychologist—so it was over a year now. She kept her true identity hidden under her favorite skin of a sexy, chic, brunette female, but the underneath . . . especially after her first loss to Jim Heron . . . was a fucking mess.

And this human was actually helping her.

Devina snapped a tissue out of the box on the table beside her. "I just . . . I hate moving. I feel totally out of control. And lost. And . . . scared."

"I know you do." Warmth positively wafted out of the woman's pores. "Changing homes is the hardest thing for someone like you to do. I'm very proud of you."

"I had no time. No time to do it right." More tears. Which she hated. But, God, she'd had to rip her collections out of their rightful places in a matter of *hours*, scrambling, throwing things into boxes. "I still haven't been able to sort through everything and make sure nothing was broken or lost."

Oh, God . . . *lost*.

Panic fanned into her chest and made the heart she had co-opted beat triple-time.

"Devina, look at me."

She had to force her eyes to focus through the panic attack. "I'm sorry," she choked out.

"Devina, the anxiety is not about the things. It's about your place in this world. It's the space you declare as yours emotionally and spiritually. You must remember that you don't need objects to justify your existence or make yourself feel safe and secure."

Okay, that all sounded well and good, but her things on the earth were what tied her to the souls she owned down below, the only link she had to her "children." Over the centuries, she had amassed personal possessions from every soul she'd taken: buttons, cuff links, rings, earrings, thimbles, knitting needles, glasses, keys, pens, watches . . . the list went on and on. She preferred things made of precious metal, but any kind of metal would do: Similar to the way the substance reflected light, it also gave off the reverberations of the one who'd owned it, worn it, used it.

The radiated imprint of those humans was the only thing that calmed her when she couldn't get down to her sanctuary for a personal visit.

God, she hated having to work on earth.

On a shudder, she blotted her tears. "I just can't stand being so far away from them."

"You need your job, though. You've told me yourself. And your ex-husband is better equipped to handle the day-to-day care of your children."

"He is." She'd had to shoehorn her backstory into some semblance of a human's situation. There was no ex-husband, needless to say, but the parallel worked: Her souls were safe where she left them. It just killed her to be away. There was no place she'd rather be than at the bottom of her well, watching the writhing, screaming throng trapped forever in her walls.

Playing with them was fun, too.

"So where did you end up?" the therapist asked. "After your boyfriend and you decided to end your relationship, where did you go here in town?"

Now her anxiety switched to anger. She couldn't believe she'd lost the first battle with Jim Heron ... or that that fucking bastard had infiltrated her private space. Thanks to him and those other two angels, she'd had to take everything she had and vacate that loft at a dead run.

"I have a friend who has a building that's vacant." Not a friend actually. Just some guy she'd fucked until he signed all the papers. Then she'd killed him, stuffed his body into a hazardous-waste drum, and sealed the thing up good. He was in his own basement now, decomposing comfortably.

"And the move is completed?"

"Yes, everything's there. But as I said, I just haven't arranged it properly." She had, however, found another virgin, which she'd promptly sacrificed and put to good use protecting the mirror that got her to back to Hell. "I've put in a security system, though."

If anyone breached the blood seal into the room where her most prized possession was, she'd find out in a heartbeat. It was how she had known the instant when Jim and his angel buddies had violated her space. How she'd saved her things.

Virgins were a pain the ass to find these days, though. With everyone having sex so much, what had once been a piece of cake to get was now becoming rarer and rarer. She never killed children; that was just wrong—it would be like someone taking one of her souls away from her. But try finding someone over eighteen who hadn't been in the sack. You could be at it for days.

Long live the abstinence movement, was all she could say.

"Wait, building?" the therapist said. "You're not staying in some building, are you?"

"Oh, no. I'm at a hotel for the time being. Work is taking me out of town. Up to Boston, actually." Because it was time for the second battle with her nemesis.

And goddamn it, she was going to win this one.

"Devina, this is such good work." The therapist clapped her hand on her knee and smiled. "You're living apart from your things. You've made a breakthrough."

Not really, considering that she could be anywhere in the blink of an eye.

"Now tell me, how's work? I know last week was rough."

Devina's hand found her bag and she stroked the soft leather. "It's going to get better. I'm going to make it better."

"Your new coworker. How are things going with him? I know there'd been some initial friction."

Friction? Yeah, you could say that.

She thought of her and Jim Heron in the parking lot of the Iron Mask, him buried deep inside of her, her riding him hard. In spite of the fact that she hated him with a passion, she wouldn't mind a little more private time with him.

Devina straightened her spine. "He's not going get the vice presidency. I don't care what I have to do, but I've worked too long and hard to have some guy barge in and take what's mine."

Seven souls. Seven chances for good or evil to win. And the first one had gone to the other side. Three more went in favor of Jim Heron and she was not only out of a "job," but the angels took over the Earth and each and every one of her souls were redeemed.

All her work for nothing: Her collections gone. Her army gone. Herself . . . gone.

She stared at her therapist. "I will not let him win."

The woman nodded. "Do you have a plan?"

Devina patted her bag. "I do. I absolutely do."

*    *    *

After the session, Devina took herself north and east, casting herself into the air as a dark shadow and winging her way through the night. She coalesced on Boylston Street, across from the Boston Public Garden, where the weeping willows over the pond were just greening up.

The demure brick box of the Four Seasons Hotel took up nearly the entire block, between its entrance, porte cochere, and windowed restaurants. Although the exterior was quite plain, the interior was all warm wood and elegant brocade, and there were always fresh flowers.

She could have just flashed up to her room, but what a waste of an outfit: her Escada lizard-print pants and Chanel blouse were stunners, to say nothing of her Stella McCartney trench.

And what do you know, only her second night here and already the doormen and front-desk staff called out greetings as she swept into the lobby, her Louboutins clipping on the marble.

Which served to remind her of what she already knew: Of all the suits of illusioned flesh she had ever worn, this one—of a brunette woman with legs that didn't quit and a set of breasts that made human men trip over their own tongues—was the one that fit her best. Even though technically she was a sexless "it," experience had proven that her arsenal of weapons was best wielded by a manicured hand.

Plus she liked the clothes for women better.

The fucking, too.

Her suite on the top floor had a magnificent view of the garden and the Boston Common, and a lot of grand rooms—as well as excellent room service. The bouquet of roses was a nice touch and supplied gratis.

Which was what you got when you paid thousands and thousands and thousands of dollars for digs.

She walked through the sitting room and the master bedroom to the marble bath. On the counter between the two sinks, she put down her bag and took out the sweat-shirt she'd taken from that MMA octagon. The hoodie was the color of fog and a size double-XL. Found at any Wal-Mart or Target, it was one of those anonymous garments that could have been worn by any man, something that was easy to find, easy to afford. Nothing special.

Except this one was unique. Especially given the blood-stains.

Thank God those cops had shown up when they had. Otherwise, she would have missed the appointment with her therapist altogether.

Quickly shedding her clothes, she tried to leave them in a wrinkly mess . . . and lasted about a minute and a half. The disorder made her head hum and she had to gather them up, stride for the closet, and hang everything where it needed to be. She'd worn a bra, so that got put in the bureau. No panties to worry about.

She was decidedly calmer as she went back to work at the bathroom counter.

Taking out a pair of golden shears from her makeup case, she cut a circle into the sweatshirt over where the heart of the man who wore it would have been. Then she diced up the fabric, the cotton fibers giving way easily and falling to the smooth marble in a little pile.

She used one side of the scissors to slice into her palm, and her blood ran dirty gray as it dropped onto the nest she'd made.

For a moment, she was transfixed with disappointment. She wished her blood ran red—so much more attractive.

Truth be told, Devina hated the way she really looked. Far better this body. And the others.

Picking up the sweatshirt's clippings and grinding them into the tainted blood on her palm, she pictured the man who had had the fabric against his flesh, seeing his hard face and the brush cut that was growing out and the tattoos on his body.

Still milling her hand and keeping an image of Isaac Rothe in her head, Devina walked naked into the bedroom and sat on the duvet. On the side table, she opened a squat ebony box and took out a hand-carved chess piece, the depiction of the queen not nearly as beautiful as her suit of flesh. She hadn't seen Jim Heron whittle the grand lady, but he had and she pictured him doing so in her mind, imagining him curled around a sharp knife, his sure hands wielding a steel edge to reveal the object within the wood. Pressing what he had made into her bleeding palm, along with the fibers from the sweatshirt, she melded them, integrated them. Then she leaned over and picked up a candle, which lit at her will. Lying down, she blew across the flame, the mingling essences of all three of them flowing over the flame.

The purple glow that emanated on the far side covered her, enveloping her in phosphorescence . . . calling the owners of the things together . . . calling them to her.

Jim Heron wasn't going to know what hit him this time. He might have won the first round, but that wasn't happening again.

# CHAPTER
## 4

When you worked in central processing at the Suffolk County jail in downtown Boston, you saw a lot of shit. And some of it was the kind of thing that put you off your coffee and doughnuts.

Other kinds . . . were just frickin' bizarre.

Billy McCray had been a beat cop in Southie first, serving alongside his brothers and his cousins and his old man. After he'd been shot on duty about fifteen years ago, Sergeant had arranged for him to have this desk job—and it had turned out that not only did his wheelchair fit just fine under the lip of the counter, he was damn good at pushing paper. He'd started booking arrests and taking mug shots, but now he was in charge of everything.

Nobody so much as blew his nose in this place but that Billy didn't tell 'em it was okay to take a Kleenex.

And he loved what he did, even if it got wicked weird sometimes.

Like first thing this morning. Six a.m. He'd booked a white female who'd been wearing a pair of Coke cans as pasties, the two aluminum numbers glued at the bottoms to her boobs and sticking straight out. He had a feeling that mug shot was going to end up on The Smoking Gun.com and she was probably going to enjoy the exposure: Before he'd taken her picture, he'd offered to get her a shirt or something, but nah, she wanted to show off her ... well, cans.

People. Honestly.

Turned out the rubber cement was easy to get off, but they were serving her drinks in a single paper cup just in case she got another bright idea—

As the steel door opened down at the end of the hall, Billy sat up a little straighter in his chair.

The woman who came in was a sight to see, all right, but not for the reason most of the freaks here were. She was about ten feet tall and had blond hair that was always up in a twist on her head. Wearing a perfectly fitted suit and a long, formal coat, he knew without asking that her purse and her briefcase were worth more than he had in his 401(k).

To say nothing about that huge gold rope around her neck.

As a couple of guards passed her, they also stretched up their spines and dropped their voices ... and immediately looked over their shoulders to get a look-see at the back of her.

And when she came up to the Plexiglas partition in front of him, he was glad he'd already slid the thing back, because he got to smell her perfume.

God ... it was always the same. The scent of rich and expensive.

"Hi, Billy, how's Tom doing at the police academy?"

Like a lot of Beacon Hill types, Grier Childe's intonation made a simple question seem better than something Shakespeare had written. But unlike those tight-asses, she wasn't a snot and her smile was genuine. She always asked about his son and his wife and she really looked at him, meeting his eyes like he was so much more than just a desk jockey.

"He's doin' great." Billy grinned and crossed his arms over his puffed-up chest. "Graduating in June. Working out of Southie. He's a marksman like his pops—kid could take out a tin can from a mile away."

Unfortunately, that reminded him of Coke Girl, but he pushed the image right out of the way. Much better to enjoy the view of Ms. Childe, Esq.

"It doesn't surprise me that Tommy's an ace." She signed into the log and braced a hip on the counter. "As you said, he takes after you."

Even after two years of this, he still couldn't believe she stopped to talk to him. Yeah, sure, the DA types and the regular public defenders chatted him up, but she came from one of those old-school, white-shoe firms—and usually that meant just the facts on where their clients were.

"So how's your Sara doing?" she asked.

As they talked, he typed her name into the system to pull up who she'd been assigned to. About every six months or so, she came up on rotation as a public defender. It was, of course, pro bono for her. Her hourly rates were undoubtedly so expensive, he was damn sure the clients she got here couldn't afford more than two words from her, much less a whole hour . . . or, Christ, even a case's worth of time.

When he saw the name that was next to hers, he frowned.

"Everything okay?" she asked.

Well, no, it wasn't. "Yeah. You're good."

Because he was going to make it his business for her to be.

He reached to the side for a stack of files. "Here's the paperwork on your client. If you go to number one, we'll bring him out to you."

"Thanks, Billy. You're the best."

After he buzzed her through the main door into the jail's receiving and processing unit, she walked off to the room he'd given her—which just happened to be right next to his office. Making a note in the computer, he picked up the phone and dialed down to holding.

When Shawn C. answered, he said, "Bring up number five-four-eight-nine-seventy, last name Rothe. For our Ms. Childe."

Little silence. "He's a big one."

"Yeah, and listen—could you have a talk with him? Maybe remind him how being polite to his counsel'll make things easier on him."

There was another pause. "And I'll just wait outside the door when he's in with her. Tony'll cover me down here."

"Good. Yeah, that's good. Thanks."

As Billy hung up, he wheeled himself around to face the security monitoring screens. In the lower left one, he watched as Ms. Childe sat down at a table, cracked open the file, and looked at the reports in it.

He was going to keep his eye on her until she was safely out of there.

The thing was, down at the jail, there were two kinds of people: insiders and outsiders. Outsiders got treated polite and all, but insiders . . . particularly nice, young insiders with beautiful smiles and a lot of class . . . they got taken care of.

And that meant Shawn C., the guard, would be parked out in the hall, looking through the chicken-wire window the entire time that that homicidal maniac who'd been arrested for cage fighting was in with their girl.

If that motherfucker so much as breathed wrong around her, well . . . suffice it to say that in Billy's shop, no one was above a little corrective action: All the guards and staff knew about the dark corner in the basement where there were no security cameras and no one could hear an asshole scream when payback turned into a bitch.

Billy leaned back in his chair and shook his head. Nice

girl in there, real nice. Course, given what had happened to her brother ... Hard lives had a way of making for nice, didn't they.

Grier Childe sat in front of a stainless-steel table on a cold stainless-steel chair that was across from another stainless-steel chair. All of the furniture was bolted to the floor and the only other fixtures were the security camera up in the corner and an overhead lightbulb that had a cage around it. The walls were concrete block that had been painted so many times it was nearly wallpaper smooth, and the air smelled like rotgut floor cleaner, the cologne of the last attorney who'd been in the room, and old cigarettes.

The place couldn't have been more different from where she usually worked. The Boston offices of Palmer, Lords, Childe, Stinston & Dodd looked like a museum of nineteenth-century furniture and artwork. PLCS&D had no armed guards, no metal detectors, and nothing was screwed into place so it couldn't be stolen or thrown at somebody.

There the uniforms came from Brooks Brothers and Burberry.

She'd been doing pro bono public defending for about two years, and it had taken her at least twelve months to get in good with the front desk and the staff and the guards. But now it was like old-home week whenever she came here, and she honestly loved the people.

Lot of good folks doing hard jobs in the system.

Opening up the file of her newest client, she reviewed the charges, intake form, and history: Isaac Rothe, age twenty-six, apartment down on Tremont Street. Unemployed. No priors. Arrested along with eight others as part of a bust the night before on an underground gambling and fighting ring. No warrant needed because the fighters were trespassing on private property. According to the police report, her client was in the ring at the time the police infiltrated. Apparently the guy he'd fought was getting treated at Mass General—

*It's nine o'clock on a Saturday morning. . . . Do you know where your life is?*

Keeping her head down, Grier squeezed her eyes shut. "Not now, Daniel."

*I'm just saying.* As her dead brother's voice drifted in and out of her head from behind, the disembodied sound made her feel utterly crazy. *You're thirty-two years old, and instead of cozying up to some hot boy toy, you're sitting here in the police station with sucky coffee—*

"I don't have any coffee."

At that moment, the door swung wide and Billy rolled in. "Thought you might like some wake-up."

*Bingo*, her brother said.

*Shut. Up*, she thought back at him.

"Billy, that's really kind of you." She took what the supervisor offered, the warmth of the paper cup bleeding into her palm.

"Well, you know, it's dishwater. We all hate it." Billy smiled. "But it's a tradition."

"It sure is." She frowned as he lingered. "Something wrong?"

Billy patted the vacant chair next to him. "Would you mind sitting here for me?"

Grier lowered the cup. "Of course not, but why—"

"Thanks, dear."

There was a beat. Clearly, Billy was waiting for her to shift around and was not inclined to explain himself.

Pushing the file across the way, she went to the other seat, her back now to the door.

"That's a girl." He gave her a squeeze on the arm and rolled out.

The change in position meant that she could see the filmy apparition of her younger, beloved brother. Daniel was lounging in the far corner of the room, feet crossed at the ankles, arms linked at the chest. His blond hair was fresh and clean, and he had on a coral-colored polo shirt and madras shorts.

He was like an undead model in a Ralph Lauren ad, nothing but all-American, sun-kissed privilege about to take a sail off Hyannis Port.

Except he wasn't smiling at her, as he usually did. *They want him facing the door so the guard outside can keep an eye on him. And they don't want you boxed into the room. Easier to get you out this way if he goes aggressive.*

Forgetting about the security camera, and the fact that to anybody else she was speaking into thin air, she leaned in. "Nobody is going to—"

*You've got to quit this. Stop trying to save people and get a life.*

"Right back at you. Stop haunting me and get an eternity."

*I would. But you won't let me go.*

On that note, the door behind her opened up and her brother disappeared.

Grier stiffened as she heard the tinkling sound of chains and the shuffling of feet.

And then she saw him.

Holy . . . Mary . . . mother . . . of . . .

What had been brought out of holding by Shawn C. was about six feet, four inches of solid muscle. Her client was "dressed in," which meant he had his prison garb on, and his hands and feet were shackled together and linked with a steel chain that ran up the front of his legs and went around his waist. His hard face had the kind of hollow cheeks that came with zero body fat, and his dark hair was cut short like a military man's. Fading bruises were clustered around his eyes, a bright white bandage sat close to his hairline . . . and there was a red flush around his neck, as if he'd very, very recently been manhandled.

Her first thought was . . . she was glad good old Billy Mc-Cray had made her switch seats. She wasn't sure how she knew it, but she had the sense that if her client chose to, he could have taken Shawn C. down in the blink of an eye—in spite of the cuffs and the fact that the guard was built like a bulldog and had years of experience handling big, volatile men.

Her client's eyes didn't meet hers, but stayed locked on the floor as the guard shoved him into the tight space between the vacant chair and the table.

Shawn C. bent down to the man's ear and whispered something.

Growled something, was more like it.

Then the guard glanced over at Grier and smiled tightly, as if he didn't like the whole thing but was going to be professional about it. "Hey, I'll be right outside the door. You need anything? You just holler and I'm in here." In a lower voice, he said, "I'm watching you, boy."

Somehow she wasn't surprised at the precautions. Merely sitting across from her client made her wary. She couldn't imagine moving him around the jailhouse.

God, he was big.

"Thanks, Shawn," she said quietly.

"No problem, Ms. Childe."

And then she was alone with Mr. Isaac Rothe.

Measuring the tremendous girth of his shoulders, she noted that he wasn't twitching or fidgeting, which she took as a good sign—no meth or coke in his system, hopefully. And he didn't stare at her inappropriately or check out the front of her suit or lick his lips.

Actually, he didn't look at her at all, his eyes remaining on the table in front of him.

"I'm Grier Childe—I've been assigned your case." When he didn't raise his eyes or nod, she continued. "Anything that you say to me is privileged, which means that within the bounds of the law, I will not reveal it to anyone. Further, that security camera over there has no audio feed, so no one else can hear what you tell me."

She waited . . . and still he didn't reply. He just sat there, breathing evenly, all coiled power with his cuffed hands set on the tabletop and his huge body crammed into the chair.

On the first meeting, most of the clients she'd had here either slouched and did the sullen routine, or they played all indignant and offended, with a lot of exculpatory talk. He did neither. His spine was straight as an arrow, and he was totally alert, but he didn't say a word.

She cleared her throat. "The charges against you are serious. The guy you were fighting with was sent to the hospital with a brain hemorrhage. Right now you're up for second-degree assault and attempted murder, but if he dies, that's murder two or manslaughter."

Nothing.

"Mr. Rothe, I'd like to ask you some questions, if I may?"

No reply.

Grier sat back. "Can you even hear me?"

Just as she was wondering whether he had an undisclosed disability, he spoke. "Yes, ma'am."

His voice was so deep and arresting, she stopped breathing. Those two words were uttered with a softness that was at total odds with the size of his body and the harshness of his face. And his accent . . . vaguely Southern, she decided.

"I'm here to help you, Mr. Rothe. You understand that, right?"

"No disrespect, ma'am, but I don't believe you can."

Definitely Southern. Beautifully Southern, as a matter of fact.

Shaking her head clear, she said, "Before you dismiss me, I'd suggest you consider two things. Right now, there's no bail set for you, so you're going to be stuck in here as your case moves forward. And that could be months. Also, anyone who represents himself truly does have a fool for a client—that's not just a saying. I'm not the enemy. I'm here to—"

He finally looked at her.

His eyes were the color of frost on window glass, and filled with the shadows of deeds that stained the soul. And as that grim, exhausted stare bored through the back of her head, it froze her heart: She knew instantly that he wasn't just some street thug.

He was a soldier, she thought. He had to be—her father got the same look in his eyes during quiet nights.

War did that to people.

"Iraq?" she asked quietly. "Or Afghanistan?"

His brows flared a little, but that was the only reply she got.

Grier tapped his file. "Let me get you bail. Let's just start there, okay? You don't have to tell me anything about why you were arrested or what happened. I just need to know your ties to the community and a little more about where you live. With no prior arrests, I think we've got a shot at . . ."

She stopped as she realized he'd closed his eyes.

Okay. First time she'd ever had a client take a snooze in the middle of a meeting. Maybe Billy and Shawn C. had less to worry about than they thought.

"Am I boring you, Mr. Rothe?" she demanded after a moment.

# CHAPTER
## 5

"**A**m I boring you, Mr. Rothe?"

Not. Hardly.

His public defender's voice was a kind of lullaby in Isaac's ears, her aristocratic inflection and perfect grammar soothing him so much he was oddly afraid of her. Originally, he'd closed his eyes because she was simply too beautiful to look at, but there had been an added benefit to the lights out. Without the distraction of her perfect face and her smart stare, he was able to fully concentrate on her words.

The way she spoke was poetic. Even to a guy who wasn't into the hearts and flowers routine.

"Mr. Rothe."

Not a question, a demand. Clearly she was getting fed up with his ass.

Cracking his lids, he felt the impact of her nail him in the sternum—and tried to tell himself that she was making such a big impression because it had been years since he'd been around a true lady. After all, most of the females he'd fucked or worked with had been rough around the edges, just like him. So this precisely coiffed, clearly educated, perfumed exotic across the table was some kind of stunning anomaly.

God, she'd probably faint if she saw his tattoo.

And run screaming if she knew what he'd been doing for a living for the last five years.

"Let me try to get you bail," she repeated. "And then we'll see where we are."

He had to wonder why she cared so much about some scrub she'd never met before, but there was an undeniable mission in her eyes, and maybe that explained it: Clearly, being down here with the riffraff was exorcising some kind of demon for her. Maybe it was a case of rich-guilt. Maybe it was a religious thing. Whatever it was, she was damned determined.

"Mr. Rothe. Let me help you."

He so didn't want her involved in his case ... but if she could set him free, he could take off and he was undoubtedly safer out in the world: His old boss would have no trouble sending a man into this jail on a charge and engineering the assassination right under the noses of the guards.

To Matthias, that would be child's play.

Isaac felt his conscience, which had been long silent, send up a holler, but the logic was sound: She looked like the kind of lawyer who could get things done in the system, and as much as he hated to involve her in the mess he was in, he wanted to stay alive.

"I'd be grateful if you could do that, ma'am."

She took a deep breath, like she was having a break in the middle of a marathon. "Good. All right then. Now, it says here you live over on Tremont. How long have you been there?"

"Just over two weeks."

He could tell by the way her brows went together that that wasn't going to help him much. "You're unemployed?"

The technical term was AWOL, he thought. "Yes, ma'am."

"Do you have any family? Here or elsewhere in the state?"

"No." His father and brothers all thought he was dead, and that was just fine with him. And them as well in all likelihood.

"At least you don't have any priors." She closed the file. "I'll go up in front of the judge in about a half hour. The bail's going to be steep . . . but I know some bondsmen we could approach to put up the money."

"How high do you think it will be?"

"Twenty thousand—if we're lucky."

"I can cover it."

Another frown and she reopened his file, taking a second gander at his paperwork. "You stated here that you have no income and no savings."

As he stayed quiet, she didn't give him flak and didn't seem surprised. No doubt she was used to people like him lying, but unfortunately, he was willing to bet his life that what he was keeping from her was far, far deadlier than what her Good Samaritan antics usually brought her in contact with.

Shit. Actually, he *was* betting her life on it, wasn't he. Matthias cast a wide net when it came to assignments, and anyone standing next to Isaac ran the risk of being in the crosshairs.

Except once he was gone, she was never going to see him again.

"How's your face?" she asked after a moment.

"It's fine."

"It looks as if it hurts. Do you want any aspirin? I've got some."

Isaac stared down at his busted hands. "No, ma'am. But thank you."

He heard the *clip-clip* of her high heels as she got to her feet. "I'll be back after I—"

The door opened and the muscle who'd taken him up from holding came barreling in.

"I'm off to talk to the judge," she said to the guard. "And he was a perfect gentleman."

Isaac allowed himself to be dragged upright, but he wasn't paying attention to the officer. He was staring at his public defender. She even walked like a lady—

His arm got yanked hard. "You don't look at her," the guard said. "Guy like you doesn't even *look* at someone like her."

Mr. Manners' death grip was a little annoying, but there was no faulting the SOB's opinion.

Even if he'd had a garden variety job and nothing more than a couple of speeding tickets, Isaac wasn't anywhere near that league of woman. Hell, he wasn't even playing in the same sport.

# CHAPTER
## 6

Jim Heron had long been aware that there were two kinds of gyms in the world: commercial and old-school. The former had coordinating color schemes and women taking spinning classes in full makeup and guys with John Mayer carp tattoos pumping weights with padded grips. You were expected to wipe down the machines after you used them and chirpy, spray-tanned trainers checked you in as you came and went.

He'd tried out one of those right after he'd left XOps. It had nearly made him go couch potato.

The old school was more up his alley and that was exactly what he and Adrian and Eddie walked into in South Boston. Mike's Gym was a man's world, baby: Place smelled like an armpit, had walls that were prison-worthy, and was hung with faded pictures of Arnold from back in the eighties. The mats were neon blue, the weights were iron, and the single stationary bike in the corner was one of those wind-resistant jobs with the caged fan.

Damn thing was a relic and had dust on the seat.

The men who were doing circuits on the machines or free-weighting it were big, quiet, and had tattoos of the Virgin Mary and Jesus and the cross. There were a lot of broken noses that had healed up cockeyed and some bad caps on gritted front teeth that were no doubt from hockey games or bar fights.

Undoubtedly everyone knew everybody else because they were all related somehow.

He felt right at home as he came up to the front desk. Guy behind it was sixty, maybe sixty-five, with ruddy skin and pale blue eyes and hair that was whiter than the froth on a Bass Black & Tan.

"What can I do for you boys?" the man said, lowering the *Boston Herald*.

A couple of the members glanced over, and kept staring. Jim and his backups weren't lightweights, but they were unknowns, which put them into *what-the-hell?* territory.

"I'm looking for a guy," Jim said as he took out the flyer with Isaac's pic on it and spread the thing flat on the chipped Formica counter. "You seen him around here maybe?"

"No, I ain't," the guy replied without looking down. "I ain't seen nobody."

Jim glanced around. A lot more eyes on them and a lot of weights pausing. Clearly, pushing the old man wasn't a smart move if he didn't want to get bum-rushed.

"Okay. Thanks."

"No problem." The *Herald* snapped up into place.

Jim turned away and refolded Isaac's picture. As he went for the door, he cursed under his breath. This was the third place they'd tried, and they'd gotten nothing but stonewalled—

"Hey. I know him."

Jim stopped and looked over his shoulder. A guy with a Boston Fire Department T-shirt came over.

"My pops don't like to get involved." The guy nodded down at the flyer. "Who is he to you?"

"My brother." And that wasn't a total lie. They were related in a visceral way because of what he and Isaac had been through in XOps—plus there was that whole debt thing.

"He was arrested last night."

Jim's brows shot up. "No shit?"

"Bunch of my cousins are cops and they busted a fight ring. Your bro's a straight-up killer. Only reason anyone ever got into the octo with him was for the big purse, but he never lost. Not once."

"How long he been in town?"

"I only saw him fight, like, three times." *Saw* was pronounced *sore*. "Listen, 'round here, bunch of fuckers want to get together and beat each other, we'll let 'em do their thing. But you gotta keep it honest—that's why they were raided. The promoter was throwing the bouts except for the ones your boy was in."

Fuckin' A. Isaac in the system was not a good thing.

"Pops, lemme have the *Herald*?" The guy reached over to his dad and took the newspaper, looking through it. "Here."

Jim read the article fast. Underground fighting, blah, blah, blah—*Isaac Rothe*? Wait, he was in under his *real* name?

Talk about a target on his chest: Matthias could easily just send someone into the penal system to off the SOB.

"If you want to find your brother . . ." The firefighter's face grew calculating. "I can tell you where he'll be as soon as he gets out."

Not more than two hours after Grier left her client and went to the judge, she was back behind the wheel of her Audi A6 and stuck in traffic around the Boston Common. Fortunately, the pace picked up through Chinatown and then she was out the other side on Tremont Street.

Part of her rush was that she didn't really have time to take this diversion. She had a meeting with a *Fortune* Fifty company at one o'clock in her office in the Financial District . . . and all those skyscrapers were at the moment in her rearview mirror and getting smaller.

But she needed to know more.

Which was the other half of her burning hurry.

As she cursed herself, she braced for Daniel to make an appearance and glanced into the backseat. When he didn't show up, she took a deep breath.

She really didn't need her metaphysical editorial board at the moment.

Daniel had died two and a half years ago and he first came to her in a dream the night before his funeral. It had been such a relief to see him healthy and clean and not in a heroin nod, and in her sleep, they had talked as they'd been able to before the addiction had really ground him down. The jump to "real life" had occurred about six months later. One morning, she'd been talking to him and her alarm had gone off. Without thinking twice about it, she'd reached over and silenced the thing . . . only to realize she was awake and he was still very much with her.

Daniel had smiled as she'd shot upright—like he was proud of himself. And then in his chilled-out way, he'd informed her that she wasn't losing her mind. There was, in fact, an afterlife, and he was in it.

It had taken some time to get used to, but two years later, she no longer questioned his periodic hi-how-are-yas—although she did keep his visits to herself. After all, just because she didn't think she was crazy, that wasn't to say others might disagree—and who needed that? Besides, if he was a hallucination and she was turning into something out of *A Beautiful Mind*, well . . . it worked for her, so to hell with the mental-health experts: She had missed Daniel so much and she had him back in a way.

Refocusing on the brick walk-ups that rose on either side of Tremont Street, she tracked the numbers when she could see them around the doors. On some level, she couldn't believe she'd gotten her client bail, but then, his lack of priors and the general overcrowding in the system had worked in their favor.

Mr. Rothe, on the other hand, had seemed neither surprised nor pleased when she'd told him. He had just asked her in his polite, quiet way to go to his apartment and get twenty-five thousand dollars in cash—because there was no one he could call to make that kind of a run.

Sure. No problem. Right.

Because handling ill-gotten cash didn't make her an accomplice or threaten her bar status in any way.

She was still shaking her head at the situation as she slowed down in front of a three-story house that had been cut up into apartments. There was no parking space for miles—naturally. With a curse, she went around the block a couple of times, wondering if she dared double-park it, when—hallelujah—someone pulled out across the street. It took her a second and a half to do an illegal U-ey and wedge her sedan into the spot. She didn't have a residential parking sticker, but she wasn't going to be long, and at least she wasn't in front of a hydrant.

Getting out, she huddled into her thin wool coat. April in New England on the ocean translated into thirty days of bitter, wet wind that chilled you to the bone and wreaked havoc on your hair. And that wasn't the worst of it—there were puddles all over the place, even when it hadn't rained. Everything in town seemed to drip, like the city was a sponge that had surpassed its capacity . . . the cars, the buildings, the spindly trees, all of it wicking the moisture out of the air and channeling it down onto the perma-damp asphalt and concrete beneath your feet.

Definitely more L.L. Bean than Louboutin.

At the front door of the house, she craned in for a closer look at a seventies-era intercom that had three little buttons. Per Isaac's instructions, she punched the one on the bottom.

A moment later, the ring was answered by a woman

dressed in a retina-busting, retro afghan the size of a bed-sheet. Her hair was cranked into corkscrew curls the color of a Halloween pumpkin and there was a cigarette between the painted fingertips of her right hand.

Evidently, her look had gotten stuck in the same era as the intercom.

"You're Isaac's girl?"

Grier stuck her hand out and did not correct the statement. Figured it was better than "attorney." "I'm Grier."

"He called here." The woman stepped back. "Told me to let you in. You know, you don't seem like his type."

A quick image of the man sitting so silent and deadly flashed through Grier's mind: on that theory, the guy should have been dating a Beretta.

"Opposites attract," she said as she looked over the landlady's shoulder. Down at the end of the tight hall, the staircase loomed in the distance like a spiritual beacon, at once apparent and yet unattainable.

"Well . . ." The landlady lounged against her flocked wall-paper. "There's opposites, like one person is a talker and the other isn't. And there's *opposites*. How did you meet?"

As her nosy stare locked on Grier's gold necklace, there was the temptation to answer, "the penal system," just to see how far the woman's eyes would bug. "We were matched up."

"Oh, like eHarmony?"

"Precisely." The main points of compatibility being his requiring someone with a law degree to get him bail and her having a JD from Harvard. "Will you let me in his place now?"

"You're in a hurry. You know, my sister tried eHarmony. The guy she met was a frickin' jerk."

It turned out that getting the landlady up the stairs took about as much effort as throwing her over a shoulder and carrying her to the third floor. However, ten minutes of question deflection later, they were finally at the door.

"You know," the landlady said as she put her keys to work and unlocked things, "you should think about—"

"Thanks so much for all your help," Grier said as she slipped inside and shut the woman out in the hall.

Leaning against the wood panels, she took a deep breath and listened to the grousing fade on its way downstairs.

And then she turned around ... Oh, God.

The barren room was as wilted and lonely as an old man, proving that poverty, like age, was a great equalizer—she could have been in any tenement or drug house or condemned building in any city in any country: The old pine floors had all the gloss of a sheet of sandpaper, and the ceiling had water stains in the corners that were the color of urine. No furniture in sight, not one table or chair or TV. Just a sleeping bag, a pair of combat boots and some clothes in precisely folded piles.

Isaac Rothe's pillow was nothing but a sweatshirt.

As she stood just inside the apartment, all she could think of was the last place her brother had stayed. At least her client's was clean and there weren't hypodermic needles and dirty spoons everywhere: This sparseness did not appear to be the result of an addict's slanted priorities.

But good Lord, it was still a shocker to remember where Daniel had ended up. The filth ... the cockroaches ... the rotting food ...

Forcing herself to get a move on, she went into the kitchen and wasn't surprised to find all the cupboards and the drawers and the refrigerator empty. Bathroom had a razor, shaving cream, toothbrush, and soap.

In the bedroom, which was totally unoccupied, she went into the closet and used the penlight on her key chain to look around inside. The panel that Isaac had described was over to the left and she got it open without a problem.

And yes, there was, in fact, a Star Market plastic bag with twenty-five thousand dollars in cash hidden in the dusty space between the framing boards. Or at least the loose collection of bills looked and weighed like that much money —

*Creak.*

Grier froze.

Listened hard.

Glancing over her shoulder, she stopped breathing. But all she heard was the thunder of her heart.

When the silence persisted, she shoved the bag back where it had been, replaced the panel and shut the closet again; then she went over to the window across the way. The glass was so damned milky with grime, it wasn't as if anyone could see in from the outside, and yet she felt as though she was being watched. . . .

Something flashed and she leaned in closer.

At the top of the window, a pair of tiny metal plates had been stuck to the cracking paint, one on the frame, the other on the sash. There was another set at the bottom and the things appeared to be made of copper that had been coated with a matte finish of some kind. If she hadn't come over, she never would have noticed them.

Grier went back through living room, the kitchen and the bathroom, and found the same thing on every single window. Top and bottom, two sets. And the doors were likewise equiped — all of them, interior and exterior.

She knew exactly what the plates were.

Her multimillion-dollar house on Louisburg Square in Beacon Hill had them on its own sashes and jambs. They were state-of-the-art security alarm contacts.

Standing in the center of the apartment, her mind ran through the math: bowling-alley empty, forty-dollar sleeping bag for a bed, no phone . . . but the place was wired for sound like it was a bank safe.

Time to dig around.

Using the soft cloth that she cleaned her sunglasses with, she went through her client's personal effects without leaving fingerprints behind — and she found the alarm's receiver in the folds of the sleeping bag. As well as a pair of forty-caliber handguns that were fitted with silencers and had no serial numbers on them and a hunting knife that was well-worn but viciously sharp.

"Jesus . . . Christ," she whispered, putting everything back just as she'd found it.

Rising up from her crouch by the "bed," she went into the kitchen. Systematically going from handle to handle, she wiped off her prints and then looked under the sink and behind the refrigerator. Next stop was the bathroom, and her hands were shaky as she got rid of any traces she might have left behind and also flashed her penlight into dark corners.

In her haze of jerky suspicion, she was well aware that she was violating her client's privacy, but the bloodhound in her couldn't stop—the frantic hunt was like a muscle that hadn't been used and needed the exercise. She had done this so many times with Daniel's apartments and cars, and by the time she finished going through Isaac Rothe's place, she felt sweaty and vaguely nauseous in a very familiar way.

No drugs, though. Anywhere.

Returning to the living room, she measured the windows once again. The twenty-five grand would be worth protecting . . . but the security system hadn't been activated.

Which meant it was used as a notifier when Isaac was sleeping.

In her experience, the only kind of criminal element with access to this caliber of equipment was a drug lord or very high-level Mafia capo. Her client's affect and physical appearance matched neither of those profiles—typically, those were older men, not under-thirties who were built like enforcers.

There was one other possible explanation, however.

She got out her cell phone and dialed up a number that she'd used too many times in the past.

When the call was answered, she took a deep, long one and felt as though she were jumping off a cliff.

"Hi, Louie, how's my favorite PI doing?.... Aw, that's sweet of you.... Uh-huh.... I'm good."

Liar, liar, liar on that one.

While the two of them played catch-up, she headed back to the money stash and wiped the doorknob of the closet with her square of cloth. "As a matter of fact I do need something. If you have some time, I have somebody I'd like you to check out for me, please?"

After she told Louie all she knew about her client, which wasn't more than a name and a birth date and this inconsequential address, she hung up.

The question was, of course, what now?

She hadn't believed Isaac Rothe when he'd told her he had cash.

So she'd posted his bail herself.

It had been her only choice: The court was willing to let her client off, but the bailsmen wouldn't touch the case. Too much of a flight risk.

Which suggested the judge might have had his head wedged when he'd made his decision.

Oh, wait . . . that would be her in this situation.

Looking around the empty apartment, she realized that her client was about as substantive as a draft. There was no way he was going to stick around for his hearings.

Hell, he probably wasn't going to be here a minute past when he was released. He clearly had resources, and his things were backpack portable.

She glanced at the door.

Good thing she could afford to lose that twenty-five grand of hers. The plan had been to pledge it on faith so that he trusted her and would let her help him.

But it was probably going to end up being a very expensive lesson in not investing in people you didn't know and shouldn't trust.

# CHAPTER
## 7

It was six p.m. when Isaac was finally brought out of holding by a guard. In spite of how long it took to come and get him—and he had a feeling the staff had been taking their own sweet time—the process for his release was smooth and quick now that they had decided to let him out: Cuffs to be unlocked—theirs. Signatures to be inked—his. Clothes to change out of—theirs. Clothes to change into—his. Wallet returned.

All he could think about was his attorney. He couldn't believe she'd gotten him bail.

Or carried money for him.

Man, he owed her. Without Grier Childe, he wouldn't be on the verge of the freedom that was going to keep him alive.

He hadn't seen her since she'd come to tell him that she'd been successful with the judge, but clearly she'd settled things with his cash or he wouldn't be back in his own boxers.

The lockdown part of the courthouse was separated from the public section by a series of gates that took him by the room he'd met with her in. The last set of don't-even-think-about-its was by central processing, where he'd been checked in and photographed.

God, he could still smell her perfume.

With a clank, the steel lock was sprung and the guard gave him a shove in lieu of a "bon voyage" —

"Do you need a ride?"

Isaac stopped dead just inside the waiting area. Ms. Childe was standing across the linoleum, looking like she belonged at a cocktail party and not the county jail: Her hair was in the same twist, but she wasn't in a suit anymore. She was wearing some kind of little-black-dress thing ... as well as a pair of sheer black panty hose that made him swallow hard to keep from groaning.

What a woman she was.

"Do you?" she prompted.

Feeling like a Neanderthal for going the goggle route, he shook his head. "No, thank you, ma'am."

She walked over to the exit and opened the way out, standing to the side, looking like a million bucks ... and as if she had nothing better to do with her time than play doorstop for him.

Isaac stepped out of the waiting room and into a hall that had just a bank of elevators and a fire exit.

"Let me give you a ride," she told him as she punched the down arrow. "I know where you live, remember? And it'll be hard for you to get a cab at rush hour."

True enough. Plus he only had five dollars in cash on him. "I'll take care of it."

"Exactly. By letting me drive you. It's cold and you don't even have a coat, for God's sake."

Also true. He'd lost his sweatshirt in the rush of getting cuffed. But like everything else about him, that was not her problem.

When she turned away, as if the decision had been made, he stared at the complicated swirls of her hair. He couldn't see any pins or anything, and yet it didn't look shellacked.

Magic, he thought.

Without being aware of it, he reached up with his busted punching hand like he was going to touch the nape of her neck. He caught himself in time, though.

And he was gone a moment later, ducking soundlessly into the stairwell.

Which had an open square layout. Perfect.

He made no noise as he slung his body over the banister and let himself free-fall two stories down, catching himself on a just-in-time grab and then swinging his torso up and over. He landed in a silent crouch and didn't wait even a heartbeat before he took the last set of steps in a leap and hit the exit. As he broke free into the cold April wind, he scared the crap out of the smokers by the door before leaving them in the dust.

Falling into a run, his path took him up through a dark maze of buildings and then down past all the jewelry stores, as well as Macy's and Filene's Basement. Rush hour meant the streets were teeming with professional people disgorged from the Financial District, all of them filing into underground T stops or streaming like ants across the park. Fortunately, there was less foot traffic in Chinatown, although more cars—which improved his time.

As he gunned for his place, the exertion helped with the fact that he had nothing but a muscle shirt on, although the wet chill in the air did keep the bruises and the cut on his forehead from pounding too much. When he got to the block where he stayed, he was almost disappointed to slow down—exercise was good for calming his mind and taking the kinks out.

Approaching the three-story house from the rear, he wound in and out of the shallow yards of the neighbors and stopped about thirty feet from the back door. The lights were on in the landlady's crib and the second floor, but everything was off on his level.

When he was reasonably sure he hadn't been followed, he bent down and picked up a stone. Staying in the shadows, he closed in, then hauled back and snapped out a throw, clipping the dangling head of the bald bulb over the stoop and putting the exterior lighting to sleep.

Isaac waited, hanging tight right where he was: Speed was often your friend, but that wasn't always the case. Sometimes going slow was the only reason you woke up the next morning.

Downstairs, a shadow got up and passed from window to window, then made a return trip to the flicker of the television. Not good news, but not a surprise. Mrs. Mulcahy never left her roost except to go get food—and she was the kind of pesky landlord who made him consider the benefits of park benches. Tonight, however, she wasn't the reason he was sneaking into his own place: Chances were damn good that with his name in the penal system, his address had been popped by XOps, and that meant this location was no longer secure.

He had to get in and out of there fast.

Ten minutes later, it was a case of over to the back steps. Key in the lock. Ghosting up the stairwell.

And on his way to the top floor, he avoided the squeaking steps—which eliminated three out of every four of the bastards.

The door to his flat opened without a sound because he'd oiled the hinges the night he'd moved in, and with a quick twist of the dead bolt, he locked himself inside. A fast listen told him that there were no sounds other than the television below, but he stayed where he was for a minute and a half just to be sure.

When there was nothing out of order that he could sense, he got down to business.

Lightning fast was the speed. Whisper quiet was the way.

Out of the kitchen. Into the front room.

He took one look at his stuff and knew Grier had rifled through it—the shift in the pile of clothes was so subtle only he would notice, but the folding system he'd developed was designed precisely for that purpose.

He put on the sweatshirt he used as a pillow, slipped his two forties into the fat center pockets in front and changed into his combat boots. Ammo, hunting blade and his cell phone went into his pants, and then he put on the black windbreaker that was all he had, coat-wise.

Down to the bedroom. Into the closet.

There had been twenty-seven thousand eight hundred and fifty-three dollars in his stash, so he should have a little something left over after the bail.

He popped off the panel and reached in—

*"Fuck."*

He didn't have to open the Star Market bag and count; by weight alone, he knew that Grier hadn't taken even a dollar out of the rolls of hundreds and twenties or the fluffy scruff of the unbundled.

But she had been here—Matthias would have taken the weapons to make him less dangerous. And waited around to shoot him in the head.

Shit ... the cash-intact crap meant either there was a bondsman involved ... or she'd bailed him out with her own money. And when he'd been processed, there had been no disclosure about a third party posting the benjamins. So she must have.

*Damn it.*

Snapping back into action, he took the bag and replaced the section of bead board. Then he went around to the windows and doors, flicking off the receptors with his knife and putting the metal plates into his pockets. No more than three minutes later, he left the way he'd come: out the back and quiet as smoke.

The five hundred dollars he left on the counter in the kitchen was going to have to cover the fact that he was breaking his lease, and Mrs. Mulcahy would have to figure out herself that he'd left when there was no sign of him after a couple of days.

The less contact with him, the safer she was.

Same with his attorney.

God *damn* it.

Down below, in the backyard, Isaac's senses were razor-sharp as he whispered around to the side of the apartment house and resumed his jog. He didn't slow his pace until he was a couple of miles away.

Ducking into an alley, the call he made was answered on the second ring: "Yeah."

"It's Rothe."

The fight promoter perked right up. "Jesus Christ, I heard you were in jail. Listen, I can't bail you—"

"I'm out. We fighting tonight?"

"Shit, yeah! We was gonna have to move from that location anyways. This is *awesome*. How'd you pull it off?"

"What's the address and how do I get there?"

The location was some six miles away in a town called Malden, which made sense—the cops in Southie were obviously dunzo with having fights on their turf. And how the promoter hadn't gotten pinched was a mystery. Unless, of course, he was the one who'd given the tip and gotten out in time.

You never knew with people like that guy.

After Isaac hung up, his next move was to find a bus shelter with a schedule. When the right ten-wheeler monolith trundled along, he boarded it and sat by the emergency exit window.

As he stared out at the apartments and businesses and buildings that passed by, he wanted to scream.

He was getting out of XOps because he'd found his conscience, and that meant he couldn't take off with Grier Childe having covered him to that extent. She'd looked rich, but twenty-five grand was a lot of cash no matter how much you were worth. Hell, he wouldn't have felt comfortable with even an anonymous bail bondsman eating that bill. But that elegant woman who he'd lied to? And sent on a dirty errand?

Nope. He wasn't about to leave her in the lurch.

And didn't that just complicate everything.

Two hours after she left the jail without her client or any clue where he had gone, Grier stood in the middle of a shindig full of people who were arguably part of her tribe. Everyone was old-money Boston and shared common *Mayflower* ancestry.

God love them, but some of these blue bloods were old enough to have come over on the boat itself.

Her mind wasn't on this ballroom at the Four Seasons, however. Or the man in front of her who was talking to her about . . . What was this party for? The MFA or the ballet?

She glanced across at the placards that had been set up. Reproductions of Degas. Which didn't necessarily help answer that one: All those fuzzy tutus could have fit into either category.

As the bow tie in front of her kept chatting away, she was not tracking. Her mind was stuck back in that hallway at the courthouse . . . when she'd turned around from the elevators and found herself alone.

She'd never even heard Isaac move, much less leave. One moment he was behind her; the next there was nothing but air where he'd been. How someone that size could pull off a disappearance like that was astounding.

Of course, it hadn't taken a genius to figure that he'd gone out the back stairwell—so she'd punched through the fire door and started after him, taking her high heels off and jogging down in her stocking feet. She went all the way to the bottom of the stairs, pushed out of the exit, and glanced over at a guy who was lighting up a cigarette. When she'd asked him if he'd seen a big man leave, he'd just shrugged, blown a milky white cloud into the air and wandered off.

After she'd put her stilettos back on, she'd gone to the underground parking garage, gotten in her car and driven over to her client's apartment again. There had been no lights on upstairs, but she hadn't expected any. The last place someone on the run went was the address they'd given the police.

She'd known her client was a flight risk. What she hadn't counted on was him being like that smoker's exhale in the breeze, gone as fast as he had appeared.

Coming back to the present, Grier put her warm chardonnay on the tray of a passing waiter—just as her phone started to vibrate against her hip.

Excusing herself, she ducked out into the hallway. "Hello?"

"Hey, Miz Childe. How you be?"

"Breathlessly waiting for your call, Louie, that's how."

"Aw, now that's sweet, right there. You're a good woman." Louie dropped the affable routine and got down to business. "You're not going to like what I have to tell you."

Why am I not surprised? she thought. "Let's get to it, then."

"He's a ghost."

No disagreement there. Still, considering she'd been chatting up her dead brother lately, ghosts could be real. "He looked pretty corporeal to me when I was sitting across the table from him."

"Well, the Isaac Rothe I was able to locate died about five years ago. Down in Mississippi. He was found dead in a ditch on a cattle farm, and he was nineteen at the time. The newspaper articles I read said he was busted up beyond recognition, but the photo of him while alive that ran with the obit matched the mug shot taken at the police station yesterday night. It's the same guy."

"Jesus . . ."

"Not for nuthin', but the disappear job back then was expensive and extensive. I mean, for him to have lasted this long undercover? Sure, you can do it—this is a big country and all—but you got to be careful, because there are a lot of central databases. He hasn't been using his own social security number—that is different than the one with the name originally—so it could be part of how he stayed gone. But my sense is, he knows what he's doing. And he has some serious backing."

"What kind of serious backing?"

"I'll give you two initials: U and S."

"Last name 'government'?"

"I was going with Uncle Sam, but yup, that fits."

"I don't get it, though. If he wanted to stay lost, why did he keep his own name? You buy a new social, usually it comes with a different first and last, doesn't it?"

"You'd have to ask him about the whys. But first thing comes to my mind—he never expected to be found. And I'll tell you this . . . I'd be careful around him. That body in that ditch in Mississippi didn't get there by accident. I'd bet my retainer on the fact that someone killed a white boy who looked enough like him to pass in a closed casket—and guess what: Your client there is still breathing. So that SOB could be a murderer."

Grier closed her eyes. Great. This just kept getting better: She'd not only bailed out a flight risk who had bolted, but a man who might well have killed somebody and faked his own death.

Polite and gentle my ass, she thought, wondering how in the hell someone like her, who'd passed nineteenth grade summa cum laude, had managed to be so stupid.

At that moment, the crowd parted to reveal Daniel in a tuxedo lounging next to one of those Degas. As he toasted her with a champagne flute, his handsome face was wallpapered in told-you-so.

The dead sonofabitch had a point. Even though he'd passed two years ago, she was still performing a kind of CPR on him: Desperate to bring him back to real life, she was caught up in other people's dramas, that urge to get in and help sometimes the only thing that kept her going.

"You okay there, girl?"

She gripped her cell phone harder and wondered what the PI would say if he knew she was staring into the all-knowing eyes of her deceased sibling. "Not really, Louie."

"He snow you?"

"I snowed myself."

"Well, I got one other piece of info for you—although I'm not sure I want to give it over. Sounds like you're in too deep already."

Bracing herself, she muttered, "Tell me. I might as well know all of it."

# CHAPTER

## 8

### *North Lawn, Heaven*

Up high above the earth, in the celestial realm, the archangel Nigel strode over cropped green grass, hands clasped behind his back, head down, eyes straight ahead. His croquet whites had not been put to proper use, his failure to concentrate rendering him a pitiful contestant against the archangel Colin's prodigious skills with a mallet.

Indeed, Nigel's balls had been rolling thither and yon, going everywhere except through the wickets.

Eventually, he'd given up the pretense. There was no training his mind upon aught save what irritated him so, and therefore he was useless but for ambulation and rumination.

Damn it, rules needed to be followed. That was why in contests of wit and wiles they were agreed upon before play began—so there were no questions or errors due to misinterpretation in the midst of the game. Verily, he had always believed that a fair contest required two things: well-matched opponents and well-defined parameters.

And in the case at hand, namely that of the future of mankind, the first criterion was met rather squarely. His side and the demon Devina's were equal in strengths, weaknesses, and focus.

Most particularly the focus part, as both "teams" knew well how high the stakes were: The very future of the world below hung in the balance, the great Creator's patience having been tried over a protracted, inconclusive course of conflict between good and evil on the planet below. Mere weeks ago, it had been declared from on high that there would be seven final opportunities to prevail—and upon a simple majority of them, dominion would be won over not only the physical world but the bucolic heavens and the fiery depths of Hell.

Nigel was in charge of the "good" side. Devina captained the "bad."

And that scurrilous demon was cheating.

The rules of the game provided that Nigel and Devina were to choose the souls "in play" and then sit back and watch Jim Heron interact and steer the course of events such that the resolution was either redemption or condemnation.

Seven chances. And the first one had been resolved in Nigel's favor.

The next six were to be conducted in the true arena. And in the course of events, Nigel and Devina were allowed a certain amount of "coaching": As Nigel had won the coin toss, so he had been permitted to approach Jim first—and for parity to be preserved, Devina had been likewise allowed to interact with the man. But now they were supposed to be off the field and on the sidelines for the most part, with interaction limited to the occasional time-out and the end-of-match recap by whoever's side won.

Devina was down there, however. Down there and mucking about.

"You interfered as well."

Nigel stopped, but did not turn around to face Colin. "My dear boy, do go fuck yourself."

Colin's laugh was deep and for once lacking in sarcasm. "Ah, there's the lad we know and love. I'd wondered where you'd gone, given how badly you'd played."

Keeping his back to his best mate, Nigel stared across the lawn at the high castle walls of the Manse of Souls. Beyond the vast stone fortification, in an infinite mansion of fine appointments and leisurely accoutrements, were the life-lights of those who had proven themselves of good and fine nature during their time on Earth.

If the angels did not prevail, all of those who so deserved what they had now would be lost to the pits of Hell. As would all else—including himself and his three associates.

"Adrian and Edward are not in the rules," Colin pointed out.

"They take direction from him. It is a far sight different from what she is doing."

"Granted. But we are not unrepresented down there."

"She is toying with the fundamentals of the conflict."

"Are you truly surprised." Colin's tone, always sharp, turned deadly. "We have battled her too long to be taken unaware by her duplicity. Which perhaps is why the Creator allows you to persist with our two emissaries."

"Perhaps also the Creator wishes us to win."

Nigel forced himself to start walking again, and his eyes could not depart from the bridge over the moat and the stout entrance to the manse. The sight of the massive, locked portal, to which only he had the metaphysical key, reassured him—but alas it was for no good reason. The souls were safe only if these contests were won.

"Are you going to take further action?" Colin asked as they made a fat loop over the lawn and headed toward the table upon which tea had been set out.

"How can I?"

"You're willing to risk losing just to be honest?"

Nigel waved at Bertie and Byron, who were seated

off in the distance before a teapot and a carousel of tiny sandwiches. As was proper, they had neither poured nor partaken, and they would not until the other two chairs at the table were filled. Meanwhile, Tarquin, Bertie's beloved Irish wolfhound, was curled into a sit at the archangel's side, the great beast staring over at Colin and Nigel, his wise, calm eyes missing nothing.

Nigel fussed with his cravat. "Victory and deceit are incompatible. And Adrian and Edward were your idea. I don't know why I'm allowing it."

Colin cursed, his aristocratic intonation adding precise corners to the naughty words. "You know damn well we don't stand a bloody chance unless we bend the rules as well. That's why you're consenting."

Nigel's form of reply was but a quiet coughing sound, his signal that the conversation was over and done with. And upon his lead, the two of them went to the table that was arranged at his will and would disappear in the same manner.

Nigel, as with the others, neither lived nor breathed; he simply was. And the food was the same, neither necessary nor extant—as was the landscape and all that the four of them did to pass their eternity. But the trappings of a gracious life were of value. Indeed, the quarters that he shared with Colin were well kitted-out and the sojourns they took therein were not for any sleep necessity, but for recharging of a different kind.

War was exhausting, its burdens ne'er-ending, and at times, one needed physical succor.

As Nigel took his place at the table, he pulled his strength about him and resumed the mantle of leadership whilst Byron smiled and poured. In front of the other two, he was ever who he had to be. Colin, however, was different—although only when they were alone.

Never when there were others present.

As he lifted his fine bone china cup off its saucer, the

perfumed steam from the Earl Grey wafted into his nose, and he worried beneath his calm exterior.

They could not risk losing even one of these contests, but a gentleman did not play dirty.

He had his standards of gamesmanship.

Damn it.

# CHAPTER
## 9

O ut in the Boston suburb of Malden, Jim and Adrian and Eddie were nothing but shadows in the dense darkness as they approached a half-finished office building. The structure was part of a shaggy, abandoned development that had some fifteen or more of the suckers ... and not a single one of them was in use or even completed. Which suggested the financer/owner was bleeding mortally from his bank account.

Assuming he hadn't already toe-tagged himself with Chapter 7 paperwork and jumped into a liquidation grave.

The unit they'd come to see had a circle of lawn that cut into the balding forest in back, and the three of them stayed among the trees while surveilling the layout: The five-story-high skeleton was up and sealed with plum-colored glass windows, but there were no lights on and nothing but packed dirt for the parking lot in the rear.

Place was utterly abandoned.

Well, by lawful visitors, that was.

Illegal trespassers were streaming in, their cars and trucks forming a surprisingly orderly row not far from where Jim and his boys were.

Looked like the intel from that fireman back at the gym had been solid.

"You know," Adrian said, "I could get in the ring. Throw some fists. Maybe a human or two."

Jim shook his head. "I don't think we need that right now."

"In an earlier life, were you a pair of brakes?"

"Try a brick wall. Come on, let's get down there."

Blending in among the other men heading for the back entrance, Jim searched for Isaac—in the unlikely event the guy had gotten out of jail and still wanted to fight. But more significantly, he kept his eyes peeled for someone who looked like a soldier: hard, tight in the head, and there to get a job done instead of play spectator.

He was after the one who was supposed to kill Isaac.

With the way the XOps team worked, it would be somebody they'd both worked with: Given the amount of screening and training and proving ground you had to go through to get on the team, there was a limited pool of guys who made it, and new recruits took years to develop. Jim had been out only about six months; he was going to know the assassin.

And so would Isaac.

"You guys head in," he said to his boys as they came up to a door propped open by a cinder block. "I'm going to hang out here. Let me know if you see Rothe."

Except he was going to bet they didn't. If the soldier was here at all, he'd be hiding somewhere and scoping out who had come before making himself known. After all, it didn't take a genius to figure out that getting popped by the police was tantamount to sticking a red flag in your ass.

Which was why in some respects, intercepting the assassin was even more important than running into Isaac.

As Eddie and Ad slipped through the fire door, Jim faded back so that he was standing in the lee of the building. Which was out of habit rather than necessity—no one could see him.

Another bene of being an angel: He could choose when he was visible to mortals.

Lighting up a Marlboro that he kept as hidden as his leather jacket and his combats, he tracked the crowd as it filed in. Tonight's peanut gallery was made up of your standard-issue Joes: Lot of junior-varsity beer guts—that in another five years were going to be state champs. Patriots and Red Sox hats only. Couple of Chelmsford High School sweatshirts.

When the influx became just a trickle, he was ready to curse. Maybe he should have infiltrated the damn jail—although that would have been complicated. Lot of eyes, and even though he could pull off the not-there, if he had to kill somebody or save someone? He'd make any audience schizoid and probably show up in a blurry "Aliens Exist!" article in the *National Enquirer*—

A lone man emerged from the ring of trees. He was huge and the black windbreaker he wore did absolutely nothing to shrink the size of his shoulders. As he approached, he walked like the soldier he'd been trained to be, swinging his gaze around and keeping both hands in his pockets—likely gripping one or maybe two guns.

"Hello, Isaac . . ." As soon as the name left his lips, Jim was struck by a powerful, inescapable pull that made the man not just a target, but a destination.

The original plan had been to find the guy and throw him on a plane out of the country with some resources—just to help him along his way.

Now, though, he realized he needed to do more than that.

Chalking up the sea change to seeing Rothe for the first time since that night in the desert, Jim did not run up to the guy or shout his name or do anything that would spook the fucker. Instead, he summoned illumination to himself, calling it out of the darkness by agitating the molecules around his body.

He made sure his hands were up and his palms were empty. And that Isaac was the only one who saw him.

Isaac's head snapped around. And a nasty-looking gun appeared from out of that windbreaker.

Jim didn't move and just shook his head, the universal sign for "I'm not here to cap your ass."

When Isaac finally came forward, he took no chances. As he stepped up, another gun came out of a pocket to hang discreetly at his side. Both weapons had silencers and blended in with his black track pants.

For a moment, the pair of them just stared at each other like a couple of idiots, and Jim had an absurd impulse to hug the motherfucker—although he doused that quick. One, there was no reason to be a nancy. And two, it would likely get him shot at point-blank range: XOps soldiers weren't snugglers—unless they planned on killing someone.

"Hey," Jim said roughly.

Isaac cleared his throat. Twice. "What are you doing here?"

"Just passing through. Thought I'd take you to dinner."

That got a slow smile, the kind that smacked of the past. "Payback?"

"Yeah." Jim's eyes traced the rear lot and saw only a couple of stragglers. "You could call it that."

"I thought you were out."

"I am."

"So . . ." When Jim didn't immediately answer, the guy's icy eyes grew shrewd. "He sent you to kill me. Didn't he."

"I needed a favor and it was expensive."

"So why are we talking?"

"I don't take orders from Matthias anymore."

Isaac frowned. "Stupid ass. He's going to hunt you now, too. Unless you blow my head off here and now."

Jim put his cigarette between his teeth and held his palms out. "I'm unarmed. Pat me down."

It was entirely unsurprising that Isaac disappeared one of his guns, and with his free hand, did a quick review of Jim's territory.

That frown rode the guy's brow even harder. "What the fuck are you thinking."

"Right now? Oh . . . let's see, that you should not be fighting in there, for starters. After all, I'm assuming you're not here as part of the popcorn-and-Raisinets set. Instead, I want you to come with me and let me help you get out of the country safely."

Isaac's voice was ancient as he shook his head. "You know I can't trust you. I'm sorry, man. But I can't."

Fucking hell.

Bottom line, though, was you couldn't fault the reasoning: In XOps, even when you were on assignments with your compadres, it was each man for himself. Decide to leave the fold? If you were smart, you wouldn't put your life or your faith in your own mother's hands.

Jim took a drag and focused on the other man's face, feeling that burning drive in his chest get hotter. Hard to explain the "why" of it . . . but he couldn't pull out now that he'd found Isaac. Even if that compromised his battle with Devina. Even if Isaac didn't want his help. Even if it put himself in danger.

Isaac Rothe had to be saved.

"I'm sorry," he heard himself say. "But I need to help you. And you're going to let me."

The other man's eyes narrowed into slits. "Excuse me?"

Jim glanced over to the door. Adrian and Eddie had reappeared and . . . the two of them were looking like this was all supposed to happen. As if they had known all along that Isaac would show up here. And Jim would talk to the guy. And . . .

On a quick tilt of the head, Jim regarded the dark heavens, and thought about the way his first assignment had gone: no coincidences in any of the chain of events. Everyone and everything he'd met up with had woven into his task. And golly gee-fuckin'-whiz, it was so not hard to imagine that Matthias was playing on Devina's team. The guy had done evil wherever he went, perpetrating acts of violence and deceit that had both shaped the world on a global scale as well as altered private lives forever.

Jim refocused on Isaac. Maybe being so damned committed to this AWOL soldier wasn't just a page out of his past . . . Hell, Nigel, his new boss, hadn't seemed easygoing in the slightest—and yet the archangel had rolled over the instant Jim had announced he was going after Isaac: Not the kind of thing that you did if you were team captain and your quarterback started running for your own goal line.

Exactly the kind of thing you did if your boy was right where you wanted him.

Holy shit . . . Isaac *was* his next assignment.

Man, that shit he'd pulled over his own corpse at the funeral home was going to prove to be a stroke of genius.

"You're going to need me," he pronounced.

"I can take care of myself."

As Isaac went to leave, Jim snagged his arm. "You know you can't do this alone. Don't be an asshole."

There was a long moment.

"What are you thinking, Jim." The guy's pale eyes were haunted. "You were out. You were free. You were the one who got away. Why would you go back into the hellhole?"

Jim led with a logic that the other man could believe in—and something that was also the truth; just not the only one. "I owe you. You know that. I owe you for that night."

Jim Heron was exactly as Isaac remembered him: big, jacked, and nothing but business. The blue eyes were the same, the blond hair was still mostly buzzed off, the face was freshly shaven as always. He even had a Marlboro quietly smoldering in his hand.

But there was something a little different, some kind of vibe that was just . . . off, though not in a bad way.

Maybe the lucky bastard had taken to actually sleeping at night, as opposed to keeping a gun in his palm and waking up at every sound.

God, when he'd heard Heron had pulled out of XOps, he'd never expected to see the man again—either because Matthias rethought the soldier's bye-bye-birdie card and put a bullet into his think tank or because Jim wisely stayed away from anyone and anything that had to do with his former life.

And yet here he was.

As Isaac stared into the guy's eyes, he found himself believing, as much as he could, that Heron had come to help because of that debt created in the land of sand and sun. Besides, if the SOB had wanted Isaac dead, that would have happened long before any of this conversating had gotten rolling.

"If I'd come to kill you," Jim murmured, "you'd be on the ground already."

Bingo.

"Okay," Isaac said. "You hold my shit while I fight. We can start there."

Well, didn't that call out the fuck-no in the guy's face. "You can't get in that ring. Between the flyer I saw and the arrest, you might as well have a GPS tracker shoved up your ass."

"I need the money."

"I have cash."

Isaac glanced over by the exit and realized that there were two big men hanging by the door. When they raised their hands in greeting, he asked, "They with you?"

Jim seemed surprised. "Ah, yeah. They are."

"You starting your own crew? Going freelance?"

"You could say that. But we were talking about you and how you're not fighting."

To piss with that. He wasn't stiffing that attorney for twenty-five grand, and the two thousand dollars he had left after that wasn't going to get him far. And although Matthias could send a guy into the ring who could kill him in front of a hundred witnesses and still make it look like an accident, what choice did he have? He was no one's charity case—he'd learned that long ago—and he wasn't about to be in debt to Jim, either, just to settle an old score.

In ten minutes, he could earn another a grand or two. And if he got shanked by Matthias's second in command, the one who'd showed up last night? It didn't really matter. He'd known the moment he bolted from the team that a funeral was waiting for him, except he was like someone with a mortal disease: The cure for going AWOL was a bitch and likely to kill him, but at least he was putting up a fight and dying on his own terms.

Staying in XOps? Shit, he was dead even though he had a heartbeat.

He was so hollow at this point he might as well be in his grave.

"I'm fighting," he said. "And I'll give you my stuff to hold while I'm in the octagon. That's as much help as I'll accept tonight."

No reason to tell the guy how much cash was in the windbreaker. And Heron already knew about the guns—but clearly wasn't of a mind to use them.

"This is a huge mistake."

Isaac frowned. "Lot of people would have told you to leave Matthias out in that desert to die, but you brought him back because you had to—and you wouldn't have let anyone talk you out of it. Same thing here. Either get on board or get out of my way."

A curse word. Then another. Finally, Jim took a last inhale on the cigarette and ground the butt out on the bottom of his combat boot. "Fine. But I will intercede—are we clear? You get in the ring with the wrong asswipe, I'm going to shut the fight down."

"Why the hell are you doing this?" Isaac said hoarsely.

"Why the hell did you go out to find me and Matthias that night?"

Memories of two years ago bubbled up and Isaac went back to the desert, back to the moment when the encrypted radio had squawked and he'd picked it up and heard Jim's thready voice.

Ten minutes was all it took to make the arrangements: medic to their tent, airlift out waiting, and a trauma team over the border, boom, boom, boom. And then he'd sat there and waited for about a minute and a half.

The Land Rover he'd found had been parked with the keys in it and Isaac had gotten behind the wheel and gone gunning. What Jim hadn't known was that when Matthias and he had left, Isaac had hung back and watched the direction they'd headed.

Something just hadn't seemed right about the trip out into the dunes: Nobody went anywhere alone with Matthias. It was like asking an Ebola patient to cough on you.

Making big fat sweeps out from camp, he'd found them an hour later a good five miles away from where he'd started: In his night-vision goggles, he'd zeroed in on something moving slowly across a rise, and considering that trolls didn't really exist, he could only assume it was a man hefting another man through the sand.

As he'd driven over to them, he'd thought about how funny deserts were: Like their polar opposite, the ocean, at night they melded into the sky at the far distance, and it wasn't until you had a reference point, like a shrub or a ship—or a dumb-ass idea like Jim's savior shit—that you had visual confirmation the earth was in fact round, and not square.

And that Heaven was not where you were.

He'd been traveling without headlights and he didn't turn them on. Instead, he took a white undershirt and held the thing out of the window, knowing that Jim would see it and hopefully not think it was the enemy. Fucker had been armed like a tank battalion when he'd left camp.

As Isaac had eased to a halt, he'd gotten out with both hands fully visible and allowed Jim to approach. The guy had looked exhausted, but then he'd been carrying Matthias's deadweight across his back for God only knew how many miles through the shifting sand.

It had not been a surprise that Jim had glared at the knight-in-shining routine—in spite of their boss's condition, which was clearly critical.

*Just passing through*, Isaac had said. *Thought I'd take you to dinner.*

With a shake, he came back to this night, here in . . . Where was he? Malden?

His voice held the same exhaustion Jim's had had way back when. "Don't get yourself killed because of me, okay?"

Jim muttered something that sounded like, *A little late for that*. But clearly, that hadn't been the words.

Forcing his head back into the game, Isaac left the past and his emotions in the dust, his focus shifting to the present as he turned away and started walking into the entrance to the building.

As he stepped inside, Jim and the guy's two buddies were tight on him and he had to wonder why Heron wasn't wearing a hat to hide his face or anything to disguise who he was. Dumb son of a bitch. Gets free . . . only to come back in.

Crazy.

Fucking nuts.

But he had his own problems to worry about, and God knew, Jim was an adult and therefore allowed to be a moron when it came to his own life.

While Isaac went along, the rear hallway of the abandoned office building was an obstacle course, thanks to countless empty drywall buckets and a thousand half-drunk bottles of Mountain Dew and Coke. But it had been a while since anyone had lifted a finger here—there was dust all over the debris.

Clearly, the money had run out just as the screwdriver-and-monkey-wrench crowd had come in: Naked electrical wires snaked across the unhung ceiling, along with partially completed HVAC ducts and plumbing pipes. Illumination came from battery-operated lanterns placed every five feet on the floor, and the air was cool to the point of being cold. At least until they got into the huge lobby of the place. In spite of the cathedral ceiling, the fifty or so guys milling around on the raw concrete floor kicked up the temp, thanks to body heat.

It was clear why this was a perfect place to fight: The architects had planned some kind of glass extravaganza for the front entrance, but like so much else, it hadn't been completed. Instead of a whole lot of see-through panes, there were plywood sheets nailed onto the girders.

So the lighting and the crowd were hidden.

The octagon had been set up in the center of the space, and as soon as Isaac walked into the crowd, the cheering started. As strangers slapped him on the back and congratulated him for getting out of jail, cell phones flipped up to all kinds of ears, the network going to town, with news that he was good to go even after the bust.

The promoter rushed up to him. "Holy fuck, they're going wild already! This rocks . . . !"

Blah, blah, blah.

Isaac scanned the faces as he went over to the far corner and settled in to wait. As Jim eased into a lean beside him, he found himself saying, "Last night, an old friend of ours showed up."

"Who."

"And what do you know," Isaac said grimly, "he's back."

Over where the bouncers were taking the gambling money and the fighting fees, Matthias's number two was getting a wallet out of his pocket. As cash changed hands, the guy looked over and smiled like a crocodile.

Then he pointed right at Isaac's chest.

"You're not getting in that ring," Jim bit out, stepping in front and blocking the sight line.

Isaac stared over Heron's heavy shoulder, right into the face of the man who'd been sent to kill him. "Yeah. I am."

# CHAPTER
## 10

It was past ten o'clock when Grier parked her Audi out in Malden and cut the engine. She'd manuevered the sedan around on the packed dirt so that it was facing out and was away from most of the other cars—although it wasn't as if the "parking lot" had any dedicated exit or entrance or spaces.

As she'd driven by the address Louie had given her over the phone, she hadn't been sure she was in the right place. The office park had been empty as far as she could tell, the dozen or so matching five-stories spiraling off from an unlit main drive like schoolchildren lined up for a head count. Evidently, the development had been intended for high-tech companies, at least according to the sign that read, MALDEN TECHNOLOGICAL PARK. Instead, it was a ghost town.

Louie never steered her wrong, though, so she'd turned in and gone all the way to the back . . . and found about twenty-five trucks and cars behind the building farthest from the main road. Made sense. If she were trespassing to put on an illegal cage fight, she'd have made sure she was as hidden as possible, too.

Getting out of her car, she went over to the fire door that was propped open by a cinder block, and walked in.

The deep, buzzing growl of a crowd of men boiled down the hallway, the testosterone forming a wall she practically had to push through. As she headed toward the sound, she wasn't worried about the meathead quotient—which was clearly going to be high. She had Mace in one pocket and a stun gun in the other: The former was legal in the state of Massachusetts if you had a valid firearm identification card and she did. The latter . . . well, she'd pay the five-hundred-dollar fine, assuming she ever had to use the thing.

If she could walk into a crack house in New Bedford at midnight, she could handle this.

As she emerged into an atrium of sorts and got a gander at the six-foot-high, chain-link walls of the fighting octagon, she was well aware she could have just called the cops on the match tonight—but then Isaac, assuming he showed up, would either be arrested again or take off. And in either of those cases, she might not have a chance to get to him. Her goal was to have him stop and think long enough to see what he was doing. Running away was never the solution, and if he went that route, he'd have a warrant out for his arrest, more charges against him, and the beginnings of a record.

Assuming he didn't already have one: That murder in Mississippi worried her—but it was, like all of his other stuff, something for the proper authorities to deal with. As his defense attorney, she had to try to get him to stay and face the music on his current charges. It was the right thing for society—the right thing for him as well.

And if she couldn't get him to see the light? Then she was going to resign from the case and tell the authorities everything she knew about him. Including the guns and the details of that security system. She wasn't going to become an accessory to crime in her pursuit of doing the right thing—

She froze as she saw her client, her hand coming up to the base of her throat.

Isaac Rothe was standing alone in the far corner, and though the chain links of the cage separated them, there was no mistaking who it was . . . and no diminishing the effect of him: He was a menace, his size and the hard expression on his face turning the other men into little boys. And whereas she'd been struck by his politeness back at the jail, now she got a true picture of who he was.

The man was a killer.

Her heart beat fast, but she didn't falter. She was here to do a job of sorts, and damn it, she was going to talk with him.

Just as she stepped forward, some smarmy guy with gold teeth monkeyed up one side of the cage. "And now . . . what you're waitin' for!"

Isaac took off his sweatshirt and his combats, leaving them on the floor, and then he prowled the ring, his chin down, his eyes glaring out from under his brows. His shirt stretched tightly across his pecs, and his arms were carved with power even as they hung loosely at his sides. Heading into the fight, he was all muscle and bone and vein, his shoulders so wide he looked like he could bench-press the damn building.

As he clawed up the cage and landed on bare feet inside, the roar of the crowd rang her head like a bell and turned her spine into an adrenaline conductor. In the glow of the eight camping lanterns that hung off the support poles, her client was part gladiator, part animal, a deadly package ready to do what he'd clearly been trained for.

Unfortunately, the opponent who swung over the top and landed across from him was nearly a mirror image of him: same brutal build, same height, same deadly look— even dressed the same way, his muscle shirt showing plenty of the snake tattoo that wound its way around his shoulders and neck. And while the audience hollered and closed in, the two circled each other, looking for an opportunity, arms and chests and thighs tensed.

Isaac went in first, his body swinging around, his foot snapping out and catching the other man in the side with a blow so vicious, she was willing to bet his target's ancestors felt it in their graves.

It all happened so fast. The two fell into a rhythm of strikes and dodges, their muscle shirts quickly dampening around the neck and down the back, the buttery yellow lamplight making it seem as if they were fighting in a ring of fire. The contacts, when made, were the kind that sounded like gunshots, the hard, resonant impacts carrying over the churning, restless crowd. Blood flew—from the cut on Isaac's head that was quickly reopened and then from a split in the opponent's lip. Neither fighter seemed to care, but the kibitzers loved it sure as if they were vampires—

A hand on her ass whipped her head around.

Moving back sharply, she glared at the guy with the wandering palm. "I beg your pardon."

He seemed momentarily surprised, and then his bouncing stare narrowed. "Hey . . . what you doing here?"

The question was posed as if he'd recognized her.

Then again, he could have been talking to Santa Claus and taking it seriously—his face was slick with sweat and half of it twitched like he had an electrical short in his cheek. He was obviously tweaking—and God knew she was an expert in making that diagnosis.

"Excuse me," she said, walking away.

He followed. Just her luck, the one idiot in the place who was more interested in hitting on her than in the fight he'd come to see.

He grabbed her arm, pulling at her. "I know you—"

"Get your hand off me—"

"What's your name—"

Grier snapped herself free. "None of your business."

He jumped at her in the space between one heartbeat and the next: The three feet between them abruptly became three inches. "You're wicked touchy. You think you're better than me, bitch?"

Grier didn't budge her body, but took the stun gun out and slipped the safety pin into the grip. Putting the weapon within striking distance of the front of his jeans, she bit out, "If you don't get the hell away from me, I'm going to shoot six hundred and twenty-five thousand volts through your jewels. On three. One . . . two . . ."

Before she got to trigger time, he shuffled back and held quaky hands up. "I didn't mean . . . I just thought I knew you. . . ."

As he wandered away, she kept the stun gun out and took a deep breath. Maybe she had met him during her searches for Daniel—but he was clearly out of his mind and she was in enough hot water already.

Refocusing on the ring, she looked up—

Just in time to see Isaac go down like a stone.

Fighting Matthias's second in command was a pleasure. Isaac had never trusted or liked the guy, and having a shot at the bastard had been an unspoken career goal.

Ah, the irony. Just as he was getting out, he got his chance—

*Wham!*

As right hooks went, the fucking thing was a bulldozer, and it caught Isaac square in the jaw, kicking his skull back and causing all kinds of trouble: Given that the brain was nothing but a loose sponge in a snow globe, his mental matter went haywire, banging around its hard bone home and rendering him senseless and off balance.

All things considered, he'd been more worried about a weapon of the metal variety, but knuckles worked. Fuckin' hell, they worked—

That was the last thought he had as the floor of the octagon leaped up to greet him, its hi-how're-ya just as much a rocket as his former comrade's fist.

Good thing he was the Energizer Bunny.

He was up a second after he back-flatted—even though his legs were numb and loose and his vision was like a TV that needed its knobs adjusted. Lunging, he was all instinct and will, proof that the mind could override the body's pain receptors—at least for a little while. He tackled his opponent around the waist and drove him into the ground; then flipped him over onto his stomach and wrenched his arm back, pulling the thing like it was rope.

On a crack, something gave out and Isaac abruptly had to catch himself from falling.

The crowd went nuts, all kinds of *fuckin' A* ricocheting around the half-finished lobby until a shrill whistle cut through the roar. At first, he assumed the sound was just an extension of the chaos in his head, but then he realized that someone had stepped into the ring. It was the promoter, and for once, the bastard's face was a little pasty.

"I'm calling the fight," he yelled as he grabbed Isaac's wrist and yanked it into the air. "Winner!" Leaning in, he hissed, "*Let go of him.*"

Isaac couldn't figure out what the guy's problem was—

His eyes finally focused properly, and well, what do you know. Matthias's number two needed an X-ray, a cast, and maybe a couple of screws: His humerus protruded out of his skin like a snapped-off, bloodied stick, the arm broken and then some.

Isaac jumped off and backed up against the chain link, his breath pumping in and out of his mouth. His opponent was on his feet nearly as quickly and he held the hand that flopped casually, like he had nothing more exciting than a bug bite wrong with him.

As their stares met and the guy smiled in that way of his, Isaac thought . . . shit, this fight had been nothing but a warning shot across his bow.

A message that they were on him.

An invitation to run.

Fine. Fuck Matthias. And that compound fracture was his response: They could take him out but he was going to do some serious damage on his way to the grave.

Isaac didn't hang around. He popped up onto the links and sprang himself over the lip. Fortunately, the crowd knew better than to get too close, so he was able to quickly head for Jim—

He slammed right into his public defender.

"Christ!" he barked, jumping back from the woman.

"Actually, it's Childe. With an 'e.'" She cocked an eyebrow. "Thought I'd try the taxi offer again—you need a ride back to Boston? Or are you not heading in that direction?"

Momentarily forgetting his manners, he bit out, "What the *hell* are you doing here?"

"I was going to ask you the same. Considering that one of the provisions of your bail is that you not participate in illegal cage fighting. And that realllllly didn't look like a game of Parcheesi you just played. You *broke* that man's arm."

Isaac glanced around, wondering what the quickest way to the door was—because she did not belong in this group of roughnecks and he had to get her out of here. "Look, can we go outside—"

"What are you thinking? Showing up here and fighting?"

"I was going to come to see you."

"I'm your attorney—I should damn well hope so!"

"I owe you twenty-five thousand dollars."

"And I'll tell how you can settle the score." She planted her hands on her hips and leaned forward, that perfume of hers getting into his nose . . . and his blood. "You can stop being a stupid ass and show up for your hearing in two weeks. I'll give you the time and date again, if you've forgotten to write it down."

Okay . . . she was *totally* hot when she was pissed.

Annnnnnnnd that was so not an appropriate reaction under the time-place doctrine. Among other things.

At that moment, Jim and his boys approached, but Grier

didn't spare them a glance—even though Jim was staring at her hard. And didn't that give Isaac an idea of what she'd be like in a courtroom. Man, she was incredible when she was focused and angry and ready to serve someone up on a plate.

"Two other things," she bit out. "You'd better pray that guy whose arm needs to be set in plaster doesn't call the police. And you need to see a doctor. Again. You're bleeding."

Just to fill in the gap, even though there wasn't one, the promoter came up with what looked like a couple thousand dollars. "Here's your cut—"

Abruptly, Grier's eyes turned pleading, even as her beautiful face remained tight. "Don't take the money, Isaac. And come with me. Do the right thing tonight and it'll save you a whole lot of misery later. I promise you."

Isaac just shook his head at her and stuck his hand out to the promoter.

"Oh, for *fuck's* sake."

As she cursed and turned away, he was momentarily struck dumb by the fact that she'd dropped the f-bomb.

Snapping back into action, he reached for her arm, but the promoter stepped in the way. "Now, before I give this to you"—he slapped the bills on his palm—"I want you to come fight two nights from now."

Which would be a no-go. He was hoping to be out of the country by then. "Yeah. Sure."

"It'll be here, assuming we got no problems. You were frickin' amazing—"

"Just shut up and gimme the cash."

Isaac rose up onto the balls of his feet and stared over the milling heads, watching Grier's fancy-dancy hairdo march out toward the back door. By and large the men got out of her way, but then, given her mood, she was probably capable of castration.

Just by force of will.

Drowning out the promoter's jock-sniffer ass-kissing,

Isaac grabbed the money, shoved his feet in his combats and took his sweatshirt and windbreaker back. As he ran off after his public defender, he buried the green in his pockets and double-checked on his guns, the silencers and his plastic bag piggy bank.

"Where the hell are you going?" Jim said as he and his boys followed at a jog.

"Wherever she goes. She's my attorney."

"Any chance of talking you out of this?"

"Nope."

"Fucking hell," Jim said under his breath as he shoved some guy out of the way. "FYI, Matthias's number two left."

"Black sedan," the man with the piercings cut in. "The quarter panels were dinged and the thing was dirty as shit, but the tires were brand-new and there were electronics in the trunk."

That was XOps for you, Isaac thought. Incognito and state-of-the-art at the same time.

As he broke free of the exit, the sound of cars and trucks starting up and taking off turned the night into a traffic disco. Amid the growling engines and flashing headlights, he looked around for her car. She'd drive something foreign, he was guessing. A Mercedes, BMW . . . Audi . . .

Where was she?

# CHAPTER
## 11

*Undisclosed location, OCONUS*

Matthias was well aware he was an agent of evil in the world.

Which didn't mean he was totally bad. In large measure, the billions of innocent people on the planet were not on his radar screen and he left them alone. He also did not take candy from babies. Or shave cats. Or give the e-mail addresses of people who'd pissed him off to European sex-toy sites.

And he had, once—back in 1983—walked an old lady across a busy intersection.

So he wasn't *all* bad.

That being said, if, in the process of getting a job done, he had to accept certain collateral damage or sacrifice an "innocent" or two, that was the way shit went: In those cases, he was no different from the car accident or the cancer or the lightning strike, nothing but life's lottery lost for the given individual.

After all, everyone's clock was ticking, and he'd played Grim Reaper enough to know that firsthand.

As he repositioned his broken body in his leather chair,

he groaned. At the age of forty, he felt more like a hundred thousand years old, but being a survivor would do that to you.

At least he didn't have to shit in a bag and still had one eye that worked.

In front of him, on the glossy desk, were seven computer screens. Some showed pictures, others streamed data, and one told him where each of his operatives were on the planet Earth. With what he was in charge of, information was mission critical. Which was an irony of sorts. He was a man with no identity operating a team that didn't officially exist in a world of shadows—and intel was the only concrete thing he had to work with.

Although even that, like people, could fail you.

As his cell phone rang, he picked up the thing and looked at its little screen. Ah, yes, perfect timing. Matthias was looking for two men—and he'd sent his second in command after one of them.

The other . . . was complicated. Even though it shouldn't have been.

He accepted the call. "Have you found him."

"Yeah, and went a few rounds with him in the ring."

"He's alive, though."

"Only because you want him to be. By the way, his lawyer showed up at the fight—and guess what. She happens to be the daughter of a friend of ours."

"Really. What *are* the chances." Actually, they were a hundred percent, because Matthias had gone into the Suffolk County court system in Massachusetts and purposely had retired captain Alistair Childe's surviving offspring assigned to the case.

They'd needed to get that traitor Isaac Rothe out from behind bars so they could kill him and keep his body for future use—and good old Albie's little girl was just the ticket: She was a fine attorney with a bleeding heart that led her into places she didn't belong. Perfect combination.

And clearly it had worked: Rothe was free less than twenty-four hours after his arrest.

Christ, it had been that easy to find the bastard. But then, who'd have thought he'd use his own last name?

Huh, Matthias thought. Maybe he was taking candy from a baby here.

"You should have let me kill him in the ring," his second in command bitched.

"Too many witnesses, and I want him flushed out of Boston."

Because now that Grier Childe had served her purpose, he had to get Isaac the hell away from the woman. Matthias had already killed the captain's son, and so he considered their score even. However, the sonofabitch had already tried to leverage his way out once and that meant the daughter had to be used to keep her sanctimonious daddy-o in line: As long as she was alive, she could be killed, and that threat was better than duct tape over a flapping mouth any day.

"Follow him out of state as only you can," Matthias heard himself say in a calm, level tone. "Wait for the right moment, and *not* around Childe's daughter."

"Why does that matter?"

"Because I fucking said so. That's why."

Matthias ended the call and tossed the phone across the desk. All of his men were good at what they did, but his number two had tricks that no one else could come close to. This of course made the guy extremely useful, but also a danger if his ambitions or thirst for blood got away from them both.

The man was a demon, straight up—

Abruptly, Matthias had to take a deep breath to ease a pain in the center of his chest. Lately, the sharpshooters had been happening with increasing frequency, rendering him breathless and slightly nauseated. He had a feeling he knew what it was, but he was going to do *nada* to stop the myocardial infarction that was coming his way.

No doctor's visit for him, no stress test, no Lipitor, no Coumadin.

On that note, he lit up a cheroot and exhaled. No Chantix to stop smoking, either. He was going to go hard with the coffin nails until he dropped dead from the big one — God knew he'd tried to kill himself with that bomb in the desert, and that had been a giant fuckup. Much better to ease into his grave the old-fashioned way, through bad diet, lack of exercise, and addictions.

As a chiming alarm went off, he braced his palms on the arms of his chair and prepared himself for getting vertical. Pain meds would have eased him tremendously, but they also would have dulled his brain, so that was a no-go. Besides, physical agony had never bothered him.

Gritting his teeth, he pushed hard on the chair and hefted his weight onto his legs. Moment to steady. Reach for the cane. Deep breath.

That night in the land of sand when he'd been saved by Jim Heron had had repercussions, and a lot of them were the lead-and-steel kind — only not weapons. Thanks to that cocksucking soldier dragging him out of that ruined, dusty building and hauling him eight miles through the dunes in a fireman's hold, Matthias was now part man, part mechanics, a creaky, clunky version of the strong, powerful fighter he'd once been. Put back together with pins and screws and bolts, he'd wondered in the beginning whether it would be a turning point. Whether the pain and suffering he'd gone through with all the surgeries would open a door to his becoming . . . a human.

As opposed to the sociopath he'd been born.

But, no. All he'd had since then were these precursors of the heart attacks that ran in his family. Which was a good thing. Unlike the bomb he'd set in the sand and deliberately stepped on, he knew a coronary would do the job — hell, he'd watched his father die from one.

Actually his father had been his first kill, courtesy of

Matthias knowing exactly what to say to cause his old man's ticker to seize up good and stop dead. He'd been fifteen at the time. Pops had been forty-one. And Matthias had sat on the floor of his bedroom and watched the whole thing, idly turning the knob on the radio that woke him up for school, looking for a good song among all the crap on the airwaves.

Meanwhile, his father had turned red, then blue . . . then faded out to gray.

Perverted fucker had deserved it. After all he'd done . . .

Pulling out of the past, Matthias drew on his coat, and as always the simple act of dressing was a production, his back straining to accommodate the shift of his arms. And then he was out of his office and walking the subterranean halls of the anonymous office complex he worked in, his body hating him for the ambulation.

His car and driver were waiting for him in the underground parking facility, and when he got into the rear of the sedan, he groaned.

Shallow breathing kept him conscious as the flaring pain grew volcanic . . . and then gradually subsided as the car eased forward.

From up front, he heard the driver say, "ETA eleven minutes."

Matthias closed his eyes. He was not entirely sure why he was making this trip . . . but he was being drawn to the northeast United States by a compulsion not even his rational side could deny. He just had to go, even as he was surprised at the need.

Then again, just as his number two had found his target, Matthias had also located the soldier he was after personally, and this long flight back over the ocean was because he wanted to look the man who had saved his life in the face for one last time—before the bastard's corpse was buried.

He told himself it was to confirm that Jim Heron had indeed died.

There was more to it than that, though.

Even if he didn't understand the whys...there was much more to this trip for him than that.

# CHAPTER
## 12

More than anything, Grier was furious at herself.

As she pounded over to her Audi, weeding through the other cars and getting heckled by a knuck dragger or two, everything came into sharp focus: where she was, what she'd done earlier at the courthouse, who she was trying to save.

Isaac had *broken* that guy's arm. In front of her and a hundred other people. And treated it with the same degree of shock and panic as someone hanging up a phone.

Like he did that every day.

And then he'd accepted money for it.

Coming up to her sedan, she got her key fob out and de-activated the alarm. And as she caught her reflection in the glass of the driver's-side door, she thought of her brother.

The kind of wild buzz that had driven her to come out here reminded her of the night he'd died.

Grier had been the one to find his body and her resuscitation efforts had made no difference . . . because he'd been dead before she'd started them. But she'd kept up the pumping on his chest and the breathing into his mouth anyway.

The paramedics had had to drag her off his body. Screaming.

And the thing was, in death, as well as in life, he hadn't cared about all her efforts to save him. He'd been transfixed by his final fix, a haunting look of ecstatic pleasure frozen on his pasty gray face, his driving addiction fulfilled.

Recklessness took a variety of different forms, didn't it.

She'd always prided herself on being the responsible one out of the pair of them, the one who had excelled at school, and worked hard to get ahead, and never done anything that her parents would have disapproved of. She'd certainly never, ever tried illegal drugs. Not even once.

And yet here she was, putting herself and her career at risk on the off chance she could talk a total stranger into going straight. If the police had shown up—or did, there was still time for that—getting arrested as a spectator would have had her booted from the Massachusetts bar faster than she could say, "But, Judge, I was only there for my client." She'd already put up twenty-five grand, which would hardly break her bank ... except how much farther could those funds have gone if put to use on some program for at-risk youth?

As her head started to pound, she regarded her actions since around nine a.m. with a clear eye. And what do you know, she saw not so much someone doing good in the world, but an out-of-control woman who was—

Daniel appeared on the far side of her car, his ghostly face dead serious. *Get in, Grier. Get in the car and lock the doors.*

"What?" she said. "Why—"

*Do it. Now.* Her dead brother seemed to focus on the air behind her right shoulder. *Damn it, Grier—*

"I remember who you are."

She squeezed her eyes shut. Oh for God's sake, this just kept getting better, didn't it. The meth head was back.

Turning around to give her erstwhile suitor another—

The man grabbed her arms, and with a shove that left her teeth singing, pushed her up against the car face-first. As he held her in place with his body, she was reminded that men were in fact built differently from women: They were a hell of a lot stronger. Especially when they were high and desperate.

"You're Danny's sister." The breath on her cheek was hot and smelled like roadkill in August. "You showed up a couple of times at his place. What happened to him?"

"He died," she croaked out.

"Oh . . . God. I'm sorry. . . ." The addict seemed honestly sad. In a Tim Burton, distorted-netherworld kind of way. "Listen, can you spare some cash? Rich girl like you . . . hafta have some cash on you. But only if you can manage it."

Uh-huh, right. She knew she was going to give him what he wanted whether she liked it or not—which was how, in spite of the way he phrased it, a mugging worked.

Rough hands rummaged around and her purse was ripped off her shoulder. She thought about yelling, but the weight bearing down on her rib cage made anything more than shallow breaths impossible, and besides, she had parked way around the side in the shadows. Who was going to hear her?

As her wide eyes tracked the departing cars and trucks that were so close and yet so far away, she had an absolutely absurd memory of the opening scene from *Jaws*— where the woman was being dragged under by the shark and saw the glowing lights of houses on the shore.

"I'm not gonna hurt you. . . . I just need money."

With his body still forcing her against the car, he dumped the contents of her bag on the muddy ground, her cell phone, wallet, keys, everything pouring free. And then he tossed her sixteen-thousand-dollar Birkin bag over the hood of the Audi.

Stupid bastard. He could have gotten more for that on eBay than any cash he'd find in her wallet.

Half of her mind was in a panic, the other part icy calm, and she went with the latter, because she was nothing if not her father's daughter: This freaked-out addict was going to spin her around at some point because he was going to want her jewelry, and when he did, she had a good chance of kneeing him where it counted.

Even if she had to pretend she wasn't about to throw up all over her shoes—

The weight crushing against her wasn't so much removed as it was vaporized, gone as if it had never been: One second she couldn't breathe. The next, she had all the oxygen in the world.

As she dragged in a tremendous gulp of air and held on to the car roof to keep standing, grunts sounded next to her.

Pushing herself around, she had to blink a couple of times to understand what she was looking at—but no amount of wait-maybe-I'm-not-seeing-this-right changed what was going on: Isaac had come out of nowhere, pinned her assailant to the ground, and was giving the guy a root canal the hard way.

Namely with his fist.

"Isaac—" Her voice cracked and she coughed. "Isaac! Stop it!"

Louie the PI's voice echoed through her head: *That SOB could be a murderer.*

"Isaac!"

She was expecting to have to jump on him or call for help to get him to stop the beating, but as soon as it started, it was over. Isaac quit the Rocky routine on his own, flipping the man onto his stomach and wrenching his arms back to immobilize him.

Nothing was broken this time.

And Isaac wasn't even breathing hard as he glanced over at her. "Are you okay?"

His eyes were sharp, his expression deadly and calm, his voice even and polite. It was obvious that he was in total control of himself and the situation . . . and it dawned on her that he might possibly have saved her from something awful. With addicts, you never knew what they were going to do.

"Did he hurt you?" Isaac said. "Are you okay?"

"No," she answered roughly, not sure which question she was answering.

With sheer, brute strength, Isaac picked the man up and gave him a shove and there was no argument, not even a comment. Her attacker scrambled away like he was damned well aware he'd narrowly missed the beat-down of his life.

And then Isaac picked up her things. One by one, he gathered what had been in her purse, wiping off the mud on his own sweatshirt, lining everything up on the hood of her car.

Falling back against the driver's-side door, she was captivated by how very careful he was, his bloody hands gentle.

Daniel appeared right beside him, seemingly struck by how he treated what was hers. *Let him take you home, Grier. You're in no condition to drive.*

"He hasn't asked me," she mumbled.

"Asked you what?" Isaac said, glancing over.

When she waved the words away, he went and got her bag, putting everything into it before holding the thing out to her. "I'd like to drive you home. If you'll let me."

*Bingo*, her brother said.

She opened her mouth to shut up Daniel, but just didn't have the energy to follow through with it.

"Ms. Childe?" With her client's Southern accent, that came out as one word, *MzChiiiilde*.

God, what to do. And of course, *Hell, no*, was the healthiest response—in spite of Daniel's opinion.

*Trust me*, Daniel said.

Isaac's voice dropped. "Just let me get you home safe. Please."

For some unknowable reason, her instincts were telling

her to trust this stranger with a bad past and a criminal present who was on the run. Or was it just a case of her savior complex overriding better judgment?

Or . . . was it the look on a ghost's face? Like Daniel was seeing something she couldn't in this collision between her and a dangerous stranger with a soft Southern drawl.

"I don't need a driver. That I can do myself." She took her bag from him. "But I do need you to stick around and face your charges."

Isaac scanned the area. "How about we talk at your house."

"I carry Mace, you know."

"I'm glad."

"And a stun gun." For all the good it had done her just now.

Good Lord, she couldn't believe she was even thinking about going home with Isaac. The meth head had been a twitchy amateur . . . and her client sure as hell seemed like a professional.

His pale gray eyes bored into hers. "I'm not going to hurt you. I swear it."

With a curse, she wrenched open the car door. "I'm driving."

The question was, Where the hell was she going? And with whom?

Jim watched the Audi drive off, its milky exhaust rising up behind both cold tailpipes. He was utterly unconcerned about where the pair went—he'd slipped transmitters into both Isaac's sweatshirt and the bag with the money.

"You could have just let me do a locator spell," Eddie muttered.

"I'm used to working with the GPS shit from my old job." And who could have guessed he'd ever suffer from technology nostalgia?

Speaking of intel—it was time for some clarity in that

department: Although he could see how and why Isaac might be up next on the list of seven souls, a little face-to-face time with his English dandy of a boss was the only way to be certain.

Lot of pressure off him if it turned out saving Isaac's ass had a larger purpose.

He swiveled his head toward Eddie. "Tell me how to get over to the Four Lads. Do I have to die again?"

If he did, he had a Beretta on him and he already knew what kicking the bucket from a gunshot was like. Snore.

"Don't bother." Adrian cracked his knuckles. "They're not going to tell you anything. They can't."

What the fuck? "I thought I worked for them."

"You work for both sides, and they've given you all the help they can."

Jim looked back and forth between the two angels: Each of them had the tight expression of a guy with a shoestring noosing up his balls.

"Help?" he said. "Where's my goddamned help?"

"They gave you us, asshole," Adrian snapped. "And that's all they can do—I've already gone over and asked them who's supposed to be next. I figured it would help you, you ungrateful bastard."

Jim popped his brows at the Mr. Thoughtful routine. First time through the park with Adrian, the guy had silver-plated Jim to the enemy—to the point where he'd ended up fucking Devina in the parking lot of a club. In his truck. Without knowing she was a demon.

"Times have changed since then," Ad said gruffly. "You know they have."

In a flash, Jim remembered what the guy had looked like just a day or so ago after Devina had finished using and abusing him in a variety of ways. He'd given himself over to her so that Jim had had half a chance at winning the first round.

"Yeah, they have." Jim offered his knuckles in guy-speak for, *Sorry I insinuated you're dog shit.*

As Ad gave them a pound, Eddie said, "We're technically against the rules."

Jim shrugged. "If it'll help me win, I'll take it. Rules are relative."

Which was why he'd been chosen, wasn't it. He was hardly a frickin' Boy Scout—

Jim's head snapped around at a metal-on-metal squeaking sound. The portable octagon had been dismantled and was being shoved through the door by four guys who then carried it over to a U-Haul van. Next trip in and out they were carrying the eight concrete corner weights and poles and then no one was left but him and Eddie and Adrian.

Which was a metaphor for the sitch he was in, wasn't it.

Fine. This was how the game was played? Cool. He was used to relying on himself and his instincts in the field . . . and *everything* was pulling him toward Isaac.

The question was: where was Devina? Assuming she was after Isaac, she'd be searching for a way into him so her parasitic nature could take him over and she could ultimately own him forever in Hell after she killed him.

Jim refocused on his angels. "If Devina is possessing someone, is there a way to tell? Any markers? Reference points?"

At least then he could get a bead on her.

"Sometimes," Eddie said. "But she can wipe away her fingerprints, so to speak—and now that she knows me and Ad are with you, she'll be extra careful. However, there are some clean souls she'll never touch, and those glow."

"Glow? You mean like . . ." Shit, that blond attorney who'd taken Isaac home with her had had a light all around her body—which was why when Jim had seen her, he'd stared at her as he had. "Like a halo?"

"Exactly like that."

Well, at least there was one thing working in their favor. He'd assumed he'd just been seeing things. Turned out he was—and thank God for it.

Jim took out his GPS receiver and called up Isaac's two little blinking dots. Sooner or later, if Devina was fucking with the guy, she was going to make an appearance in one form or another—and they were going to be there when she did.

"Are there such things as protective spells?" he asked. "Anything I can put around Isaac to keep him safe from her?"

"We can work something out," Eddie said with an evil little smile. " 'Bout time to start teaching you that stuff."

You got that right, Jim thought.

Closing his eyes, he unfurled his wings, their great weight settling on his spine and shoulders as they became visible. "They're heading into town. Let's go—"

"Hold up," Eddie said, his wings appearing. "We need to go by the hotel and get some supplies. Assuming you don't want us going inside the house?"

"As long as Devina doesn't show, I'll stay on the out."

"This won't take all that long."

"It'd better not."

As he grabbed a couple of running steps to get the momentum working for him, he felt the irony of everything like a great gust under his body: He never would have believed that angels existed or that the eternal battle between good and evil was not only real, but something he'd be fighting in.

Then again, when you weighed in at about two hundred and twenty pounds of solid muscle and were able to haul yourself off the ground with a network of metaphysical feathers . . . the crazy-ass reality you were in had a fuckload of credibility.

He was going to be goddamned if Devina got her claws

into Isaac—in whatever form she was currently copping to. Isaac was *his* boy, and the idea of that man falling into his enemy's hands was not acceptable—especially if that demon happened to be wearing a familiar face.

Which just happened to have an eye patch.

# CHAPTER
## 13

Isaac had been in the Boston vicinity only twice, and both times had been for pass-through trips on his way overseas—the kind of thing where all he did was walk across a tarmac at Otis Air Force Base down on Cape Cod.

That being said, as Grier hung a left off something called Charles Street, he didn't need to have had a guided tour of the city to know they were in prime real estate–land. The town houses on both sides of the hill they went up were all pristine brick with glossy black shutters and doors. Through clean windows, he could see interiors that were antiqued up to within an inch of their lives and had enough crown molding to crush a king's head.

Clearly, he was in the natural habitat of the blue-blooded Yankee.

As ancient *Saturday Night Live* sketches of Dan Aykroyd doing Kennedy impressions about "chowdah" rolled through his head, Grier took a left into a small square that was demarcated by a wrought-iron fence and brick lanes on all four sides. In the middle, its little park had graceful trees with tiny buds already showing, and the surrounding walk-ups were the best of the best in this bestest-ever neighborhood.

So not a surprise.

After she parked her Audi parallel to the fence, they both got out. She hadn't said much on the trip here, and neither had he. But then again, he wasn't a big talker to begin with—and she had a fugitive for a passenger. Not exactly a so-how-about-this-weather? kind of gig.

The house she indicated was hers was a bow-front on the corner and had white marble steps up to its black front door. Fluted black planters the size of Great Danes sat on either side of the entrance, and the brass knocker was as big as his head. One light glowing on the third floor; several on the exterior. And as he surveyed the area, there appeared to be nothing out of place—no unmarkeds trolling by, no sounds that were wrong, nobody suspicious lurking.

As they walked over the uneven bricks of the street, he wanted to reach out and steady her, given her heel situation—but he didn't dare. First of all, she probably still wanted to slap him . . . and second, he had palmed up both his guns inside his windbreaker on a just-in-case.

He was always careful with himself. Having her in tow? He took vigilance to a whole new level.

Besides, Grier handled the trip to her front door just fine, in spite of the fact that she was walking in stilettos and had been attacked by some drugged-up asswipe.

Too bad they hadn't met in a different world. He would have really liked to—

Yeah, right. Take her on a date?

Whatever. Even if he had gone the law-abiding, I'm-not-an-assassin route, they were from opposite ends of the spectrum: he was all farm boy and she was all fabulous.

And he really had to cut the double-think when it came to how attractive she was.

Her security alarm went off the moment she opened the way in and he was glad, although he didn't approve of her letting riffraff like him in the house. And how was that for fucked-up?

As she punched in her code at the ADT panel, he looked down at the soles of his combats—which were caked with chunky mud and fuzzy sod. Bending down, he unlaced them, slipped them off, and left them outside.

Her black-and-white marble floor was warm under his socks—

Looking up, he found her staring at his feet with an odd expression on her beautiful face.

"I didn't want to track in," he muttered, shutting the door and locking it.

After he took off his windbreaker, he got out the Star Market bag with his life savings in it and they just stood there: her in her black designer coat and her soiled purse that had one strap hanging loose; him in his sweatshirt with a load of dirty money in his bloody hand and two guns she didn't know about in his pockets.

"When was the last time you ate," she said softly.

"I'm not hungry. But thank you, ma'am." He glanced around, looking into a tall-ceilinged room that was painted a rich red. Over the regal marble fireplace was an oil painting of a man sitting up straight in a gilded chair with a pair of old-fashioned spectacles perched on his nose.

It was so quiet here, he thought. And not just because there weren't any sounds.

Peaceful. It was . . . peaceful.

"I'll make you an omelet, then," she said, putting her bag down and starting to shrug out of that coat.

He stepped up to her to help, but she moved back. "I've got it. Thanks."

The dress underneath . . . Dear *God,* that dress. Modest and black had never looked so sexy, as far as he was concerned, but then that was more about her than the design or the fabric.

And those legs. Fuck him, but those legs with the sheer black stockings . . .

Isaac snapped his man-whore back into place with a re-

minder that it would be an open question whether someone like her would let him so much as wash her car—much
less allow him take her to bed. Besides, would he have any
clue what to do to a woman like her? Sure, he was good at
raw fucking—he'd been begged for repeats enough times
to have confidence on that front.

But a lady like her deserved to be savored—

Damn him to hell. He had a feeling he was licking his
lips.

"Kitchen's in the back," was all she said as she picked up
her bag and walked away.

He followed her down the hall, taking note of the rooms
and the windows and the doors, noting escape routes and
entryways. It was what he did in any space he went through,
his years of training with him sure as the skin on his back.
But it was more than that. He was looking for clues about
her.

And it was weird . . . the peaceful thing kept at it, which
surprised him. Old-fashioned and expensive usually meant
tight-assed. Here, though, he breathed deep and easy—
even though that made no sense.

In contrast to the rest of the house, the kitchen was all
about the white and stainless steel, and as she set to work
pulling out bowls and eggs and cheese, he put his money
down on her counter and couldn't wait to get out of the
room: Across the way, there was a wall of windowpanes
that were probably six by eight feet apiece.

Which meant anyone with a pair of eyes could go all
looky-looky on them.

"What's in the back?" he asked casually.

"My garden."

"Walled in?"

Her arms full, she stepped up to the cooktop in the granite island. "Security conscious?"

"Yes, ma'am."

She went over, turned on an exterior light, and canned

the inside ones—which gave him a perfect view of the back without a lot of hassle. God, she was smart.

And her garden was surrounded by a ten-foot-high brick oh-no-you-don't that he totally approved of.

"Satisfied?" she said.

In the darkness, her voice took on a husky quality that made him want to track her body through the room and ease her up against something so he could get under that black dress.

Man, her question wasn't one she wanted to ask him tonight.

"Yes, ma'am," he murmured.

When the lights came back on, there was a faint touch of red in her cheeks—the sort of thing he might not have noticed if he hadn't made it his business to stare at her as much as he could. But maybe the color was just her being keyed up because of everything that had happened tonight.

No doubt that was it.

And the fact that he'd noticed at all made him less than impressed with the male species: Somehow, even in the midst of great chaos, even when it was tacky as hell, men still managed to get the hots for a female.

"Sit down," she told him, pointing with her wire whisk to a stool under the lip of the island, "before you fall down. And don't even try the I'm-fine, clear?"

Man . . . total hots for this woman.

Complete hots.

"Hello?" she said. "You were just about to sit down over there?"

"Roger that."

As she returned to the cooktop and got cracking— literally—he did as he was told.

To keep his eyes off her, he looked over her purse, which she'd left next to where he'd parked it. What a goddamn shame something so nice and expensive had been trashed.

There was dried mud all over the leather and that handle had been really mangled.

Idiot meth head.

Rising up, he went over to the sink, pulled a paper towel free, and got the thing damp. Then, resettling, he went to work, trying to get the mung off.

When he glanced up, she was staring at him again and he stopped what he was doing to hold up his hands. "I'm not going to steal from you."

"I didn't think you were," she said in that quiet voice.

"Real sorry about your purse. I think it's done ruined."

"I have others. And even if I didn't, it's just stuff."

"Expensive stuff." And on that note, he leaned over to the island and pushed his money toward her. "I need you to take this."

"And I need you not to go on the run." She cracked another egg on the rim of the bowl and split it using only one hand. "I need you to follow through on what you agreed to do when I got you bail."

Isaac ducked his eyes and resumed his largely unsuccessful cleanup routine.

She let out an exhale that was just a syllable or two away from being a curse. "I'm waiting. For you to answer me."

"Wasn't aware there was a question, ma'am."

"Fine. Will you please stay here and stick with the system?"

Isaac rose up and headed back to the sink. As he snapped a clean Bounty off the roll, the truth leaped out of his mouth. "My life isn't my own."

"Who are you running from?" she whispered.

Maybe she'd dialed down the volume because the lawyer in her was knee-jerk discreet. Or perhaps she was guessing right: The types who were after him could hear and sometimes see through even solid walls. Glass ones like the kind in this kitchen? Piece of cake.

"Isaac?"

There was no response that he could give her so he shook his head and went back to wiping the mud off her bag . . . even though she was probably just going to throw the damn thing out in the morning.

"You can trust me, Isaac."

His reply was a long time in coming. "It's not you I'm worried about."

Grier stood on the far side of the island, the Humpty-Dumpty eggs scattered around and drooling on the granite, a red bowl full of yellow yolks and transparent whites ready to take a beating.

Her client was absolutely huge as he perched on her stool, his busted-up hands taking care of her Birkin. And yet in spite of his size and the regard he was showing her bag, she wanted to crack his head on something hard. The solutions were so clear to her: Stay in the system, come clean with whatever military agency he'd bolted from, sort out the repercussions, do the time . . . start over.

Whatever he'd done could be redressed.

Society could forgive.

People could move on.

Unless, of course, they were stubborn assholes determined to flout the rules and go it alone.

She picked up a final egg and slammed it against the bowl's rim, shattering the shell. "Ah, hell's bells."

Isaac's eyes lifted. "It's okay. I don't mind a little crunch."

"It's *not* okay. None of this is okay." She bent over and fished out the little white specks with her fingernail.

When things looked acceptable in the bowl, she heard herself say, "Would you like to have a shower before we eat?"

"No, ma'am," was his quiet, unsurprising response.

"I have clothes you could change into." That got his eyebrow to peak briefly even if he didn't look over at her. "My brother's. He used to stay here with me sometimes—not exactly your size, of course."

"I'm good. But thank you, ma'am."

"You need to lose the 'ma'am' crap. We were over that the minute you got into my car."

As that brow went up again, she grabbed a block of cheddar and started grating. Hard. "You know . . . you remind me of him. My brother."

"How so?"

"I also want to save you from what your choices are doing to your life."

Isaac shook his head. "Not a good idea."

True enough. God knew she'd failed once at that already.

Shaking the cheese from the grater, she put the thing aside and diced up some Canadian bacon. As they both worked at their tasks, it didn't take long before the silence got to her . . . but more to the point, it wasn't in her nature to quit.

Which suggested that if she'd been born a car she'd be in the demolition derby.

"Look, I can try to help with more than just the charges against you. If you're—"

"I got most of the dirt off." He lifted the purse while meeting her straight in the eye. "But there's nothing I can do about the strap."

"Where are you going to go?"

When he didn't reply, she sliced off a chunk of sweet butter into the pan and fired up the burner. "Well, you can stay here for the night if you want to rest up. My father's had this place wired so tightly not even a mouse could get in without triggering the system."

"ADT is good. But not that good."

"That's just the dummy system." That got both his brows to pop and she nodded. "My father was in the military. The Army, actually. When he got out, he went to law school and then ... well, he's kept current, let's just say. Current and protective of me."

"He wouldn't approve of my being here."

"You've been a gentleman so far and that, more than what you wear or where you're from, has always been what's mattered to him. And to me, by the way—"

"I'm leaving this money behind when I go."

Lifting the pan off the heat, she tilted its flat face, sending the butter on a little ride that was ultimately its undoing. "And I can't accept it. You must know that. It would make me an accessory." She thought she heard a soft curse, but maybe it had only been an exhale. "After all, I'm willing to bet that cash came from fighting. Or was it drugs?"

"I am not a dealer."

"Which means it's the former. Still illegal. By the way, I looked into your background." She did a rewhisk on the eggs and then poured more than half of them into the pan, a quiet whoosh rising up. "There was nothing except for a newspaper article from five years ago about your death. It came with a picture of you, so don't bother denying it."

He went utterly still, and she knew his eyes were on her sharply.

For a moment, she wondered exactly what she'd welcomed into her home. But then, for some reason, she thought about him taking his combat boots off and leaving them by the front door.

Time to get real, she thought. "So are you going to tell me what branch of the government you work for or should I just guess?"

"I'm not with the military."

"Really. So I'm supposed to believe that you fight like you do and secured your apartment as you did and are on a fast track out of town just because you're some kind of casual street thug or low-level mob enforcer? I don't buy it. Incidentally, seeing you in that ring was how I knew for sure—that and the fact that you called off your own dog next to my car when I was attacked. You were utterly in control of yourself and the situation with that druggie, not some sloppy, emotional bouncer type doing a save-the-day. You were a professional—are, actually. Aren't you."

She didn't need him to say a word because she knew she was right. And yet, when there was no comment, she glanced up, half expecting him to be gone in a breath of air.

But Isaac Rothe, or whatever his name was, remained seated at her island.

"How do you like your eggs?" she said. "Hard or soft?"

"Hard," he bit out.

"Why am I not surprised."

# CHAPTER
## 14

Dead to rights, Isaac believed the expression was.

As he met the eyes of his public defender, hostess, and short-order cook, it was clear she knew she'd pegged him on all accounts.

And didn't that make him feel stripped naked.

"I think you should resign from my case," he said grimly. "Effective tonight."

She sprinkled cheese and Canadian bacon onto the bubbling circle of an omelet. "I'm not a quitter. Unlike yourself."

Okay. That pissed him off. "I'm not either."

"Really? What do you call running from your responsibilities."

Before he knew it, he'd leaned across the countertop, and was looming over her. As her eyes flared, he said roughly, "I call it survival."

To her credit, or her stupidity, she didn't relent. "Talk to me. For God's sake, let me help you. My father has connections. The kind that run deep and into the shadows of the government. There are things he can do to help you."

Isaac remained outwardly calm. Inside, though, he was scrambling. Who the hell was her father? Childe . . .

Childe ... The name didn't spark anything in his data banks.

"Isaac," she said. "Please—"

"You got me out so I can keep going. That has helped me. Now you gotta let me go. Let me go and forget you ever met me. If your father is the kind of man you say he is, you know damn well there are branches of the service where AWOL is a death sentence."

"I thought you weren't in the military."

He let that one lie where it landed ... which was on top of the pile of shit he'd brought to her door.

In the silence, she added a little seasoning, the saltshaker making no sound, the peppermill crackling. And then she folded the omelet in half and let it hang out on the heat for a bit.

Two minutes later, the plate that was presented to him was white and square and the fork was sterling silver and had curlicues on it.

"I know you're polite," she said, "but don't wait for me. It's better hot."

He didn't like eating before her, but considering he'd shut her down on everything else, he figured now was an opportunity to be accommodating. Going to the sink, he washed his hands with soap and water; then he sat down and ate every last bite.

It was gorgeous.

"Stay the night," she said after she'd fixed her own and started in on it while she stood at the counter. "Stay the night and I'll resign from your case—but not until you have breakfast with me tomorrow morning. And you'll be taking your money with you when you go. I won't be a part of that. If you leave, you're going to have to have that debt on your conscience."

A wave of weariness blew through him, sucking him down hard onto the stool. Among his many sins, owing her the money seemed a curiously unsupportable burden, far over and above the number of bodies he'd put into graves. But that was what decent people had always done to him . . . they made him see too clearly who and what he was.

Just as he was gearing up to argue about the B-and-B thing, she cut him off. "Look, if you're here, I know you're safe. I know you've had a meal or two and that you're going to leave stronger. Right now, you need medical attention for your face, another omelet, and a bed that you can rest in. As I said, this house is wired way beyond civilian standards and there are a couple of tricks in the interior—so you don't need to worry about a break-in. Besides, nobody with ties to the government is going to hurt me because of my father."

Childe . . . Childe . . . Nope, still nothing. Then again, he'd been a grunt in XOps who'd been preoccupied with two things: getting his target and getting out alive. He was hardly the type to know about military hierarchy.

Jim Heron would, though. And the guy had slipped him his number. . . .

"So do we have a deal?" she demanded.

"You'll resign," he countered gruffly.

"Yes. But I'll have to tell them everything I know about you when I do. And before you ask, since you've neither confirmed nor denied a connection to the government . . . I'll just forget we ever talked about that."

He wiped his mouth with a napkin and wanted to curse at his lack of options: Man, her determination was in the angle of her jaw—clearly, it was her way or no way.

"Show me your security system." As her shoulders visibly eased up, she put down her fork, but he was having none of that. "No, finish your food first."

While she ate, he got up and paced around, memorizing everything from the pictures on the walls to the photos around the couch and sitting area. Finally, he stopped in front of all that glass.

"Let me show you."

At the sound of her voice, his eyes focused on the reflection of her as she stood behind him in that black dress, a beautiful specter of a woman. . . .

In the quiet silence of the house, with his belly full of food she had prepared for him, and his eyes drinking in the sight of her . . . things went from complicated to completely chaotic.

He wanted her. With a hunger that was going to put them both in a hell of a bind.

"Isaac?"

That voice of hers . . . that dress . . . those legs . . .

"I need to go," he said roughly. Actually, he needed to come . . . inside of her. But that was *not* going to be part of this. Even if he had to cut his own cock off and bury it in that lovely backyard of hers.

"Then I'm not going to resign from your case."

Isaac wheeled around and was entirely unsurprised when she didn't step back or budge one inch.

Before he could open his mouth, she held up her palm to stop him before he started. "It doesn't matter that I don't know you and I don't owe you. So you can stop that argument right there. You and I are going to check out my security system and then you're going to sleep in my guest room and leave in the morning—"

"I could kill you. Right here. Right now."

That shut her up.

As her fingertips lifted to that heavy gold necklace of hers, like maybe she was imagining his hands around her throat, he walked over to her.

And this time she did back away . . . until the counter where her empty plate sat stopped her.

Isaac kept coming until he put his arms on either side of her, locking his hands on the granite, effectively imprisoning her. Looking right into those wide blue eyes of hers, he was desperate to scare some sense into her.

"I'm not the kind of man you're used to."

"You're not going to hurt me."

"You're trembling and you've got a death grip on your neck right now. So you tell me what you think I'm capable of." As she swallowed hard, he figured the wake-up call was way overdue—except he felt like a thug putting on the show of aggression. "I know you're into the savior thing. But I'm not the kind of charity case that'll feed your soul. Trust me."

A humming energy started to vibrate between them, the air molecules in the space between their bodies and their faces agitating.

He leaned in even closer. "I'm more the type to eat you alive."

Her breath exhaled in a rush and he felt it fan over the skin of his neck in a tickle.

And then she floored his ass.

"So do it," she bit out.

Isaac frowned and pulled back a little.

Her eyes were burning, a sudden anger suffusing her beautiful face with a passion he was shocked and titillated by.

"Do it," she growled, grabbing at one of his arms.

She yanked his hand up and put it to her throat. "Go ahead—do it. Or are you just trying to scare me, huh?"

He snapped his wrist out of her grip. "You're out of your mind."

"That's it, isn't it." Her anger really shouldn't have been a total turn-on again. Really. Truly. "You want to try to bully me into getting scared and letting you off the hook. Well, good luck with that. Because unless you're prepared to follow through on the threat, I'm not backing down and I'm not scared of you."

His lungs started to burn . . . and whereas it would have been a hell of a lot smarter for him to step off and use one of her doors, he ended up putting his hand right back where it had been on the granite . . . so she was once again stuck between his heavy arms.

He liked her right where she was, all but blanketed by his body. And he respected her show of strength; he really did—even as it made him worried about how reckless she was.

"Guess what," he said in a low, gravelly voice.

She swallowed hard once again. "What."

Isaac moved in close, putting his mouth right to her ear. "Killing you isn't the only thing I could do to you . . . *ma'am*."

It had been a long time since Grier had felt every square inch of her body—at the same time. Good God, though, she did now, and it wasn't just the skin she was in. She felt every bit of Isaac Rothe, too, even though nothing of his was touching her.

There was just so much of him. And maybe she should have been turned off by the raw, masculine thing he had going on . . . but instead, the brutal reality of his power just drew her in tighter and tighter. Separated by mere inches, with both of them breathing hard, she was utterly unhinged, her emotions unleashed sure as if he had in fact popped her head off her body and let it roll on the floor.

God, she was desperate for him: She wanted to hurl herself right into him and get knocked out by the impact. She wanted him to be the brick wall that she slammed into. She wanted to be senseless and reeling and out of touch with her reality . . . because of him and the sex he threw off like a scent and the wild ride he would be.

Yeah, sure, it wouldn't last. And when she came to, she was going to feel like hell. But in this electric moment, she didn't care about any of that.

"Isaac—"

He backed off. The moment she said his name hoarsely, he not only moved away, he pulled out of the vortex.

Pacing around, he rubbed his short hair like he was trying to scrub his brain raw, and the physical distance gave her a clue about how she would feel in the aftermath if she ever were with him: very empty, vaguely nauseated, and definitely ashamed.

"That won't happen again," he said roughly.

As his pronouncement hung in the still air between them, she told herself that she was relieved she wouldn't have to deal with the sex stuff.

Annnnnnnnnnnnnd . . . the throbbing between her thighs told her that was a bald-faced lie.

"I still want you to stay," she said.

"You never give up, do you."

"No. Never." She thought of the number of times she'd tried to pull Daniel out of his tailspin. "Not ever."

Isaac's face was ancient as he looked across the kitchen at her, his frosty eyes nothing but pits of darkness. "Word to the wise. Letting go can be an important survival mechanism."

"And sometimes it's a moral failing."

"Not if you're being dragged behind a car. Or being pulled down a rat hole. Sometimes to save yourself, you have to get out."

She knew they were getting close to his truth and she kept her voice as steady as she could. "What are you getting out of, Isaac. What are you saving yourself from?"

He just stared at her. And then . . . "Where's your security system."

The deflection was a disappointment, but the concession that he was staying was a win of sorts. And as she took him to the front of the house, she pulled herself together as best she could, even though her knees were loose and her skin overheated and her mind spinning.

There was a terrible familiarity to the way she felt, one that she refused to dwell on . . . but might well bring up to her dead brother when she saw him again. Daniel never spoke of the night he had died, or all the self-abuse that had gone on before that. Maybe, though . . . they needed to talk about everything.

"As I mentioned, this is just for show," she said, sweeping a hand past the ADT pad that was mounted on the wall. "The real unit is in the back of my bedroom closet. Each window and every door has the ADT receivers, but the real system is secured by radio waves and infrared beams and copper plates. Just like yours."

"Show me the connectors. And I want to see the motherboard. Please."

Which would mean taking him upstairs.

As she glanced over at the carpeted steps, she found it hard to believe that she was wondering whether she could be trusted with him. . . .

That close to a bed.

What the hell was happening to her?

# CHAPTER
## 15

As Isaac was led into a cozy library-type room, he knew this was where Grier spent her downtime. There were sections of the *New York Times* and the *Wall Street Journal* in a wicker basket next to a stuffed chair, and the wide-screen TV on the far wall no doubt had CNBC or CNN or FOX News on it most nights.

Who sat here and watched with her? That brother of hers?

"See?" she said, pulling one of the Black Watch tartan drapes aside.

Isaac went over and leaned in—and the whiff of her perfume was precisely the kind of thing he didn't need right now.

Forcing himself to focus on the tiny flashes of copper, he approved of what he was eyeing. Very current stuff.

Who the *hell* was her father?

Before he did something stupid, like touch her, he moved away, and as he wandered by the TV, he was entirely unsurprised by the collection of DVDs tucked into the shelves. Lot of foreign titles and serious movies he'd never heard of, much less seen. Then again, he hadn't been to the cinema since the late eighties.

Last thing he knew, Bruce Willis was a cop desperately looking for a pair of shoes that fit, Arnold was a cyborg with sunglasses, and Steven Seagal had a real hairline.

"Will you take me to the motherboard," he said, turning around to her.

The *and into your bed* part he left off. What a gentleman.

"Of course."

Following her up the stairs, he gave her a wide berth—which was good in that he kept his hands to himself, and not so hot because his eyes had plenty to look at. Jesus, her hips had a way of making him grind his molars.

When they passed the second floor, he took a quick pause and snagged an impression of three bedrooms with open doors. The decorations were done in the same old-money routine as downstairs, but there was a cozy vibe to it all. Much more "family" than "hotel."

He certainly hadn't lived like this. He'd shared a room the size of her front hall with two of his brothers growing up. In XOps, he'd grabbed sleep where he could—usually sitting upright in a chair facing a door with a gun in his hand.

"I'm on the third floor," she said from a number of steps up on the landing.

He nodded and got his ass in gear. It turned out she was actually the *whole* third floor. The master bedroom was a sprawl with its own sitting area, fireplace, and French doors that opened to what he guessed was a private terrace.

"In here."

He tracked the sound of her voice, going over to the walk-in closet she'd disappeared into. The damn thing was as big as some people's living rooms, with wall-to-wall creamy carpeting and legions of clothes lined up and hanging by category.

The air smelled like her perfume.

She was at the back, shifting aside a dozen or so serious-looking suits to reveal ... a four-foot-high, three-foot-wide grate that appeared to be nothing more than an old-fashioned radiator cover. But what do you know, the thing slid back and revealed a crawl space.

Little click and the light came on.

She went in first and he was tight on her going into the cramped confines—and there it was.

Holy . . . shit.

As they knelt down side by side, he thought, Man, good thing he wasn't a techie type or he'd be swooning. The setup was as sophisticated as it got—no little pad with ten numbers and *off*, *stay*, or *away* to choose from. This was a computer-linked system that monitored the various zones in the house on multiple levels. And if he was reading it right, the only way to get at the components was all the way up here, and disarming would be tricky.

Except . . . "I didn't see you turn it off when we came in."

She handed over something that looked like the key fob to a car. "The pad is calibrated to my thumbprint. I take this with me wherever I go, and the system's engaged now."

As he turned the thing over in his hand, she said, "Good enough?"

He flipped his eyes up to hers. "Good enough."

Long moment. Too long for where they were.

Way too long for who they were.

"Anything else," she said.

Yes. "No."

Grier nodded and worked her way around to step out of the confines. After he emerged, they put the grate back and walked into her room—go fig, he couldn't help but look at her bed. Big. Lot of duvets and pillows. On the far side, there was a small TV on top of a choice antique table, and a bookcase lined with precisely ordered DVDs.

He frowned and went over, even though it was none of his business—because he couldn't possibly be seeing the titles right.

*Pretty in Pink. Breakfast Club. Sixteen Candles. Die Hard. Under Siege.*

Even he knew these.

"That's my nighttime viewing," Grier said, as she came across and straightened the thin boxes even though they were perfectly straight.

"Different from what you have downstairs." And he found it hard to believe she was a poser who wanted to be all Jane Austen in public and Jerry Seinfeld here in her room.

She picked up *When Harry Met Sally* . . . and smoothed her hand over the autumn scene on the front. "I don't sleep well and these help. It's like . . . my brain goes back to the time when they came out. I see the cars . . . the supermarket scenes with cheaper prices . . . the clothes that used to be in style . . . hair that no one wears anymore. I go back to when I was the age I first saw them, back to when things were . . . simpler." She laughed in an awkward rush. "Cinematic knockout drops, I'd guess you'd call it. It's the only thing that works for me."

Staring at her as she looked at Meg Ryan, he had such an image of her curled on her side, the blue flicker of the screen playing across her features, the trip into the past calming her nerves and slowing her brain down.

Did she have a lover to watch with her? he wondered. A boyfriend?

No ring, so he assumed she wasn't married or engaged.

"What," she said, tugging at her beautiful black dress.

He cleared his throat, hating that he'd been caught staring. "Which shower do you want me to use."

That made her smile. For the first time.

And yeah, sap that he was . . . his breath caught and his heart stopped.

Grier put the movie back in its slot. "More food first," she said as she turned and led the way back downstairs.

Jim and his boys landed in the rear garden of a three-story brick house that both screamed old money and apologized for making any fuss at the same time. Everything about it, and its neighborhood, was refined and super-well cared for . . . and brick. For God's sake, the whole zip code looked like the three little pigs had gone hog wild: brick houses, brick walls, brick walkways, brick lanes.

It was enough to make the Big Bad Wolf go iron lung.

Through plate-glass windows, a kitchen that was pretty damn spank spread out in all kinds of directions, and there was some kind of food thing going on at the counter — but no people. Stepping back, Jim looked not at the house, but *through* the house, closing his eyes and concentrating.

Yes, he could sense the pair of them . . . as well as something else. There was a . . . ripple . . . inside.

His lids flipped open and just as he lunged for the back door, Eddie caught him by the arm. Which, considering the guy's strength, was like running into a parked car. "No, it's not Devina. That's a wayward soul."

Jim frowned and focused his feelers on the disturbance. "Wayward?"

"It's a soul that has been released from the body, but has yet to go to its destined eternity. It's trapped here on earth."

"A ghost."

"Yeah." Eddie slipped his backpack off his shoulders, his thick braid falling forward. "It's hanging around, waiting to be free."

"What keeps the thing here?"

"Unresolved business."

"And you're sure that's what it is." As the angel's red eyes went rock-hard, Jim raised his hands. "Okay, okay. But can we go with calling them 'ghosts'? That 'wayward' shit is straight-up granny-speak."

"Agreed," Adrian chimed in.

"Oh, for the love . . ." Eddie muttered. "You can call them Fred if it gets you off."

"Deal."

At that moment, Isaac and Grier walked into the kitchen. As the guy parked it on a stool, she resumed cooking for him and the tension between them was obvious ... as was the attraction: The pair of them were playing eye tennis — each time one looked over, the other glanced away — and that blush on the woman's cheeks sealed the deal on the ooh-la-la undertone.

Staring through the glass, Jim felt utterly ancient and apart. Guess now that he was an angel any dreams of ever getting married and doing the kid thing were dead and gone — to say nothing of dating anyone ... although, Christ, when had he ever dated?

And he'd never been the marrying kind, so what the hell was he bitching about?

Besides, this was no Lifetime movie going down in RL on the far side of the glass: what he was staring at was a hunted man and a woman who was in over her head.

Hardly something to be envious of.

In fact, he wondered what in the hell the guy was thinking. Anyone who had worked with their old boss knew that collateral damage was a very real possibility in this scenario.

"Man, let's just move in with them," Adrian groaned. "Screw protective spells — I love a good omelet and I'm starved."

Jim glanced over. "Seriously."

"What? Gotta have plenty of bedrooms in this place." Abruptly the angel's voice grew deeper. "And I can partake of my extracurricular exercises discreetly."

Yeah, and he wasn't talking about basket weaving there. Read: sex with anonymous women. Sometimes with Eddie riding shotgun.

Jim had spent only one night with the pair of them, but he already knew what the drill was. Even though Ad had allowed himself to be used and abused by Devina at the end of the first match, it hadn't taken him long to go trolling again. The guy was frickin' obsessed with the females.

"Can you please focus?" Jim glanced over at Eddie. "So what can we do here—"

Adrian cut in with a growl. "Oh, yeah, she's making him another one."

"You can *so* drop that food-as-porn voice."

"Hey, when I'm into something, I go with it."

"Try learning to cook then—"

Eddie cleared his throat. "Right. So there's a tradeoff to protecting this place—the stronger spells will flag the site for Devina."

"She already knows," Jim said quietly. "I will bet my balls that she's already found him."

"Still think we should lie low."

"Agreed."

Eddie reached out. "So give me your hand."

As Jim offered his palm, he glanced at the pair inside. They seemed insulated from the hurricane swirling on their horizon, and he had the oddest urge to make it so they stayed that way—

"*Shit*," he hissed, yanking his arm back. Looking down at the sting on his hand, he found a thick cut down his life line, one that was oozing . . . blood . . . or something like it.

There was a sheen to the welling red flow, like iridescent car paint in sunlight. Funny, he hadn't noticed anything strange back at the funeral home—then again he'd been a little distracted by his old body's imitation of a sandbag on that slab.

Eddie resheathed his crystal dagger. "Go around and mark each of the doors. Keep in mind the image of the two of them and see them safe and at peace, protected, calm. Same as before—the stronger your image is, the better it works. It'll form a kind of emotional barometer within the house—so that if there's a major disturbance, you'll feel it. It's a low-level spell and will get you here fast if something happens—and it shouldn't get Devina's attention. 'Course, it won't keep her out of there, but you can get here in the blink of an eye if she breaches the barrier."

With his hand dripping, Jim went up the steps to the back door, keeping himself cloaked so that he would appear to Isaac and his lady friend as nothing but a passing shadow. Pressing his palm to the cold painted panels, he focused on the two of them, catching them at a moment when their eyes locked and held. Then he lowered his lids and concentrated on nothing but that image . . .

The world went away, everything from the breeze on his face to the creak of Adrian's leather jacket to the distant sounds of traffic just disappearing . . . and then his body went as well, his weight lifting off his feet, even as he stayed on the ground.

There was nothing for him, around him, or about him but the picture in his mind.

And it was from out of the vacuum that his power boiled up.

An immense groundswell of energy channeled into the blank space he'd created and without understanding it, he knew precisely what to do with the force, sending it around the house, giving part of it away only to find that even more streamed in.

Dropping his arm, he stepped back—

Jim went statue. The shimmer in his blood was on the door . . . and spreading in all directions in waves, covering the panels and the jambs and moving onto the brick. Upward and out to the sides it surged, gaining ground, taking over.

Sealing the house up.

"Not bad for a first try," he muttered, getting ready to go around to the front.

As he turned, he paused. The two angels were looking at him as if he were a stranger.

"What." He glanced over his shoulder. The shimmery

red wave was still spreading, going up and over the roofline. "Sure as shit looks like it worked."

Eddie cleared his throat. "Ah, yeah. You could say that."

"To the front—"

"Not necessary," Eddie said. "You've covered the house."

As Adrian muttered something under his breath and shook his head, Jim thought, What the hell?

"You two look like someone pissed on your boots. You want to tell me the problem." Pause. Cue response . . . which didn't come. "Fine. Whatever."

"We should go now," Eddie said as he put his knife back in the pack. "With the spell in place, we're not a value-add. She's got beads on all of us."

"How?"

The two angels looked at each other. Ad was the one who answered. "We've all been with her. If you know what I mean."

Jim narrowed his eyes on Eddie, but the angel just busied himelf with his damn luggage.

Well, what do you know. Devina got around.

Putting the thought out of his mind, Jim walked through the garden's back gate and went around to the front entrance. After making note of the number and street, he took to the air in spite of an impulse to stay put.

He was satisfied with his little sealant spell, however— plus Dog had been back at the hotel for quite a while, and Jim needed to take him out. Maybe he'd get them both a pizza. . . .

While Adrian and Eddie no doubt enjoyed a different kind of pie.

# CHAPTER
## 16

As Isaac was having his second omelet—and wondering how in the hell he was going to get through the night—Grier went to get his room ready. When they were both finished, she took him up to what was clearly the men's guest bedroom suite: The walls and drapes were done in navy blue and chocolate brown and there were leather chairs and a lot of leather-bound books.

He felt like a total intruder.

"I'm going to change and then clean up the kitchen," she said as she stepped out and pulled the door partially shut. "If you need anything, you know where to find me."

There was a brief pause. Like she was searching for something to say.

"Good night, then," she murmured.

" 'Night."

After she closed him in, he listened to her going to her room, her footfalls soft and steady. Overhead, he couldn't hear her walking around, but he imagined her heading into that massive closet and taking off her black dress.

Yeah ... that zipper inching down, showing him her back. The shoulders of the top part sliding off her arms ...

the material pooling at her waist and then slipping from her hips.

His cock twitched.

Then got fully hard.

*Shit.* Just what he didn't need.

Going into the bathroom, he stopped and had to shake his head at his host. On the marble counter, she'd left out fresh towels, a collection of toiletries, a tube of Neosporin, and a box of Band-Aids. There was also a fleece that was man-sized and a set of drawstring flannel pajama bottoms that sent a spike of jealousy straight through his chest.

He hoped like hell they really were her brother's. And not some slick-suited lawyer type who slept with her.

Cursing himself, he ducked into the glass shower and turned on the water. It was no business of his who her lovers were—what flavor or how many or when and where. And as for the flannel pj thing? They were clean and going to keep him from flashing his ass.

Didn't matter whose they were.

He took off his sweatshirt and double-checked his guns. Then he pulled his muscle shirt over his head, slid his pants off and got a gander at his reflection in the mirror: lot of black-and-blues on his shoulders and chest interspersed among the network of old scars that had healed up just fine.

Hard not to wonder what Grier would think of him.

Then again, if they hooked up in the dark, he wouldn't have to worry about—

"Fuckin' *A*." He so needed to cut that crap.

Getting into the shower, he wondered exactly what it was about her that got him thinking like a fifteen-year-old. And decided it had to be the fact that he hadn't had sex in a year and had been in a fight tonight—both of which were the kind of things that juiced a guy up.

Really.

They so did.

He couldn't possibly be jonesing for his attorney just because she was five-feet-nine of all woman, wrapped up in a Tiffany-style package.

Unfortunately, whatever the cause, it turned out soap and hot water didn't help his hormone overload. As he washed himself off, his hands on his skin were slippery and warm . . . and the soap ran down between his legs, dripping off his hard cock and tickling over his tight balls.

He was used to his body being full of aches and pains—it was easy to ignore all that crap. What he was feeling toward that woman? It was like trying to pretend someone wasn't screaming in church. . . .

His soapy hand wandered where it shouldn't, going in between his thighs, sweeping up the underside of his erection.

"Fuck," he gritted as he let his palm slide back down, the friction amping him up—

It took all he had in him to derail that damn hand. And he ended up washing his hair three times in an attempt to keep himself busy. Conditioned the hell out of the stuff as well. Of course, the best solution was getting out of the treacherous privacy and seductive warmth of the shower— but he couldn't quite convince his body to head in the bath mat direction.

Before he knew it, his erection was doing the magnet-to-steel thing again and his palm was all about heading home . . . and he gave up the fight.

Dirty. Lecherous. Bastard.

It felt so good, though, that grip that he imagined was hers, the hold, that slide, that twist at the tip.

Besides, what were his options? Try to ignore it? Yeah, right. He threw on those pajama bottoms, he was going to be Barnum & Bailey obscene—a tent and then some. And he had to go see her downstairs before he crashed.

He had a warning to give his lovely attorney.

The last of his internal arguments hung around for . . . oh, maybe two strokes and then he got on the ride. Facing the showerhead, he planted one hand on the marble wall and leaned into his shoulder. His cock was heavy and stiff as his frickin' forearm as he started to work it properly, his hand moving up and down. And the blast of fire that flashed up his spine made him drop his head and open his mouth to breathe.

In the gathering maelstrom, he refused to think of Grier. She might have been the cause of the arousal, but he was *not* going to fantasize about her while he jacked off in her shower. Just not going to happen. It was too skeevy and disrespectful—she deserved so much more even if she never found out what he'd done.

That was the last conscious thought he had before he was all about the orgasm: The head of his sex was so sensitive each swipe over the thing was a sweet sting that shot through his erection and dove into his balls. Spreading his legs farther apart, he got good and braced as he found his rhythm, the hot spray hitting his hair and running down his face as he began to pant—

From out of nowhere, and against management's memo to the contrary, the memory of having Grier up close and personal grabbed hold of his brain and went bulldog. No matter how much he tried to forget or focus on something else, there was no detaching what it felt like to have been that near to her.

God, her lips had been an inch from his own. All it would have taken was an incline of the head and he would have kissed—

The release came on fast and powerful, ramming into him so hard, he had to turn into his biceps and bite down to keep from barking her name out loud.

And damn him to hell, he rode it to the last jerking spasm, milking himself until his knees went loose and he tasted blood from the biting.

In the aftermath, he sagged and felt like a wasteland

on the inside, as if coming had drained him of not just the sexual impulse, but everything else.

He was so tired.

So very, very tired.

With a curse, he reached out the hand that had done the work and made sure there were no traces of anything on the marble or the glass. Then he rinsed off one last time, cut the water, and stepped from the misty confines that had gotten him into trouble.

He was still hard. In spite of the exhaustion. And the exercise.

Clearly, his cock hadn't bought the bribe.

And yup, he was right: Flannel did absolutely nothing to conceal the hey-could-we-do-some-more-of-that. If anything, that pole thing made him look twice the size he was—which, considering he was hung to begin with, was not the direction he wanted to go in.

Folding up his erection and nailing it flat against his belly with the waistband of the pj's, he reached for the fleece and prayed it came down on him far enough to hide that flushed head of his.

Which was still just full of bright ideas—

Okay, total no-go on the conceal. The pullover might have been long enough if his chest hadn't been so big. As it stood? He was more *naked* than naked as he flashed his goods.

Isaac ditched the fleece and threw on his sweatshirt; the muscle shirt was just too nasty after the fight. Damn thing should be burned, not cleaned.

And before he made the return trip downstairs, he hit the first-aid supplies, although not because he cared: Sure as shit, if he didn't use them, she was going to insist on coming up here and playing Florence Nightingale.

So not a good plan, considering what he'd just done.

The butterfly bandage he'd gotten from the med-tech

guys in jail hadn't stood a chance in the ring and God only knew where it had ended up. Whatever, though, the cut was nothing special, just a split in the skin that was deep enough to give a blood show, but nothing to get hysterical about. He was going to have a scar—like that mattered?

He slapped a Band-Aid on the thing, and didn't bother with the antibiotic stuff. He was far more likely to die from Smith & Wesson–related lead poisoning than any skin infection.

Out of the guest room. Down the stairs. By the time he got to the front hall, things had begun to ease off slightly at the hip level.

Until he came around the corner of the kitchen and saw Grier.

Oh, *man*.

If she was gorgeous in a little black dress, she was totally beddable in what was evidently her version of pajamas: men's flannel boxers and an old green sweatshirt that read, CAMP DARTMOUTH. With white socks and a pair of schleppy slippers on her feet, she looked closer to college age than any kind of thirty . . . and the absence of makeup and fancy hair was actually a plus. Her skin was satin smooth and her pale eyes popped rather than got lost behind her horn-rimmed glasses.

Guess she wore contacts.

And her hair . . . it was so long, much longer than he'd thought, and vaguely wavy. He bet it smelled good and felt even better. . . .

She glanced over from the red bowl she was drying at the sink. "Find what you need upstairs?"

Not. Even. Close.

For good measure, he yanked at the bottom of the sweatshirt to make sure Mr. Happy was covered. And then he just watched her. Like he was some kind of idiot.

"Isaac?"

"Have you ever been married," he asked quietly.

As her eyes flipped up to his, he knew how she felt: He couldn't believe he'd thrown that out there, either.

Before he could backpedal, she pushed her glasses up higher on her nose, and said, "Ah, no. No, I haven't. You?"

He shook his head and left it at that, because God knew he shouldn't have opened the door in the first place.

"A girlfriend?" she asked, picking up the pan to dry it off.

"Never had one." As her eyes shot back to his, he shrugged. "Not saying I haven't had . . . er, been with . . ."

Holy. Hell. Was he blushing?

Okay, he so had to get away from her and out of town—and not just because Matthias was after his ass. This woman was turning him into someone he didn't know.

"You just haven't met the right person, I guess?" She bent down and put the bowl away, then came over with the pan to tuck it into the cabinets under the island. "That's always the thing, isn't it."

"Among others."

"I just keep thinking it'll happen for me," she murmured. "But it hasn't. Although I do like my life."

"No boyfriend?" he heard himself say.

"No." She shrugged. "And I'm not a one-night-stand kind of girl."

That didn't surprise him. She was much too classy.

As a curiously gentle silence bloomed between them, he didn't have a clue how long he stood there, staring across the island at her.

"Thank you," he said eventually.

"For what? I haven't really helped you."

The hell she hadn't. She'd given him something warm to think about when he was alone in the cold night: He was going to remember this moment with her now for the rest of his days.

However few of those he might have left.

Moving around so that he was closer to her, he reached out and touched her cheek. As she inhaled sharply and went still, he said, "I'm sorry about . . . earlier."

Yeah, not sure which "earlier" that would be: the twenty-five grand he'd cost her, the running from the law, the attempt to scare some sense into her . . . or The Shower.

He was surprised when she didn't pull away. "I still don't want you to go."

Isaac gave that one a pass. "I like your hair down," he said instead, running his fingers through it to her shoulder. As she flushed, he stepped back. "I'm going to bed. If you need me, knock first, okay? Knock first and wait for me to answer the door."

She blinked quick, like a fog was lifting from her inner riverbank. "Why?"

"Just promise me."

"Isaac . . ." When he shook his head, she crossed her arms over her chest. "Okay. I promise."

"Good night."

"Good night."

He turned and left her in the kitchen by herself, taking the hall and the stairs fast, because his self-control was threadbare, and in spite of the two omelets, he was starved.

Not for food, though.

Like a total nancy, he ducked into the guest room and waited behind the closed door just so he could listen to the sound of her going up the softly creaking old stairs. When he heard her shut herself in, he pivoted around . . . and wondered what in the hell he was going to do for the next eight hours.

His cock twitched like it was raising a hand to be called on by the teacher, the erection all oh-oh-oh-oh-I-got-an-answer-for-that.

"So not going to happen, big guy," Isaac snapped at himself.

Rubbing his eyes, he couldn't believe he'd fallen so low

as to be talking to his dumb handle. Or trying to reason with it.

And on top of that, he also couldn't believe he'd agreed to stay—especially given who had stepped into the ring with him. But he couldn't argue with what he'd seen in the back of Grier's closet—and although Matthias didn't mind collateral damage, he sure as shit wouldn't seek it out. Especially if her dad was military: Matthias knew everyone—and was fully aware of any complications that could arise if he killed the daughter of somebody important.

With yet another curse, Isaac went into the bathroom and brushed his teeth; then he stretched out on top of the duvet and turned off the light. As he focused on the ceiling, he imagined her in that cozy bed up above him, with the television on and something from the *Magnum P.I.* era playing in front of her closed lids.

He wanted to be up there with her.

He wanted to be up there . . . and all over her.

Which meant he had to leave at the crack of dawn before she even woke. Otherwise he might not be able to go without trying to take something he had no right to . . . much less deserved.

Closing his eyes, he made it about fifteen minutes before his tossing and turning rode those pj bottoms so far up his crotch he felt like he could cough flannel.

If he was doing the mattress and pillow thing, he usually slept naked and now he knew why. This was f'in' ridiculous.

Half an hour later he couldn't stand it anymore and stripped down completely. The only thing he kept near were the pair of guns tucked just inside the blankets. After all, he might be flashing his ass, but there was no reason to be vulnerable.

# CHAPTER
# 17

The Comfort Inn & Suites in Framingham, Massachusetts, had corridors that stank of Febreze, windows that were caulked shut, and sheets that were a little itchy. But at least the quietly humming Coke machine by the elevator spit out an endless stream of glacially cold caffeinated heaven.

Adrian Vogel loved a good Coke, preferring the old-school glass bottles to cans. But he'd take the plastic long-necks happily enough.

And he was going to buy two as soon as he got off on his floor. One for himself and one for . . . "What did you say your name was?"

The redhead next him was exactly his type: totally stacked, partially wasted, and under no illusions that this was going to be anything but sex.

"Rachel." She smiled, showing teeth that were sparkly and superwhite. "And I think I'll keep my last name to myself."

Man, those chompers of hers were incredible—as lined up and shiny as bathroom tile. Then again she was a dental hygienist, so she probably got a discount.

Hell, with her looks, she could be a model for their product lines.

There was a ding and the door slid back, revealing

the red-and-white vending machine of his dreams. As he stepped aside and let lovely, sparkly Rachel-with-no-last-name pass, he was well aware that he was using her, but that was a two-way street: Their conversation at the bar next to the hotel had started up over the fact that she was wrenching her wedding band off.

Apparently, her husband was fucking a friend of hers.

And it had taken Adrian 'bout a minute and a half to come up with the perfect payback.

He'd bought her a couple of drinks and then one more, and he knew he had her when she asked if he was staying in the hotel. He told her yes, he was . . . with his best friend. Who was a lot better-looking than he was.

Right, total lies-ville on that one. But he liked to share with Eddie if the women were up for it. Given the state of his buddy's game, the fucker would never get laid if Ad didn't bring 'em home.

"Hold up," he said as he stopped at his machine, got his wallet out, and peeled free a couple of bills.

"You know," his date said, "I've never been with any-body like you."

Yeah, he was damn sure of that one. "Really?" As he smiled at her over his shoulder, she focused on the loop in his lower lip—and to oblige, he deliberately licked over the dark gray metal. "I ain't so bad, am I?"

Her eyes were hungry. "Not at all. Hey, do you have a girlfriend? I never asked."

Adrian turned back to the machine and fed the money in, listening to the little *whirrrrrr* as the George Washing-tons were sucked into the thing's gullet.

"No," he said, pushing the pad for a regular. "I'm not with anyone."

Actually he had been . . . all too recently. Which was why, even though he always liked his sex, he'd been so hell-bent on picking the chick up last night and hitting on Ra-chel tonight.

Washing off after Devina had used him was always a process. Sure, right after she released him, the hot water and soap got rid of his blood and the other stuff that coated his skin . . . but the filthy dirty thing always persisted.

This lovely little morsel of humanity, however, was going to help replace the sensations that lingered in his body.

The ones that had nothing to do with the fading bruises on his skin.

The shit with Devina stayed with him, lingering in the back of his mind, festering. To the point where there were now two of him: the one who bantered with Jim and stayed alert and was ready to fight for Isaac Rothe's soul . . . and the one who was curled up in the recesses of his mental park, shaking and numb and all alone.

"Diet?" he asked.

"Yes, please."

This time, his hand shook as he fed the machine's mouth. To the point where it took him a couple of tries to get the bill in. "Hey, could you do something for me?"

"Sure."

"Wrap your arms around me."

There was a soft laugh and then he felt a gentle compression around his waist as Rachel No-Last-Name did what he'd asked. As she leaned into the back of him, her soft breasts pressed against his hard muscle and the warmth of her body was one hell of a contrast to what was doing inside of him.

He was so damn cold. Cold as the Coke he was buying.

Adrian let his head drop and braced one hand against the machine, holding them both upright.

Devina was going to kill him. If not when she was actually fucking him, then because of the aftermath: His brain wasn't working right anymore, and as the days went by and it didn't return normal, he was starting to worry. He didn't think Jim knew; he worried that Eddie did—and here was the problem: He had no intention of getting benched by the powers that be again. He was a fighter and he had a personal vendetta against Devina . . . and that meant he had to pull it together.

"You know," Rachel murmured against his shoulder, "if you wanted to feel my breasts, there's a better way."

He swallowed hard and put his mask back in place. Turning around in her arms, he swept her red hair off her neck and tilted her chin up. "You're so right."

He was utterly empty as he kissed her, but she didn't know that, and he was so desperate to make a connection that he didn't care.

"Adrian. . . ." As she drew out his name, he guessed she liked the way the metal bar through his tongue felt against her own.

Running his hands down her hips to her ass, he pulled her in tight to his body and tried to break through his arctic circle with her curves and the way she moved against him and the smell of her perfume and the taste of the cranberry and vodkas she'd been drinking.

Keeping to the rhythm, he punched the "diet" button and the machine coughed up another bottle.

"Come on," he growled, grabbing her soda. "Let me introduce you to Eddie. Like I told you, you're going to love him. Everyone loves him."

He gave her a wink in an attempt to flirt, and going by the way she giggled, it was clear she bought the charm . . . and was really open to what she was walking into.

"You know, I've never done this before," she said, as he led her down the corridor. "Well, with . . . you know."

"Two people?" She giggled again and he smiled down at her. "That's okay—we'll treat you very, very well."

This was going to work, he told himself as he got out his plastic key to the door. This *had* to work. Last night just hadn't been enough, but after this, his slate was going to be clean and his head was going to be back in the game and he was going to get to take his pound of flesh out of Devina.

When they came up to his room, Adrian stopped, slipped the card in the slot, and opened the way just a crack. "We've got some company. You decent?"

Eddie's reply was quick and annoyed. "Of course I am."

Adrian pushed in with that manufactured smile nailed on the front door of his face. "Where are you, buddy?"

As his roommate came out from the loo, Eddie's hard look changed the instant he saw the female.

Noooooooot so annoyed anymore. But Adrian knew the guy had a thing for redheads—which was why the lovely Rachel had been a slam dunk.

While Eddie stepped up to introduce himself, Ad went over and put his head through the open connector into Jim's room.

The angel was sitting in front of the laptop he'd bought earlier in the day. On one side of him, there was an open box of half-eaten pizza, and on the other, a Marlboro quietly smoldered in an ashtray. In his lap, Dog was a scruffy pile of gray-and-blond-colored fur—to the point where you couldn't tell what end was tail and what was muzzle.

Going by Jim's frown, it was pretty clear what he was doing on the compy: He was searching for info on that girl Devina had murdered, desecrated, and hung upside down in that tub back in Caldwell—the virgin girl who had been sacrificed to protect the demon's turf. The one Jim had tried to save . . . and been too late for.

"Jim."

At the sound of his name, the guy who was responsible for saving the world looked up. His eyes were red rimmed from lack of sleep and he was looking hollowed out—so yeah, he was pretty much what you'd expect, given how much was on his shoulders. And yet he was clearly up to the task. That spell the guy had pulled out of his ass at the brick house? Unbelievable. First try out of the gate and he did it on a oner. Eddie or Ad? Would have had to go all around the place marking the entrances to ensure proper coverage.

Kind of made you wonder what else the bastard could do.

"What's up, Ad?" the guy said as he picked up his cig and took a draw. The exhale was slow and tired.

Adrian thumbed over his shoulder. "We're gonna be busy for a little bit."

"Are you, now."

As if on cue, Rachel let out one of her giggles and right on the heels of it came a low purring growl. Which usually meant Eddie was going in for something. A kiss. A palm up. A sucking . . .

Jim's stare narrowed. "Are you okay?"

Adrian stepped back and started to shut the door. He didn't want Jim involved in his drama. It was one thing to be undone before Eddie—who he'd lived through hell with. Literally.

But not Jim. He liked the guy . . . trusted him . . . was willing work with him. That was it, though.

"Hold up a minute," Heron demanded.

"I gotta go—"

"You can spare me a frickin' minute. Something tells me they won't go far without you."

Adrian was having problems.

Jim could sense it clearly as the guy stood in the doorway with that faker smile on his puss and a body that was strung tight as a bridge cable. Sure, he'd appeared to be keeping shit together, but that wasn't the truth under his Mr. Rough Guy routine, was it.

And battle fatigue was not a joke; it fractured your brain and presented a danger to yourself and others. After all, walking around with a noggin that wasn't working right was like having a weapon in your holster that could misfire at any moment—and blow up in your hand.

"Adrian."

"What." The guy's reply was not an opening for discussion. And neither was the hand with long red nails that snaked across his hip and began to drag up his shirt.

"Come in here for a sec," Jim said, well aware he was pushing water uphill. No way the angel was going to turn away from Ms. Fancy Fingers over there.

"Little busy right now, buddy." Adrian's eyes were nothing but glass, like whatever lit up the inside of him had taken off for a vacation.

"This is more important."

"FYI, I'm not a big talker. I'm a doer."

This got yet another giggle and the shirt pushed up past the angel's pecs . . . and then there was a pause, like the female was surprised with what she'd found. Made sense. Ad's nipples were pierced with bars, and a gunmetal gray chain connected the set—and didn't stop there. The links ran down his six-pack and beneath the waistband of the jeans.

Jim had pulled a hey-wait-a-minute when he'd first gotten a gander at the connect-the-dots, too.

"Look, Adrian," he began, prepared to start in, even if it was with an audience.

Ad twisted around to the woman. "Go say 'hi' to Eddie for minute, honey."

The redhead took the suggestion and ran with it, crossing over to the other guy and pulling him in for a kiss. Through the crack in the door, it was a hell of a show as Eddie maneuvered her to the bed, laid her out and covered her with his heavy body. Going by the gasping, she was in straight-up heaven as she pulled his muscle shirt—

Jim frowned and jacked forward, wondering if he was seeing right . . . and yeah, he was. Eddie's back was heavily scarred . . . but not as in a burn or a random whipping. It was the same symbology that had been on the stomach of the girl at Devina's place—

As Jim burst to his feet, Adrian stepped into the line of sight, blocking the view. As well as the way in.

"What the fuck is on him?" Jim hissed, hanging on to Dog.

Adrian just shook his head as the lights went out in the far room and something hit the floor. Like one of Eddie's combat boots.

"We're not talking about anything," the angel said quietly. "We'll work for you and do what we have to to help you win, but you're not welcome in our cesspool, Jim. He and I have been together too long, and in case you haven't noticed, you just showed up on the job."

A deep, guttural voice rose through the darkness: "Come on, Adrian."

That sure as hell wasn't the female sending out the demand. And for once, Ad, who wasn't into taking orders, seemed in the mood to comply.

"We're right next door if you need us," the guy said before he disappeared into the darkness and the sex. "Just holler."

And then everything was shut up tight.

Jim sank back down onto the chair and resettled Dog in his lap. Stroking the animal's rough fur, he had to force himself to stay where he was. He wanted to break into that other room and demand that Adrian see a shrink and Eddie talk about what those markings were. But come on—everyone was half-naked and soon-to-be totally naked. And then pneumatics were going to get started.

"Hell . . . fuckin' hell."

Closing his eyes, he saw the patterns carved into Eddie's back and remembered the moment he'd busted into Devina's bathroom and found that innocent young girl upside down over the tub. Her blood had been bright red against the white porcelain and all over her pale skin and her blond hair. She'd been slaughtered and marked by the demon, her skin scratched raw with symbols.

Just as Eddie's had.

Devina had obviously gotten her claws into that angel. And Jim was going to need the details on that one.

Refocusing on the laptop he'd bought that afternoon, he cleared the screen saver with a swipe of his finger. The Dell had only civilian speed and memory, but then again, it wasn't like he was going to be commanding satellites off its keyboard—and the *Caldwell Courier Journal* Web site had come up easily enough.

As he returned to the archives, that picture of the girl was a raw wound on his brain. Dead bodies were nothing new to him, and yet that one had burrowed into his brain stem and set up shop in the heart of his CPU.

He wished he could have at least given her a proper burial. But when he'd entered the room, he'd broken the spell that had protected Devina's sacred mirror so they'd had to leave. After that, the remains of the girl had disappeared.

Which was what brought Jim to the newspaper. Somebody would be looking for their daughter, and the body—or at least pieces of it—would eventually be found: Adrian maintained that Devina usually just dumped what was left as opposed to destroying it because that would cause more pain to the family and friends.

Such a peach that female was.

And it made him wonder whether permanently missing was better than defiled and destroyed. Hell of a choice.

In the search box, he entered things like "blond woman found dead" and "blond woman homicide" and "blond female killed." Nothing—well, a lot of somethings, just none that fit what he was looking for. The results were too old either in age, because his victim had looked to be only about eighteen/nineteen, or the articles were from six months to a year ago whereas his girl had been killed very recently: The blood had been fresh, and her body, though mutilated, had appeared to be in relatively good health, which made him assume she hadn't been tortured or starved for a period of time prior to her death.

When the *CCJ* didn't give him what he wanted, his next stop on the information superhighway was the national database of missing persons. He searched the state of New York.

Oh . . . man. So many.

So much damn suffering out there in the world: nights that were filled with parents or husbands or wives or sisters and brothers wondering if the one who had been taken from them was dead or alive or in agony caused by another.

"Christ," he whispered.

And he had been part of this, hadn't he. On a worldwide scale, he had perpetrated crimes that had created holes in other people's lives. Yes, the vast majority of his targets had been evil men, but he knew for a fact that many had had families, and now he wondered what he'd left behind. Even if the paterfamilias had deserved to die, what kind of trickle-down chaos had he created? He knew that a couple of his targets had been renowned for loving their kids: They might have been enemies with dangerous resources on a political calculus, but they hadn't been bastards at home.

"Shit, Dog . . ." There was a snuffle and then a cold wet nose bumped against his hand. "Yeah, let's start wading through all this."

Dog raised his scruffy head and yawned so wide he let out a sound like a hinge squeaking. Then with another snuffle, the mutt rearranged himself in Jim's lap, curling his little paws in and relaxing.

Jim tried to smooth the fur that had been messed up by the repositioning, but Dog's wiry coat made that wasted effort. Silly animal always looked like he'd been blown dry by a set of box fans and then hit with four cans of Aqua Net.

Faces . . . names . . . stories . . .

As a moan percolated up from next door, he thought

of the last time he'd had sex and got nauseated. The idea that'd he'd come inside his enemy was enough to give his cock a case of the never-again shrivels.

To think the other two had done her as well—

At first, the sensation was hard to place. Something was . . . just off. And then the vague huh-what? coalesced to the back of his neck until he was convinced cold air was being exhaled on his nape.

He wrenched around, but nobody was there. And the chills persisted, flickering down his spine, turning into a fleet of ants that teemed over his back.

Jim got to his feet and set Dog on the carpet.

Isaac, he thought. Isaac and Grier . . .

*That house . . .*

*The spell at the house.*

He was out of the hotel and back to Beacon Hill in the work of a moment, landing in the rear garden. The incantation he'd thrown remained in place, the outside of the town house still glowing, and now that he was in range, he knew he'd been right to come.

Devina was here. He could sense her evil, parasitic presence.

And yet everything appeared quiet: Through the plate-glass windows in the back, the kitchen was dark, with nothing but a distant hall light throwing illumination. No shadows moving, no alarm screeching, no guns going off, no screaming.

With a great beat of his wings, he levitated up to the third-floor terrace and landed in silence. Walking over to the French doors, he kept himself invisible to the human eye and peered in. The blond attorney was in her bed, lying on her side facing a little TV, apparently sleeping.

She seemed just fine.

Matter of fact, everything appeared just fine. Yeah, sure, he could sense that ghost hovering around—but it wasn't a threat to her or Isaac. . . .

The vibrating alarm in his spinal cord was still going strong, however, and he was inclined to listen to it rather than go with this illusion of A-OK. On a blink, he walked through the glass door and stood in the center of her room, braced for action.

Which appeared to be a waste of muscle tension.

Again, there was nothing out of place, no sounds. . . .

Frowning, he walked past the bed and through the closed door across the way. On the landing at the head of the stairs, he paused, and the ant farm on his back went crazy, the tickle so intense it turned his whole body into a tuning fork. Jogging downward, he knew he was headed in the right direction as the sensation got even worse — and then he ghosted into the room Isaac was using.

And there was the disturbance.

His fellow soldier was on the bed, twisting and turning in the sheets, his body contorting, his face screwed up tight in a mask of agony. As his big hands gripped the duvet, his arms strained, and that heavy chest of his pumped air hard.

Devina was here, all right, but she was *in* the man, not around him: The demon had sucked Isaac into a nightmare and trapped him in some kind of torture. And the result was a torment all the more real for its unreality, Jim imagined, because the bitch could custom-fit the abuse to Isaac's weaknesses, whatever they were.

At least there was a simple solution: Wake the poor bastard up.

Jim rushed forward —

Nigel, his new boss, appeared in the corner of the room and held his hand up like a crossing guard. "If you rouse him, she'll get into more than just his mind."

Jim pulled out of the lunge, yanking his weight back onto his heels and confronting the English lordship-type who was his CO Tonight, the archangel was dressed in a 1920s-era tuxedo, and sporting a cigarette in a holder in his right hand and a martini glass in the other. But this wasn't a party to him: In spite of his Gatsby duds and his 007 drink, his face and his voice were death's-door grim.

Jim pointed to the bed. "So I was right. Isaac is my next assignment."

Nigel took a draw on his coffin nail and exhaled—which made Jim realize they actually had something in common. Although given that they were both immortal, guess it wasn't a bad habit anymore.

"Indeed, saving his life is the answer," was the eventual reply.

"But I can't leave him like this," Jim said as Isaac let out a groan. "Even if he'll live through it, it's cruel."

"You cannot wake him, however. You relate to humans through their souls. That is your conduit—the way you touch them when you interact with them. Right now, his mind is contaminated by her—if you open the door by disturbing him, she shall waltz right on your heels."

Hardly the kind of assist he was looking to provide the enemy.

And yet as Jim stared at the thrashing man, he worried whether the experience would actually kill the sorry SOB. He looked as if someone were ripping his arms and legs off. "I'm not going to let him suffer like this."

"Use the tools you have. There are many."

Damn it, he should have brought Eddie and Adrian with him. "Tell me."

"I cannot. I shouldn't be here a'tall. If I provide too much guidance, I risk affecting the outcome and thus having the round disqualified—or worse."

Down on the bed, Isaac let out a rippling scream.

"Shit, what do I do?"

When there was no answer, Jim looked over to the corner and saw nothing except a fading curl of smoke left by the archangel's cigarette. His boss had disappeared the same way he'd arrived: quickly and in silence.

"Fucking hell, Nigel . . ."

ROUTING SLIP 13/04/16 11.03

Item 1802750188
Crave / Ward, J.R.

Reservation for 0407010539
Miss Scarlett Gohri

At SGYA/Yate Library

 South Gloucestershire
Staff Reservation
      update_to_cag 13/04/16

Standing there all by his little lonesome, while his back screamed in alarm and Isaac suffered, Jim took out his phone and tried Eddie. Adrian. Eddie again. He was about to go back to the hotel and drag them out of bed—naked if he had to—when the solution came to him.

# CHAPTER

## 18

Bolting up off the pillows, Grier grabbed her chest and felt her heart pound against her palm as she woke on a gasp. With her free hand, she pushed her hair out of her face and looked around. Her room was all in shadow, nothing but the floating DVD logo on the TV screen shedding any light.

"Isaac?" she asked, her voice cracking.

No answer. And no footsteps coming up the stairs.

As disappointment slowed her heartbeat, she corrected herself: It was relief. *Relief*.

"Daniel?" she said softly. When her brother didn't make himself known, she figured she'd come awake because her nerves were shot—

Grier froze. There was a man in her room. A huge man who was standing in front of the French doors, just outside the light of the TV. He was utterly still, like a photograph, and the only reason she knew he was there was the silhouette he cut through the ambient glow of the city.

Opening her mouth to scream, she . . . stopped herself.

He had wings.

Great wings that lifted above his shoulders and shimmered like moonlight over water, hypnotizing her eyes.

He was an angel, she thought. And as an odd, disassociated peacefulness eased over her, she decided this had to be a dream. Right? Had to be ...

"Why are you here?" she asked, her voice sounding far, far away.

As he took a step forward, his face emerged from shadow and she was struck by how hard he looked. No cherubim sweetness. No airy-fairy, beneficent-messenger expression. No robes, either—he was dressed in a tight black shirt and ... blue jeans?

This was a warrior.

And he reminded her of Isaac.

"Why are you here?" she asked again, unsure whether she'd just thought the words the first time.

Looking straight into her eyes, he pointed to the door that led out into the hall.

*Isaac*, she thought—or perhaps heard in her mind.

Grier shot out of bed and ran for the stairwell, urgency driving her feet deep into the carpet, her hand barely catching the banister as she skidded around and tore down the stairs.

At the door to the guest room, there were the sounds of some kind of struggle. *Oh, God ...*

Bursting in, she couldn't see much in the darkness and called out, "Isaac? Are you okay—"

It happened so fast she couldn't track the movement. One second she was just inside the doorjambs; the next she was wrenched around, shoved onto the ground, and totally incapacitated, her arms pulled behind her back and held there hard.

A cold piece of metal pushed into her temple as a heavy weight sat on her hips.

Fear choked the air right out of her lungs, even as she was sure it was Isaac, because he smelled like her soap. "P-p-please ..." She dragged in a breath. *"It's me ... Grier."*

He didn't move. Just started to pant like he was struggling.

Tears slicked over her eyes. "Is . . . aac . . ."

"Oh, *fuck*." In a flash, he was off her and the gun disappeared.

As she tried to catch her breath, he bent down to her and croaked, "I'm so sorry—"

She jerked away and leaped to her feet, moving back until she slammed into the wall. Putting shaking hands to her face, she tried to inhale nice and slow, but her lungs were jamming up against her ribs, and her throat was so tight she felt like she was being choked.

Isaac gave her plenty of space and didn't say another word. He just stood where he was, in the slice of light that cut in from the hall fixture. As the roar between her ears dimmed, she realized he was naked, that sweatshirt of his held over his privates, his pecs and his stomach muscles standing out in stark relief.

No doubt he'd traded the gun for modesty.

"I didn't know it was you," he said. "I swear."

In her head, she heard him telling her not to come in until he answered.

"Grier . . ." His voice cracked, his expression one of physical pain—like it killed him that he'd done that to her.

When she felt like she could speak, she met him straight in the eye. "Just answer one thing . . . are you on the run for a good reason or a bad one?"

The response was long in coming and quiet as breath. "Good. I promise you." And then he surprised her. "I needed the money and I can't work legally—that's why I was fighting. I also happen to be well trained."

Well, yeah.

He cursed and ran a hand through his short hair, his biceps bunching up thick and stretching a bright, angry bite mark on his muscle. "I have to leave the country because I've got a better shot that way. If I'm found, they're going to kill me." He put his palm over his heart, as if taking a vow. "I'll never hurt you intentionally. I swear. When you came in, I didn't know it was you. I was having a dream. Nightmare. Shit—" He winced "Crap, I mean. Sorry 'bout the cuss word."

She had to smile a little. "Sometimes they're the only thing that fits."

"What made you come down? Was I . . . making some noise?"

As if he'd been known to do that.

Grier frowned and decided to keep her winged visitor to herself. "I guess I just knew you needed me."

For a long beat, they stared at each other in the soft darkness.

"Can I do anything to help at all?" she whispered.

"Just take the money I owe you and resign. Please. And if anyone comes asking about me, tell them everything you know."

"Which would be next to nothing," she thought out loud.

"Exactly."

Shaking her head, she went over to him and put her hand on his forearm. "I can't stop you if you're going to run, but I can't afford to be contaminated by how you got the money. If you leave it with me, I'll just turn it in—"

"It's to pay you back."

"I can't accept it—you know I can't. My license to practice is at risk—frankly, I'm walking the accomplice line here already. I should have called the police back in Malden. And tomorrow morning, I'm going to have to tell them that I harbored you for a time while trying to get you to turn yourself in. All that is bad enough."

But God help her, she believed him. She believed that he was running for his life. And damn it, she was going to do as much to help him as she could.

As Isaac stood naked in front of his defense attorney, he was still trying to replug into reality. The nightmare had a way of unwrapping his snow cone so that he came out on the other side a drooling mess. Or at least that's what it felt like. For a while after he woke up, everything always seemed to move too fast and take too much energy to figure out.

God, the damn thing was always the same when it came to him, and even after two years, it was still as freshly horrifying as it had been the first time: in a pit of darkness, a living corpse with lidless eyes worked him over until he was bloodied from head to foot and screaming around whatever had been shoved into his mouth. There was never any escaping. He was pinned to some kind of table and no one could hear him—and though he could handle the physical pain, what undid him was the knowledge that the torture would go on forever. There was no end to it . . .

Grier squeezed his arm and brought him back to the here-and-now. "That newspaper article," she said. "The one from five years ago. Who was responsible for the body in the ditch?"

"I didn't kill him."

But he'd heard about the death—and provided Matthias with his wallet and a set of clothes without asking a whole lot of questions. And as soon as he'd turned over those markers of his life, he'd walked into the XOps fold and disappeared. Leaving his family had been an easy thing to do. His father had been raising five hellacious boys on the farm by himself and one less was a blessing to that bunch of Neanderthals. Plus he and his old man had never gotten along.

Which was why, when he'd gone AWOL, he'd used his own name on the fake ID he'd bought. No one was looking for him from back home—and he sure as shit hadn't planned on getting arrested. But the thing was, if he was starting over, he wanted to return to the person he'd been before Matthias had come along. So stupid, though. No label was going to get him back to that place and time, and nothing was going to erase the past five years.

What he needed was forgiveness.

Abruptly, Grier's face came into sharp focus. God, her eyes were clear. And smart.

And so beautiful.

"Grier . . ." The sound of her name on his lips was hungry even to his own ears. Hungry and desperate.

"Yes . . ."

That was so not a question, he thought. It was an answer . . . but, man, it was the wrong one.

Pulling himself out from under her palm, he tried to derail what was happening between them. "I think you'd better go."

She cleared her throat. "Yes. I should."

Neither of them moved.

"Go," he told her. "Now."

When she turned away, he crossed his free arm over his chest to keep himself from grabbing her and pulling her into him.

And she didn't go nearly far enough, as it turned out. She stopped in the doorway, the light from the hall hitting her profile and drawing over her perfect features ever so gently.

She deserved that kind of carefulness in a lover, he thought.

But he was too raw, too needy . . . too starved to be tender with her.

As she stood on the threshold, with the hand that had been on him gripping the doorknob, her hold tightened until her knuckles went white.

"What's wrong," he said in a voice so deep it nearly disappeared.

Stupid goddamn question.

Especially as he traced the curve of her breast with his eyes and wanted to do the same with his mouth.

"Have you ever wanted something you shouldn't?" she asked.

Fucking hell. He had half a chance at resisting her if it was all one-sided—namely, his: There was nothing like telling yourself you were a nasty bastard to get a choke hold on your libido. But if he'd woken up in some parallel universe where she somehow wanted him that badly, too?

They were both screwed—even without the sex part.

"Have you?" she demanded.

"Yes, ma'am." Like right now.

Now her voice was as husky as his. "What did you do?"

*I took two steps forward and turned her around by the hips. I yanked her in tight and then I kissed her for about a minute and a half before I stripped her naked from the waist down. After I got on my knees, I threw one of her legs over my shoulder and worked her with my mouth until she came all over my tongue and—*

"I walked away." His throat was so tight the reply was strangled. "I walked away and I didn't look back."

Her shoulders straightened as if she'd resolved herself. "Very smart."

He released his breath, relieved that she wasn't as insane as he was feeling—

When she shut the door, she was on his side of it. And then she came at him through the darkness, drifting over like a shadow . . . and bypassing him to go lie on the bed.

Isaac couldn't breathe and couldn't think. But he could move.

Damn right, he could move.

All that let's-be-smart went right out the window as he approached and loomed over her, seeing her pale skin against the dark navy sheets. She'd stretched out in the place he'd warmed not from some cozy-ass dream, but in his exertions to get away from his nightmare. And didn't that remind him of what they were both going to wake up to.

"You sure about this?" he asked in a guttural voice. "I get down on that mattress right now, I'm not stopping until I'm inside of you."

He meant every word.

And as she opened her mouth, he cut her off. "Make sure you give me an answer you can live with. Because what happens now will not change tomorrow."

"I know. And you have my answer. Right here."

With that, she pulled her T-shirt over her head and lay back down.

# CHAPTER
# 19

Grier couldn't draw a breath as the cool air hit her bare breasts and her nipples tightened up on a quick sting of pleasure—although her body's response was more from the way his hot eyes latched onto her than the temperature.

And yet she had to wait for him to speak, move, do something . . . *anything*—

He dropped the sweatshirt.

A gasp sucked down her throat.

Male. Animal. That was all that came to her.

She hadn't seen a lot of men naked, but she was very sure the number could have been a hundred thousand and none of them would have compared to Isaac Rothe: He was built heavy in the shoulders and the chest, and tight in the stomach and hips . . . and fully erect?

His sex more than lived up to the rest of him.

He came down to her through the inky darkness, sliding in against her, his body harder and bigger than her eyes had let on, her breasts cushioning his pecs as his weight settled on top of her.

God, he smelled good.

And damn her, she was panting to have him.

His hand burrowed in, going under her waist, pulling her

even tighter into those strong, strong arms of his. And as they drew up hip to hip, the boxers she had on were no barrier at all to the blunt head of him pushing at her core — which was so very ready for him.

"Oh, God—"

He cut her off, his mouth finding hers and taking her lips like he owned her. He kissed her with none of the awkward first-time stuff she was used to; there was nothing hesitant or polite or tentative at all: Isaac kissed her like he meant to have her, and she was ready to be taken.

She'd never wanted anything this badly before.

Abruptly, he rolled over onto his back and took her with him until she was sprawled across his body. Splitting her legs, she straddled his hips and he cursed as she settled on his arousal and rode him up and back, stroking them both. As she moaned, his tongue slipped into her and she dragged her hands down to his lower half, feeling the curling of his muscles as he pushed rhythmically against her.

Before she could touch him, though, he was shifting her up his body, his mouth on her neck, then her collarbone, then—

He latched onto one of her nipples, the hot, wet suction throwing her into a wild arch that nearly cracked her spine. To stay in control of her, his hands dug into her hips and held her steady—and she needed it as he dragged his tongue over her and then resumed the tugging pull.

"I want to be naked," she moaned. "I want—"

He was right on that, hooking his thumbs into the waistband of the boxers and moving them south. She rose up to help him and had to shamble around to dismount him and get the things down ... because his mouth was still at work, sticking with her, moving to her other breast, nipping and then sucking again.

When she resettled across his belly, her wet sex sealed on the hot skin of his waist, and as his hips surged, the tightening weave of his stomach muscles moved against her, driving her higher sure as if it was his palm between her thighs. With the dueling onslaughts at her breasts and her core, he seemed to be all over her, touching every inch of her body.

And it wasn't enough. There would be time for exploration later—all she wanted was him inside. . . .

Isaac clearly thought the same thing, too. Without her saying a word, he returned her to the mattress, his erection a hot brand on her thighs as he moved into position. Parting her knees with one of his own, he made room for himself—

They both groaned as they brushed against each other down below.

"I'm clean," he said in her ear.

"I know." She raked her nails over his shoulders. "Saw . . . medical record . . . I'm on . . . pill. . . . now!"

They joined together in a rush, his body going rigid above her as he pushed in deep and hit home. He was big and thick inside of her, heavy on top of her, hot against her skin: This may have been wrong on so many levels, but when it came to the fit, he was perfect.

Isaac dropped his head onto her neck and started to move, his body rolling against hers, her head moving up and back on the pillow as he stroked in and out. Sliding her hands down to his lower back, she could feel the growing tension in him already—and he wasn't the only one getting close to release.

On a moan, she widened her legs and gave him more, her nails sinking into his skin, the tips of her breasts and the depths of her core tingling. She breathed through her mouth hard as his rhythm of broad strokes swept her up into the heavens even as she stayed on earth.

And then she was free. Flying and free on a wild ride that made the real world seem so blissfully far away. It was just what she needed, an explosive shattering that took her out of herself and the too-structured life she led and the powerful mind that had gotten her so far and yet trapped her, too.

As she began to come down, Isaac's thrusts got shorter and faster, his arms going all around her and tightening up hard. She was crushed against him but she didn't care—and she was glad she'd gone over the edge first so she could concentrate fully on what was happening to him.

Except . . . he slowed.

And then stopped altogether.

Lifting his head, he braced his torso up on his arms, but didn't look at her.

Just as she was going to ask him what was wrong, he pulled out of her, still fully erect, and got off the bed. The air that rushed in to fill his place was like an arctic blast across her naked skin—and the deep freeze only got worse as he strode into the bathroom and closed the door.

Left alone, she lay in the dark, every muscle tensed up and her whole body flushed with a very different kind of heat.

She waited, and when she didn't hear water turn on or the toilet run, the idea that it might have just been an equipment malfunction of some sort dwindled. And it couldn't be embarrassment over some kind of performance thing because God knew he'd satisfied her and been erect.

Her hands shook as she covered her face, and damn it if reality didn't come rushing back. This should never have happened.

Perfect fit? More like a perfect *fix*: She'd been in a reckless frame of mind ever since she'd looked into Isaac Rothe's frosty eyes, and just as it had been with her brother, she'd had to take a hit of something very dangerous.

Where had her brain gone? Having sex with some man she didn't know— No, worse than that: a *client* of hers— who was up for assault? With no protection—even though she was on the pill and she did know he wasn't HIV positive, it was still risky as hell.

In the heat of the moment, she'd made a choice that was hard to defend, much less comprehend.

For some reason, Daniel came to mind, and she remembered the pair of them being thirteen and sixteen and stealing their father's car. It had been down at Hyannis Port in the summer—where night wasn't just dark; it was pitch black. They'd pushed the Mercedes two-seater down the drive, started it up, and gone for a ride, changing places, each taking the wheel. They'd ended up on the breakway in front of the marshes, on the sandy road right on the lip of the ocean. With the sea wind in their hair and the whoosh of the air and the sense of electric freedom, they'd laughed until they couldn't see.

Which was how they'd crashed into a shack.

They'd both been hardwired wrong, hadn't they—Daniel a little wronger than her, granted, but it wasn't just her brother who did crazy things. And in a way, his descent into the seedy needle underlife had been her drug: The peaks and valleys as she made progress with him and then lost it and then got through to him once more became the drum section in her life's orchestra, the driving force that marked all the other notes.

And now that he was gone . . .

She dropped her hands and looked over at the closed door, picturing Isaac on the other side.

He was the perfect fit for the vast hole her brother's death had left behind, a wave of drama sweeping into her life and becoming the thing she could throw herself into. After all, Daniel as a ghost wasn't half as vivid as he'd been alive.

Isaac was pure octane.

Yanking the covers over herself, she sat up and drew her hair back behind her ears. The reality was, that man in there had had more sense than she did. He'd wanted to go and leave her; she'd made him stay. He'd given her a chance to go back to bed alone; she'd shut them in together. He was going to take off without looking back; she was going to want to see him after tomorrow. . . .

Frowning, she realized there were still no sounds in the bathroom. Nothing.

What was he doing in there? It had been a while.

Grier dragged a sheet with her as she got up and walked over to the door. Knocking softly, she said, "Are you okay?"

No answer. "Isaac? Is there something wrong?"

Well, other than the fact that he was on the lam from both the federal government and now the state of Massachusetts and was staying at his soon-to-be former attorney's house . . . having had sex with her.

Details, details.

Or wait, did the lack of orgasm on his part mean the hookup didn't count? She had finished, though . . . so maybe she'd been with four and a half men now?

"Isaac?"

When there was no response, she rapped quietly. "Isaac?"

Without much hope, she went for the knob, but the thing turned easily—to her relief, he hadn't locked himself in. Cracking the door, she saw a bare foot and an ankle in the dim light from outside. He was evidently sitting on the floor in the corner by the shower.

"Mind if I come in?" she asked, pushing her way into the room . . .

Dear God . . . he was curled into himself, his face on his biceps, his arm up and blocking his face, his bruised hand lying on his hair. He was breathing hard, his shoulders rising and falling.

He was sobbing. Sobbing in that restrained, manly way where he barely let any of it out, his choked inhales the only thing that clued her in.

Grier approached him slowly and sat down beside him. When she put her hand lightly on his bare shoulder, he jumped.

"Shhh . . . it's just me."

He didn't look at her and she was willing to bet if he'd been able to, he would have told her to get out. But he couldn't. And all she could do was sit with him and gently soothe him with touch.

"It's okay," she murmured, knowing there was no reason to ask about the whys: There were a lot to choose from. "You're all right. . . . It's okay. . . ."

"It's really not," he said hoarsely. "It's so not. I'm . . . not. . . ."

"Come here." She tugged at him, not really expecting him to give in . . . but he did. He turned to her and let her wrap her arms around him as if he were a wild beast who had decided to be tamed for a short time. He was so big that she couldn't reach far, but she made what contact she had count and put her face in his cropped hair.

"Shhh . . . you're all right. . . ." As she murmured the lie over and over again, she wanted to say something else, but that was the only thing that came to her—even though she had to agree with him. Nothing about the situation was fine. Neither of them was all right.

And she had the sense that "okay" was not going to fit the way things ended between them. Or for him.

"I still don't know how," he said after a while.

"How what?"

"That you knew I was having my nightmare."

As she frowned in the darkness, she stroked his hair. "Ah . . . you wouldn't believe me if I told you."

"Try me."

"An angel came into my room." There was a beat of silence. "He was . . . magnificent. A warrior . . . he woke me up and pointed to the door and I knew it was because of you." Just so she didn't sound freakish, she tacked on, "I guess I was dreaming, too."

"Guess so."

"Yeah." Because angels didn't exist any more than vampires and werewolves did.

At least ... she'd believed that until tonight. Except what she'd seen certainly hadn't felt like a dream.

God only knew how long they stayed like that, curled around each other, their collective warmth amplifying for a different reason than it had out in the bedroom: now, it was skin-on-skin comfort.

When Isaac finally sat up from her, she braced herself for him to thank her awkwardly and tell her to go. But instead, he traded places with her, his arms wrapping around her body, one behind her knees, the other at her back. Then he rose from the floor as if she weighed nothing and carried her out past the messy bed into the hall. He took the stairs without slowing or seeming to exert himself; his breathing barely changed even while he held her.

Up in her room, he laid her out in between her sheets and then just stood over her.

She could feel the hunger in him, but this time it wasn't sexual. It was for something that seemed even more important than all that desperate heat.

Grier moved over to make space, and after a moment, he slipped inside with her. Now, she was the one being cradled, that muscled chest of his somehow making all her problems magically seem smaller. And yes, the idea that she was falling into some kind of Cinderella state made her cringe, but she was too relaxed to put up a fight.

Closing her eyes, she tucked her arm around his waist.

As exhaustion slammed into her and knocked her out cold, her last thought was that it was okay to sleep. There would be time to say good-bye in the morning.

Isaac lay beside Grier, and waited for her to sink down solidly into REM territory. To pass the time, he reviewed vocabulary terms, because his mind was cannibalizing itself and he needed to redirect his neurons.

In the male lexicon of labels, the term *nancy* usually referred to guys who were a little light in their loafers: the kind who made women kill spiders for them, worried about how much starch was in their dry cleaning, and might possibly have a spice rack that was alphabetized.

Real men did not have spice racks. Or even know how to find them in a kitchen—much less what to do with what was in 'em. . . . At least, that was what his father had taught him and his brothers. And actually, in retrospect, that opinion sort of explained why their mother had gone off, married someone else, and started a new family before she'd died. Clearly, she'd known that a reboot of the system was going to get her nowhere and the only solution was to get fresh components—

What had he been thinking about? Oh, right. Nancys.

Next step up the vocab ladder—or down, as it were—was probably *pantywaister*. He wasn't exactly sure where that little ditty had come from, but it was synonymous with terms like *sissy*, the old-school *pencil-necked geek*, and the newer *little bitch*. These were the guys who might well have the impulse to change a tire for a woman, but would have trouble lifting the spare out of the trunk—and forget about working the lug wrench. They were also the sort who threw like girls, shrieked when they saw rats, and would call the police in a bar brawl instead of getting in there to start punching.

His father had always believed women were weaker, and maybe when it came to hefting bales of hay for six to eight hours straight in the ninety-degree heat, he might have had a point. But Isaac knew a lot of females in the service who could not only pitch baseballs like a man; they could punch as good as one, too—and had better aim.

Strength didn't have to be identical to be equal. . . .

God, why the hell was he thinking about his father?

Right. Back to the Dictionary of Dickless Wonders. Which apparently his pops had been an editor of.

The lowest of the low . . . the bottom rung . . . the ball shriveler of them all . . . had to be *pussy*. That was the kind of thing that, if your buddy was joking with you and busting you for something, he could throw it out and the shit was funny. If the word was said seriously, however, it was a leveler. In general, nonspecific terms, *pussy* could refer to a guy who, say, couldn't perform in bed with a woman he had the hots for. And then capped that lack of follow-through with . . . oh, say—and this was purely a hypothetical— maybe collapsing naked on the floor of said woman's loo and crying like a motherfucking baby.

Until she had to come and comfort him after he had let her down. After endangering her life and her professional career.

Yeah. Something like that.

As he groaned in the dark, he couldn't believe the fucking mess he'd made out of the whole thing. Stopping in the middle? Going into the bathroom and pulling a hankie routine?

Why didn't he just put a dress and some nail polish on and call himself Irene?

Shit, the sex . . . the sex had blown his mind. Literally. And that had been the problem. Some kind of fissure had been opened in him the instant he'd sunk into her wet heat, and with each pumping thrust, what had started as a hairline fracture grew into a vast divide.

It wasn't about fear. Or second-guessing his AWOL status.

It was the fact that when you were on the job with Matthias, you were so damn busy keeping yourself alive that you had no clue how under-the-gun you were.

And what do you know, bolting from the fold was just more of the same. Having that dream? More of the same.

But making love to a beautiful, warm woman in a soft

bed that smelled of lemon in a house even he couldn't doubt the security of?

Too close to normal. Too safe. Too good to be true.

The juxtaposition of that and where he'd been and where he was going in the morning had peeled him wide—which kind of proved what he'd always suspected: It was just too hard to dip even a foot into the civilian way of life. The straddle to be in both worlds was unsustainable.

And on that note . . .

Shifting around to the side table, he reached for the remote of the DVD and hit *play*. When the menu came up, he chose *play all*, and after a beat, the *Three's Company* logo came on over the shot of a beach scene. As the intro credits ran, John Ritter ogled a chick and ended up falling off a bike—and as he hit the sand, Grier's brows tightened . . . then relaxed completely.

Perfect. She'd trained herself to associate the TV with deep sleep, and the bubble of noise and soft flickering light was going to help cover his tracks.

About fifteen minutes into the episode, Isaac slowly slid his arm out from under her head and then he eased from between the sheets. In his absence, Grier rolled over to face the TV and resettled with a sigh. Which was his cue to get a move on.

Hitting the stairs, he went down to the room he'd been given.

Ten minutes later, he headed back to her, fully dressed, with his weapons. Standing over her, he watched her sleep for too long and had to force himself to bend down and pick up her hand. Moving her carefully, he put her thumb on the remote to the security system and deactivated it. After a green light flashed, he reengaged the alarm to see what kind of delay there was.

Which would be none: Immediately the red light glowed, and he was stuck inside.

Made sense. She'd just trigger it after she locked the front door.

He checked his watch. Four a.m.

Grier made a little snuffle and eased her head deeper into the pillow, her blond hair falling onto her cheek.

He didn't trust himself to stay with her until she woke up.

Now or never, asshole.

*Thank you*, he mouthed to her.

And then with a curse, he disarmed the system and left without looking back.

Downstairs, he was silent and quick as he went and checked the ADT keypad in the front hall. Just as he'd hoped: disengaged. After all, when you had a rottweiler guarding your house, did you really need a yellow Lab as backup?

The front door was solid wood and three inches thick—so even though he couldn't engage the dead bolt, it was going to take a battering ram to get inside. His only concern was the glass doors and windows, but the frames were super sturdy and locked—and if you shattered panes the size of the ones in the kitchen, they made a hell of a noise.

So she was safe as she could be.

After cutting the exterior lights, he took his muscle shirt from his pocket and tore off a strip; then he stepped out and cranked that big ol' door into place. Quick pause to double-check the handle was locked and secure and he tied the strip of cloth around the wrought-iron lantern to the left.

Next move was to walk off into the chilly April morning.

Not a moment too soon, either. As this was New England, the sun rose real early, and he probably had only an hour or so of good darkness before the dawn's rays started to chase away the shadows. Going left, he headed across something called Pinckney Street, and less than ten yards down the hill, he found what he was looking for—one of the smaller town houses was under reconstruction, its windows on the first floor boarded up, a pathway of plaster dust running in and out of the front door.

And there were no lights on, inside or out.

Going in all Spidey and shit, he grappled up the house, using the moldings around the door and the windows to brace his feet and yank his weight up. A quick punch through a dusty pane and he waited for the scream of a security alarm. None came. So he flipped the latch, shoved the sash up, and hello, Lucy, he was home.

Total elapsed time: a minute and a half.

The place was rock cold and covered with more plaster dust, and he hoped like hell that this was a union job, given that it was Sunday—so he could stay as long as he wanted.

Casing the joint didn't take long, and similar to Grier's setup, the back of the house opened to a courtyardy thing that was gated—and there were no chalky footprints on the red brick there. Obviously, the workmen arrived and left the front way.

To clear the exit route for some parkour action if he needed it, he popped the latch on the window above the rear door's transom; then he returned to where he'd broken in and picked out all of the glass shards on the pane he'd smashed—because no glass at all looked, from a distance, like nothing was wrong.

The vantage point he took was by the window on the far front right of the house, and to hide most of himself, he moved a piece of plywood over for cover. From where he took up res, he could see about seventy percent of Grier's bow-front. What was missing was the rear door and the upper terrace, but this was as good as it was going to get.

Leaning up against the cold wall, his eyes scanned the little park with its wrought-iron fence and statue and gracefully limbed trees. Might as well enjoy the view. He wasn't

leaving until he saw Grier get into her car and drive away—
without anyone on her tail.

Twenty minutes later what he feared most rolled up. The
black unmarked was not what Jim's buddy had described
from the night before: no dings or dust on this bad boy.
And the darkened windows prevented him from seeing the
driver or any passenger.

But he had a feeling who it was.

Shit, he hated when he was right.

And this was all his fault.

# CHAPTER
## 20

Grier woke up at six a.m. and knew as soon as she saw the tail end of a *Three's Company* episode that Isaac has left: She hadn't restarted the DVD when they'd come up to her room . . . and yup, the security system was off.

She'd obviously slept through his going.

Arching over, she checked her bedside table, thinking that maybe he'd written her a note. But the only thing he'd left behind was the scent of the shampoo and soap he'd used: the cedar-y fragrance was on one of her pillows and some of her sheets.

Getting up, she pulled on her sweatshirt and went down to the second floor. The guest room was neat as a pin, the bed made to military precision. The only sign he'd been there at all was the single towel that had been hung to dry on the rack in the bath. He'd even wiped down the glass walls of the shower so there weren't any water marks on the inside.

The man was a total ghost and she was a pathetic loser to think he'd make some gesture of good-bye.

She headed downstairs to the kitchen and stopped in the archway.

Well, turned out he had left one thing behind: On the counter was the plastic bag of cash.

"Damn it. God*damn* it."

She stood there for a time, staring not at the twenty-five grand, but at the Birkin he'd tried to clean up for her.

Eventually, she went and got the home phone. The number she dialed was one she'd memorized two years ago.

The public defender's office always had someone on call, because crime, like illness and accidents, didn't recognize any distinction between weekdays and weekends. And the guy who answered was an attorney she knew well. Although her resignation from Isaac's case was a surprise to him, when she stated that she had approximately twenty-five thousand dollars from the cage-fighting racket on her kitchen counter, he got on board PDQ.

"Jesus."

"I know. So I have to resign."

"Wait, he left that cash at your house?"

Might as well practice her stab at revisionist history. "Last night, Mr. Rothe came over here. I'd posted his bail and he wanted to pay me back—and I got the impression it was because he was thinking of running. I didn't notify the police because I thought it was my duty to talk him out of taking off and I believed that I'd dissuaded him. Except then I found what he'd left for me this morning on my back porch." She drew a deep breath, the weight of the lies not sitting well on her empty stomach. "Given the money, I feel strongly that he is going to leave the state immediately. I'm calling the police next and I'll drop the cash off at the precinct house as evidence when I go there to give a statement this morning."

"Grier—"

"Before you ask, I'm listed in the white pages, which is how Mr. Rothe found my house, and no, I didn't feel threatened at all. I asked him to come in and he did for a little while—and he left without a fuss." At least that part was the whole truth.

"Well, hell . . ."

"Yes, I do believe that covers it. I wanted you to know what I was going to do and I'll keep you posted. I don't know where this is all going, to be honest."

Ding, ding, ding, another truth.

Her colleague made a dismissive sound. "Look, you've never had a blemish on your record and you're keeping it all aboveboard. You haven't done anything wrong."

No comment on that one. No reason to ruin the veracity trend.

"You are getting independent counsel, however?" he said.

"Of course." Fool for a client and all that stuff. Just like she'd told Isaac back at the jail.

After she got off the phone with the other attorney, she was on with the cops moments later. And they, of course, fit her right into their schedule.

In hopes of bracing herself, she fired up the coffee machine—and then realized she wasn't alone.

Hanging her head, she wondered what if anything Daniel had seen the night before in the guest room.

*Nothing,* her brother said. *I know when to leave.*

Thank God, she thought to herself as she hit the power button. "I wish I could give you some of this. I loved when we could have coffee together."

*It smells good.*

She usually sought him out with her eyes whenever he appeared, but not this morning. She really couldn't face him, and not because she'd hooked up with someone. Well, the sex was part of it. The real driver, though, was that reckless burn; it was just too close to what had destroyed him.

*Yeah, you and I are the same. We got it from Dad.*

"You know, you never talk about your death," she said as the Krups machine burbled and hissed.

His voice got hard. *What's done is done, and that score needs to be settled between other people.*

"Score?" When he said nothing more, she gritted her teeth. "Why won't you ever answer anything? I've got a list as long as my arm of things I want to know, but all you do is deflect or evade."

The further silence had her glaring over her shoulder: Daniel was leaning against the stainless-steel refrigerator, his translucent form throwing no reflection in the buffed finish. His blue eyes, the ones that were an identical color to her own, were staring at the floor.

"I don't understand why you're here," she said. "Especially if we can't really talk about the things that matter. Like how you died and—"

*This is about your life, Grier. Not mine.*

"Then why did you tell me to take that soldier home," she groused.

Now Daniel smiled. *Because you like him. And I think he's going to be good for you.*

She was not sure about that at all. She was feeling shattered already, and she'd known him for only a day. "Do you know what he's done? Who he's trying to get away from?"

Her brother's frown was not encouraging. *That I'm not talking about. But I can tell you he's not going to hurt you.*

God, she was tired of being surrounded by men who had duct tape over their mouths.

"Will I see him again?"

Daniel started to fade away, which was what he did whenever she put him on the spot about something.

"Daniel," she said sharply. "Stop running out on me—"

When all she got back was a clear shot at the refrigerator door, she looked up at the ceiling and cursed. She never had any control over when he showed up or how long he stayed. And she had no idea where he was when he wasn't haunting her.

Did he hang out at the undead's equivalent of a Starbucks? Speaking of coffee . . .

Determined to follow through on something, *anything*, she got a mug and the sugar bowl and went to town on the hot and steamy—all the while wondering whether caffeine was a good idea given her nerves.

At nine o'clock, she left the house with the cash and a headache that seemed to have put its feet up on her frontal lobe and had plans to stay the day. After initializing the ADT system, she stepped out, closed the door and turned the dead bolt with her key—

Frowning, she stared up at one of the two wrought-iron lanterns by the entrance. A small strip of white cloth had been wound around its base.

Pivoting on her heel, Grier looked all around and saw nothing but parked cars she recognized . . . and a neighbor walking a chocolate Lab . . . and a couple strolling arm in arm . . .

*Get a grip, Grier.*

She was not in a Hitchcockian world where people were followed and planes dive-bombed from midair and secret signals were left on light fixtures.

Unwinding the scrap of fabric, she shoved the thing in her coat pocket so as not to litter and went over to her Audi. As she walked off, she engaged the big alarm—even though she didn't usually do that if she wasn't in the house.

Down at the police department, she met with a detective, turned the money over, and gave a statement. Attorney-client privilege did not extend to ongoing criminal activity, so she was required to say what she knew about the fighting ring, Isaac's participation in it, and the location where she believed they would still convene out in Malden.

While time passed and she talked, she had a growing conviction that Isaac was far gone by now—and chances were good no one from Boston would find him.

She had to wonder who would, however.

Two hours later, she stepped out of the precinct and stared up at the yellow sun in the cloudless spring sky. The warmth on her face made the cold breeze feel even more frigid, and the rest of the day loomed over her.

Her car didn't take her home.

It was supposed to. She sent it in the direction of Beacon Hill with the intention of crawling back into bed and getting some more sleep.

She ended up on Tremont Street.

As she went around the block where Isaac's apartment was, naturally there was no place to dump the Audi, and it was probably a sign for her to stay away. Persistence got her into trouble, though, when a VW Bug shuffled out and left a void. After wedging in, she locked up and went over to the house.

Knocking on the front door, she hoped that the landlady was home—and never thought she'd be glad to see someone like that again—

The woman opened up and Grier made the connection she hadn't the day before: It was Mrs. Roper from *Three's Company*. From the fake red curls to the plastic bangles.

"You're back," was the greeting.

"I just need to get in one last time."

"Where *is* he?" the landlady said, blocking the way.

Ah, yes, an information tollgate, Grier thought. "He was here last night. Didn't you hear him?"

Cue *Jeopardy* theme. Then . . . "The man's like a ghost," Mrs. Roper-esque bitched. "Never makes a noise. Only way I know he's there is that he already paid next month's rent. He's in jail, isn't he. Are you his attorney?"

"No." She hated lying. She truly did.

"Well, I think—"

As the sound of a phone ringing cut her off, Grier was ready to kiss whoever was calling.

Except the landlady batted the air with a dismissive hand. "That's just my sister."

Great. "Will you take me upstairs, please? I won't be long."

The ringing went silent. "Look, I'm not going to keep doing this. Get your own key."

"Oh, I agree—I need one. And I apologize."

The woman mounted the stairs like a bull, pounding up and grunting, today's muumuu swinging like a flag.

At the top, she unlocked the door with her key. "Now, I'm telling you—"

The phone started ringing again downstairs, and as that wig went to and fro, it was like a dog stuck making the choice between two tennis balls.

"I'll be back," Mrs. Roper announced gravely.

Kind of like the Terminator had gone drag queen.

Left on her own, Grier stepped inside Isaac's place and closed herself in, throwing the lock in the hopes that if the call didn't last long, that woman would assume it was a come-and-gone situation.

A quick review of the living room proved that he'd been by, but that was an of-course: The gun he'd pulled on her last night had to have been one of the ones she'd found and the sweatshirt he'd been wearing was what he'd used as a pillow. He hadn't taken everything, however. The sleeping bag was left behind, as well as some workout pants and a pair of Nikes—although the sensors on the windows and doors were gone.

In the kitchen, she found a neat pile of bills—clearly, they were an offering so that when no more rent was paid the score would be settled.

Leaning against the counter, she had no idea what she'd expected to find—

A soft creaking sound brought her eyes over to the rear door. When there was nothing else, she figured she'd imagined the footstep . . . but then the latch to the dead bolt turned slowly.

She straightened, her heart going haywire as she put her hand into her purse and got her Mace ready, which was better than the stun gun, given the distance. "Isaac?"

Except it was not her AWOL soldier.

The man who entered the apartment had black hair and tanned skin and he was wearing a dark suit under a trench coat. A patch covered his right eye, and he used a cane to balance his tall body.

"I'm not Isaac," he said, in a very deep voice.

The chilly smile he gave was the sort of thing that made you want to take a step back. Unfortunately, she was already against the counter, so there was nowhere to go.

And that was before he shut them both in together.

How much noise did she have to make to get Mrs. Roper back up here? she wondered.

"You must be the defense attorney."

Oh, Christ, she thought. This was what Isaac had wanted to protect her from, wasn't it.

Grier Childe looked just like her brother, Matthias thought as he stared across a galley kitchen at her.

And say what you would about the elder Childe's bleeding-heart politics and nosy predilections, he and that wife of his had done right on the procreating end. Both their kids were blond, blue eyed, with perfect bone structure. Cream of the old-school crop, as it were.

Plus the daughter evidently had half a brain, going by her résumé. And was without all those messy addiction problems.

He felt his lips stretch a little wider. "What's in your purse? Gun? Mace?"

She took out a thin leather-bound tube and flipped the top cover off. Putting it up in position, she let the defense weapon speak for itself.

"Make sure you aim at my good one," he said, tapping his left eye. "The other side won't get you shit." When she opened her mouth to speak, he cut her off. "Did you expect to find Isaac here?"

"We're not alone. The landlady is downstairs."

"Oh, I know. She's talking to her sister about their brother's wife." Those patrician blue eyes of hers widened. "They don't like her because she's too young for him. I'd give you the details, but it's private. And not very interesting. Now, tell me, did you expect to find Isaac here."

She took a moment to reply. "I'm not answering any of your questions. I suggest you unlock that door and leave. You're trespassing."

"If you own the world, there's no such thing as trespassing. And a word of advice—you want to come out of this alive, you'll be a little more accommodating." Matthias casually wandered over to the window above the sink and looked out of the milky glass. "But I suspect I know the answer anyway. You didn't think you'd find him here because you believe he's left Boston. You're basing this assumption on the cash he left behind with you—and don't bother to deny it. I listened to you talk to your buddy at the public defender's office—"

"It's illegal to tap someone's phone without a warrant."

Pushing against his cane, he straightened back up. "And I would say to you again that words like 'trespassing' and 'illegal' and 'warrant' don't apply to me."

He could feel her fear . . . and see it, too. She had her fingers cranked down so hard on that cylinder that the knuckles were white. But really, she didn't need to worry all that much. It seemed highly unlikely that Isaac had told her anything material—that would be her death sentence, and the guy knew it: Nothing would keep her breathing if she had intel on XOps. Not even a desire to shut her father up for good.

"I think you and I should come to an agreement," he said, putting his hand inside his coat. "Hold it—don't go crazy with your bug spray. I'm just getting you a business card."

He pulled one out, holding it between the tips of his index and middle fingers, leaving the guns he was packing right where they were holstered. "If you see your client again, call this number, Ms. Childe. And know that it's the only reason I came here to see you. I just figured you and I should meet in person so you understand how serious I am about Isaac Rothe."

She kept the Mace with her as she came forward and tilted in, as if she wanted to stay as far away from him as possible. And he knew damn well as she took the card what she was going to do with it. But that was part of the plan.

As she studied what little had been imprinted, Matthias left his free hand where she could see it. "Isaac Rothe is a very dangerous man."

"I have to go," she said as she shoved what he'd given her into her purse.

"No one's keeping you. Here, I'll even get the door."

Opening the thing wide, he stood to the side and approved of the way she measured both him and the stairs that were revealed. Cautious, oh so cautious . . .

She went to hurry by him . . . and at the last moment before she was free, he snatched her arm and held her back. "I left something for you in the trunk of your car. After all, most accidents happen in the home, and you might need to call for help."

She ripped herself out of his hold. "Don't threaten me," she snapped.

As Matthias stared into those beautiful eyes of hers, he felt ancient. Ancient and broken and trapped. But as he had learned two years ago, he couldn't stop the trajectory of his life. It was like putting your palms up to an avalanche: You got crushed and the rush of snow and ice didn't even notice.

"I am not afraid of you," she said.

"You should be," he replied grimly, thinking of the twelve different ways he could make it so she didn't come down for breakfast tomorrow morning. "You should be very afraid."

He let her go, and she took off like a rocket, her blond hair flowing out behind her as she raced down the stairs.

Going back to that window over the sink, he watched her head around the house and go out to the street.

She was going to be so very useful in this situation, he thought.

On a number of levels.

# CHAPTER
## 21

As Grier walked up to her Audi, she had the key remote in her hand and her heart in her throat.

She'd seen that man before; there was some kind of flicker in the back of her mind, some memory of him. He hadn't had the eye patch or the cane—she would have remembered those. But she had definitely seen him.

Approaching the car, she stood beside it, every muscle in her body braced as if at any moment the thing was going to go *Sopranos* on her and blow sky-high. And just as she finally raised her key to unlock it, a black sedan with darkened windows eased by her on Tremont. Looking into the glass . . . she got nothing. All of it was impenetrable, and the sunlight glinted off the windshield so she couldn't see who was driving.

She knew damn well who was inside, however. And she'd bet that he was lifting a hand in a little wave.

The sedan didn't even have a license plate.

As the thing took off, all kinds of smart ideas went through her head, including the ever-present 911 call or doing a dial to her friends at the Boston Police Department or getting her father to come over. But she didn't think whatever was in the trunk was going to kill her. That man had already had his shot at her, so to speak: He could have easily drugged her and dragged her out the back or killed her outright with a silencer.

Letting her fingers do the walking would only lead to complications—and although the first thing she was going to do when she got home was get in touch with her father about this card, she wasn't sure she needed him to come screaming over here in a panic.

Shit, her cell phone might be tapped, too.

Hitting the remote, she released the trunk latch and slowly lifted. . . .

Frowning, she bent down and wondered if she was seeing things right. Sitting on the dark gray felt of the trunk's interior was . . . well, it appeared to be one of those Life Alert buttons that old people used, nothing but a cream-colored plastic transmitter in the shape of a triangle with the logo across the front in red. The chain it was on was silver, and long enough so that if you put it around your neck it would dangle below your heart.

She got a tissue out of her bag and picked the thing up for closer inspection; then she went around, got behind the wheel, and laid it out on the seat next to her. When she hit the ignition, she did flinch—in the event the Audi burst into flames—except her heart rate settled fast. But come on, she was an innocent bystander when it came to whatever was going on with Isaac, and she had to imagine that an American civilian on American soil was not the kind of collateral damage the U.S. government wanted to deal with.

As she drove over to Beacon Hill, she put a call in to her father, and when she got voice mail, she tried to leave a message, but what could she say given that she didn't know who was listening? She ended up deleting the fits and starts and figured he'd see the missed alert on his phone and get back in touch with her.

At home on Louisburg Square, she parked in her spot

against the fence and looked around through the car windows. Who was watching her? And from where?

No wonder Isaac had been twitchy. The idea of getting from her Audi to her front door made her wish she had a Kevlar vest on.

Grabbing her purse and palming the Life Alert with the tissue, she got out and hurried over—except as she got closer to her house, she slowed. On the lantern, wrapped tightly around the base, was another strip of white cloth.

Pivoting fast, she stared up at all the brick buildings and wished she could see inside them.

She was not alone anywhere she went, was she.

As her heart got back on the Pony Express and her blood rushed through her veins and her brain, she ducked into her front door, disengaged the big alarm, and put the Life Alert on the breakfront. Dropping her bag, she quickly shut up the ADT's beeping, and then leaned out of the house only long enough to pull the cloth free.

One, two, three: she shut herself in, locked the door and reengaged the monster system—something that she never did in the daytime when she was at home.

With grim purpose, she went into the kitchen with her bag and put everything on the counter: the business card, the pieces of cloth, and the transistor. All of which she was careful to handle with a tissue.

The two sections of fabric were identical and had clearly been ripped off the same source—and she had a feeling where they were from. Isaac's muscle shirt.

What do you want to bet it was a signal that he was—

As her cell phone went off, she yelped and nearly blew out of her shoes. When she checked who it was, she answered and didn't waste time.

"Dad . . . we need to talk."

There was a silence and then Alistair Childe's patrician voice came over the connection. "Are you all right? Shall I come over?"

Cradling the phone in the crook of her shoulder, she picked up the Life Alert by the chain and watched it dangle. Clearly, she was under surveillance—so it wasn't like there was any hiding who she saw or where she went. And besides, having her father show was probably a good idea. She'd always sensed that he had serious power in high elevations, because politicians and military men alike treated him with something more than just respect: They were vaguely afraid of him, in spite the fact that he was an Ivy League–educated gentleman.

Might not hurt to throw him in the mix, and besides, there was no one else she would have gone to with this situation.

"Yes," she said. "Come now."

In the house on Pinckney Street, Isaac stared out from behind his sheet of particleboard with an urge to kill. And that burning drive wasn't in the civilian sense that he was frustrated and wanted to let that shit out in the hypothetical.

He wanted to slit Matthias open from throat to scrotum and gut him like a pig.

Motherfucker was *not* going after his woman.

It didn't matter what Isaac had to do or sacrifice: Grier Childe, with her good heart and her smart eyes, was *not* going to become a notch on Matthias's belt.

Clearly, however, she was in the guy's crosshairs. She'd taken off well over two hours ago, and she'd had the cash with her. Which should have been Isaac's cue to leave as well . . . except the black sedan that had driven by at dawn had rematerialized from an alley off Willow Street and gotten right on her bumper.

With no wheels of his own, he'd had to let them both drive away, his goddamn heart pounding with impotent rage. His first instinct was to call Jim Heron—but he still wasn't sure he could trust the guy.

The only thing he'd been able to do was replace the

signal he'd tied to her lantern. Picking up a painter's hat that had been left behind, he'd put it on to cover his face and slipped out briefly to tie another piece of that muscle shirt around the iron fixture—just in case whoever was in that car hadn't seen the first one before she'd taken it away. Although that was unlikely. The question was whether the XOps method of marking a situation as clear would matter: In the field, when an assignment was finished and the team member had taken off, he always left a white mark somewhere on the premises or the vehicle or the scene.

Isaac was hoping that it would get his past and his present redirected away from Grier. But, yeah, whatever: When she'd come back home, she'd been sporting a frown so deep it was as if she were squinting, and she'd had something in her hand that she was carrying with a tissue.

Like she didn't want to get her handprints on it or smudge the ones that were there.

Then she'd removed the second mark he'd left on her lantern.

And . . . now the black sedan returned, oozing past her house, going up the street. Coming back. Parking.

"Fuck. *Fuck* . . ."

He wanted to break cover, march across the street, and knock on the window of that unmarked with the muzzle of his gun. Then he wanted to stare into the eyes of whoever it was while he pulled the trigger and turned the bastard's frontal lobe into a milk shake.

He had a feeling who it was, too.

He hoped that bastard's arm was feeling better.

Man, to hell with leaving Boston now; he wasn't going anywhere until he was sure Grier was out of the line of fire . . . and yet, shit, he was the one who'd put the target on her chest.

He was chewing on that little slice of happiness when a Mercedes the size of a small house drove up to her front door. No nosing around and looking for a parking spot for that bad boy; the thing stopped at the curb and stayed there, the only concession to the illegality being its flashers.

The man who got out was over six feet tall and soldier trim. His gray hair was full and combed back from a side part, and even in the fleece and workout gear, he oozed money. And what do you know, he strode up and used the lion's-head door knocker like he owned the place.

Grier's father. Had to be.

The instant she opened up, he stepped inside, and then just like that, they were shut in together and he couldn't see anything more.

Generally speaking, in a stakeout situation, you wanted to find a single perch and keep still. Moving around increased the likelihood of being spotted—especially in broad daylight in an area you weren't familiar with, when people were already looking for you.

And in his case, it wasn't just bad form to get eye-balled—it was suicide.

So as much as his body was screaming for him to get a move on, close in, change locales, he had to stay put.

Nightfall. He had to wait until nightfall, and even then, he needed to be careful. That security system of hers was a no-break sitch: His specialty was killing people, not disarming state-of-the-art wiring, so the chances of his getting in without triggering it were nil.

Assuming he even wanted inside where she lived. The issue was how to best protect her, and it was hard to know what was worse—her in there alone with him on the perimeter. Or him in there with her.

Dimly, he heard his stomach growl and the sound made him feel keenly the number of hours that had passed since he'd eaten last. But he shrugged that off, just as he had countless times in the field.

Mind over matter, mind over body . . . mind over everything.

He just wished like hell he knew what Grier and her pops were talking about.

Standing in her kitchen and staring at her father as he looked at her little lineup of what-the-hells, Grier had so many questions she didn't know where to start.

One thing was certain: When her father reached out to pick up the business card, his hand was trembling ever so slightly. Which in anybody else was the equivalent of a full-blown epileptic seizure.

Alistair Childe was a warm man with a good soul, but he rarely showed emotion of any kind. Especially if it was an upset kind of thing. The only time she'd ever seen him cry had been at her brother's funeral—which had been bizarre not just for the rarity of his tears but because the two hadn't really gotten along.

"Who gave this to you?" he asked in a voice so thin it didn't sound like him in the slightest.

Grier sat down on one of the stools at the island and wondered where to start. "I was assigned a public-defender case yesterday. . . ."

The story was a quick tell, but it got a big reaction: "You let that man come over *here*?"

She crossed her arms over her chest. "Yes, I did."

"Into the house."

"He's a human, Dad. Not an animal."

Her father all but fell onto the other stool and then he struggled to unzip the neck of his fleece. "Dear God . . ."

"I've resigned from the case, but I went to Isaac's apartment just now—"

"What in the *world* made you go there?"

Okay, she was going to ignore that outraged tone. "And that was when I was given the card and told to call if I saw Isaac again. And I also got that Life Alert thing." She shook her head. "I'd seen the man before. I swear . . . a long time ago."

If her father had been pale before, now he turned the color of fog, not just blanching, but going opaque gray. "What did he look like?"

"He had a patch over his eye and he—"

She didn't finish the description. Her father bolted up off the stool and then abruptly had to catch his balance on the counter.

"Father?" She grabbed his arm in alarm. "Are you all—"

She was not surprised when he just shook his head.

"Talk to me, please," she said. "What is going on here?"

"I can't . . . discuss it with you."

Grier dropped her hold and stepped back. "Wrong answer," she bit out. "Totally wrong answer."

As she glared at him and all his resolute silence, she realized why she'd felt so oddly comfortable around Isaac: Her father was a ghost as well. Always had been. She'd literally grown up and now lived under the fear that at any moment he could disappear forever.

And her client had given off that exact same vibe.

"You've got to talk to me," she said grimly.

"I can't." The eyes that looked at her were those of a stranger in familiar garb—as if someone had taken a mask of her father's features and stepped in behind the surface dressing to stare outward. "Even if I could . . . I couldn't bear to contaminate you with . . ."

He sagged as if bowing under a great mountain of weight.

Strange, she thought. There were definitely times as you got older when you began to see your parent as a person rather than Father or Mother. And this was one of them. The man in her kitchen was not the all-powerful lord of house and office . . . but someone who was caught in some kind of bear trap, the jaws of which were seen only by him.

"I need to go," he said roughly. "Stay here and don't let

anyone in. Turn the security system on and do not answer the phone."

As he went to leave, she blocked his way to the front hall. "Unless you tell me what the hell is going on, I'm going to walk out that door the moment you leave and parade around Charles Street until I either get mowed down in traffic or am found by whatever you're so afraid of. Do not push me on this. Because I will do it."

There was a moment of glower-to-glower. And then he laughed harshly. "You are my daughter, aren't you."

"Through and through."

He started walking, doing laps around the granite-topped island.

It was time, she thought. Time to get the answers to all those questions that she'd wanted to ask about him and what he did. Time to fill the voids of mystery and shadow with tangible answers that were long overdue.

God, as much as Isaac was a complication, he was almost like a blessing from above.

"Just talk, Dad. Don't be a lawyer—don't think everything through."

He stopped on the far side of the cooktop and stared over at her. "My mind is the only thing I've got, my dear."

After a moment, he returned to the stool he'd dropped onto earlier, and as he sat down, he rezipped the neck of his fleece—which was how she knew she was going to get the truth, or some measure of it: He was pulling himself back together, regaining who he was.

"When I was in the army as an officer, I served in Vietnam, as you know," he said in the direct, matter-of-fact tone that she'd heard all her life. "Then I went to law school, and I was supposed to go back to civilian life. But I didn't really get out of the military. I've never really been out."

"The people who came to the door?" she said, realizing it was the first time she'd ever spoken about them.

"It's the kind of thing that you never really leave. You *can't* get out." He pointed to the card. "I know that number. I've dialed that number. It takes you right into the heart . . . of the beast."

He went on to speak in general terms, offering loose description instead of clear definitions, but she filled in the blanks: It was government ninja-style, the kind of thing that justified the paranoia of conspiracy theorists, the sort of organization that you were likely to see in movie theaters and comic books, but that sane civilians didn't believe really existed.

"I don't want that"—he jabbed his finger at the card again—"anywhere near you. The idea of that . . . man . . ."

When he didn't finish, she felt compelled to point out, "You haven't really told me anything."

He shook his head. "But that's the thing—it's all I've got. I'm on the fringes, Grier. So I know just enough to be clear about the danger."

"What exactly did you do for . . . whoever 'them' is?"

"Information gathering—I was strictly in intelligence. I never killed anybody." As if there were a whole murder department. "A big part of what drives the machine is information, and I have gone out and gotten it, and brought it back. I have also been called upon from time to time for my opinion on certain international figures or corporations or governments. But again, I've never killed."

She was incredibly relieved there was no blood on his hands. "Are you still involved?"

"Like I said, you're never truly out. But I haven't had an assignment in . . ." Long pause. "Two years."

Grier frowned, but before she could ask anything further, he got up and said, "Your former client is in over his head if he's gone AWOL from them. He can't save himself and you can't help him or save him, either. If that Isaac character shows up here again, call me immediately." He swept the card, the cloth strips, and the transmitter up and put them in the pocket of his fleece. "I won't let you get into this mess, Grier."

"What are you going to do with all that?"

"I'm going to make sure it is clear that you no longer represent Isaac Rothe, that you are going to have nothing to do with him, and that if you see him again, you will be contacting me directly. I will explain that you chose none of this and that you are eager to move along. And most important, I will state emphatically that you were told absolutely nothing by him. Which is the truth, isn't it?"

The hard look in his eye told her that even if that wasn't the case, she'd better be damned sure to maintain it was.

"He never said a word to me about what he'd done or why he was on the run. Not one word." As Grier watched her father sag with relief, her frustration eased up. "Dad . . ."

She went to him, slipping her arms around his waist and hugging him for a long moment.

"I'll call you in one hour," he said. "Turn the system on."

"The phone lines are tapped."

"I know."

Grier stiffened. "How long have they been?"

"Since the very beginning. Some forty years ago."

God, why was she even surprised . . . and yet the violation left a bad taste in her mouth. Like so much of this did.

After she showed him the door, she locked herself in and hit the alarm, then went into the study and peeked out the window to watch his Mercedes pull away from the curb and take off down Pinckney Street toward Charles.

When she could no longer see his taillights, she put her hand into her pocket and got out the things she'd taken from his when they'd embraced: The Life Alert and the business card and the strips of cloth had not in fact left with him.

Alistair Childe had been absolutely correct about one thing: She was nothing if not his daughter.

Which meant she wasn't going to be sidelined in this.

*You're crazy, you know that*, her ghostly brother said from beside her.

"Not a news flash." She glanced over at him. "I've been talking to a dead guy for the past two years."

*This is serious, Grier.*

She looked down at the things in her hands. "Yes. I know."

# CHAPTER
## 22

When night finally fell, Isaac was ready to scream, *About fucking time,* at the top of his lungs.

But instead of going the Tarzan route, he ducked out the back way of the townhouse, slipping from the window he'd unlatched that morning, closing it up behind himself, and dropping without a sound onto the rear brick terrace.

He was lucky that it was a cloudy night, because that drained the light even faster from the sky. And yet he was screwed, because the neighborhood was lit up like a god-damn jewelry store: From the streetlamps to the fixtures around all those shiny black doors to the headlights of cars, he was going to have hell's own amount of trouble hiding himself.

He made the trip to Grier's at turtle speed, finding all the shadows to be had and taking advantage of them.

Forty-five minutes.

That was how long he spent going no more than twenty yards across the street and into her backyard. Then, again, he went up the hill two blocks and doubled back before dropping down another street past her and taking an alley over to her walled garden.

A jump up . . . a quick hard grip on the top of the brick

lip...a full-bodied swing...and he was in among her rhododendrons.

He froze where he landed in a crouch.

There was no one that he could see or sense. Which meant he could scope the place through the glass panes—

As Grier entered the kitchen, he took a deep breath, the kind that gave him a powerful shot of energy and focus in spite of the fact that he hadn't eaten or taken a drink in almost twenty-four hours.

It felt like forever since he'd seen her last, and he hated how exhausted and pale she looked as she paced around, like a bird in the wind searching for a branch to perch upon. She was on the phone, talking with animation, gesturing with her hands....Then she ended the call and tossed the receiver across the counter.

He waited to see if anyone came to check on what had undoubtedly been some noise. When nobody did, he assumed she was alone—

Something moved. Over on the left.

His eyes shot across the garden, but his head didn't shift and his weight didn't pivot. It was hard to pinpoint exactly what had changed positions, because there were a lot of—

Jim Heron stepped out of the darkness. And wasn't that a surprise, given the wall that ran around everything. Then again, maybe he'd been there before Isaac had come— which was even more disturbing because Isaac should have teased out his presence.

Although the guy had always been very, very good at making like the landscape.

"What are you doing here?" Isaac demanded, his hand finding the butt of a gun as he straightened.

"Looking for you."

Isaac glanced around and didn't see anyone else. "Well, you found me." And shit, maybe Heron could help on a limited scale. "Your timing is good, by the way."

"And yet you didn't call? I gave you my number."

Isaac nodded up to Grier. "Complications."

Jim cursed under his breath. "Without even knowing the particulars, I can tell you your solution. Leave. Now. You're worried about her? Let me put you on an airplane."

"They gave her something."

"Fucking hell. What."

"I don't know." He stared through the glass at Grier. "And that's why I'm not leaving."

"Isaac. Look at me." When he didn't comply, Jim grabbed his biceps and squeezed. "Now."

Isaac slid his stare over. "I can't have her . . . hurt."

Another curse. "Okay, fine, so let me clean up the mess. You're too valuable to sacrifice. We need to get you to somewhere safe, far, far away from anyone or anybody who knows you or could find you. I'll take care of her—"

"No." God, he couldn't explain it and he knew it wasn't logical. But when it came to Grier . . . he couldn't trust anyone.

"Be reasonable here, Isaac—you're the gun pointed at her head. You're the trigger and you're the bullet and you're the shot that's going to kill her. You hang around here? You're putting paid to her tombstone."

"I'll get myself in between her and Matthias. I'll—"

"The only way to save you both is for you to get the fuck out of here. Besides, maybe if we can keep you hidden for long enough, he'll give up—he won't be able to afford the diversion of resources for an endless search."

Isaac slowly shook his head. "You know what Matthias has been like the last couple of years. He's running XOps like a clubhouse, moving his own agenda. He used to take orders . . . but lately? He's been making them up. He's out of control. The assignments now are about . . . something else. I don't know what. And that means he'll hunt me until he dies. He has to—it's the only way to protect himself."

"Then let him track you all over the globe. We'll make sure you stay two steps ahead of him for the rest of your natural life."

Isaac refocused on Grier through the glass. She was bracing herself against the counter he'd sat at, her head dropping down, her shoulders bowing as if they bore all her weight. Her hair had been left loose and the long, wavy lengths nearly touched the granite.

"I'm beginning to think that I made a mistake," he heard himself say. "I should have stayed in XOps."

"Your mistake is staying in this garden."

Probably. But he wasn't leaving.

"Oh, for fuck's sake," Jim bit out. "Take this."

At the sound of a rustling, Isaac glanced over and found a paper bag being held out to him.

"It's a turkey sandwich," Jim said. "Mayo. Lettuce. Tomato. And a cookie. From DeLuca's on the corner. I'll even take a bite to prove I haven't poisoned it."

Jim shoved his hand into the bag, pulled a reveal on the sandwich, and peeled back the cellophane with one hand. Then he cranked his jaw around the thing, bit hard, and chewed with his mouth closed.

Which naturally caused Isaac's gut to go two-year-old and start howling. "What kind of cookie."

Jim talked around his mouthful. "Chocolate chip. No nuts. Fucking hate nuts in chocolate-chip cookies."

"I'm much obliged," Isaac said softly. Holding out his left palm, he took what was offered and ate with efficiency.

"Cookie?" Jim murmured.

It pained him to say it, but he had to: "You take a bite first. Please."

That big mitt disappeared into the bag again and came out with something the size of a car wheel. Unwrap. Bite. Chew.

"Thank you kindly," Isaac said as dessert changed hands.

"I have a bottle of water in my back pocket." Jim took the thing out, made a show of cracking the lid, and grabbed a healthy swig.

Isaac leaned forward, and accepted the FIJI bottle. "You've saved me."

"That's the plan," the guy muttered.

Inside the kitchen, Grier started to make dinner, and damn, she was vulnerable as hell over that cooktop—all the glass turned the room into a TV set that stayed tuned to the Childe Channel twenty-four/seven.

"I'm leaving her undefended if I take off."

"You're making her a target if you stay. You shouldn't be here now. You shouldn't have spent all day in that house across the street."

Isaac looked over sharply. "How did you know?"

Jim just rolled his eyes. "Remember what I did for a living for over a decade? Look, be realistic. Let me watch over her once we get you settled."

"FYI, I know you a little too well—so this Boy Scout routine's kind of hard to buy."

"You can choke on the shit as far as I care. Just take advantage of it—"

A cold breeze wafted in from an indiscernible direction ... and Isaac felt a chill run up his spine that had nothing to do with air temperature and everything to do with instinct.

Beside him, Jim stiffened and looked around—

Two huge men came out of the shadows behind him.

Isaac was quick on the draw, palming his other gun and leveling a muzzle at each of them. But it turned out they were just Jim's boys, the one who was pierced like a pincushion and the other who was the size of a mountain.

"We got company, my man," Mr. Needle Fetish hissed to Jim. "Bad company. ETA about a minute and a half."

"Get him into the house," the one with that rope-thick braid said. "He'll be safe there."

Right, time to cut in, boys: "Hi, my name is Isaac. This is Lefty ... and Bob." He lifted his guns accordingly to make the introductions. "And none of us take orders well anymore."

Jim's eyes burned as they shifted over. "Listen to me, Isaac ... get in the house ... get in the fucking house and stay there. No matter what you see or hear—do not leave. We clear?"

From out of nowhere, the guy pulled a knife that made no sense. Damn thing was made of glass . . . ? What the—

A low whistle started to hum through the air, and Isaac glanced over his shoulder in the direction of the sound. It was the kind of thing that had to be just the wind. . . . There was no other explanation for it. And yet he didn't feel any breeze on his skin.

"Get in the house if you want to live," someone said.

Jim grabbed his arm. "You can't fight this enemy, but I can. If you're inside there, you'll be safe—and you can protect that woman. Keep her with you and keep her safe."

Well, that was one order he could follow—

All at once, Grier's house seemed to glow with an ethereal light, as if it had been hit with red floodlights from the foundation up. As his eyes struggled to comprehend what he was seeing, a buzzing on the back of his neck grew so intense he worried his head was going to play 7-Up and pop off his spine.

Isaac didn't stick around.

He tore across the backyard as the unholy wind got louder and louder, praying he got inside and to Grier in time.

Grier hated fighting with her father. Absolutely despised it.

Flipping her omelet in the pan, she centered the thing and then stared at the cell phone she'd just tossed across the island.

Their first call had taken place about an hour after he'd left, and he'd done the dialing. Naturally, he'd discovered her little sleight-of-hand trick and that had led to all sorts of trouble—none of which had been resolved, because she wasn't giving the stuff back and he wasn't taking no for an answer and they'd had to cover that rocky ground in code because God knew who was listening.

After going around and around for a while like boxers

in a ring, they'd taken a time-out; she'd tried to work while her father had gone into that shadowy world of his.

Although she was just guessing at that part. It wasn't as if he told her anything concrete.

Still.

Like always.

Second trip through the phone park, and her fingers had done the walking. Her intent had been to make some kind of peace and find out what he was doing, but that had quickly devolved into more half-assed accusations in a language that appeared to be one part pig latin and one part charades.

The former working only slightly better than the latter over the connection.

As her omelet sizzled softly and she took a sip from her wineglass, a gust of wind hit the back of the house, whistling through the shutters, and fondling the wind chimes by the door. Frowning, she looked over her shoulder. Hell of a breeze, she thought, the subtle music of the clay pieces for once not calming her.

Which was what happened when you were being paranoid. Everything went creepy, even the —

A huge shape jumped up to the back door and filled the glass panes. As she let out a scream and leaped for the panic button on the security system remote, Isaac's face was illuminated out of the darkness by the motion-activated light he triggered.

He started pounding with his fist, but he didn't do that for long. He wheeled around to face the backyard, flattening against the house as if something were coming at him.

As she rushed over, she disarmed the system, and he all but fell into the kitchen when she opened up. He was the one who slammed them in together, locking the dead bolt and then putting his body against the panels as if someone were going to try to get in.

Between breaths, he commanded, "The system . . . put it back on. . . ."

She did so without hesitation—

Everything went dark.

Except for the blue glow of the flame under the pan on the stove and the yellow halo of the light over the stoop, the kitchen went utterly black—and it took her brain a second to catch up to the fact that he'd canned the lights.

The gun he brought up by his chest didn't throw much reflection or shadow, but she knew exactly what was in his palm as he shifted over and settled against the wall by the door. He didn't point the weapon anywhere near her—he wasn't even looking at her. His eyes were trained on the rear garden.

When she tried to come over to look, he put his heavy arm out and held her back. "Stay away from the glass."

"What's going on?"

A blast of wind hit the house, the chimes going haywire to the point where they were twisting around on their strings, all but screaming in pain.

And then a strange creaking noise beat out the racket.

Bracing herself on the counter, she looked up to the ceiling and realized it was the whole house. . . . Her family's brick house, which had stood without budging on its solid foundation for two hundred years, was groaning as if it were about to be torn off from its hold on the ground.

Her eyes went to the glass wall. She couldn't see anything but shadows moving because of the wind . . . except they weren't right. They didn't . . . move right.

Transfixed by the sight of dark patterns shifting around over the ground like thick oil, she felt her mind bend as it tried to form an explanation for what her eyes were taking in.

"What is . . . *that?*" she breathed.

"Get down behind the counter." Isaac glanced up to the ceiling as the house let out another curse. "Come on, baby, hold your own."

Falling to her knees, she looked at the old mirror across

the way. On its wavy plane, she could see out the windows into the garden and watch those all-wrongs wending around.

"Isaac, get away from the door—"

A pealing scream filled the air, and Grier let out a shout and covered her ears. Isaac didn't even flinch, however—and she took strength from him.

"Fire alarm," he yelled. "It's the fire alarm!"

He lunged for the cooktop and shoved the smoking omelet to the side, canning the flame on the burner with a quick twist. "Do what you have to," he barked. *"But make sure the fire department doesn't show up!"*

# CHAPTER
## 23

Matthias drove the last leg of the trip himself.

He'd been flown into this town from his little detour over in Boston because although he could pilot a number of different aircrafts, he'd been stripped of his wings since his injuries.

But at least he was still able to drive, goddamn it.

The flight from Beantown to Caldwell had been short and sweet, and the Caldwell International Airport was a breeze—although when you had his level of clearance, the TSA types never got anywhere near you or your bags.

Not that he'd brought any luggage with him—other than that which he carried around in his brain.

His car was yet another black-on-black unmarked with armor plating and glass thick enough to give any bullet a concussion. It was just like the one he'd had when he'd paid Grier Childe a visit . . . and just like the one he'd have in any city he went to, at home or abroad.

He'd told nobody but his number two where he was going—and even his most trusted didn't know the why behind it. There were no problems with the secrecy, however: The good thing with being the darkest shadow among a legion of them was that when you up and disappeared, it was part of your fucking job and no one asked any questions.

And the truth was, this trip was beneath him, the kind of thing he'd ordinarily have assigned to his right-hand man — and yet he had to do this himself.

It felt like a pilgrimage.

Although if that was what he was on, things had better get inspiring pretty frickin' quick. The road he was currently following was just a generic stretch of boutique shops and Walgreens and gas stations that could have been any city, anywhere. Traffic was light and of the pass-through variety; everything was shut up for the night, so you were here only if you were going somewhere else.

For most of the people, that was. Unlike the rest of them, his destination was . . . right here as a matter of fact.

Easing off on the accelerator, he pulled over to the side and parked parallel to the curb. Across a shallow lawn, the McCready Funeral Home was dark inside, but there were exterior lights on all over the place.

Not a problem.

Matthias placed a call and was routed around from person to person, skipping like a stone through the phones of others until he found the decision maker who could get him what he wanted.

And then he sat and waited.

He hated the silence and the darkness in the car — but not because he was worried that there was someone in his backseat or that somebody was about to go click-click, bang-bang from the shadows outside. He liked to keep moving. As long as he was in motion, he could outrun the twitchies that inevitably T-boned his adrenal glands when he was at rest.

Stillness was a killer.

And it turned the Crown Victoria into a coffin —

His phone rang and he knew who it was before he

checked. And no, it wasn't going to be the people he'd just spoken with. He'd finished his business with them.

Matthias answered on the third ring, just before voice mail kicked in. "Alistair Childe. What a surprise."

The shocked silence was so satisfying. "How did you know it was me?"

"You don't honestly think I would let just anyone get through to this phone." As Matthias stared through the windshield at the funeral home, he found it ironic that the pair of them were talking in front of the thing—given that he'd put the man's son in one. "Everything's on my terms. Everything."

"So you know why I've spent all day trying to find you."

Yes, he did. And he'd deliberately made himself hard to reach for the guy: He firmly believed that people were like pieces of meat; the longer they stewed, the softer they became.

The tastier, too.

"Oh, Albie, of course I'm aware of your situation." A soft rain started to fall, the drops dappling the glass. "You're worried about the man who stayed with your daughter last evening." Another shot of quiet. "You didn't know that he'd been there at your house all night? Well, children don't always tell their parents everything, do they."

"She's not involved. I promise you, she knows nothing—"

"She didn't tell you she had a guest during the dark hours. How can you really trust her?"

"You can't have her." The man's voice cracked. "You took my son. . . . You cannot have her."

"I can have anyone. And I can take anyone. You know that now, don't you."

Abruptly, Matthias became aware of a strange sensation in his left arm. Glancing down, he saw his fist had cranked on the steering wheel so hard his biceps were doing the shimmy.

He willed the grip to release . . . but it didn't.

Bored with his body's little spasms and tics, he ignored this newest one. "Here's what you have to do if you want to be certain about your daughter. Give me Isaac Rothe and I go away. It's just that simple. Get me what I want, and I leave your girl alone."

At that moment, the entire block went dark—courtesy of his little phone call.

"You know I mean every word," Matthias said, going for his cane. "Don't make me kill another Childe."

He hung up and put the phone back in his coat.

Swinging his door wide, he groaned as he got out, and chose to stick to the concrete sidewalk as opposed to the lawn, even though it was a less direct route to the back. His body ambulating over grass? Not a good thing.

After picking the dead bolt on the rear door—which proved that even though he was the boss, he hadn't lost his nuts-and-bolts training—he sipped inside the funeral home and set about finding the body of the soldier who had saved him.

Confirming the identity of Jim Heron's "corpse" felt as necessary as drawing his next breath.

Back in Boston, in that defense attorney's rear garden, Jim braced himself for the fight that was coming, literally, on the wind.

"It's just like killing a human," Eddie shouted over the gale. "Go for the center of the chest—watch out for the blood, though."

"The bitches are sloppy as shit." Adrian's grin had an edge of madness to it, his eyes sparkling with unholy light. "It's why we wear leather."

As the brick house's kitchen door slammed shut, and the lights went out, Jim prayed that Isaac kept himself and that woman in there.

Because the enemy had arrived.

From the midst of the shoving gusts, black shadows

rippled over the ground and boiled up, forming shapes that became solid. No faces, no hands, no feet—no clothes, duh. But they did have arms and legs and a head, which he guessed ran the program God, the stink. They smelled like rotten garbage, a combination of sulfurous egg and sweaty, spoiled meat, and they growled as wolves did when hunting in a coordinated pack.

This was evil up and moving, darkness in tangible form, a four-set of nasty, festering infection that made him want to take a bath in bleach.

Just as he settled into his fighting stance, the back of his neck went off, that ringing alarm he'd felt the night before tweaking its way into the base of his brain. His eyes shot up to the house in a fuck-no . . . except he was certain that wasn't the source.

Whatever—he needed his game head on big-time.

As one of the shadows rolled up into his space, Jim didn't wait for the first strike—not his style. He swung wide with his crystal knife and kept going as he ducked under a blow that snapped out farther than he'd expected.

Got some elastic in 'em evidently.

Jim did make contact, though, nicking something that caused a spray of liquid to shoot in his direction. In midair, the splash morphed into buckshot pellets that then dissolved when they hit him. The sting was instant and intense.

"Fuck!" He shook off his hand, momentarily distracted by the smoke rising from his exposed skin.

The blow landed on the side of his face and made his head ring like a bell—proving that he might be an angel and all that shit, but his nervous system was still decidedly human. He immediately went on the offensive, outing a second knife and double-blading the bastard, forcing the thing into the bushes while he ducked those punches.

As they engaged, the back of his neck continued to holler, but he couldn't afford to be distracted.

Fight what was in front of you first. Then deal with what came next.

Jim was the first one to get a kill in. He lunged when his opponent arched forward, his crystal dagger going in at the gut level. As a rainbow explosion of light flared, he twisted away, covering his face with his arm to block the deadly spray, his leather-covered shoulder taking the brunt of the impact. The splattering of shit steamed and stunk like battery acid—burned like it, too, as the blood of the demon ate through the cowhide and headed for his skin.

He immediately fell back into fighting stance, but the other three oilers were covered: Adrian was handling a pair and Eddie was all over his guy . . . demon . . . whatever the fuck it was.

With a curse, Jim reached up and rubbed his nape. The sensation had graduated from tingle to roar, and he bowed under the agony now that his adrenaline ebbed a little. God, it just got worse . . . to the point where he couldn't handle it and sank down on his knees.

Putting his palm on the ground and bracing himself, it dawned on him what was doing. In a case of perfectly bad timing, Matthias had acted on the spell he'd put on his corpse back in Caldwell—

"Go!" Eddie hissed as he slashed and retracted. "We've got this! You get to Matthias."

At that moment, Adrian offed one of his pair, his crystal dagger going deep into the thing's chest before he jumped up onto the stoop to avoid the spray. The sprinkle of buckshot hit the other demon he was fighting—

Oh, shit. The black oily bastard absorbed the spray—and doubled in size.

Jim glanced back Eddie, but the angel barked, "Go! I'm telling—" Eddie dodged a strike and threw one of his own with his free fist. "You can't fight like this!"

Jim didn't want to leave them, but he was quickly becoming worse than useless—his buddies were going to have to defend him if this ringy-ding-ding got any more acute.

"Go!" Eddie shouted.

Jim cursed, but stood up, unfurled his wings, and took off in a shimmer ...

Caldwell, New York, was more than two hundred miles west—assuming you were a human on foot, bike, horseback, or in a car. Angel Airlines covered the distance in the blink of an eye.

As he touched down on the front lawn of McCready's joint, he saw the unmarked parked at the curb ... and the fact that an entire block was without electricity ... and knew he was right.

Matthias had come calling.

Just the man's style.

Jim headed across the grass, and felt like he was going back in time ... to that night in the desert that had changed everything for him and Matthias.

Yeah, his summoning spell had worked.

The question was what to do with his prey.

# CHAPTER
## 24

S tanding in Grier's kitchen, Isaac totally approved of the way she took care of business. In the midst of the chaos, she was calm as she worked the phone and the security system: A quick one, two, three, and she had cut off the fire alarm, called in a false report, and reset the system. And she did it all crouched behind the counters, protected and hidden.

Definitely his kind of woman.

With her on top of things, he was free to try to figure out what the hell was doing in her backyard. Twisting around so that his body remained tucked away, he searched through the glass . . . but all he got was just the wind and a whole lot of shadows.

Yet his instincts were screaming.

What was Jimmy doing back there with his buddies? Who had shown up? Matthias's crew usually rolled up in unlicensed unmarkeds. They didn't hop on broomsticks and dive-bomb from out of a stormy sky. Besides, there was no one out there anymore that he could see.

As time dragged and a whole lot of nothing-but-wind went on, he thought maybe he'd lost his mind altogether.

"You okay?" he whispered without turning around.

There was a rustling and then Grier was shoulder-to-shoulder beside him on the floor. "What's going on? Can you see anything?"

He noted she didn't answer the question—but come on, like she had to? "It's nothing we need to be a part of."

Nothing, period, it seemed. Although ... well, actually, if he squinted, the shadows did seem to form patterns consistent with fighters engaging in hand-to-hand combat. Except, of course, there was nobody out there—and he was seeing logic to the way things moved. To get the effect he was seeing, a legion of lights would have had to be shining in from all different directions to get even close to the optics.

"This doesn't feel right to me," Grier said.

"I agree." He looked over at her. "But I'm going to take care of you."

"I thought you were going to leave."

"I didn't." The *couldn't* part was something he kept to himself. "I'm not going to let anything hurt you."

Her head tilted to the side as she stared at him. "You know ... I believe you."

"You can bet your life on it."

In a quick move, he put his mouth to hers on a hard kiss to seal the deal. And then just as he was pulling back, the wind stopped—sure as if the industrial fan causing all the blowing had been unplugged: In the back forty, there was nothing but utter silence.

What the *hell* was going on?

"Stay here," he said as he stood up.

Naturally, she didn't take the order, but rose to her feet, her hands resting on his shoulder as if she were prepared to tail him. He didn't like it, but he knew arguing wasn't going to get him anywhere—the best he could do was keep his chest and shoulders front and center to block any shot at her.

He inched forward until he could see outside better. The shadows had disappeared and the tree limbs and bushes were still. Distant sounds of traffic and the far-off wail of an ambulance were once again an ambient city song playing like Muzak all around the neighborhood.

He glanced over at her. "I'm going out there. Can you handle a firearm?" When she nodded, he took out one of his two guns. "Have this."

She didn't hesitate, but man, he hated the sight of her pale, elegant hands on his weapon.

He nodded down at the thing. "Point and shoot using both palms. Safety's off. We clear?"

When she nodded, he kissed her again because he just had to; then he moved her back into position in the shelter of the floor cabinets. From that vantage point, she could see anyone coming in from the front or the rear, but also cover the interior door that he had a feeling led to the basement stairs.

Palming his other gun, he exited in a quick shift—

His first breath brought an unholy stench into his sinuses and down the back of his throat. What the . . . ? It was like a chemical spill—

From out of nowhere, one of the pair who'd been with Jim appeared. It was the guy with the braid and he looked like he'd been spray-painted with WD-40—and had dry ice shoved in all his pockets: Tendrils of smoke were steaming up from his leather jacket, and shit . . . the *smell*.

Before Isaac could what-the-fuck him, Jim's boy cut the question off. "Do us a favor and stay put. Coast is clear for now, though. If you understand what I'm saying."

As Isaac met the man's eyes, there was no question that even though they were strangers, they spoke the same language: The guy was a soldier.

"You want to tell me what the hell just happened out here?"

"Nope. But I wouldn't mind some white vinegar if she has it?"

Isaac frowned. "No offense, but I think making salad

dressing is the least of your concerns, buddy. Your jacket needs a hose-down."

"I've got burns to take care of."

Sure enough, on the side of his neck and on his hands there were raw, red patches on his skin. As if he'd been hit with some kind of acid.

Hard to argue with the steaming bastard, considering he was injured. "Give me a sec."

Ducking back in the house, Isaac cleared his throat. "Ah . . . do you have any white vinegar?"

Grier blinked and then pointed with the gun muzzle to the sink. "I use it to clean the hardwood. But why?"

"Damned if I know." He headed for the sink and found a huge jug with a Heinz label on it. "But they want some."

"Who's they?"

"Friends of a friend."

"Are they okay?"

"Yeah." Assuming the definition of *okay* included a section for roasty-toasted.

Outside, he handed over the stuff, which was promptly thrown around like cool water on a sweaty football player. It did kill the smoking and the stench, though, on both Braid Guy and the pincushion.

"What about the neighbors," Isaac said, glancing around. The brick-to-window ratio on the backs of the buildings worked in their favor, but the noise . . . the smell.

"We'll take care of them," Braid Guy answered. Like it was no biggie and something they'd done before.

What kind of war were they fighting? Isaac thought. Was there another organization past XOps? He'd always assumed Matthias was the shadiest of the shady. But maybe here was another level. Maybe that was how Jim had gotten out.

"Where's Heron?" he asked them.

"He'll be back." The one with the piercings returned the

vinegar. "You just stay where you are and take care of her. We got you."

Isaac waved his gun back and forth. "Who the hell are you?"

Mr. Braid, who seemed the leveler of the pair, said, "Just part of Jim's little group."

At least that made some sense. Even though they'd clearly been in a rough-and-tumble, neither seemed bothered at all. No wonder Jim worked with them.

And Isaac had a feeling he knew what they were doing— Jim might just be after Matthias. Which would certainly explain the guy's desire to get involved and play Orbitz with the plane tickets.

"You need another soldier?" Isaac asked, only half-joking.

The two glanced at each other and then back to him. "Not our call," they said in unison.

"Jim's?"

"Mostly," Mr. Braid replied. "And you've got to be dying to get in—"

"Isaac? Who are you talking to?"

As Grier walked out of the kitchen, he wished like hell she'd stay inside. "No one. Let's head back into the house."

Turning to good-bye Jim's boys, he froze. Nobody was around. Heron's wingmen were gone.

Yup, whoever and whatever they were, they were definitely his kind of soldiers.

Isaac went up to Grier and walked them both back inside. As he threw the lock and turned on one track of lighting waaaaaay across the room, he grimaced. Man, the kitchen didn't smell much better than those two out back had: burned egg, charred bacon, and blackened butter were not a party for the ol' sniffer.

"Are you all right?" he asked, even though once again the answer was self-evident.

"Are you?"

He ran his eyes down her from head to foot. She was alive and he was with her and they were safe in this fortress of a house. "I'm better."

"What's in the backyard."

"Friends." He took his gun back. "Who want both of us to be safe."

To keep himself from dragging her into his arms, he sheathed both guns in his windbreaker and picked the pan off the stove. Dumping the remains of her almost-dinner in the sink, he washed the thing out.

"Before you ask," he murmured, "I don't know anything more than you do."

Which was essentially true. Sure, he had a leg up on her when it came to certain things—but as for the shit in the backyard? Fucking. Clueless.

He popped a dish towel off a hook and . . . realized she hadn't said anything for a while.

Pivoting around, he saw that she had taken a seat on one of the stools and wrapped her arms around herself. She was utterly self-contained, having retreated into her skin and turned to stone.

"I'm trying . . ." She cleared her throat. "I'm really trying to understand all this."

He brought the pan back over to the stove and braced himself on his arms, thinking here it was again, the great divide between the civilian and the soldier. This chaos and scramble and deadly danger? To him, it was business as usual.

Except it was killing her.

Like a complete lame-ass, he said, "You want to give dinner another shot?"

Grier shook her head. "Being in a parallel universe where everything looks like your life, but is actually something else entirely is an appetite killer."

"Been there." He nodded. "Done that."

"Made it your profession, matter of fact. Didn't you."

He frowned and left that one right where it had landed on the counter between them. "Listen, are you sure I can't make you—"

"I went back to your apartment. This afternoon."

"Why." Fuck.

"It was after I dropped your money off at the police department and gave a statement. Guess who was at your place."

"Who."

"It was someone my father knew."

Isaac's shoulders tightened up so hard, he found it difficult to breathe. Or maybe his lungs had frozen solid. Oh, Jesus Christ, no . . . not—

She pushed something across the granite at him. A business card. "I'm supposed to call this number if you show up here."

As Isaac read the digits, she laughed with a sharp edge. "My father had the same expression on his face when he read what was on it. And let me guess, you're not going to tell me who'd answer the ring, either."

"The man at my apartment. Describe him." Even though Isaac knew.

"He had an eye patch."

Isaac swallowed hard, thinking that whatever he'd assumed she'd had in that tissue when she'd gotten out of her car . . . he'd never considered that it would have been given to her by Matthias himself.

"Who is he?" she asked.

Isaac's reply was just a shake of the head. As it was, she was already standing at the precipice of the rat hole he and her father were sucked into. Any explaining would be the size-thirteen boot in the ass that sent her over the edge and into a free fall—

With a sudden surge, she burst up from the stool and grabbed the glass of wine she'd been nursing. "I am so god-damn tired of all this silence!"

She pitched the chardonnay across the room, and when the glass hit the wall, it shattered, leaving a bomb burst of wet stain on the plaster and shards all around on the floor.

As she wheeled toward him, she was breathing hard and her eyes were on fire.

There was a beat of raw silence. And then Isaac came around the island toward her.

He kept his voice low as he approached. "When you were in the police station today, did they ask you about me?"

She seemed momentarily nonplussed. "Of course they did."

"And what did you tell them?"

"Nothing—because short of your name, I don't know a goddamn thing."

He nodded, bringing his body even closer to hers. "That man at my apartment. Did he ask about me?"

She threw her hands up. "Everyone wants to know about you—"

"And what did you tell him?"

"Nothing," she hissed.

"If someone from the CIA or the NSA comes to your door and asks about me—"

"I can't tell them anything!"

He stopped so close, he could see each individual lash around her stunning blue eyes. "That's right. And that's what is going to keep you alive." As she cursed and went to turn away, he grabbed her arm and snapped her back around. "That man at my apartment is a cold-blooded killer and he let you go only because he wants to send a message to me. The reason I'm not telling you anything—"

"I can lie! Damn it—why do you assume I'm naive?" She glared up at him. "You have no idea what it's been like my whole life, seeing all these shadows and never having them explained. I can *lie*—"

"They'll torture you. To make you talk."

That shut her up.

And he kept going. "Your father knows this. So do I—and believe me, during training I got put through an interrogation session, so I know *precisely* what they'll do to you. The only way I can be sure you don't get that is if you really don't have anything to say. Frankly, you're too close to this anyway—through no fault of your own."

"God . . . I *hate* this." The trembling in her body wasn't about fear. It was rage, pure and simple. "I just want to hit something."

"Okay." He tightened her fist and drew her arm back over her shoulder. "Take it out on me."

"What—"

"Hit me. Tear my eyes out. Do anything you have to."

"Are you mad?"

"Yes. Insane." He dropped his hold on her and braced his weight, staying close . . . close enough so she could cork him a good one if she wanted to. "I'll be your punching bag, your Kevlar vest, your bodyguard . . . I'll do anything to help you get through this."

"You're crazy," she breathed.

As she stared up at him all flushed and alive, the heat in his blood surged—and took them into even more dangerous territory. For fuck's sake, like he needed to get sexed up? Now, yet again, was not the time or the place.

So naturally, he asked, "What's it going to be . . . Do you want to hit me or kiss me?"

In the wake of the demand, Grier ran her tongue over her lips and Isaac tracked the movement like a predator. Yet it was clear as he stayed where he was that what happened next was up to her.

Which proved what kind of man he was in spite of the profession he'd fallen into.

On her side, she wasn't thinking anything remotely professional. She was confused and off-kilter—this was last night all over again with the reckless buzzing. But that wasn't what compelled her now.

This could be the only time she had with him. Ever. She'd spent all afternoon wondering where he was, if he was okay . . . if she would see him again. If he was still alive. He was a stranger who had somehow become very important to her. And though the timing was horrible, you couldn't schedule the opportunities you had.

Dropping her arm, she uncoiled the fist he'd made for her, and as it came down, she wished she could keep it to herself because that was a more responsible choice. Instead, she leaned into him and put her palm between his legs. On a growl low in his throat, his hips thrust forward.

He was hard and thick.

And had to hold himself up as he swayed.

"I won't stop this time," he growled.

She tightened her grip on him. "I just want to be with you. Once."

"That can be arranged."

They met in the middle in a blaze, lips crushing, arms winding around, bodies coming together. In the dim kitchen, he picked her up and took her down onto the floor between the island and counter, rolling over at the last moment so he was the bed she lay upon. As her legs settled between his, the hard ridge of his erection dug into her and his tongue entered her mouth, taking, owning. As they kissed in desperation, his body undulated beneath her, rolling and receding, the powerful contours of him achingly familiar in spite of how little time she'd spent against him.

God, she needed more of him.

In a fumbling move, she yanked up her shirt and he was right on it, pulling down the lacy cups, freeing her nipples, and then moving her up so that his lips latched onto one, sucking, pulling, licking. His hair was thick against her fingers as she held him to her, his mouth wet and hot, his hands grabbing her hips and digging in.

"Isaac ..." The groan was strangled and then cut off altogether by a gasp as his palm swept between her legs and cupped her sex.

He rubbed her in tight circles as he flicked his tongue, and only the raging need to have him inside gave her the focus she needed to go for his nylon sweatpants. Shoving the waistband down, she kicked off her loafers, hooked a toe, and peeled them all the way off.

No boxers. No briefs. Nothing in the way.

Wrapping her palm around his thick shaft, she stroked him and he moved with her, counterthrusting to increase the friction. And the sound he made ... holy heavens, the sound he made: that growl was all animal as he inhaled against her breast.

Grier sat up, his lips popping off her breast, and with a curse, she all but ripped her yoga pants and her panties off. As he gripped himself and stood his erection up, she restraddled him and sat down, lowering herself onto him, joining them together, moving his windbreaker up so she could get to more skin. The feel of him kicked her head back, but she watched his reaction, hungry to see what he looked like—and he didn't disappoint. With a great hiss, his teeth clenched and he sucked in air through them, the cords in his neck straining, his pecs popping up into tight pads.

As she took over and set the pace, it was as if she were owning him in some primal way, marking him with the sex.

"God ... you're beautiful," he panted as his hot eyes watched her from lowered lids, tracking the movement of her breasts as they peeked out from between the shirt and the crammed-down bra cups.

He didn't stay down for long, though. He was fast and strong and sure as he sat up and kissed her hard, pushing in even deeper and holding her to him. At first she panicked that he was stopping again, but then he burrowed into her neck and spoke to her.

"You feel so good." His Southern drawl was low and

husky and it went straight into her sex, heating her even further. "You feel . . ."

He didn't finish the sentence, but slipped his big palms under her to lift her up and down, his massive biceps handling her weight as if she were nothing but a toy—

She came so hard she saw stars, a bright galaxy exploding where they were joined and sending a shower of sparkling light throughout her body. And just as he'd promised, he didn't stop this time. He went rigid and jerked against her, his arms shooting around her waist and tightening until she couldn't breathe—not that she cared about oxygen. As he twitched inside of her and shuddered against her, she sank her nails into his black windbreaker and held him.

And then it was all over.

As their breathing slowed, the stillness afterward was much the same as the departure of that great, sourceless wind: oddly traumatic.

Silence. God . . . the silence. But she couldn't think of anything to say.

"I'm sorry," he bit out roughly. "I thought this would help you."

"Oh, no . . . I—"

He shook his head, and with his tremendous strength lifted her off his body, separating them easily. In a quick move, he set her aside, yanked his waistband back up, and reached for a clean towel. After he gave the thing to her, he settled with his back against the cupboards and put his knees up, arms balanced on the tops of them, hands hanging loose.

It was then that she noticed the gun on the floor beside where they had been. And he must have seen it at the same moment she did because he grabbed the weapon and disappeared it into the windbreaker.

Squeezing her eyes shut briefly, she cleaned up quick and redressed. Then she settled in an identical pose next to him. Unlike Isaac, however, she didn't stare straight ahead;

she looked at his profile. He was so beautiful in that male way, his face all angles and bone—but the weariness in him bothered her.

He'd lived on the edge for too long.

"How old are you really?" she asked eventually.

"Twenty-six."

She recoiled. So that was the truth? "You seem older."

"I feel like it."

"I'm thirty-two." Still more silence. "Why won't you look at me."

"You've never had a one-night stand. Until now." Like he'd cursed her in some way.

"Well, technically, it's been two nights with you." As his jaw clenched, she knew that wasn't a help. "Isaac, you didn't do anything wrong."

"Didn't I." He cleared his throat.

"I wanted you."

Now he looked at her. "And you had me. God . . . you had me." For a brief second, his eyes flared with heat again, and then he refocused on the cabinet in front of him. "But that's it. It's over and done with."

Okay . . . *ouch*. And for a guy who seemed bitched that he'd indoctrinated her into the one-night club, you'd think his conscience would feel better if they did it a few more times.

As her sex heated again, she thought . . . they'd just see about the "over and done with" part.

"Why did you come back?" she asked.

"I never left." As she felt her brows flare, he shrugged. "I spent all day in hiding across the street from you—and before you think I'm a stalker, I was watching the people who were—and are—watching you."

As she blanched, she was glad for the darkness in this valley of cabinets and cupboards. Much better for him to think she was holding it together. "The white strips were put there by you, weren't they. Your muscle shirt."

"It was supposed to be a signal to them that I'd taken off."

"I didn't know. I'm sorry."

"Why haven't you married?" he asked abruptly. And then he laughed in a hard burst. "Sorry if that's too personal."

"No. It isn't." All things considered, nothing seemed out-of-bounds anymore. "I never fell in love. Never had time to, really. Between chasing after Daniel and my work . . . no time. Plus . . ." It seemed at once perfectly normal and completely foreign to speak so candidly. "To be honest, I don't think I ever wanted anyone that close to me. There were things I didn't want to share."

And it wasn't like she was hoarding her family's name or position or wealth. It was the bad things that she kept to herself—her brother . . . and her mother, too, if she was honest. Just as she and her father were both lawyers and very focused, the other two in the family had suffered from similar demons. After all, just because alcohol was legal, didn't mean it couldn't destroy a life as much as heroin did.

Her mother had been an elegant drunk for all of Grier's life and it was hard to know what had put her there: biological predisposition; a husband who disappeared regularly; or a son who at an early age started to walk the path she did.

The loss of her had been just as horrible as Daniel's death.

"Who's Daniel?"

"My brother."

"Whose pj's I borrowed."

"Yes." She took a deep breath. "He died about two years ago."

"God . . . I'm sorry."

Grier glanced around, wondering if the man—er, ghost—in question would choose now to show up. "I'm sorry, too. I really thought I could save him . . . or help him save himself. It didn't work out that way, though. He, ah, he had a drug problem."

She hated the apologetic tone she always assumed when talking about what had killed Daniel—and yet it crept into her voice every time.

"I'm really sorry," Isaac repeated.

"Thank you." Abruptly, she shook her head as if it were a saltshaker that had caked up. Maybe this was why her brother refused to talk about the past—it was a terrible downer.

Switching gears, she said, "That man? Back at your apartment—he gave me something." She leaned up and patted around for the Life Alert, finding it under the sweater she'd taken off after the first fight with her father. "He left it in my trunk."

Although she handled it with the tissue, Isaac took the thing with his bare hands. Guess fingerprints were a nonissue to him.

"What is it?" she asked.

"Something for me."

"Wait—"

As he shoved it into his pocket, he talked over her objection. "If I want to turn myself in, all I have to do is hit the button and tell them where to find me. It's got nothing to do with you."

Give himself over to that man? "What happens then?" she asked tightly. "What happens if you . . ."

She couldn't finish. And he didn't answer.

Which told her everything she needed to know, didn't it—

At that moment, the front door unlocked and opened, the sounds of keys and footsteps echoing down the hall as the security alarm was turned off by someone else.

"My father!" she hissed.

Jumping up, she tried to straighten her clothes—oh, God, her hair was a wreck.

The wineglass. *Shit.*

"Grier?" came that familiar voice from the front of the house.

Oh, damn, Isaac *really* didn't need to meet what was left of her family right now.

"Quick, you have to—" When she looked back, he was gone.

Okay, usually, she was frustrated by his ghost routine. At the moment, it was a godsend.

Moving fast, she flipped on the lights, grabbed a roll of paper towels, and headed for the mess on the floor and wall.

"In here!" she replied.

As her father came into the room, she noticed he'd changed into his casual uniform of a cashmere sweater and pressed slacks. His face, however, was anything but easygoing: Stark and cold, he looked as he did when he faced an opponent in court.

"I received notification that the fire alarm went off," he said.

Undoubtedly he had, but he'd probably been on his way over here anyway: His house was out in Lincoln—no way he could get to Beacon Hill this fast.

Thank God he hadn't gotten here ten minutes earlier, she thought.

To keep her blush out of the sight, she concentrated on picking up the sharp shards. "I burned an omelet."

When her father didn't say anything else, she stared over at him. "What."

"Where is he, Grier. Tell me where Isaac Rothe is."

A sliver of fear trickled down her spine and landed in her gut like a rock. His expression was so ruthless, she was willing to bet her life on the fact that the pair of them were on opposite sides of the table when it came to her client.

Houseguest.

Lover.

Whatever Isaac was to her.

"Ouch!" She brought up her hand. A piece of glass was sticking straight out of the pad of her forefinger, her blood bright red as it pooled into a fat, welling drop.

As she headed over to the sink, she felt the presence of her father across the kitchen like a gun pointed at her back.

He didn't even ask how badly she'd hurt herself.

All he did was say once again: "Tell me where Isaac Rothe is."

# CHAPTER
## 25

Back in Caldwell, inside the funeral home, Jim was an old pro at the McCready floor plan and he worked his way down to the basement on quick feet. When he got to the embalming room, he walked through the closed doors . . . and all but skidded to a halt when he came out on the other side.

He hadn't realized until now that he never expected to see his old boss again face-to-face.

And yet there Matthias was, across the way at the refrigerator units, looking at the nameplates on the latched doors just as Jim had done night before last. Shit, the guy was frail, that once tall, robust body now angled over his cane, the previously black hair showing gray at the temples. The eye patch was still where it had been after the initial round of surgeries—there had been hope that the damage wasn't permanent, but clearly that had not been the case.

Matthias stopped, leaned in as if to double-check, and then unlatched a door, braced himself against his cane, and pulled a slab out of the wall.

Jim knew it was the right body: From under the thin sheet, the summoning spell was at work, the pale phosphorescent glow bleeding through and glowing like his corpse was radioactive.

As Jim walked over to stand on the other side of his remains, he wasn't fooled by the fact that Matthias seemed to have wilted around his skeleton and was relying on the cane even as he stood without moving: The man was still a formidable, unpredictable opponent. After all, his mind and his soul had been the drivers of all those bad deeds, and until you were in your grave, they were with you wherever you went.

Lifting a hand, Matthias pulled the sheet back from Jim's face and laid the hem with curious care on his chest. Then, with a wince, the guy gripped his left arm and massaged as if something hurt.

"Look at you, Jim."

As Jim stared at the guy, he reveled in the instability he was about to create. Who knew being dead would be so useful?

On a shimmer, he revealed himself. "Surprise."

Matthias's head jerked up—and to give him credit, he didn't even flinch. There was no jump back, no flap of hands, not even a change in breathing. But then again, he probably would have been more surprised if Jim hadn't made an appearance: The currency of trade in XOps was the impossible and unexplained.

"How did you manage this." Matthias smiled a little as he nodded down at the body. "The match is uncanny."

"It's a miracle," Jim drawled.

"So you were just waiting for me to show up? Wanted a reunion?"

"I want to talk about Isaac."

"Rothe?" Matthias's one eyebrow lifted. "You're past your deadline. You were supposed to kill him yesterday—which means tonight we don't have anything to say to each other about that. We do have business, however."

So not a surprise that Matthias outed an autoloader and pointed it squarely at Jim's chest.

Jim smiled coldly. And it so wasn't hard to imagine that Devina had taken this man over and was using him as a walking, talking weapon in her bid to get Isaac. The question was how to disarm her nasty little puppet, and the answer was easy.

The mind . . . as Matthias had always said, the mind was the most powerful force for and against someone.

Jim leaned forward over his corpse until the muzzle was all but kissing his sternum. "So pull the trigger."

"You're wearing a vest, are you?" Matthias twisted his wrist so that the weapon pivoted and made a little knot out of Jim's black T-shirt. "Helluva lot of faith you're putting in it."

"Why are you still talking." Jim braced his palms on the cold steel table. "Pull the trigger. Do it. Pull it."

He was well aware he was creating a problem for himself: If Matthias popped him, and he didn't pull the standard-issue drop-and-flop that humans did, there was going to be hell to pay on the holy-shit front. But it was worth it just to see—

The gun went off, the bullet shot out . . . and the wall behind Jim ate the lead. As the ringing sound echoed around the tiled room, rank confusion flickered over the cruel mask of Matthias's face . . . and Jim felt a fuckload of pure triumph.

"I want you to leave Isaac alone," Jim said. "He's mine."

The sense that he was bartering with Devina over the guy's soul was so strong it was like he'd been destined to have this moment with his former boss . . . as if the sole reason he'd dragged the bastard out of that sandy hellhole and risked his own life to get him to a clinic had been for this conversation, this negotiation, this exchange.

And the feeling got even sharper as Matthias balanced on his cane and eased forward to put the business end of that gun right back against Jim's chest.

"The definition of insanity," Jim murmured, "is doing the same thing over again and expecting a—"

The second shot went off exactly as the first had: loud sound, slug in the wall, Jim still standing.

"—different result," he finished.

Matthias's hand shot out and grabbed onto Jim's leather jacket. As the cane dropped on the floor and bounced, Jim smiled, thinking this shit was better than Christmas.

"You want to shoot me again?" he asked. "Or are we going to talk about Isaac?"

*"What are you."*

Jim grinned like a crazy motherfucker. "I'm your worst nightmare. Someone you can't touch and you can't control and you can't kill."

Matthias slowly shook his head back and forth. "This isn't right."

"Isaac Rothe. You're going to let him go."

"This doesn't . . ." Matthias used Jim's jacket as a counterbalance while he shifted to the side and looked at the wall that had been cosmetically wounded. "It isn't right."

Jim gripped that fist and squeezed hard, feeling the bones compress. "Do you remember what you always tell people?"

Matthias's eye flipped back to Jim's face. "What. Are. You."

Jim jerked the two of them together so their noses were an inch apart. "You always tell people there's no one you can't take, nowhere you can't find them, nothing you won't do to them. Well, that would be a right-back-at-you. Let Isaac go and I won't make your life a living hell."

Matthias stared hard into his eyes, probing, seeking information. God, this was a head trip in a good way. For once, the man who had all the answers was off his game and floundering.

Christ, if Jim was still alive, he'd take a picture of that puss and make a calendar of the damn thing.

Matthias rubbed the eye that was visible, like he was hoping what vision he had left would clear and he'd find himself alone—or at least the only person standing in the embalming room.

"What are you?" he whispered.

"I'm an angel sent from Heaven, buddy." Jim laughed low and hard. "Or maybe I'm the conscience you were born without. Or maybe I'm a hallucination from all the prescription meds you need to control your pain. Or maybe this is just a dream. But whatever the case, there is only one truth you need to know—I'm not letting you take Isaac. That's not going to happen."

The two held eyes and stayed that way as Matthias's brain clearly churned.

After a long moment, the man apparently decided to go with what was in front of him. After all, what was it that Sherlock Holmes had said? When you eliminate the impossible, whatever remains, however improbable, must be the truth.

Therefore, he clearly concluded that Jim was some flavor of alive: "Why is Isaac Rothe so important to you?"

Jim released the grip on his old boss. "Because he is me."

"Just how many more of 'you' are out there? We've got this thing on the slab—"

"Isaac wants out. And you're going to let him go."

There was a long silence. And then Matthias's voice changed, growing softer and grimmer. "That soldier is full of state secrets, Jim. The knowledge he's accumulated is worth a shitload to our enemies. So, news flash, it's really not a case of what you or he wants. It's what is best for us—and before you go all bleeding-heart indignant on my ass, the 'us' is not you and me, or XOps. It's the fucking country."

Jim rolled his eyes. "Yeah, right. And I'll bet all that patriotic bullshit gives Uncle Sam a hard-on. But it doesn't do shit for me. The bottom line is . . . if you were in the civilian population, you'd be a serial killer. Working for the government means you get to wave the American flag around when it suits you, but the truth is, you do what you do because you enjoy picking the wings off of flies. And everybody's an insect in your eyes."

"My proclivities don't change a thing."

"And because of them, you serve no one but yourself." Jim brushed at the pair of burn marks on the front of his shirt. "You've taken XOps over as your own personal death factory, and if you're smart, you'll duck out yourself before some of these 'special assignments' come back to bite you on the ass."

"I thought you were here to talk about Isaac."

Little too close to a nerve, huh? "Fine. He's smart, so he can keep himself out of enemy hands, and he's got no incentive to turn."

"He's alone. He has no money. And people get desperate quick."

"Fuck that—he's got a sterling record and he's going to disappear."

The corner of Matthias's mouth inched up. "And how would you know that. Oh, wait, you've already found him, haven't you."

"You can let him go. You have the power to do this—"

"No, I don't!"

The explosion was a surprise, and as the words faded in the same way the gunshots had, Jim found himself looking around the room for verification that he'd heard that right. Matthias was all-powerful. Always had been. And not just in his own eyes.

Hell, the bastard had enough clout to turn the Oval Office into a mausoleum.

Now Matthias was the one leaning in over the corpse. "I don't give a fuck what you think about me or how your inner Oprah has spun this whole situation. It is *not* about what I want. . . . It's what I'm compelled to do."

"Innocent people have died."

"So that the corrupt could! Christ, Jim, this whaaa-whaaa bullshit coming from you is ridiculous. Good people die every day and you can't stop it. I'm just a different kind of bus mowing them down—and at least I have a larger purpose."

Jim felt a wave of anger crest—but then as he thought about it all, the emotion ebbed into something else. Sadness, maybe.

"I should have let you die in that desert."

"Which is what I *asked* you to do." Matthias grabbed onto his own left arm again and dug in, like he'd just been sucker punched in the pit. "You should have followed the orders I gave to leave me there."

So hollow, Jim thought. The words were so hollow and dead. As if they were about someone else entirely.

"Compelled," indeed. The guy had wanted to get out so much he'd been willing to kill himself to do it. But Devina had pulled him back in; Jim was sure of it. That demon and her thousand faces and her countless lies were at work here. Had to be. And hadn't her manipulations set the scene perfectly for the battle over Isaac: that solider had done evil, but was trying to start over, and this was his crossroads, this tug-of-war between Jim and Matthias over his what-next.

Jim shook his head. "I'm not going to let you take Isaac Rothe's life. I can't. You say you work with a purpose—so do I. You kill that man and humanity's lost more than an innocent."

"Oh, come on. He is *not* innocent. His hands drip with blood just like yours and mine. I don't know what's happened to you, but don't romanticize the past. You know *exactly* what he's guilty of."

Pictures of dead men flashed in front of Jim's eyes: stab wounds, gunshots, leaky faces and crumpled bodies. And those were just the messy jobs. The stiffs who'd been asphyxiated or gassed or poisoned had just been gray and gone.

"Isaac wants out. He wants to stop. His soul is desperate for a different way and I'm going to get him there."

Matthias winced and went back to rubbing his left arm. "Want in one hand, shit in the other—see what you get the most of."

"I'll kill you," Jim said simply. "If it comes down to it— I'll kill you."

"Well, what do you know ... there's a news flash. To quote yourself, do it now."

Jim slowly shook his head again. "Unlike you, I don't pull the trigger unless I have to."

"Sometimes getting a jump on the showdown is the smartest move, Jimmy."

The old name momentarily flipped him back into the past, back to basic training, back to sharing a bunk with Matthias. The guy had been cold and calculating then ... but not through and through. He'd been as loyal as someone could be to Jim, given their situation. Over the years, however, any trace of that limited slice of humanity had been lost—until the man's body was now as mauled and decrepit as his soul.

"Let me ask you something," Jim drawled. "You ever met a woman named Devina?"

That one eyebrow arched. "Now why would you ask that?"

"Just curious." He straightened his leather jacket. "FYI, I've had a devil of a time with her."

"Thanks for the dating advice. That's *really* my priority right now." Matthias returned the sheet back over Jim's cold gray face. "And feel free to kill me anytime. You'd be doing me a favor."

Those last words were spoken softly—and proved that physical pain could bow even the fiercest of wills if it was strong enough and lasted long enough. Then again, Matthias had had a shift of priorities even before that explosion, hadn't he.

246 J. R. Ward

"You know," Jim said, "you could take off as well. I did. Isaac's trying. There's no reason if you don't have the stomach for this anymore that you can't get out, too."

Matthias laughed in a burst. "You left XOps only because I let you go temporarily. I always intended to get you back. And Isaac is not getting away from me—the only way I would consider not offing him is if he would continue to work for the team. In fact, why don't you tell him that for me? Given that you two are so buddy-buddy and all."

Jim narrowed his eyes. "You've never done that before. Once someone's broken the trust, you've never let them back in."

Matthias exhaled on a raw shudder. "Times change."

Not always. And not about that shit. "Sure enough," Jim said on a lie. "Let's put me back in there, shall we?"

The two of them slid the slab into the refrigerator unit and Jim relatched the door. Then Matthias slowly bent down to pick up his cane, his spine cracking a number of times, his breath hitching as if his lungs couldn't handle their job as well as the pain he was feeling. When he righted himself, his face was an unnatural red—proof of how much the simple movement had taken out of him.

A broken vessel, Jim thought. Devina was working with or through a broken vessel here.

"Did any of this really happen?" Matthias said. "This conversation."

"The whole damn thing is real, but you're going to take a little nap now." Before the guy could ask, Jim brought up his hand and summoned power to his forefinger. As the tip began to glow, Matthias's mouth dropped open. "You'll remember what was said, however."

With that, he touched Matthias on the forehead and a shimmer of light went through the man like a struck match, flaring fast and bright, consuming both the broken body and the evil mind.

Matthias went down like a stone.

Angel Ambien, baby, Jim thought. Knocks out the best of 'em.

And as he stood over his boss, the back-flat was just too fucking metaphorical: The man had fallen in more ways than just in the here and now.

Jim didn't believe for one second that the guy was sincere about taking Isaac back into the fold. That was just a draw to get the soldier within shooting range.

God knew Matthias was an excellent liar.

Jim bent down and put the man's gun back into its holster; then he slipped his arms behind the guy's knees and under his shoulders—shit, the cane. He reached across, picked it up, and laid the thing right down the center of the man's chest.

Standing up was a breeze, and not just because Jim had strong shoulders. Damn . . . Matthias was so light; too light for the size of his frame. He couldn't have weighed more than a buck fifty, whereas in his prime he'd been well into the two hundreds.

Jim walked through the closed doors of the embalming room and went up the stairwell to ground level.

Back in the desert, when he'd done this the first time with the fucker, he'd been prickling with adrenaline, on a race to get his boss back to camp before the fucker bled out—so that he wouldn't be accused of murder. Now, he was calm. Matthias was not about to die, for one thing. For another, they were both in a bubble of no-can-see and safely in the States.

Passing through the locked front door, he figured he'd take Matthias over to the guy's car—

"Hello, Jim."

Jim froze. Then twisted his head to the left.

Strike that about the "safely," he thought.

On the far side of the funeral home's lawn, Devina stood on the grass in her black stilettos, her long, gorgeous brunette hair curling down to her breasts, her little black dress hugging all those curves. Her perfect facial features, from those black eyes to those red lips to that alabaster skin, positively glowed with health.

Evil had never looked so good.

But then again, that was part of her surface appeal, wasn't it.

"What you got there, Jimmy," she said. "And wherever are you going with him."

Like the bitch didn't already know, he thought, wondering how in the hell he was going to get out of this one.

# CHAPTER
## 26

From his vantage point in Grier's pantry, Isaac could hear what was being said out in the kitchen—but he couldn't see a damn thing.

Not that he needed a visual.

"Tell me where Isaac Rothe is," Grier's father repeated in a voice that had all the warmth of a January night.

Grier's response was just as chilly. "I was hoping you'd come here to apologize."

"Where is he, Grier."

There was the sound of running water and then the flapping of a dish towel. "Why do you want to know."

"This isn't a game."

"I didn't think it was. And I don't know where he is."

"You're lying."

There was a heartbeat of a pause, during which Isaac squeezed his eyes shut and counted the ways in which he was an asshole. For shit's sake, he'd brought a wrecking ball into the woman's life, crashing through her relationships both personal and professional, creating chaos everywhere—

Footsteps. Hard and sharp. A man's. "You tell me where he is!"

"Let go of me—"

Before he knew he was blowing his cover, Isaac burst out of hiding, throwing the door wide. It took him three leaping steps to get to the pair of them and then he was all over Grier's pops, swinging the man around and shoving him face-first up against the refrigerator. Palming the back of the guy's head, he pushed that patrician piehole into the stainless steel so hard, good ol' Mr. Childe's panting breath left little clouds of condensation on the panel.

"I'm right here," Isaac growled. "And I'm a little twitchy at the moment. So how about you don't handle your daughter like that again, and I'll consider not opening the freezer section with your face."

He expected Grier to pull a let-him-go, but she did no such thing. She just took a box of Band-Aids out from under the sink and fiddled around choosing the right size.

Her father heaved a deep breath. "Get away . . . from my daughter."

"He's just fine where he is," she answered, as she wrapped a strip around her index finger. Then she put the box away and crossed her arms over her chest. "You, however, can leave."

Isaac briefly frisked her father's fancy-ass sweater and superpressed pants, and when he didn't find a weapon, he stepped away, but stayed close. He had a feeling the guy had gotten physical because he was scared to death and about to crack—but no one handled Isaac's woman like that. Period—

Not that Grier *was* his woman. Of course not.

Damn it.

"You know you're giving her a death sentence," Childe said, his eyes boring into Isaac's. "You know what he's capable of. He owns you and he'll mow down whoever he has to in order to get to you."

"Nobody owns anybody," Grier cut in. "And—"

Mr. Childe didn't spare his daughter a glance as he cut her off. "Give yourself up, Rothe—it's the only way to be sure he doesn't hurt her."

"That man's not going to do anything to me—"

Childe wheeled around on Grier. "He already killed your brother!"

In the aftermath of that drama bomb, it was as if someone had slapped her—except there was no one to hold back from her, no guy to yank free and disarm and immobilize. And as Grier went white, Isaac felt a paralyzing impotence. You couldn't protect people from events that had already happened; there was no rewriting history.

Or . . . people, either. Which was the root of so many problems, wasn't it.

"What . . . did you say?" she whispered.

"That was no accidental overdose." Childe's voice cracked. "He was killed by the same man who's going to come after you unless he gets this soldier back. There is no negotiating, no bargaining, no terms to trade. And I can't—" The man started to break down, proving that money and class were no protection against tragedy. "I can't lose you as well. Oh, God, Grier . . . I can't lose you, too. And he will do it. That man will take your life in the blink of an eye."

Shit.

Shit, shit, shit.

As Grier braced herself against the counter, she was having trouble processing what her father had said. The words had been short and simple. The meaning, however . . .

She was half-aware that he was still talking, but she'd gone deaf after, "That was no accidental overdose." Stone deaf.

"Daniel . . ." She had to clear her throat as she cut in. "No, Daniel did it himself. He'd OD'd at least twice before. He . . . It was the addiction. He—"

"The needle in his arm was put there by someone else."

"No." She shook her head. "*No*. I was the one who found him. I called nine-one-one and—"

"You found the body ... but I saw it happen." Her father let out a sob. "He made me ... watch."

As her father buried his face in his hands and lost it completely, her vision flickered in and out like someone was playing disco with the lights in the kitchen. And then her knees went loose and—

Something caught her. Kept her from hitting the floor. Saved her.

The world spun ... and she realized she'd been picked up and was being carried over to the couch across the way.

"I can't breathe," she said to no one in particular. Wrenching at the neckline of her shirt, she gasped. "I can't ... breathe. . . ."

Next thing she knew, Isaac was putting a paper bag up to her mouth. She tried to bat it away, but her arms just flopped uselessly and she was forced to breathe into the thing.

"You need to shut the fuck up," Isaac said to somebody. "Right now. Pull it together, my man, and zip it up good."

Was he talking to her father? Maybe.

Probably.

Oh, God ... Daniel? And her father had been forced to *see* it happen?

Questions that needed answers did more for her than the carbon dioxide influx. Shoving the bag away, she pushed herself up.

"How? Why?" She shot both of them hard stares. "And listen, I'm already pretty damn deep in this situation, right? So some explanations are not going to hurt—they will, however, keep me from going insane."

Isaac's jaw got to grinding, like his foot was being chewed raw by a Doberman but he didn't want to let a scream out.

Not her problem. "I will go insane," she said before turning to her father. "Do you hear me? I can't live like this for one minute, one second . . . one *moment* longer. Not after that bombshell. You'd better start talking. Now."

Her father all but fell into the armchair beside her, as if he were ninety years old and making the descent to his deathbed. But just as he had not cared about the cut on her hand, she didn't grant him any mercies—and that was a shame. They had always been alike, in tune, of one mind. Tragedies, secrets, and lies, however, frayed even the closest of ties.

"Talk," she demanded. "Now."

Her father looked at Isaac, not her. But at least when Isaac shrugged and cursed, she knew she was going to get *a* story. Although probably not *the* story.

And how sad not to be able to trust her own father.

His voice was not strong when he finally began to speak. "I was first recruited to join XOps back in 1964. I was graduating from West Point and I was approached by a man who identified himself as Jeremiah. No last name. The thing I remember most about the meeting was how anonymous he was—he looked more like an accountant than a spy. He said there was an elite military arm that I qualified for and asked if I would be interested in learning more. When I wanted to know why me—after all, I was third in the class, not first—he said grades were not everything."

Her father paused for quite a while, as if he were remembering the exchange nearly fifty years later word for word. "I was interested, but ultimately I said no. I'd already joined the army as an officer and it seemed dishonorable to pull out of the commitment. I didn't see him again . . . until seven years later, when I had transitioned back into civilian life and was getting out of law school. I don't know why I said yes exactly . . . but I was getting married to your mother, and I was joining the family firm . . . and it felt like my life was over. I craved excitement, and there didn't seem . . ." He frowned and abruptly glanced over at her. "This is not to suggest that I didn't love your mother. I just needed . . . something more."

Ah, but she knew how he felt. She lived with that same itch for an edge that ordinary life didn't seem to offer.

The consequences of feeding it, however? Not worth it, she was coming to believe.

Her father took out a monogrammed handkerchief and dried his eyes. "I told Jeremiah—the man who had come to see me—that I couldn't disappear from life altogether, but that I was interested in something, anything else. That's how it started. Eventually, I was regularly going on intelligence missions overseas and our law firm gave me leeway because I was the founder's grandson. I never knew the full scope of the assignments I was given as an operative . . . but from newspapers and television, I was aware that there were consequences. That actions were taken against certain individuals—"

"You mean murders," she cut in bitterly.

"Assassinations."

"Like there's a difference?"

"There is." Her father nodded. "Murders are purposeless."

"The result is the same."

When he didn't say anything else, she was so not willing to have the story end there. "What about Daniel."

Her father exhaled long and slow. "About seven or eight years into it, it dawned on me that I was a part of something I couldn't live with. The phone calls, the people coming to the house, the trips that would last for days, weeks . . . to say nothing of the consequences of my actions. I stopped being able to sleep or concentrate. And God, the toll on your mother had been tremendous and it impacted the two of you as well—you were both young then, but you recognized the tensions and the absences. I started trying to get out." Her father's eyes flipped to Isaac. "That's when I discovered . . . that you don't get out. Looking back on it, I was naive . . . so damned naive. I should have known better, given what I'd been asked to do, but I'd gotten caught up in it all. Still, I had no choice. It was killing your mother . . . she was drinking heavily. And then Daniel started . . ."

*Doing drugs*, Grier finished in her mind. It had begun in middle school for him. First booze, then pot . . . then LSD and 'shrooms. And then the hard-core contact sport of cocaine, followed by the mellow morgue feeder that was heroin.

Her father refolded his handkerchief with precision. "When my initial overtures about leaving were met with a resounding 'no,' I became paranoid that on one of my assignments they were going to kill me and make it look like an accident. I stayed silent for years. But then I learned something I shouldn't have, something that was a game changer for an important man of power. I tried . . . I tried to use it as a key to unlock the door."

"And . . ." she interjected, her heart was pounding so loudly she wondered if the neighbors could hear it.

Silence.

"Go on," she prompted.

He just shook his head.

"Tell me," she choked out, hating her father as she remembered walking in and seeing Daniel that last time. He'd had a needle sticking out of a vein in the back of his arm and his head had been back, his mouth slack, his skin the color of winter snow clouds.

"If you don't answer me . . ." She couldn't finish. The idea that she might lose all of her family right here, right now closed her throat up tight.

That handkerchief was unbound once more with shaky hands. "The men approached me in the firm's parking garage downtown. I'd been working late and they . . . they put me in a car and I figured this was it. They were going to kill me. Instead, they drove me south to Quincy. To

Daniel's place. He was already high when we all walked in—I think ... I think he believed it was a practical joke. When he saw the syringe they'd brought, he offered them his arm—even though I was screaming for him not to let them—" Her father's voice broke. "He didn't care. . . . he didn't know. . . . I knew what they were doing—but he didn't. I should have ... They should have killed me, not him. They should have ..."

Rage made Grier's vision white out briefly. When it came back, the center of her chest was ice cold and she didn't care that he had suffered. Or had regrets or ...

"Get out of this house. Now."

"Grier—"

"I don't want to ever see you again. Don't contact me. Don't come near me—"

"Please—"

"Get out!" She shifted to Isaac. "Take him out of here— just get him away from me."

She'd do it herself, but she barely had enough strength to stand up.

Isaac didn't hesitate. He walked over to her father, hitched a hand under the guy's arm, and lifted him out of the armchair.

Her father was talking again, but she was deaf as he was escorted from the kitchen: The image of her brother's body on that ratty couch consumed her.

The small details were the killer: His eyes had been partially open, his pupils staring off sightlessly into the middle distance, and his faded blue T-shirt had been stained with dark patches under the armpits and vomit on the front. Three rusty spoons and a grubby yellow Bic lighter had littered the coffee table, and there had been a half-eaten pizza that looked a week old on the floor by his feet. The stuffy air had smelled of stale urine and cigarette smoke as well as something chemically sweet.

The thing that had stuck out the most, though, was that

she'd noticed his watch had stopped: When she'd called 911, they'd told her to see if there was a pulse and she'd gone for his nearest wrist. As she'd pulled it up and dug her fingers in, she'd seen that the timepiece was not the one their father had given him upon his graduation from U Penn—that Rolex had long ago been pawned off. What he'd had on was just a battery-operated Timex and the hands had frozen at eight twenty-four.

It was the same way that Daniel's body had just stopped. After all the beatings it had taken, it had finally run out of life.

So ugly. The scene had been so ugly. And yet his lovely hair had been the same. He'd always had a blond angel mop, as their mother had called it, and even on the slide into dead-and-gone, the curls on his head had retained their perfect circular nature: though the color was dingy from lack of washing, Grier had been able to see past that to the beauty that was.

Or had been, as it were.

Snapping out of the past, she rubbed her face and stood up from the sofa.

Then with all the grace of a zombie, she put the back stairs to use and went to her room—where she got a suitcase and started packing.

# CHAPTER
## 27

On the lawn at the McCready Funeral Home, Jim didn't waste a lot of time trying to figure out how Devina had known where to find him: She was here and the issue was how to get rid of her.

"Cat got your tongue, Jim." Her voice was just as he remembered it—low, smooth, deep. Sexy—provided you didn't know what was inside her skin.

"Nah. Not hardly."

"How have you been, by the way."

"I'm fan-fucking-tastic."

"Yes. You are." She smiled, showing perfect pearlies. "I've missed you."

"What a sap."

Devina laughed, the sound rolling through the chilly night air. "Not in the slightest."

As a car turned the corner and went by on the street, its headlights illuminated the front of the funeral home and the patches of brown in the lawn and the barely budding dogwood—and did absolutely nothing to Devina. Then again, she didn't really exist in this world.

The demon's eyes ran down him and then focused on Matthias. "Back to the issue at hand."

"There is no issue, Devina."

"I love when you say my name." She took a lazy step forward, but Jim wasn't fooled by the nothing-special. "Whatever are you going to do with him?"

"I was going to put him in his car to wake up. But now I'm thinking I'll fly him back to Boston."

"You'll find that he's too heavy, I'm afraid." Another step forward. "Are you worried that I'll do something bad to him?"

"Like you're a naughty little girl and are going to tie his shoelaces together? Yup. That's right."

"Actually, I have other plans for your old boss." A third step.

"Do you." Jim held his ground—literally and figuratively. "FYI, I'm not sure his plumbing works after all the injuries. I've never asked, but Cialis only goes so far."

"I have my ways."

"Undoubtedly." Jim bared his teeth. "I'm not going to let you take him, Devina."

"Isaac Rothe?"

"Both of them."

"Greedy. And I thought you didn't like Matthias."

"Just because I can't stand the bastard doesn't mean I want you to have him—or use him like a toy. Unlike the pair of you, I have a problem with collateral damage."

"How about we make a deal." Her smile was way too self-satisfied for his liking. "I let Matthias go along his merry way tonight. And you spend a little time with me."

His blood turned cold. "No, thanks. I have plans."

"Found someone else? Been unfaithful to me?"

"Not a chance. That would require a relationship."

"Which we have."

"Not." He glanced around just to double-check that she didn't have reinforcements. "I'm outta here, Devina. Have a nice night."

"I'm afraid Matthias is not going to make it."

"Nah, he's going to be just fine—"

"Will he." She extended her long, elegant hand.

All at once the man started to moan in Jim's arms, his face screwing down in agony, his frail limbs spasming.

"I don't have to even touch him, Jim." Curling her fingers up tight, like she was squeezing his heart in her palm, Matthias torqued hard. "I can kill him here and now."

With a curse, Jim combed through what he'd learned from Eddie, trying to pull a spell or an incantation or . . . something . . . out of his ass to stop the onslaught.

"I have toys by the thousands, Jim," she said softly. "Whether this one lives or dies? Means nothing. Affects nothing. Changes nothing. But if you don't like collateral damage? Then you better give yourself to me for the rest of the night."

Shit, put like that, why was he protecting the guy? She'd just find another source to influence Isaac's outcome. "Maybe it's better for you to put him in a grave."

At least Matthias would be out of his hair. Then again, maybe whoever was next in line would be worse.

"If I kill him now," Devina tilted her pretty head, "you'll have to live with the fact that you could have saved him but chose not to. You'll have to add another notch to that tattoo on your back, won't you. I thought you'd given that kind of thing up, Jim."

Rage boiled through his body, frothing his blood until his vision started to get wavy. "Goddamn you."

"What's it going to be, Jim."

Jim glanced down at his old boss's ruined face. The skin across the bone structure had turned an alarming gray color, and his mouth had cranked open even though his breath was shallow.

Fucking A . . .

Fucking *hell*.

On a curse, Jim turned away, started walking . . . and was entirely unsurprised when Devina materialized in his path.

"Where are you going, Jim?"

Christ, he wished she'd stop saying his frickin' name.

"I'm taking him to his car. And then you and I are leaving together."

The smile she gave him was radiant and made him sick to his stomach. But a trade was a trade and at least Matthias would live to see the next dawn—yeah, sure, there was undoubtedly some kind of death waiting in the wings for him, whether it was a physical collapse or his dirty deeds coming back to haunt him. Jim, however, wasn't going to make the call as to the "when" if he could avoid it. That was up to Nigel and his ilk—or whoever the hell was in charge of destinies.

Tonight, he was going to keep the man alive, and that was all he knew. Because even a sociopath deserved something better than falling prey to the likes of Devina.

And hopefully, Jim would make it through whatever she had planned for him with a little more information about what made her tick—and how to take her down.

Intel remained everything.

Back in Boston, Isaac put the hood of his windbreaker up to hide his face, and then frog-marched Grier's dad through her front door. Once they were outside, he was very aware of how exposed he was—hood or no hood, his identity was pretty damn obvious. But it was a cost/benefit situation: he didn't trust Childe and Grier wanted the guy gone.

So do the math.

As he hustled father dearest around to the driver's side of the Mercedes, the cold air seemed to tighten the man up, the remnants of the hard-core confron with his daughter getting replaced with a determination Isaac had to respect.

"You know what he's like," Childe said as he took out his key fob. "You know what he'll do to her."

The image of Grier's smart, kind eyes was inescapable. And yeah, he could just imagine the sort of shit Matthias would hurt her with. Kill her with.

Might even make the father watch again.

Might make Isaac play witness, too.

And didn't that make him want to throw up.

"The solution is within you," Childe said. "You know what the solution is."

Yes, he did. And it was a bitch.

"I beg you . . . save my daughter—"

From out of the shadows, Jim Heron's buddy with the piercings stepped forward. "Evenin', gents."

As Childe recoiled, Isaac grabbed the man's arm and held him in place. "Don't worry, he's with us." More loudly, he said, "What's up."

Shit, he needed to get back in the house here, boys.

"Thought you might like some help."

With that, the man stared at Childe like his eyes were a phone jack and he was plugging into a wall. Abruptly, Grier's father started to blink, his lids working Morse code, flip-flip, fliiiiiip, flip, flip. . . .

And then Childe said goodnight, calmly got in his car . . . and drove away.

Isaac watched the taillights turn the corner. "You want to tell me what you just did to that man?"

"Nope. But I've bought you some time."

"To do what?"

"Up to you. At least her father no longer believes he just saw you in that house—which means right now daddy-o isn't hopping on his cell phone and calling your old boss with where you are."

Isaac glanced around and wondered how many eyes were on him. "They already know I'm here. I'm about as undercover as the Vegas Strip at this point."

A large palm landed on his shoulder, heavy and strong, and Isaac froze as a flush went through him. The sense that the guy was powerful was not a surprise—like Jim would hang with anybody else? But there was something freaky about him, and it was not the dark gray metal hoops in his lower lip and his eyebrow and his ears.

His smile was positively ancient, and his voice suggested there were secrets all over his syllables as he spoke: "Why don't you go inside?"

"Why don't you tell me what the hell's going on?"

The guy didn't look thrilled with the hit back, but Isaac was so NMP'ing that one. He didn't give a shit if Jim's buddy gave birth to kittens from the upset—he needed some intel so things made sense.

Some sense.

Any sense.

Christ, this must be how Grier felt.

"I've bought you a night—that's all I can say. I strongly suggest you get in there and stay put until Jim comes back, but obviously I can't make you grow a brain."

"Who the fuck are you?"

Pierced leaned in. "We're the good guys."

With that, he jogged his hooped brow and Cary Granted it with a grin—

Then just like that, he was gone. Sure as if he was a light turned out. Except, come on, he must have walked off?

Isaac wasted a split second looking around, because, hello, most bastards—even the high-level spooks and assassins he'd been in the service with—couldn't disappear into thin air.

Whatever. He was a sitting duck out on this front stoop.

Isaac flashed back into the house, locked the door, and went into the kitchen. When he didn't find Grier, he leaned up the rear stairwell.

"Grier?"

He heard a distant reply and took the rear stairs two at a time. When he got to her room, he stopped in the doorway. Or skidded to a halt was more like it.

"No." He shook his head at her rich girl's flavor of Samsonite: That monogrammed luggage was so not going any-where. "Absolutely not."

She glanced over from the nearly filled suitcase. "I'm not staying here."

"Yeah, you are."

She pointed her forefinger at him like the thing was a gun. "I don't do well with people trying to order me around."

"I'm *trying* to save your life. And staying here where you're known and visible to a lot of people, where you have a job that you'll be missed at and appointments to keep and a security system like the one in this house is the way to stay alive. Going off to anywhere else just makes it easier for them."

Turning away, she pushed at the clothes she'd packed, her slender body bowing as she leaned into the shoving and made more room. Then she picked up a sweater and folded it in half and then in quarters.

As he watched how her hands shook, he knew he would do anything to save her. Even if it meant condemning himself.

"What did you say to my father?" she demanded.

"Not much. I don't trust him. No offense."

"I don't trust him, either."

"You should."

"How can you say that? God . . . the things he's kept from me—the things he's done . . . I can't . . ."

She began to tear up, but it was clear she didn't want the old haven-in-strong-arms routine from him: She cursed and marched into the bathroom.

Dimly, he heard her blow her nose and run some water. While she was in there, his hand went into his windbreaker's pocket and he palmed up the Life Alert. Death Alert was more like it: Help, I haven't fallen and I'm standing up—can you come and rectify this problem?

Grier remerged. "I'm leaving here with or without you. It's your choice."

"It's going to be without me, I'm afraid." He took his hand out.

She froze when she saw the device. "What are you doing with that?"

"I'm ending this. For you. Right now."

"*No!*"

He pressed the summons as she lunged for him, sealing his fate—and saving her—with a one-touch.

A little red light on the device started blinking.

"Oh, God . . . what have you done?" she whispered. "*What have you done?*"

"You're going to be fine." His eyes traced her face, memorizing yet again what was already etched into his mind forever. "That's all that matters to me."

As her eyes welled up, he stepped forward and captured a single, crystal tear on the pad of his thumb. "Don't cry. I've been a dead man walking since I bolted. This is nothing more than what would come to me eventually. And at least I can know you're safe."

"Take it back . . . undo it . . . you can—"

He just shook his head. There was no undoing anything— and he was realizing that fully now.

Destiny was a machine built over time, each choice that you made in life adding another gear, another conveyor belt, another assemblyman. Where you ended up was the product that was spit out at the end—and there was no going back for a redo. You couldn't take a peek at what you'd manufactured and decide, Oh, wait, I wanted to make sewing machines instead of machine guns; let me go back to the beginning and start again.

One shot. That was all you got.

Grier stumbled back and hit the edge of her bed, sinking down like her knees had gone out. "What happens now?"

Her voice was so quiet, he had to strain to catch the words. In contrast, he spoke loud and clear. "They'll be in touch with me. The device is a transmitter that sends a signal and it will receive their call. When they hit me back, I arrange for a place to turn myself in."

"So you could fake them out. Leave now—"

"It has a GPS in it so they know where I am every second."

So they knew he was here now.

But he didn't think they would kill him in her house—too much exposure. And Grier didn't know it, but as long as he turned himself in, she was going to be okay because her brother's death was going to keep her alive. Matthias was the ultimate chessman and he was going to want control over her father, given what the guy knew. Having already offed the son, it went without saying that XOps could do the same to the daughter—and as long as that threat was out there, the elder Childe was neutralized.

The man would do anything to keep from burying a second kid.

Grier's life was her own.

"My advice to you," he said, "is stay here. Work things out with your father—"

"How could you do that? How could you turn yourself over to—"

"I wasn't one of the team who murdered your brother—but I've done things like that." As she recoiled, he nodded. "I've gone into homes and killed people and left them where they landed. I've stalked men through forests and deserts and cities and oceans and I've taken them out. I'm not . . . I'm not an innocent, Grier. I've done the worst things one human can do to another—and I got paid for it. I'm tired of carrying all those deeds around with me in my head. I'm exhausted from the memories and the nightmares and the on-edge twitch. I thought running was the answer, but it's really not, and I just can't live with myself any longer. Not one more night. Besides, you're a lawyer. You know the statutes for murder. This"—he dangled the Life Alert by its chain—"is the death sentence I deserve . . . and want."

Her eyes stayed locked on his. "No . . . no, I know the way you've protected me. I don't believe you're capable of—"

Isaac whipped off the windbreaker and sweatshirt and turned around, flashing her the massive tattoo of the Grim Reaper that covered every inch of skin on his back.

At her gasp, he hung his head. "Look at the bottom. You see those marks? Those are my kills, Grier. Those are . . . how many brothers and fathers and sons I've put into graves. I am . . . not an innocent to be protected. I'm a murderer . . . who's simply getting what's coming to him."

# CHAPTER
## 28

As Adrian reappeared in the back forty of the lawyer's house, he once again took up res next to Eddie—who was doing an excellent imitation of an oak tree.

"You send the father off?" the other angel murmured.

"Yeah. I gave us enough time for Jim to get back here. He call yet?" Like, in the five minutes he'd been out front with Isaac.

"No."

"Damn it."

Frustrated at everything, Ad brushed at his arms, which were still steaming a little. Man, he hated smelling like vinegar—and gee, what do you know, the skirmish with Devina's Disposable Posse had ruined yet another fucking leather jacket. Which pissed him off.

He'd really liked this one.

Giving up, he refocused on the back of the house. Jim's superstrength spell was all ashimmer, the red glow sparkling in the night.

"Where the *hell* is Jim," Eddie growled as he checked his watch.

"Maybe a fight will come find us again." Ad forced himself to crack a smile. "Or I could go get us another girlie."

As Eddie cleared his throat and made like he was all Mr. I-So-Don't-Do-*That*, Ad knew better. The angel was a ferocious motherfucker once he dropped the buttoned-up routine—Rachel of the perfect teeth and no last name had been floating on air as they'd sent her off at dawn. And as much as it pained Ad to admit it, he had a feeling a lot of that postcoital blissed-out shit had been from Eddie's ministrations.

Bastard had a hell of a tongue, evidently—and good job he did. Ad had tried to get into the sex, but he'd ended up just going through the motions.

Eddie rechecked his watch. Looked at his phone. Glanced around. "What did you do to the father?"

"He thinks he came here and Isaac was gone already."

Eddie rubbed his face like he was exhausted. "I hope like hell Jim gets back soon—that Isaac character is going to bolt. I can feel it."

"Which is why I hit him with my magic palm." Adrian flexed the thing. "Jim likes GPS. I don't."

"At least TomToms don't sing like you do."

"Why is everyone else in the world tone-deaf?"

"I think it's the other way around."

"Feh."

A breeze whistled through the bare limbs of the budding fruit trees and both of them stiffened . . . but it wasn't round two of Devina's disposables rolling in. Just the wind.

The long wait grew longer.

And even longer-er.

To the point where Adrian's natural tendency to be in movement itched up his spine and had him cracking his neck. Over and over again.

"How you doing?" Eddie said softly.

Oh, great. Like the caring-sharing shit would help him relax? Even on a good night, that routine gave him the urge to run around the block a couple hundred times.

"Ad?"

"I'm fine. Dandy. Yourself?"

"I'm serious."

"And we're not going there."

Little pause . . . liiiiiittle happy pause that was drenched and dripping in Eau de Disapproval. "You can talk about it," Eddie countered. "I'm just saying."

Oh, for chrissakes. He knew the guy was just being all about the buddy-I-got-your-backs, and it wasn't that he didn't appreciate the effort. But after Devina had had at him this last time, his insides were loose and sloppy, and if he didn't weather-strip his door, dead-bolt it and toss out his welcome mat, things were going to get messy. In ways that couldn't be cleaned up.

"And I'm telling you, I'm good. But thanks."

To cut off the convo, he focused on the house. God, that "low-level" spell of Jim's was so strong . . . as strong as anything Adrian and Eddie could pull off under the full leverage of their powers. Which might well mean that that angel had tricks which could seriously fuck with Devina—

The soft chiming of Eddie's phone was good news: There was only one person who could be calling and that was Jim.

Adrian glanced over when Eddie didn't accept the call. "You're not answering?"

Eddie shook his head. "He sent us a picture. Network's slow tonight—it's still coming up."

You'd think with all the shit they could do, they'd be able to communicate telepathically—and to some degree, they were able to. But long distances were kind of like shouting across to the other side of a football stadium. Also, if someone was injured or dying, the ability to pull off stuff like spells and incantations and mind thoughts—

"Oh . . . God . . ."

As Eddie's voice broke, Adrian felt a premonition pour over his head like cold blood. "What."

Eddie started to scramble with the phone's buttons.

Ad grabbed for the cell. "Don't you erase it—don't you fucking—"

A couple of quick lunges and they were in a full-out fight for the phone—and Adrian won only because desperation made him lightning fast.

"Don't look at it," Eddie barked. "Don't look—"

Too. Late.

The little image on the glossy screen was of Jim naked and splayed out on a huge wooden table, arms wide, legs wide. Metal wire was wound around his wrists and ankles to pin him down, and his skin was lit by candlelight. His erect cock had a leather strap wrapped around the base to keep it hard—but although he was technically aroused, he wasn't juiced for the sex; that was for sure. . . . and Adrian knew exactly what Devina did to get the initial blood flow where she wanted it.

That tourniquet was going to give her something to play with for hours and hours.

Adrian swallowed, his throat tightening up sure as if he were on those hard, oily boards himself. He knew all too well what was coming next.

And he knew what those shadowy figures lurking in the background were.

The texted caption under the photo: *My New Toy*.

"We've got to get him out of there." Adrian nearly crushed the phone from the way his hand tightened around it. "That fucking *bitch*."

Lying on Devina's "worktable," as she called it, Jim didn't bother looking at her—not even when she got his phone out and a flash went off. What he was primarily concerned with were the dark figures that circled the periphery like they were dogs about to get set loose: He had a feeling they were the same things he and the boys had fought outside of that lawyer's house, because they moved with that shifty, snakelike undulation.

Whatever. Chances were good he was going to know one way or the other in not long at all.

Thanks to the curtain of darkness that surrounded him, he had no conception of the number of them or the size of the room: The candlelight threw only so much illumination, and the wax-and-wick numbers were set at intervals of a couple of feet around him.

So this was how a birthday cake felt: kinda worried, given that all your delicate frosting was damn close to open flames.

Plus you were on the verge of getting eaten.

Devina stepped into the light and smiled like the angel she absolutely wasn't. "Comfortable?"

"I could use a pillow. But other than that, I'm good."

Hell, if she could lie, so could he. The truth was those wires around his ankles and wrists had barbs on them, so there were bands of pain at all his pulse points. He also had a high-fashion necklace of the same shit that made swallowing just a boatload of fun. And the table under him was coated in some kind of acid—most likely the blood from the things around the periphery.

Clearly, Devina had worked out a lot of demons on these planks, too.

He was willing to bet Adrian had been here. Eddie as well.

Oh, God . . . had the blond girl?

Jim closed his eyes, and on the backs of his lids, saw that lovely innocent strung up over that tub again. Shit, to hell with saving the world. He wished he could have traded himself for her.

Cold fingers drifted up the inside of his leg, and as they got closer and closer to his cock, sharp nails scraped his skin.

A strange sound percolated up, and for some reason it reminded him of deboning a chicken—lot of loose flapping and muffled cracking. Then there was an odd smell . . . like . . . what the fuck was it?

When Devina spoke next, her voice was warped, the tone deeper . . . lower and raspy. "I liked being with you before, Jim. Remember that? In your truck . . . but this is going to be so much better. Look at me, Jim. See the real me."

"I'm good like this. But thanks—"

Nails gouged into his balls, and then his sac was twisted hard. As the driving pain hit the neuron superhighway of his pelvic girdle, its fumes created a curdling nausea in his gut. Which of course had nowhere to go thanks to the collar clamped around his neck.

Yup, dry heaves were all he had to offer, because nothing was going to evac up his throat.

"Look at me." More with the wrenching.

His gaping mouth took its own sweet time getting his reply out. Then again, it was busy trying to accommodate the gulps of air he was taking. ". . . No . . ."

Something mounted him. He didn't know who or what it was, because there were suddenly hands all over him, the gates unleashed—

No, not hands. Mouths.

With sharp teeth.

As his cock penetrated something that had all the softness and slickness of a rusted-out sink drain, the first of the cuts were made on his chest. Might have been a blade. Might have been a long fang.

And then something blunt was forced into his mouth. Tasting salt and flesh, he figured it was some kind of cock and he started to choke, air suddenly becoming a scarce commodity.

Riding the crest of suffocation, he had a moment of total, autonomic flip-out. It was, however, a case of mind over body. The faster his heart pounded, the worse the lack of oxygen was and the brighter and hotter the flaring agony inside his rib cage.

Slow down, he told himself. Slow it all down. Just slooooooooooooooooooow down. . . .

Higher reasoning reigned and got the reins on his body: His pounding blood cooled and his lungs learned to wait for the withdrawals from his mouth to sneak a breath.

Frankly, he wasn't impressed. Sexual shit was so unimaginative when it came to torture.

This wasn't going to be a walk in the park, for real. But Devina wasn't going to break him with this violation bullshit. Or by trying to fillet his fish with the knife work. The thing with pain was, yeah, sure, it lit up your switchboard, but really, it was nothing more than a loud sensation — and like going to a concert and having your eardrums compensate over time, eventually you got used to it.

Besides, he had vast reserves of strength: Matthias had lived another day, his boys were hanging with Grier and Isaac, and while he would have preferred a time-out at Disney World or Club Med instead, the power of doing the right thing and sacrificing himself for another's well-being was sustenance for every cell in his body.

He was going to make it through this.

And then he was going save Isaac's soul and laugh in Devina's face at the end of this round.

The bitch couldn't kill him and was not going to get the best of him.

Game on.

# CHAPTER
# 29

As Grier stared across her bedroom at the tattoo that covered Isaac's back, her hands crept up and curled around her neck.

The image in his skin was done in black and gray and was so vividly drawn, the Grim Reaper seemed to be staring right out at her: The great black-robed figure stood in a field of graves that stretched in all directions, skulls and bones littering the ground at its feet. From beneath the hood, two white spots glowed above the hard jut of a fleshless jaw. One skeletal hand was on the scythe handle, and the other reached forward, pointing at her chest.

And yet that wasn't the most terrifying part.

Underneath the depiction, there was a row of lines grouped in bundles of four with a diagonal line bunching each one. There had to be at least ten of those. . . .

"You've killed . . ." She couldn't get the rest of the sentence out.

"Forty-nine. And before you think I'm glorifying what I've done, each of us has this in our skin. It's not voluntary."

That was nearly ten a year. One a month. Lives lost at his hands.

With a quick, slashing movement, Isaac pulled his windbreaker and sweatshirt down—and just as well. That tattoo was terrifying.

Turning to face her, he met her squarely in the eye and seemed to be waiting for a response.

All she could think about was Daniel ... God, Daniel. Her brother was a notch on the back of one or some of those soldiers, a little line drawn by a needle, marked permanently in ink.

She had been tattooed, too, by the death. On the inside. The sight of him dead and gone—and now the stain of the details of that night—were forever on her mind.

And it was the same for what she'd found out about her father's other life. And Isaac's.

Grier braced her hands on her knees and shook her head. "I don't have anything to say."

"I don't blame you. I'm going to leave—"

"About your past."

As she cut him off, she shook her head again. She'd been on a whirlwind since the moment he'd walked into that attorney-client room back at the jail. Caught up in a buzz, she'd spun faster and faster, from the run-in with that man with the eye patch to the sex to the showdown with her father ... to Isaac hitting the self-destruct button sure as if he'd pulled the pin out of a grenade.

But somehow, as soon as he'd done that, she felt as though the storm was over and done, the tornado having moved on to someone else's cornfield.

In the aftermath, everything seemed so clear and simple.

She shrugged and kept staring at him. "I really can't say anything about your past ... but I do have an opinion on your future." Her exhale was long and slow and sounded as exhausted as she felt. "I don't think you should turn yourself in to die. Two wrongs don't make a right. In fact, nothing can make what you did right, but you don't need me telling you that. What you've done is going to follow you around all the days of your life—it is a ghost that will never leave you."

And the dark shadows in his eyes told her he knew that better than anyone.

"To be honest, Isaac, I think you're being a coward." As his lids popped, she nodded. "It's so much harder to live with what you've done than go out in a blaze of self-righteous glory. You ever hear of suicide by cop? It's where a cornered gunman will fire once on a police barricade, and effectively force the badges to pump him full of bullets. It's for people who don't have the strength to face the reckoning they deserve. That button you pushed? Same thing. Isn't it."

She knew she'd hit the target by the way his face closed up, his features becoming a mask.

"The way to be brave," she continued, "is to be the one who stands up and exposes the organization. That is the right course of action. Shine the light no one else can on the evil you've seen and done and been. That is the only way to come close to making amends. God . . . you could stop this whole damn thing—" Her voice cracked as she thought of her brother. "You could stop it and make sure no one else gets sucked into it. You could help find the ones who are involved and hold them accountable. That . . . that would be meaningful and important. Unlike this suicidal bullshit. Which solves nothing, improves nothing . . ."

Grier got to her feet, closed the top of her suitcase, and snapped the brass latches down tight. "I don't agree with anything you've done. But you've got enough conscience in you to want to get out. The question is whether that impulse can take you to the next level—and that's got nothing to do with your past. Or me."

Sometimes reflections of yourself were exactly what you needed to see, Isaac thought. And he wasn't talking about the puss-in-the-mirror kind.

More like the eyes-of-others variety.

As Isaac frowned, he wasn't sure which was more of a shocker: the fact that Grier was totally right or that he was inclined to act on what she'd said.

Bottom line? She was spot-on: He had been on a suicidal bender ever since he'd broken away from the fold, and he wasn't the kind to hang himself in the bathroom—no, no, it was much manlier to be gunned down by a comrade.

What a pussy he was.

But that being said, he wasn't sure how coming forward would work. Who did he talk to? Who could he trust? And while he could see himself going all-info on Matthias and that second in command, he was not going to give up the identities of the other soldiers he'd worked with or knew about. XOps had gotten out of control under Matthias's rule and that man had to be stopped—but the organization wasn't entirely evil and did perform a necessary and significant service to the country. Besides, he had a feeling that if that boss of theirs was put away, most of the hardcores like Isaac would dissolve into the ether like smoke on a cold night, never again to do what they had done or speak of it: There were many like him, those who wanted out but were trapped by Matthias one way or another—and he knew this because there had been so much comment on Jim Heron's release.

Speaking of which . . .

He needed to get to Heron. If there was a way to do this, he needed to talk it over with the guy.

And Grier's father as well.

"Call your dad," he said to Grier. "Call him and get him back here. Right now." When she opened her mouth, he cut her off. "I know it's a lot to ask, but if there's another solution here, I'm damn sure he has better contacts than I do—because I've got *nada*. And as for your brother—shit, that's rat awful and I'm so very sorry. But what happened to him was the fault of someone else—it was not your father's doing. That's the thing. When you're being recruited, they don't tell you everything, and by the time you work out the reality for yourself, it's too late. Your father is way more innocent in this than I am, and he's had to lose a son over it. You're angry and you're devastated and I get that. So is he, though—and you saw it for yourself."

Even though her face went hard, her eyes welled up, so he knew she was listening.

Isaac grabbed the phone on the bedside table and held it out to her. "I'm not asking you to forgive him. Just please don't hate him. You do that and he's lost both his children."

"He already has, though." Grier swept a quick hand over her tears, wiping them clean. "My family's gone now. My brother and mother dead. My father . . . I can't bear the sight of him. I'm all alone."

"No, you're not." He jogged the receiver at her. "He's just a call away—and he's all you've got left. If I can man up . . . so can you."

Sure, he was taking a chance in presenting the idea of coming forward to her father, but the reality was that Childe's interests and his were aligned: They both wanted him the fuck away from Grier.

Staring into her eyes, he willed her to find the strength to stay connected to her blood, and he was very aware of why it was so important to him: As usual, he was being selfish. If he did come clean to some judge or congressional hearing, he was going to stay breathing for a while, but he'd be essentially dead to her as he got swept up into a witness protection program of some sort. Therefore, her father was the best shot she had at being protected.

The only shot.

Isaac shook his head. "The bad guy in this is the one you saw in the kitchen back at my apartment. He's the true evil. Not your father."

"The only way . . ." Grier wiped her eyes again. "The only way I can be anywhere around him is if he helps you."

"So tell him that when he gets here."

A moment later she straightened her shoulders and took the phone. "Okay. I will."

As a burst of emotion hit him, he had to stop himself from leaning in for a quick kiss—God, she was strong. So very strong. "Good," he said hoarsely. "That's good. And I'm going to go find my buddy Jim now."

Turning away, he went down the back stairwell, and rounded the landings with speed. He was praying that either Jim had returned or those two hard-asses out in the backyard could bring him in from wherever he was at.

Bursting through the kitchen, he hit the door out into the garden, opening it wide—

Over in the far corner, Jim's buddies were bookending a glowing cell phone, looking like they'd been kneed in the balls.

"What's wrong?" Isaac asked.

The pair glanced up and he immediately knew by those tight expressions that Jim was in the shit: When you worked on a team, there was absolutely nothing more gut-wrenching than if one of you got captured by the enemy. It was worse than a mortal wound in yourself or a teammate.

Because the enemy didn't always kill first.

"Matthias," Isaac hissed.

As the one with the thick braid shook his head, Isaac jogged down to them. Pierced was looking green, positively green. "Who then? Who has Jim? How can I help?"

Grier appeared in the open doorway. "My father will be here in five minutes." She frowned. "Is everything okay?"

Isaac just stared at the two guys. "I can help."

The one with the braid shut that right down: "No, I'm afraid you can't."

"Isaac? Who are you talking to?"

He glanced over his shoulder. "Friends of Jim's." He looked back—

The two men were gone, as if they had never been there in the first place. Again.

What. The. Fuck.

As the creep-o-meter on the back of Isaac's neck went wild, Grier walked over. "Was there someone here?"

"Ah ..." He looked all around. "I don't ... know. Come on, let's get inside."

Ushering her back into the house, he thought it was entirely possible he'd lost his damn mind.

After locking the door and watching Grier reengage the alarm, he sat down on a stool at the island and took out the Life Alert. No response yet and he hoped Grier's father got here before Matthias hit him back.

Best to have a plan.

In the silence of the kitchen, he stared at the cooktop as Grier took up res across the way, leaning back against the counter by the sink. It felt like a hundred years had come and gone since she'd made him that omelet the night before. And yet if he followed through on what he was contemplating, the next few days were going to make that seem like the blink of an eye in comparison.

Running through his brain, he tried to think of what he could say about Matthias. He knew a lot when it came to his old boss ... and yet the man had purposely created black holes in every operative's mental Milky Way: You were told only what you absolutely, positively had to know and not one syllable more. Some shit you could deduce, but there were vast patches of huh-what? that—

"Are you okay?" she said.

Isaac looked up in surprise, and thought he was the one who should be asking that of her. And what do you know, she had her arms around herself—a self-protective pose she seemed to fall into a lot when she was with him.

"I really hope you can patch it up with your father," he replied, hating himself.

"Are you okay?" she repeated.

Ah, yes, so both of them were playing dodge 'em.

"You know, you can answer me," she said. "With the truth."

It was funny. For some reason, maybe because he wanted to practice . . . he considered doing that. And then he actually did.

"The first guy I killed . . ." Isaac stared down at the granite, turning the slick expanse of stone into a TV screen and watching his own actions play out across the speckled surface. "He was a political extremist who had bombed an embassy overseas. It took me three and a half weeks to find him. I tracked him across two continents. Caught up with him in Paris, of all places. The city of love, right? I took him out in an alleyway. Sneaked behind him. Slit his throat. Which was a messy mistake—I should have snapped his—"

He stopped with a curse, well aware that his version of talking shop was hardly like some tax attorney yammering on about the IRS code.

"It was . . . shockingly uncomplicated for me." He looked at his hands. "It was like something came over me and put a lockdown on my emotions. Afterward? I just went out to eat. I had a steak with pepper—ate all of it. Dinner was . . . great. And it was while I was having that meal that I realized they'd chosen wisely. Picked the right guy. That was when I threw up. I went out the back of the restaurant, into an alley just like the one I'd murdered that man in an hour before. You see, I hadn't really believed I was a killer until it didn't bother me."

"Except it did."

"Yeah. Fuck—I mean, hell, yeah, it did." Although only that once. After that, he was good to go. Stone-cold. Ate like a king. Slept like a baby.

Grier cleared her throat. "How did they recruit you?"

"You won't believe it."

"Give it a shot."

"sKillerz."

"Excuse me?"

"It's a video game where you assassinate people. About seven or eight years ago, the first online gaming communities were getting big and integrated play had really caught on. sKillerz was created by some sick bastard—no one's ever met the guy, apparently—but he's a genius at graphics and realism. As for me? I had a head for computers and I liked"—to kill people—"I liked playing the game. Pretty soon there were hundreds of people in this virtual world—with all these weapons and identities in all these cities and countries. I was at the top of all of them. I had this, like . . . knack for knowing how to get to people and what to use and where to put the bodies. It was just a game, though. Something I did when I wasn't working on the farm. Then, about . . . about two years into it . . . I started to feel as though I was being watched. That went on for, like, a week, until one night this guy named Jeremiah showed up at the farm. I was working the back rails, mending fences, and he drove up in an unmarked."

"And what happened?" she asked when he paused.

"I've never told anyone this before."

"Don't stop." She came over and sat beside him. "It helps me. Well . . . it's disturbing, too. But . . . please?"

Right, okay. With her looking up at him with those big, beautiful eyes, he was prepared to give her anything: words, stories . . . the beating heart out of his chest.

Isaac rubbed his face and wondered when he'd become a sap—oh, wait, he knew that one: the moment he'd been escorted into that little room back at the jail and she'd been sitting there all prim, and proper, and smart as hell.

Sap.

Wuss.

Nancy.

"Isaac?"

"Yeah?" Well, what do you know—he could still answer to his own name and not just a bunch of ball-less nouns.

"Please . . . keep talking to me."

Now he was the one clearing his throat. "The Jeremiah guy invited me to come work for the government. He said he was with the military and they were looking for guys like me. I was all, 'Farm boys? Y'all looking for redneck farm boys?' And I'll never forget it . . . He stared right at me and said . . . 'You're not a farmer, Isaac.' That was it. But it was the way he said it—like he knew a secret about me. Whatever, though . . . I thought he was a moron and I told him so—I was wearing mud-soaked overalls and a John Deere hat and work boots. Didn't know what the hell else he thought I was." Isaac glanced over at Grier. "He was right, though. I was something else. Turned out the government had been monitoring *s*Killer*z* online and that's how they found me."

"What made you decide to start . . . working . . . for them?"

Nice euphemism.

"I wanted out of Mississippi. Always had. I left home two days later and I still have no interest in going back. And that body was of a kid who'd run his motorcycle off the road. At least, that's what they told me. They switched my ID and my Honda for his and there you go."

"What about your family?"

"My mother . . ." Okay, he had to really clear his throat here. "Mother had moved on from us before she died. Pop had five sons, but only two with her. I never got along with any of my brothers or him, so leaving was not a problem— and I wouldn't approach them now. Past is past and I'm okay with it."

At that moment the front door opened and from down the hall, her father called out, "Hello?"

"We're back here," Isaac answered, because he didn't

think Grier was going to: As she checked the security system, she suddenly looked too self-composed to speak.

As her father came into the room, the man was the opposite of his daughter: Childe was unraveled, his hair messed up like he'd been tearing at it with his hands, his eyes red-rimmed and glassy, his coat off-kilter.

"You're here," he said to Isaac in a tone full of dread. Which seemed to suggest whatever mind game Jim's buddy had played out front hadn't just been for show.

Nice trick, Isaac thought.

"I didn't tell him why I wanted him to come," Grier announced. "The cordless phone isn't secure."

Smart. So damned smart.

And as she remained quiet, Isaac decided he'd better drive the bus. Focusing on the other man, he said, "Do you still want a way out?"

Childe looked over at his daughter. "Yes, but—"

"What if there was a way to do it where . . . people"— read: Grier—"were safe."

"There isn't one. I've spent a decade trying to find it."

"You ever think of blowing the doors off Matthias?"

Grier's dad went stone still and he stared into Isaac's eyes like he was trying to see into the future. "As in . . ."

"Helping someone come forward to spill every single thing he knows about that fucker." Isaac glanced at Grier. " 'Scuse my mouth."

Childe's eyes narrowed, but the McSquinty routine wasn't in offense or mistrust. "You mean testifying?"

"If that's what it takes. Or shutting them down through back channels. If Matthias isn't in power anymore, everyone"—read: Grier—"is safe. I've turned myself in to him, but I want to take it one step farther. And I think it's about time the world got a clearer picture of what he's been up to."

Childe looked back and forth at him and Grier. "Anything. I'll do anything to get that bastard."

"Right answer, Childe. Right answer."

"And I can come forward, too—"

"No, you can't. That's my one stipulation. Set up the meetings, tell me who to go to, and then disappear from the mess. Unless you agree, I'm not going to do it."

He let dear old Dad put up a fight about that and spent the time looking at Grier in his peripheral vision. She was staring at her father, and though she stayed quiet, Isaac was willing to guess that the great chill was defrosting a little: Hard not to respect her old man, because he was dead serious about blabbing—if given the chance, he was prepared to spill everything he knew as well.

Unfortunately for him, however, the choice wasn't his. If this plan went tits up, Grier didn't need to lose the only family she had left.

"Sorry," Isaac said, cutting off the chatter. "That's the way it's going to be—because we don't know how this is going to go and I need you ... to still be standing at the end. I want you to leave as few fingerprints as possible on the rollout. You're already more involved than I feel comfortable with. Both of you."

Childe shook his head and held up a hand. "Now, hear me out—"

"I know you're a lawyer, but it's time to stop arguing. Now."

That gave the man pause, as if he wasn't used to being addressed in that kind of tone. But then he said, "All right, if that's what you insist."

"It is. And it's my only nonnegotiable."

"Okay."

The guy paced around. And paced around. And ... then he stopped right in front of Isaac.

Holding up a hand to his chest, he formed a circle with his forefinger and thumb. Then he spoke, his words crystal clear and tinged with appropriate anxiety. "Oh, God, what am I thinking . . . I can't do this. This is not right. I'm sorry, Isaac . . . I can't do it. I can't help you."

Just as Grier opened her mouth, Isaac caught her and squeezed her wrist to shut her up: Her father was now surreptitiously pointing in the direction of what had to be the basement stairs.

"Are you sure," Isaac asked him in a warning tone. "I need you and I think you're making a huge mistake."

"You're the one making a mistake, son. And I'd be calling Matthias right this second if you hadn't already done it yourself. I will not be a part of any conspiracy against him—and I refuse to help you." Childe let out a curse. "I need a drink."

With that, he turned away and headed across the room.

At which point, Grier grabbed the front of Isaac's windbreaker and yanked him head-to-head with her. In a nearly silent hiss, she said, "Before either of you even *thinks* of hitting me with another round of classified-info crap, you can shut it."

Isaac popped his brows clear to his hairline as her father opened the door to the cellar.

Shit, he thought. But she obviously was not going to budge on this one. Besides, maybe being involved would help her and her father patch things up.

"Ladies first," Isaac whispered, indicating the way with a gallant hand.

# CHAPTER
## 30

*Heaven, South Lawn*

Nigel granted an audience to his two favorite warrior angels not out of the goodness of his heart and not with anticipation—and in spite of the fact that he and Colin, Bertie, and Byron were in the midst of a repast. There would be no turning these visitors away, however: He knew why Edward and Adrian were coming and they were not going to like what he had to say.

Thus he felt as though he should handle them in person.

And indeed, when the two angels took form far across the lawn, they strode o'er to the grove like the avengers they were.

"I'm terribly sorry," Nigel murmured to his advisors, "but will you please excuse me for a moment."

He folded his damask napkin and rose, thinking there was no reason to ruin the meal for the others—and what was about to transpire verbally was going to be a gastronomic murder of the very bloodiest sort.

Colin got up as well. Nigel would have much preferred to do this alone, but there would be no dissuading the angel. No one and nothing could change Colin's mind about what to have for his pudding, much less on matters of import.

He and Colin met their visitors halfway between where the pair had entered and where the fine table was set amongst the elm trees.

"She has him," Edward said as the four of them came together. "We don't know how it happened—"

Nigel cut the angel off. "He gave himself so that another could have a chance at life."

"He shouldn't have done that. He's too valuable."

Nigel glanced in Adrian's direction and found that the angel was silent for once. Which was a surer sign of trouble than any other.

Nigel tugged at his cuff links, smoothing the sleeves of his silk shirt inside his linen suit. "She shan't kill him. She cannot."

"Are you positive about that?"

"There are few things you can trust her on, but the rules were not laid upon us by her. If she kills Jim, she forfeits not just the match, but the game in its entirety. That will keep her in check."

Adrian's voice drifted over, thin and hard. "There are some things worse than death."

"Verily, you are correct."

"So fucking do something." The angel was all but vibrating, his body like a Christmas popper on the verge of being pulled asunder.

"We could get him out, though," Edward said. "That's not against the rules."

"Of course you may."

Long silence.

Edward cleared his throat and appeared to gird his tongue for polite restraint. "The picture she sent us suggests that he is held within her world."

"He is not upon the earth, 'tis true."

"So how can we get to him."

"You cannot."

As Adrian cursed, Edward clapped a hold on the other angel's arm, but that didn't shut the male up. "You said we could get him out."

"Adrian, I said you 'may.' As in, you are permitted under the rules to do so. I did not, however, make a comment upon your ability. In this case, you are unable to reach him without sacrificing yourselves, thus leaving him with no support and no guidance during this crucial, early time—"

"You little *prick*."

Before Adrian could do something daft, Edward transferred his hold to the male's heavy chest and kept him back.

Nigel cocked a brow at the two of them. "I did not make the rules, and I have no more wish to be disqualified than my opponent."

"Do you have . . ." Adrian choked on his own words and had to breathe deep to finish. "Do you have any idea what she's doing to him. Right now. As we're standing on your fucking lawn and dinner is waiting for you?"

Nigel chose his words with care. The last thing he needed was the pair going vigilante. Anew. They'd already been through that mistake once, hadn't they.

"I know precisely what she is bringing to the table, so to speak. And I also know that Jim is very strong—which is the worst tragedy of all. Because she shall resort to tortures that . . ." There was no reason to go on: Adrian's eyes carried the glassy look of someone reliving his own nightmare. "I would say unto you, however, that Devina cannot keep him for long or she risks a forfeit. Things are coming to a head, and if she prevents Jim from participating fully in the outcome, then there is no fair contest."

"What about Jim?" Adrian demanded, shoving himself free of his best mate. "What about his suffering. What about him!"

Nigel glanced over at Colin, who was utterly silent. Then again, the expression on his gorgeous, familiar face said enough: His fury was so deep and wide, oceans would pale in comparison. He'd always hated Devina and this was not going to be of aid on that front.

There were enough hotheads herein, however.

Nigel shook his head with honest disappointment. "There is naught I may do. I am sorry. My hands are tied."

"You're sorry. You're fucking sorry." Adrian spit on the ground. "Yeah, you look it, you cold bastard. You look really fucking torn up. Asshole."

With that, the angel dematerialized.

"Shit," Edward muttered.

"A coarse but accurate word for it." Nigel stared at the space Adrian had just filled. "'Tis early for him to be so battle-fatigued and fragile. This does not bode well."

"You're kidding me, right?"

He glanced over at the angel. "Surely you must see the madness in him—"

"FYI, big shot, not less than four days ago, Devina worked the guy over but good. And you think he's going to be head-tight now that Jim's being put through the same wringer? Are you serious?"

"May I remind you that you swore to me he could handle this." Nigel found himself leaning forward in confrontation. After all, he might have been the captain of this side, but that didn't mean he was above fisticuffs. "You told me he could withstand the stress. You *promised* me and I believed you. And if you think it shall get easier as we proceed, then you are as crazy as he appears to be."

Edward raised his arm and drew back like he was going to throw a punch. "Fuck you, Nigel—"

Colin was all over the angel in the blink of an eye, attacking from the right, tackling the male, restraining him facedown on the bright green grass.

"You don't hit him, mate," Colin growled. "I know you're pissed off, and you want to get Jim sorted, but I can't let you pop Nigel. Not going to happen."

Nigel glanced back at the dining table. As Bertie and Byron looked over, he saw they were both sitting like worried birds, their bodies stretching up long, their arms down at their sides, their eyes wide. Tarquin had lain down on the ground and put his long-muzzled face under the tablecloth so he couldn't see anything.

The meal was beyond ruined. And not just because the show o'er here was a dramatic disaster to watch: indeed, Nigel wasn't going to be able to stomach a thing. This match with Devina was heading in bad directions on so many levels . . . and he was paralyzed by the rules.

"Let me up," Edward grunted.

Colin might have been a stone or two lighter in the frame than the other angel, but he had tensile strength beyond measure. "You're going to be nice, mate. No more fists or you'll get another bullocking."

*"Fine."*

The one word was not a capitulation of any sort, but Colin jumped free anyway—likely because he knew he could just subdue the male again if that was necessary.

Edward brushed off the blades of green that stuck to his leather coat like tinsel. "Just because Jim can live through it, doesn't mean it's fair."

With that, he disappeared into thin air.

Upon a vicious curse, Nigel regarded the disappearing imprint of Edward's heavy body, the grass springing up, righting itself.

"They have a point," Colin said gruffly. "And that bitch is not playing fair."

"Jim volunteered himself to her."

"In a situation she engineered. It's not right and you know it."

"Do you want *us* to run the risk of forfeiture?" He glanced over. "Do you want to lose because of that?"

Colin clapped the grass off his palms. "Bloody hell. Fucking bloody hell."

Nigel looked back down at the fading body mark on his lawn. "My sentiments precisely."

# CHAPTER
# 31

The wine cellar was not a place Grier went very often. First of all, the twenty-dollar bottles of chard she
poured in her glasses at night were hardly worth the trip
up and down the stairs. Second, with its bank-vault door,
low ceiling, and shelving that ran all around the walls, she'd
always felt like it was a prison.

And what do you know . . . as her father shut the three
of them into the tight confines, Isaac's heft dwarfed the
place down to the size of a Kleenex box, and she felt like
she couldn't breathe.

There was a polished table in the center of the space and
she took one of its four chairs. As Isaac sat across from her,
it was hard not to remember meeting him at the jail: It had
been just like this, the two of them facing off with each other.

Except now, in spite of the fact that neither was in cuffs,
she couldn't lose the feeling that they were both tied up
together . . . and that the foiled corks of all the bottles were
a firing squad on the verge of getting the let-loose signal.

God, when he'd been brought in to meet with her that
first time, she'd had no idea what she was getting into.

Then again did you ever? As people went through their
daily lives, off-the-cuff choices and random events could

sometimes spiral into a kind of centrifugal force that sucked you in and then spun you out into a different zip code altogether.

Even if you never left your own house.

Her father sat closest to the door and linked his hands together as he put his elbows on top of the table.

"We're safe down here," he said, nodding to an air vent up by the short ceiling that had two little red flags trembling on its breeze. "The HVAC system draws blocks away from here, so there's no worry of a contamination. There's also a tunnel out and a radio-wave transmitter that will scramble our voices if we're being recorded."

The tunnel was a news flash and Grier looked around. As far as she could tell, all the shelving was bolted in and the floor was solid stone, but given the other little tricks in the house, she couldn't say she was surprised.

Isaac spoke up. "If I was to go to someone and talk, who would it be?"

"That depends on how—"

"What about Mother." As Grier cut in, cut off, derailed, she stared at her father's face, looking for subtle twitches around his eyes and mouth. "What about when she died. Was that really cancer?"

Although it had been seven years ago, those horrible final days were still so vivid and she sifted through them, looking for cracks in the walls of the events, searching for places where things that seemed one way were really another.

"Yes," her father said. "Yes . . . she . . . Yes, that was the cancer. I swear."

Grier exhaled and found it hard to imagine that she was actually relieved by that dreadful disease. But far better for Mother Nature to have been the culprit. Far better that that tragedy didn't need rewriting. One was more than enough.

She cleared her throat. Nodded. "Okay, then. Okay."

A warm palm covered her own and squeezed. As her father's hands were both on the table, she realized it was Isaac. When she looked over at him, he broke the connection, his touch lingering just long enough so that she knew he was with her, but not so much that she felt restrained.

God, the contradiction of him. Brutal. Sexual. Protective.

With a mental slap, she refocused on her father. "You were in the middle of saying something?"

He nodded and pulled himself together before glancing back at Isaac. "How far are you willing to go?"

"I won't comment on other operatives," Isaac said, "but when it comes to my assignments, I'll go all the way. The things I did for Matthias. What I know about him and his second in command. Where the two of them sent me. The trouble is, it's a patchwork—there's a lot that I only know part of."

"Let me show you something."

Her father got up from the table, and before she could see what he did, a section of shelving came forward and wheeled left, exposing a safe set into the stone walls. The sturdy door was opened by his handprint on a panel and the inside was not very big—little more than the dimensions of a legal pad horizontally and no greater than six inches high.

He came back to the table with a thick folder. "This is everything I've been able to piece together. Names. Dates. People. Places. Pehaps this will help jog your memory." He tapped the front cover. "And I'll figure out who to go to. There's no way of knowing for sure who's involved in Matthias's inner circle—government conspiracies have thick roots, but also tendrils you can't see. The White House is not an option, and it's a federal issue, so state contacts won't help us. But here's what I think. . . ."

Her father's voice grew more powerful with each word, the gathering strength of purpose turning him into the pillar she had always believed him to be. And as he spelled out plans, she felt a shift in the center of her heart.

Although that was just as much because of something Isaac had said. *None of us know what we're getting into until it's too late. . . .*

Her brother had been a beloved junkie, an addict of the first order who likely would have died by his own hand at some point—although that was *not* a justification for what had been done to him, simply the reality of what the situation had been. And she had been surprised, at the time, with how upset her father had been at the loss. He and Daniel had had no contact for at least a year before that horrid night: after the latest stint at yet another high-priced rehab facility had fallen by the wayside, her father had hit the wall as a lot of parents and family members did. He'd given all he could to his son, limped through a decade of patches of recovery that gave treacherous hope, but were inevitably followed by long, dark months in which no one knew where Daniel was, or even whether he was alive.

Her father had been inconsolable at the death, however. To the point where he had spent a week sitting in a chair with nothing but a bottle of gin by his elbow.

And now she knew why. He believed he was wholly responsible.

As she watched him speak, she noted the age on his face . . . the wrinkling around the far corners of the eyes and the mouth, the slight droop of the jawline. He was still a handsome man and yet he'd never remarried. Was it because of the mess he was in? Probably.

Definitely.

Those signs of aging on him were not just a matter of time passing. It was stress and heartache and . . .

Shifting her focus to Isaac, his narrow and laserlike stare was intense, his pale irises positively glowing with a go-to-war light. Funny, he was nothing at all like her father in terms of background, education, exposure, experience. And yet they were identical in so many ways.

Especially united in the common mission to do right.

"Grier?"

Shaking herself, she glanced at her father. He was holding something out to her . . . a handkerchief? But why—

When she felt something hit her forearm, she looked down. A silver tear was collecting itself after the fall from her eye, coalescing into a little shimmering circle on her skin.

Another one dropped and messed up all its effort—but then the pair joined forces and the critical mass doubled.

She took the handkerchief and dried her tears.

"I'm so sorry," her father said.

She mopped her face and refolded the fine linen, remembering him doing exactly the same when upstairs in the kitchen.

"You know what," she murmured. "Apologies don't mean a thing." She laid her hand on the file he'd put on the table. "This . . . what you two are doing . . . this is everything."

The only thing that could have made any of it right.

To cut off the conversation, she cracked open the cover. . . .

She frowned and leaned in. The first page was a printout of four mug shots. All men. All of whom looked like different ethnic versions of Isaac. Underneath the pictures, in her father's handwriting, there were names, dates of birth, social security numbers, last sightings—although not every one was complete. And three of them had DECEASED across the bottom.

She flipped to the next page and the next. All the same. So many faces.

"I want to bring Jim Heron in on this," Isaac said. "The more who come forward, the better—"

"Jim Heron?" her father said. "You mean Zacharias?"

"Yeah. I saw him earlier tonight and the night before. I thought he'd been sent to kill me, but it turns out, he wants to help me—or so he says."

"You *saw* him?"

"He was with two guys. I don't recognize them, but they look like they could be XOps."

"But—"

"Oh, my God," Grier whispered, moving one of the sheets closer. "That's him."

As she pointed to one of the pictures, she heard her father say, "Jim Heron is dead. He was shot in Caldwell, New York. Four nights ago."

"That's him," she repeated, tapping at the picture.

Isaac's voice sounded confused. "How did you know? Grier . . . how did you know?"

She looked up. "Know what?"

"That's Jim Heron."

Moving her finger aside, she saw the name Zacharias below the picture. "Well, I don't know who he is, but that's the man who showed up in my bedroom last night. As an angel."

# CHAPTER
## 32

This was not working.

Deep down in the anus of Hell, where her captured souls were kept in flypaper walls, and the still air echoed with the oily moans of her servants, Devina was suffering from a serious case of buzz kill.

Which was why she'd sent everyone away.

Hanging back, she regarded the piece of meat wired to her table. In the candlelight, Jim Heron was Jackson Pollocked with blood and black wax and other liquids of various descriptions, and he was having trouble breathing through his swollen, cracked lips. On his stomach, there was a road map of carvings she'd done with her own claws, and his thighs were marked as well with her name and her symbols.

His cock had been used until it was as raw as the rest of him.

And yet he hadn't cried out or begged or even opened his eyes. No curses, no tears. Nothing.

She wasn't sure whether to be pissed off at herself and her minions for not working him hard enough . . . or to fall in love with the bastard.

Either way, she was determined to get a piece of him. The question was how.

She was well aware that there were two ways of breaking someone. The first was from the outside in: You whittled away at the individual's skin and bones and sex until the physical pain and exhaustion and shame annihilated their inner mental core. The second was the inverse: Find the fissure inside and tap it with a proverbial hammer until everything crumbled.

For her, usually the first was enough, given all the tools at her disposal—and it was also more fun and therefore always where she started. The second was trickier, although no less satisfying in its own right. All people had keys to open their interior doors; she just needed to sort through and find the one that got her inside a given individual's head and heart.

In Jim Heron's case . . . well, it was clear he was going to make her work for it. And didn't that give her Adrian some competition for Favorite Toy.

What to choose, what to choose . . .

His mother. His mother was a good one, but Devina wouldn't be able to get ahold of the real thing, and he might just be smart enough to figure out she was faking it.

Fortunately, there was another solution that happened to be under her control.

Outside of the pools of candlelight, trapped in her viscous walls, the souls of those she'd captured writhed. Hands and limbs and feet and heads made undulating appearances that never quite broke the surface of the suspension, the tortured ever searching for a way out.

The satisfaction of seeing her collection distracted her, but also made her hungry: She had to have Jim in and among her trophies. Was desperate to get him into her. At first it had been merely a case of the game; now, after this session, it was so much more than that.

She wanted to own him.

Refocusing on his face, she found his calm expression nearly impossible to comprehend. How a man could have gone through so much . . . and there wasn't even a grimace. And no fear of what was to come, either.

She would fix that, however.

And she liked to think this power in him came from that portion of his makeup that was hers. Those bleeding-heart angels with their holier-than-thou morals and strictures — weak, so weak. To the point where she didn't want to lose the game against Nigel not only because she could rule the earth and the heavens and all that was betwixt the sun and moon . . . but because what an ass slap to be bested by that bunch of pussies.

Jim, however . . . he was better than that. He was more like her at his core.

What a tragedy that he had to be sent back up to Earth soon; but play, after all, had to be resumed. Before he went, though, she was determined to make an imprint on him, give him more of a taste of what their Hell Ever After was going to be like. After all, the cuts in his skin were relatively shallow. Marks on the mind, however, went far, far deeper.

And immortals were especially satisfying in this regard because, as the brain persisted, so did memory — and that meant she could leave eternal scars in her wake.

Glancing at her wall, which stretched upward for miles, Devina thought of her therapist and the work they were doing together. This was one domain that was off-limits to her "recovery" and this situation with Jim was proof yet again of how her little hoarding problem came in handy.

You never knew what you'd need.

Extending her hand, she pulled down from the upper reaches one of the more slender shapes, moving it in and around the other souls, calling it to her. When it was by the floor, she summoned forth the soul and clothed it in the corporeal form it had worn on Earth.

Devina smiled at it. So much utility in such a bland and forgettable little package.

Turning to her table, she said, "Jim? I have someone here who you'll want to see."

As Jim lay on Devina's table, he doubted that. Very sincerely doubted that.

Besides, at this point, vision was probably a no-go.

Nothing hurt anymore, which made shit so much easier. The trade-off for that blissful numbness, however, was that his consciousness had receded into a dim corner of his inner house. It hadn't quite put its head down for a nap, but it was getting there: Hearing had hit the cotton-wool stage where everything was muffled, and things were pretty fucking cold inside his skin.

The classic signs of shock made him wonder if she did in fact have the ability to kill him.

She hadn't finished off Adrian, but had that been a whim of affection?

"I'll just leave you two to get acquainted."

Devina's satisfaction was not good news, considering she'd done everything inhumanly possible to break him down for the last . . . how long? Hours? Had to be.

Footfalls. Retreating.

A door. Shut.

Silence.

Something was with him, though. He could sense the presence to the left of him.

From behind his closed lids, he knew two things for sure: Devina couldn't have gone far, and whatever she'd locked him in with was close by.

The breathing was the first thing he noticed. Soft, hitched. The kind you drew when you were in recovery mode. Maybe it was his breath?

Nope. Rhythm was different.

He turned his head carefully toward the thing and drooled, his mouth clearing of what he couldn't swallow because of the wire around his neck.

Whatever was with him let out another hitch of breath. And then he heard a subtle clicking.

What the fuck was that?

Curiosity eventually got the best of him and he cracked one of his lids ... or gave that a shot, as it were. Took two tries and he had to push his eyebrows all the way up into his forehead before the fucker opened—

At first, Jim couldn't fathom what he was looking at. But the blond hair couldn't be denied ... that long blond hair that fell to fragile shoulders.

Last time he'd seen it had been just days ago. In Devina's bathroom.

It had been streaked with blood.

The girl who had been sacrificed to protect Devina's mirror was dressed in a stained sheath, her thin arms covering her breasts, a small hand protecting the juncture of her thighs. She appeared to be miraculously unmarked, but the trauma was there: Her eyes were wide and horrified. . . .

Except they were not on the room. They were on him ... on his body and the glossy, sticky remnants of everything that had been done to him.

"Don't ..." His voice was too damn weak, so he forced more air through that wire roadblock at his throat. "Don't look ... at me. Turn away ... for God's sake, turn away. . . ."

Shit, he needed more oxygen. He needed to make her—

Her eyes met his. The shock and terror on her face told him more than he needed to know, not just about what had been done to her by Devina, but what the sight of him was doing to the poor girl.

"Don't look at me!"

As she flinched and cringed away, he reeled his temper in. Not that there was much to throw reins on—he'd used all the strength he had on that yell.

"Cover your face," he said hoarsely. "Turn away and just ... cover your face."

The girl put her hands up and pivoted around, her delicate spine standing out against the sheath as she trembled.

Jim had pulled at his binds involuntarily during Devina's little exercise session. Now he yanked.

"You're hurting yourself," she said as he grunted. "Please . . . stop."

Pain cut off his capacity for speech and it was a while before he could say anything. "Where . . . where does she keep you? Down here?"

"In . . . in the . . ." Her voice was so very reedy, and in between the words, her teeth chattered—which explained the clicking he'd heard. "In the wall . . ."

His eyes shot toward the darkness, but the candlelight formed a luminous blockade his eyes couldn't get through.

"How does she do that?" Not chains, he hoped.

And fuckin' A, he was so going to get Devina for this one.

"I don't know," the girl said. "Where am I?"

Hell. But he kept that to himself. "I'm going to get you out of here."

"My mom and dad . . ." She choked on tears. "They don't know where I am."

"I'll tell them."

"How will—" As she glanced over her shoulder, her eyes locked on his degraded body and she paled.

He shook his head. "No looking. Promise me . . . no more looking at me."

Pale hands went back up to that beautiful face and she nodded. "My name is Cecilia. Sissy Barten—with an 'e.' I'm nineteen. Almost twenty."

"You live in Caldwell?"

"Yes. Am I dead?"

"I want you to do something for me."

Now she dropped her arms and stared at him hard. *"Am I dead."*

"Yes."

She closed her eyes as another wave of shaking shot through her body. "This isn't Heaven. I believe in Heaven. What did I do wrong?"

Jim felt something hot at the corners of both his eyes. "Nothing. You did nothing wrong. And I'm going to get you there."

If it was the last fucking thing he did.

"Who are you?"

"I'm a soldier."

"Like in Iraq?"

"Used to be. Now I fight that bitch—er, female who did this to you."

"I thought I was helping . . . when the lady asked me to carry a bag for her. I thought I was helping. . . ." She inhaled sharply as if she were trying to compose herself. "You can't get out of here. I've tried."

"I'm going to save you."

Abruptly, her voice got stronger. "They hurt you."

Shit, she was looking at him again.

"Don't worry about me—you worry about yourself."

A sound, like something dropping or maybe a metal door shutting, echoed up, startling her and focusing him. Undoubtedly, Devina was going to come soon enough and put Sissy back wherever she had been so he had to act fast. He didn't know when he was going to return here or how exactly to free his girl.

Sissy, that was.

"Is that her?" Sissy asked tightly as footfalls sounded from far away. "It's her, isn't it. I don't want to go back into the wall—please, don't let her—"

"Sissy, listen to me. I need you to calm down." She had to have something to focus on, something to keep her head together while he figured out how to get back to her. Searching his mind, he tried to pull an image out of his ass, something to ease her. "I need you to listen carefully."

"I can't go back there!"

Fuck, what could he give her to concentrate on? "I have a dog," he blurted.

There was a beat, as if he'd surprised her. "You do?"

As the footsteps drew closer, he wanted to curse. "Yeah, I do."

"I like dogs," she said in a small voice, her eyes locking on his.

"He's gray and blond and he's shaggy. His fur . . ." The footsteps grew ever louder and Jim spoke quicker. "His fur is kind of rough—like it's made up of old-man eyebrows, and he has little paws. He likes to sit in my lap. He has a limp that comes out if he runs too fast and he likes to eat my socks."

Sniffle and a hitch of breath. Like she knew what was approaching and she was going to do her best to hang on to the lifeline he was trying to give her. "What's his name?"

"Dog. I call him Dog. He eats pizza and turkey subs and he sleeps on my chest." Faster. Faster with his words. "You're going to meet him, 'kay? You're going to take him out onto a patch of grass and . . . You know how you can tuck one sock into another?"

"Yes." Urgent now. Like she wanted as much as he could give her. "A sock ball."

"Sock balls—that's right." Fast, fast, fast. "You've got a sock ball and you're going to throw it and he's going to bring it back to you. Sun is out, Sissy. You can feel it on your face—"

"When are you coming back?" she whispered.

"Soon as I can." He was talking at a blur now, the footsteps so close he knew they were stilettos with sharp, pointed heels. "You remember Dog. You hear me? When you feel like you're losing it, you remember my dog—"

"Don't leave me here—"

"I'll come for you—"

Sissy's face was slick with tears as she reached out for him. "Don't leave me here!"

In an instant, she morphed into the condition she'd been in when he'd seen her over that tub, that sheath disappearing and leaving her naked, her body desecrated, her blond hair tangled and matted with blood.

Abruptly, her eyes shot to the far corner and her stained lips trembled. "No!"

She put her hands up as if to ward off blows, bowing away—

Just like that, she was gone. And Devina, beautiful, evil Devina, walked into the candlelight.

Jim fucking lost it.

Snapped in half.

Broke like a motherfucker.

As he screamed bloody murder, it was all about the girl. The innocent girl who had been taken from her family by a demon, and pulled into a shithole, and imprisoned here . . . and forced to see the aftermath of a grown man defiled.

Rage was a nuclear blast that went off inside him—

White light poured forth from his eye sockets, exploding in the room, illuminating the glossy black walls that ran upward into infinity. The release consumed his physical form, freeing him from Devina's constraints, carrying him around the space in a rush-gust of loose molecules that blew out the candles and knocked over their stands.

Coalescing, he whirled around . . . and went gunning for Devina.

Now she was the one bracing for impact, her brunette hair stripped back from her scalp under the hurricane blast of him, the skin on her face flapping against the bone structure underneath as she lost her balance and went over onto the stone floor.

Just as he reached her, Jim pulled his new form together into a spearing lance and hurled himself right for her chest.

He entered her body and blew that bitch away, all of her parts going flying, pieces of her skin and tangles of slippery innards and pounds of dark red meat spackling the walls of her dungeon.

What was left was a black hole of equal mass and energy as that which made up him—and he was ready to go at it with her.

Except, evidently, she wasn't up for a head-to-head fight: Her warping shadow shot out of the room and down a hall, making an escape.

Fuck. That.

Jim rushed forward after her—

And slammed into the metaphysical equivalent of a brick house.

The shocking impact of the nonvisual barrier sent him backward and he became corporeal once again as he skidded over the stone floor on his raw ass.

He had one brief moment of what-the-hell, before his body's Game Over sign flashed and he fell flat on his back in utter exhaustion.

With his anger spent, there was nothing left in him, and a fatal fatigue bled out from his wonky-beating heart and spread through him sure as a weed taking root and thriving. No longer able to hold his head up, he let the thing rest on the stone and just breathed, dimly noting that the air was saturated with both the copper scent of fresh kill and the acrid pinch of still-smoking candlewicks.

"Sissy," he said into the darkness. "I'm right here. . . ."

He had no clue whether she could hear him and there was no response. Just an eerie, molten sound . . . no doubt the souls trying to get free of their prison.

He hated the idea that his girl was trapped in there.

Hated that she had seen what he'd looked like.

At that thought, pain bored into him as surely as if he'd been stabbed with a crowbar. Oh, God . . . that poor child . . .

A sudden surge of emotion fell upon him in a tidal wave: Naked and broken and filthy, Jim curled onto his side and wept in great heaving gags, his tears hot and salty on the broken skin of his face.

He had never cared about any damage to himself. Ever. But his failings ... his failings were unsupportable. And now there were two women he had not been able to save, his beloved mother and Sissy. . . . Both times, he had walked into a room too late; both times the damage had been done before he'd arrived.

With horrid acuity, he saw his mother on their kitchen floor at the farmhouse, all but slaughtered ... and Sissy over the tub.

Sissy just now as well, trying to ward off the demon.

It was too much to bear, the weight of his failures too great for him to withstand, much less go on fighting—

The sound of his name opened his eyes and slowed the raw sobs.

With vast effort, he turned his head and looked up.

Far, far, far above, a galaxy away from where he lay, a pinpoint of light gathered and grew stronger, starting first as the tiny flicker of a blinker on a Christmas tree ... and then growing to a twenty-five-watt, then a sixty-watt, then a hundred-watt bulb.

The illumination drifted down to him with all the speed and efficiency of a feather falling through still air ... of dandelion puffs blown from a child's mouth ... of milk-weed caught on a gentle breeze. . . .

The disconnect between his epic despair and the delicate path of the light was a span too great for his mind to straddle. Closing his eyes, he stopped watching and gave himself over to the random shudders of his beaten body.

"Jim."

A male voice. Above him.

He cracked his lids to see that the light had become a dark-haired man with magnificent golden wings.

Colin.

The archangel. Nigel's number two.

"Hey, mate," the guy said as he knelt down. "I've come to get you out of here."

From somewhere, God only knew where, Jim called up enough energy to speak. "Take her instead. Leave me ... take her instead. Sissy. The girl ..."

"That I can't do. I shouldn't be here even now." The angel leaned forward and gathered Jim's broken form into his arms. "But you're going to need some recovery time before you can so much as sit up, much less drag ass out of here. And the war is proceeding without you."

No argument there on his energy level, but God, he'd rather have Sissy a million miles away from here.

"Leave me," he moaned.

"Not on your life. You want Sissy free? You beat Devina. That's how you unlock this nightmare for your girl."

As they began to levitate, Jim's head lolled to the side and he watched as up, up, up they went, past yards and yards—hell, miles—of the black walls. Along the way, Colin's glowing form illuminated the shifting, churning surface, and faces pushed against the opaque, liquid barrier, as if those trapped were trying to see them, get to them, join them in the escape. From every direction, hands reached out, contouring into grotesque shapes as the tensile strength of the prison proved too hard to get through.

Where was his girl? His beautiful, innocent girl who ...

Jim's brain ran out of gas, the weave of his thoughts unraveling, consciousness giving up the ghost and going in for a deep lie-down in the hard-walled crib of his skull.

As he passed out, his last mental missive was a prayer— that Sissy would remember Dog in this hellish place and hold on until Jim could get to her.

# CHAPTER
## 33

Down in the wine cellar, with Jim Heron's picture staring up out of a dossier, Isaac was pretty damn sure both Childes had lost their minds.

"He's not dead." Isaac glanced between father and daughter. "I'm not sure what you saw or what you heard—"

"He was in my room." Grier shook her head. "That's how I knew you were having the nightmare. He pointed the way so I would go to you. I thought it was a dream, but why would I have pictured his face so clearly?"

"Because you saw him. Last night at the fight. He was with me."

"No, he wasn't."

Right. The guy had stood directly in front of her. "You said he was an angel."

"Well, it appeared as if he had wings."

It was theoretically possible that Heron had paid her a visit—but with the security alarm, you'd have to assume that if he had, he'd merely been on the far side of her French door. In her disorientation from waking up, she'd no doubt only thought he was inside. And that had been just a coincidence with Isaac's nightmare. . . . As for the wings? Jim Heron had been no saint, much less an angel.

Whatever she'd seen had to have been reflections in the glass. Had to be.

Grier's dad spoke up. "I'm telling you, he's dead. I keep alert tracers on the Internet on the names of the operatives I know of—and he was shot in Caldwell, New York, four days ago."

Isaac rolled his eyes. "Don't believe everything you read. I spoke with the guy in the back garden here at nightfall. Face-to-face. Trust me, he's alive, and we need him." Isaac got to his feet. "His buddies are watching this house as we speak, and personally, I think Heron's declared a vigilante war on Matthias—so I'm pretty damn sure we can get him to work with us—assuming they haven't killed him already. I believe he's MIA at the moment."

"I hope he turns up then because the more you have to go on, the better." Childe tapped the dossiers. "You should plan on reviewing all of this tonight, filling in the blanks, trying to piece together what you know—even if you don't want to turn in your fellow soldiers, it may aid your own recollections. I'll go upstairs into the hall bath and use my secured phone there to make some calls and get things set as fast as I can."

"Roger that. But I want you to stay away from the windows and not leave the house."

"I'll be careful." Childe glanced at his daughter. "I promise."

As Grier's dad disappeared up the stairs, Isaac checked the Life Alert. The transistor was still showing that the signal had been sent, but there was no answer yet. Which meant either he was too far underground in this wine cellar to receive it . . . or Matthias was taking his own sweet time getting back in touch.

He looked at Grier. "I'd better stay aboveground for a while in case they're trying to reach me."

"What are you going to do? If they want to meet with you right away?"

"Until I turn myself in, I've got a little leeway. But your father needs to work a couple of miracles fast." And please, Lord, let Jim Heron be okay—and show up *soon*.

She stroked the dossiers with her elegant hand. "He's good at miracles. It's actually his specialty. You should see him in negotiations." Her eyes went down to the file. "I'm going to stay here. I want to see which if any of these men I recognize. There were a number who came to the door when I was growing up and I always wondered who they were."

As she fell silent, he took a step forward. And then another. Around the table he went, until he was by her side.

When she looked up to him, he carefully brushed back a strand of hair from her face. "I'm not going to ask if you're okay, because how could you be."

"Have you ever felt . . . like you don't know your own life?"

"Yeah. And that's what got me to change."

Well, that had been the first step. He was starting to believe that she was the second. And between her father and Jim Heron . . . three was the magic number. God willing.

"You know what?" she said. "I'm really glad I met you."

Isaac recoiled. "How in the good Lord's name can you say that?"

"You were the key that unlocked the lies." She went back to staring at Jim Heron's picture. "I feel like without you it would never have come to light. Only something so shattering . . ."

As she let that drift, he stepped back. "Yeah. That's me."

She nodded absently, turning the page and getting lost in the faces of men who were just like him . . . men who had ruined her family.

Shattered it.

Were the operatives who had killed her brother in there? With notes?

Somehow he doubted her father would put her through that.

"Can I bring you some wine?" he asked before he made himself go.

Grier smiled a little. "I'm surrounded by it."

"True enough." He should have offered coffee. Water. Beer. An oil change. Anything he could do for her or give to her to ease her.

Well now, on that note, there was an improvement he could make. He could leave her.

"I'll be upstairs." When he got to the door, he looked back. She was buried in the dossiers, brows tight, arms in her lap as she leaned forward over the table.

Yeah, leaving her was going to make things so much better.

He turned away and took the stairs up to the kitchen two at a time. Pausing at the base of the back stairwell, he listened. Not a sound. Which made sense if her father had locked himself up in a secured bathroom.

Shit, he couldn't believe that he was going to shine a light on Matthias. But then sometimes natural death was too good for someone. Better that they rot behind bars or get lit up like Times Square in an electric chair.

It was almost as if he was supposed to have met Grier and her father at this precise junction in his life—that the pair of them had been preordained to show him a way out that was far more honorable than what he'd planned.

Jim Heron was going to be important as well, however.

Palming up one of his guns, he slipped out the back door into the garden.

Sidestepping the motion-activated light, he waited in the shadows without making any noise, and sure enough, one of Jim's pals stepped up a moment later. The instant he laid eyes on the guy, it was clear the vibe remained off: This one with the braid had the tight lips and hard stare of a man who still didn't know where a member of his team was.

"Jim not come in for a landing yet?" Isaac asked. Even though the answer was clearly, *Fuck no*, given that expression.

"I'm hoping you can see him in the morning."

Isaac glanced at his watch. "I don't know if I've got that kind of time."

"Make it."

Easy for him to say. "Will you let me know if he shows?"

As the guy nodded once, Isaac got pretty frickin' worried. "Is he all right?" When the man shook his head slowly, Isaac cursed. "You going to tell me what's doing?" Silence. "You know, FYI, people think he's dead."

"All I can say is . . . right now, he wishes he was."

Adrian watched as Eddie talked to Rothe up near the back door, and whereas Ad was usually nosy as hell, he didn't care what they were saying.

Nigel. Cocksucking Nigel.

Mr. Holier-than-thou-aboveboard.

Who was more than willing to let his best asset get used and abused by the enemy just because he was too much of a little bitch to roll up his sleeves and pound Devina into the ground.

Meanwhile Jim was gym equipment for a bunch of pervert assholes.

Man, he just didn't get this do-nothing. If one of his boys was captured and he could spring them? Didn't matter what he had to do, what sacrifice there was to make, where he went: He would get the sorry sonofabitch back. And yet where was their boss man? Having dinner.

Made a guy want to feed Nigel his dessert right up the ass.

Adrian rubbed his face so hard he nearly sanded his nose off. The trouble was, Devina's little workshop wasn't accessible to him and Eddie unless they jumped through her mirror—otherwise she had to take you there herself . . . and she released you only when she was good and ready.

And not before.

That was why they'd gone to Nigel. There was a rumor that the archangels could go down to Hell under certain circumstances—no one knew exactly what those dandies had to do or how it worked. Bottom line, though, was that those four lightweights were their only hope—

As if he knew his name was being taken in vain, Colin appeared from out of nowhere, the dark-haired archangel poofing it up right in front of Adrian's face.

"Shit!" Ad hissed while he leaped back and caught himself on a bush—which promptly broke in half under his heavy body.

He landed like a bag of sand, but didn't stay there. Springing up, he was all about the what-the-fuck: Those boys didn't usually show up willy-nilly on the Earth. "What are y—"

"I got him out."

Ad blinked, the English language suddenly escaping him. Wait a minute. Did he just hear— "Jim? You're talking about Jim?"

"Is out."

"But Nigel said—"

"I'm not discussing that. I got the chosen one out of Devina's lair and I left the poor sod off at your hotel—he needs care."

Eddie came over. "You got him out? But I thought Nigel—"

"I have to go." Colin stepped back and started to fade. "Go help him. He needs it."

"Thank you," Ad breathed, both relieved and sick to his stomach: the recovery from one of Devina's seshes was a bitch. Mostly because the memories were just too damn vivid.

Colin shook his head as he disappeared, his voice all that lingered: "It just wasn't right."

"I'm going to the hotel," Adrian said, unfurling himself to take to the air. "Don't let Isaac out of your—"

Eddie grabbed his arm hard. "Let me handle Jim."

"*No.*"

"You're not up to this, Adrian." Eddie's grip held him to the ground, that big hand squeezing into bone and muscle. "And you know it."

"The hell I'm not."

Breaking free, he took three running leaps and winged up into the air, grabbing onto the night and propelling himself west. The flight back to where they were staying was bumpy and rough—but not because of the wind. It was more like Eddie probably had a point, the SOB.

When Ad got to the Comfort Inn & Suites, he wanted to just barge into their rooms through the walls, but he decided not to chance it: Given that his inner Kit Kat wrapper was loose and flapping, he landed on the lawn and stalked in through the lobby. He had a feeling he was just too scatterbrained and nauseous to successfully push himself through wood and concrete.

The problem was, he knew exactly what kind of shape Jim was going to be in.

As he hit the lobby, a chirpy woman behind the desk "Good evening, sir"'d him, but he waved her off and broke into a jog. There was no waiting for the elevator; a couple was checking in with their kids and they had a cart full of luggage. But even if there had been a clean shot, he wouldn't have been able to wait for so much as the doors to open for him.

Up the stairs. Two at a time. Sometimes three.

When he got to the top floor, his ticker was going a mile a minute, and not just because he'd exerted himself. He didn't have a key to Jim's room, so he took his own and slipped it in and out of the lock of his crib.

He opened the way in on a burst. "Jim? *Jim?*"

The glow from his bathroom illuminated the rumpled

bed that he and Eddie had worked that girl out on the night before, as well as the clothes that were scattered around.

The connector to Jim's was half open, the room beyond dark.

"Jim . . . ?"

He knew the angel was in there. He could smell the candle smoke and the fresh blood and . . . the other things.

The rush to get to the guy evaporated as the reality of what he was about to walk in on clawed its way into his chest and suffocated him. But he was not turning back. He was an asshole of the first order, always had been. He was not, however, a pussy to turn away from the hard stuff.

Adrian walked to the doorway between the two rooms and leaned in. "Jim."

The light in the bathroom behind him cut a path into all the pitch-black, the illumination stopping at the foot of the angel's bed . . . as if it were too polite to show his condition.

After Adrian rounded the jamb, it took a moment for his eyes to adjust—

On a hiss, he vowed, "I'm going to kill that bitch. . . ."

Jim was lying on his side, curled into himself as if to conserve body heat, and he was trembling in fits and starts. A blanket had been pulled over his big, battered body—no doubt by the archangel—and Dog was right by his face, pretzeled into a ball, going nowhere.

As Adrian came over, he got a little wag, but the animal didn't lift his head, staying nose-to-nose with Jim.

The angel appeared to be breathing, his chest rising and falling, a soft wheeze breaching his busted mouth. His hair was matted and there was blood on his face, the features of which no longer looked like his own, thanks to a Michelin Man–like swelling.

Adrian sat down slowly. "Jim?"

No response, so he tried the name game a couple more times. Eventually, Jim's lid cracked.

"Hey," Adrian whispered.

He got a croak and then the eye shut and the body under the blanket shivered in a great seizure.

If this was anything like what Adrian went through—and given the way the guy looked, it was a one-for-one if he'd ever seen it—what Jim really wanted was a bath followed by a shower. But it was too early for that shit. Healing time first—there were just too many broken-and-bruiseds to move him—which was the burden of an angel's dual nature: being both real and unreal meant that at least half of you could get fucked-up but good, and shit didn't spring back right away.

Adrian stood and went over to the heating unit that was under the windows. Turning the dial to "sauna," he ditched his leather jacket and shut the connector to the other room, locking them in together. Then he got on the bed, stretched out on top of the thin blanket, and put his chest to the angel's back to warm him.

As he lay there and heard the heater come on with a whir, he felt the earthquakes in Jim's torso and limbs. Part of it was the healing process, which in some ways was more painful than the injuries. And part of it was the deep freeze of shock.

And part of it was the memories, no doubt.

He wanted to put an arm around the guy, but that was just going to be too uncomfortable for Jim: When he'd been in this condition, he'd lain naked without even a sheet on his clawed skin.

After a while, the billowing warmth that fanned out from the heater reached them, arcing over and raining down. Jim obviously felt the flow because he drew in a long breath and exhaled on a ragged sigh.

Lying next to the other angel, Adrian should have expected that this was where Jim would end up, and he had, to a degree. He'd known Devina had wanted the guy . . . back on their first assignment, back on that first night in the club in Caldwell. And he'd served Jim up to her.

With everything but the "to and from" tag.

Hard not to feel responsible for this.

Reallllllllly tough.

"I've got you, Jim," he said hoarsely. "I'm right here for you, man."

# CHAPTER
## 34

Down in the wine cellar, Grier went through the dossiers one by one while she waited ... and waited ... and waited some more....

*Finally.*

"Why didn't you tell me," she said, without looking behind herself.

Daniel took a long time in answering, but he didn't disappear: Whenever he was around, she could feel the slightest of drafts, and as long as that was brushing the back of her neck, she knew he was still with her.

*I thought you would hate him. And then you and he would have no one left.*

"So you knew what happened."

Daniel came around the table, one hand planted on his hip, the other buried in his blond hair so that the curls went halo on him. *I was high when it all went down ... so I just thought it was so funny, Dad bursting in with three guys in black. I figured it was his version of an intervention—all comic-book hard-core. But as they put the needle in my arm, he started to scream and that's when I realized ... it wasn't funny.*

Daniel's eyes met hers. *I'd never seen him that way be-*

*fore. To me, he was always so aloof and unemotional. It was . . . the reaction I had been looking for all my life, the visceral love I'd been after. See, I was like Mom, not you and him. I wanted more than that chilly disapproval and I got it, only it was too late. . . .* He shrugged. *In retrospect, I was too needy, and he didn't know what to do with a son who wasn't cut from military cloth. Oil and water. I should have handled it differently, but I didn't.*

"And neither did he."

*It's not anyone's fault. It just . . . was.*

Grier leaned back in her chair, thinking of the way their family had aligned, she and their father on one side, Daniel and their mother on the other.

*It wasn't his fault*, her brother said with a kind of stern tone she'd never heard from him before. *The way I ended . . . he screamed, Grier . . . and then as I was dying, I heard him say, over and over again, Danny boy . . . my Danny boy—*

As Daniel's voice broke, she was compelled to get up and go to him. Before she knew what she was doing, she put her arms around . . .

Herself.

*Please don't hate him*, he said from the far corner, having shifted quick as a blink.

"Please don't run," she countered.

*I'm sorry. . . . I have to go . . .*

He disappeared before her as if he couldn't hold his emotions in any longer, his despair lingering in the cold spot he left behind.

She stood for a time, staring at the vacant space he'd just occupied. She and her father had been two of a kind, and in their intellectual accord, they'd locked the others out, hadn't they. Her mother and brother had taken to their addictions while she and her father had been in lockstep with the law and their careers and their external passions.

She'd known it on some level . . . and maybe that had been part of her drive to save Daniel. Her brother's addiction and her efforts to pull him out of it had been the link they hadn't found outside of childhood: She had always blamed herself—and for a brief moment tonight, she had blamed her father.

Now . . . she was angry at that man with the eye patch. Viciously angry. If Daniel had lived, maybe they'd have figured it all out. Forgiven each other, all three of them, for the past. Moved along to . . . something that their family had had only on the surface. After all, privilege and money and breeding could cover up a multitude of problems—and didn't ensure that the closeness on a Christmas card was actually more than a pose once a year for a photographer.

Shaking her head, she went back to her seat and stared at the dossiers.

Isaac was going to even the score for her family, she thought. By being the one who brought down that maniacal bastard who had killed her brother and all but ruined her father.

Flipping through the photographs, she recognized each of the men now, because she'd gone through the pages over and over again while waiting for Daniel to show. There were a hundred or so pictures, but only a total of some forty men, with multiple shots illustrating them through the years. Out of the lot of them, there were five that she recognized—or at least thought she'd seen before. Hard to know . . . on some level, they looked so similar.

Isaac's picture was in there and she returned to it. The photo was a candid, caught on the fly. He was looking directly into the camera, but she had the impression he didn't know he was being photographed.

Hard. God, he looked so hard. As if he were prepared to kill.

The birth date under his name validated the age she knew him to be, and there were a couple of notes about foreign countries he'd been to. And then there was one line that she kept coming back to: *Must be provided moral imperative.* She had seen the phrase under only two other men's profiles.

"How are you holding up?"

Grier jumped at the sound of Isaac's voice, the chair under her butt screeching across the floor. Grabbing her chest, she said, "Jesus . . . how do you do that?"

Because, all things considered, she would have preferred not to get caught staring at his picture.

"Sorry, I just thought you might like a coffee." He came over, put a mug down, and then retreated back to the door-way. "I should have knocked."

As he paused between the jambs, he was now just in the hooded sweatshirt he'd used as a pillow, his shoulders oh, so wide beneath its gray expanse. And considering what the last forty-eight hours had been like, he looked amazingly strong and focused.

Her eyes went to the coffee. So thoughtful. So very thoughtful. "Thank you . . . and sorry. I guess I'm just not used to . . ." A man like him.

"I'll announce my presence from now on."

She picked up the mug and took a sip. Perfect—with just the right amount of sugar she liked in it. He'd watched her, she thought. Saw how much she'd added at some point, even though she hadn't been aware of it. And he'd remembered.

"You lookin' at me?" When she glanced up, he nodded down at the dossiers. "My picture?"

"Ah . . . yes." Grier tapped the phrase. "What exactly does this mean?"

He walked over and leaned in. As he stared at the de-tails under his face, the tension in him was palpable, his big body tight all over. "They had to give me a reason."

"Before you'd kill someone."

He nodded and began to walk around, going over to the wine bottles. He took one out, looked at the label, returned it . . . moved on to another one.

"What kinds of reasons did they give you?" she asked,

well aware that his answers about this meant way too much to her.

He paused with a Bordeaux cradled in his hands. "The kind that made it seem right."

"Like what."

His eyes flipped toward her and she had a moment of pause. They were so grim and hollow.

"Tell me," she whispered.

He put the bottle back. Went a couple of feet farther down the wooden racks. "I only did men. No women. There were some who could do the females, but not me. And I'm not going to give you specific examples, but the political-affiliation nonsense just wasn't enough for me. You kill a bunch of people or rape some women or blow some shi—er, stuff . . . up? Very different story. And I needed to see some proof with my own eyes—video, photograph . . . bodies that were marked."

"Did you ever refuse an assignment?"

"Yes."

"So you wouldn't have killed my brother."

"Never," he said without hesitation. "And they wouldn't have even asked me. The way Matthias saw it, I was a weapon that worked under prescribed circumstances, and he took me out of his holster at appropriate times. And you know . . . I realized I had to leave XOps when it dawned on me that I was no different from the people I was killing. They'd all felt as if whatever atrocities they were committing were justifiable. Well, so did I and that made us mirror images of each other really. Sure, an objective viewpoint would have agreed with me over them, but that wasn't enough."

Grier let out a long exhale. He was what she'd always believed in, she thought.

"How so?" he said.

With a flush, she guessed she'd spoken aloud. "I always told Daniel . . ." She paused, wondering if she had the stuffing left in her to go there. "I told him that it was never too late. That the things he'd done in the past didn't have to define his future. I think toward the end, he'd given up on himself. He'd stolen from my father and me and his friends. He'd been arrested burglarizing a house and also on felony theft of an auto and then while trying to hold up a liquor store. That's how I got involved with doing pro bono. I was in and out of various jails for the five years before his death. I felt like I wasn't helping him—but maybe I could someone else, you know? And I did . . . I did help people."

"Grier—"

She waved him off as her voice hitched. She was finished with crying. There was going to be no more of that and no more dwelling on what couldn't be changed. "Do you want to go through this now?"

As she indicated the dossiers, he shrugged and went to the door, settling into a lean against the jamb. "I really just came to check on you."

In the still air, his low-lidded eyes warmed her from the inside out. Such a contradiction he was . . . between his trained-killer job and his Boy Scout heart.

She glanced down at his picture. "You look like you're tracking something here."

"I was about to get on a plane, actually. I had the feeling someone was watching, but I couldn't tell from which direction. I was waiting at an airbase to go overseas." He cleared his throat like he was sweeping the memory from his mind. "Your father's passed out upstairs. He spent about two hours on the phone, as far as I can tell."

"It's been that long?" She glanced at her watch, and as she shifted her wrist around, she became aware of all the kinks in her body. Stretching her arms over her head, her spine popped. "How are things going?"

"I don't know. Before he lay down, he told me that as long as we can make it until tomorrow night, we're in business. He's pulled multiple contacts from the CIA, NSA, and the presidential cabinet, and we're meeting right here so that I don't have to move. The missing piece is Jim Heron—we're still waiting for him to get back—although if we have to, we'll go forward without him."

"Have you gotten a . . . response? You know, from them."

"No."

Fear tickled across her ribs and hit her heart like a battery charge. "Can you last until tomorrow night."

"If that's the way it has to be, yes."

He seemed so sure, and she needed to believe in that confidence: It would be a tragedy beyond measure for him to be cut down now, when he was so close to the freedom he sought.

Strange, that someone she had met only days before suddenly seemed so important to her.

"I'm proud of you," she said, running her finger down his photograph.

"That means a lot to me." Pause. "And thank you for showing me the way. I never would have been able to do this without you."

"Without my father, you mean," she countered softly. "He has the contacts."

"No. You're the one."

She frowned, thinking that was a funny way of phrasing it. "I want you to answer something for me."

"Name it."

Her eyes flipped up to his. "What are your chances. Realistically."

"Of getting out of this alive?"

"Yes." When he just shook his head, she frowned at him. "Remember, we're so done with the whole 'shelter the little woman' routine."

"Fifty-fifty."

Well, didn't that give her a knot in her throat. "That bad, huh."

"Do you want something to eat along with the coffee? I'm no chef, but I saw some leftovers in the fridge and I can work a microwave." When she begged off, he tacked on, "You have to eat."

"I'd rather have sex with you," she blurted.

Isaac coughed. Actually *coughed*, like someone had punched him in the solar plexus.

"Sorry if that's too blunt." She shrugged. "But social graces are waaaaay down my list of things to worry about right now. And I have a feeling I'm not going to see you after tomorrow night, either because you're swept up into federal custody or because . . ." She took a deep breath. "I want a proper piece of you before you go. Something to remember you with that's in my skin, not just my brain. Upstairs was so fast and furious . . . I want to pay attention and remember."

He was silent for a long time. "I'd think you'd want to forget as much of this as you can."

"Not you . . . I don't want to forget you." The corner of her mouth lifted a little. "Although I don't think I could."

When he stayed where he was, she pushed her chair back and stood up. The distance between them took three strides to cross, and as she came at him, he straightened; then he tugged his sweatshirt down like he was tidying himself up.

Grier rose onto her tiptoes and touched his face, putting her palms on his five o'clock shadow. "I'm never going to forget you."

As he licked his lips, like he was hungry for exactly what she was after, she took his hand and drew him deeper into the wine cellar, pulling him fully inside, shutting them in together.

Unlike the first time, when she'd been all wound up and seeking only more of the cyclone, this was about him, the man, not her own internal buzzing.

This was *all* about him.

As she leaned in to kiss him, he put his big hands on her thin wrists and held her off gently. "This didn't help upstairs."

"Yes. It did. You just didn't believe me."

"Grier . . ." Her name was a combination of confusion and desperation: *why* spelled with five new letters instead of the usual three.

"I don't want to talk anymore," she murmured, fixated on his mouth.

"You sure?"

When she nodded, he bent down and pressed his lips against hers, drawing her into him. He was fully aroused, more than ready for her, and yet he moved her back.

Before she could protest, she heard the click of the lock sliding into place and then those warm hands slipped under her shirt and slid around her rib cage, going to the small of her back. As she felt a gentle, lifting pressure, her feet came up off the floor and she was carried over to the table.

Pushing the dossiers to the side, Isaac laid her out flat, his palms moving to her breasts as he bent over her and kept their mouths fused. Her yoga pants were off her legs a moment later, but instead of tossing them, he put them over the chair she'd been in. Smart. No telling whether she was going to have to get dressed fast in the middle.

A subtle pull and her hips were right at the edge of the table . . . and then he broke their kiss and sank down onto his knees.

If she'd thought she'd seen his eyes burn before, it was nothing compared to what they were doing now. Frost had never been so hot.

As she got an idea where he was headed, she sat up. "But I want this to be for both of us—"

"You said you wanted to remember something." His palms slid up to the tops of her thighs and squeezed. "So lie back and let me do my thing."

That tongue of his made a reappearance—and didn't that make her get on board with the plan.

"G'on now," he murmured with that Southern drawl.

"Lie on back and let me take care of you. I promise to go slow . . . real slow."

His hands drifted down to her knees and spread her legs . . . and she gave herself up to him. Following his instructions to the letter, she felt the hard table against her shoulder blades and the cool air on her thighs and a wild heat in her blood.

As he stared at her from beneath his brows, he looked as if he were going to consume her.

And she was ready to be his meal.

Ducking his head, he went right where she needed him, putting his mouth on her sex through the thin silk panties she wore. A rush of delicious heat bloomed and her hand snapped out, grabbing the pants, dragging them over, putting them in her mouth to keep herself from calling out.

If it felt this good already, she was going to get noisy: Yes, the door to the cellar was heavy and her father was supposedly asleep, but she didn't want to take any chances.

Isaac groaned against her as he nuzzled at her through the silk, and then he ran his tongue up the fragile strip that covered her. On a curse, she arched hard, her nails scratching the wood beneath her as his hands dug into her thighs and her teeth bit into the cotton. And then there was nothing separating them. One moment his mouth was on the silk; the next, she felt a yank on her hips and heard a tearing sound as the panties gave way—

Oh, God . . . his wet tongue slipped into the heart of her and dragged upward, parting her, sliding slick against slick.

He did go slow.

As his big palms locked on her hips and held her down, he took his sweet time, kissing her and sucking at her, that tongue of his working its magic, only to be replaced with the hot, locking suction of his lips. All the while, he stared up at her, watching her breasts surge as she writhed under his mouth.

Abruptly, as if he needed to touch what he was seeing, his hands went under her shirt again and honed in on what he seemed captivated with. Unleashing the front clasp of her bra, he took possession of her on both sides, his thumbs rubbing at her nipples.

Her breath pumped in and out of her open mouth, and just as she was about to orgasm, Isaac inched back and licked his glossy lips.

"Come for me," he said. "I want to feel it."

And then he was against her once more, his tongue penetrating her—which was all it took. Her release rocked her, rolling out from her sex and taking over every inch of her body. As the swirl of sparks consumed her, she was dimly aware of him groaning, as if he felt her clenching pleasure firsthand.

He didn't stop there. Swirling, lapping, sucking ... he kept going, spreading her legs even wider, holding her in place as he marked her memory as sure as he marked her sex. She would never forget this—

One of his long fingers, or maybe two, eased inside, and the pressure and stretching sent her right over the edge again. As another orgasm fired off, her hands locked on his forearms, her nails sinking into his flesh as her spine torqued and that blast of pleasure flooded her from the inside out.

And still he didn't stop.

He was hot and he was wild and he was relentless.

He was the lover she would never, ever forget.

Much less get over, she feared.

*Oh, sweet Jesus ...*

Isaac looked up from between Grier's legs and nearly climaxed just at the sight of her. She was all woman undone, the remnants of her white panties around her hips, her black shirt around her throat, her bra halves lying to the sides. Her breasts were tight at the pink tips and her face flushed and her belly moving on a rhythm of surges and relentings as she worked herself against him.

Those pants in her mouth were one of the sexiest parts of it.

And the taste of her was even hotter than that.

Isaac could have stayed where he was for hours, but with each passing moment he ran the risk of an interruption and he wanted to finish this properly.

Rising up and looming above her, he bent her knees to her chest, his cock twitching on the edge of orgasm at the sight of the glistening heart of her all swollen and open for him. There was no ditching his pants—he pushed them down just enough to spring his erection . . . which wept at the tip as he thought of where he was going. Sweeping his hand over his wet mouth, he brought his palm to the head of his shaft, slicking himself up even more before he curled the end of his spine and brought them together.

Pushing in, he watched as he made the connection, seeing her part to accommodate his girth, hearing her moan as he went deeper and staked his claim.

"Oh, f—" The gentleman in him swallowed the curse. The caveman in him had to keep talking. "Look at you. . . . I want to leave something behind . . . *in* you."

His eyes shot to hers as he began to move, pulling in and out, in and out . . . and then he went back to looking at where they were joined, the gloss on him making his balls tight. Bending down to her breasts, he sucked a nipple into his mouth and worked it with his tongue . . . until the rhythm below made keeping that lock on her impossible: He'd meant what he'd said about going slowly, but the good intention didn't last. The sex had a momentum of its own, and it wasn't long at all before the table groaned under the force of his thrusts and he had to grip her waist to hold her where he wanted her.

As she went rigid under him, Isaac came hard as well, clamping down on his molars to keep from making noise, his lids squeezing shut even though he'd wanted to watch her face as what he was doing to her took her to another release.

With his body jerking into hers and him filling her up . . . he was as satiated as a man in the desert who'd had a sip of water.

He wasn't nearly finished with her. She wanted memories? Roger that.

Keeping them joined, he tugged the pants out of her mouth, scooped her up, and brought her lips to his, kissing her deeply as he easily carried her weight off the table. Positioning her against the smooth door, he gripped the back of her legs and started moving once again. With her hands tangled in his hair, and the blazing heat and urgent energy taking over again, the kiss couldn't last—and he didn't last much longer than the seal of their lips did. He came hard into her, collapsing against her as her own orgasm milked at him.

Recovery was a luxury he didn't allow himself much of, because he was well aware of his weight against her and the fact that her back was pressing into something hard and also that her father was in the house and . . .

So many damn *ands* with them.

Isaac slowly eased her down until her feet were on the ground, and as he slipped out of her, he didn't like the cold air on his cock. Her sex was much better . . . far, far better.

As he kissed her, the way her lips moved over his told him that in a different world, in different circumstances . . . this definitely would have been a beginning for them—in spite of all that should have kept them apart like family and money and education.

But that was not their reality, was it.

"Let me get you something to clean up with," he said quietly as he tugged his pants back into place.

After he kissed her again, he ducked out the door, and as he shut her up inside, he paused and bowed his head.

He'd lied to her.

His chances were nowhere close to fifty-fifty: Matthias was absolutely, positively going to get him. The question was just how much talking he could do into the right ears before his old boss came out of the shadows and claimed him. One thing had always been true about the head of XOps: Matthias never gave up. Ever. And even if his world was crumbling around him, he would still take his vengeance. Somehow, someway.

That wasn't going to stop Isaac from taking a shot at spilling the beans, however.

Much better to die having tried to do the right thing . . . and leave his woman thinking something less than bad of him.

Much better.

# CHAPTER
## 35

As the morning sun roused from its cloudy slumber and a halo of rays poured over Caldwell, New York, two young boys, ages twelve and nine, were hoofing it to school.

And neither one of them was impressed by all the "spring splendor."

Whatever that was.

Their mom kept going on and on about *spring splendor*, *spring splendor* . . . bleh. What Joey Mason cared about was gym: Mondays he usually had gym, but today they were having a special assembly. So no matter how "spring splendor" it was outside, he was still on his way to a day of school with nothing to look forward to.

His little brother, Tony, on the other hand, liked assemblies more than gym, so he was psyched. But he was a geek who slept with books, so what did he know about anything.

The walk from home to school was about eight blocks long and nothing big . . . just down St. Francis Street by the church and some other stuff. They were supposed to stay on the right side, because there was a gas station on the left that had lots of traffic in and out of its driveway. And they were supposed to stop at every corner curb. Which Joey did—usually while grabbing Tony's collar to keep him from walking right into a car.

Tony always walked with a book open. Just like he ate reading and went to the bathroom reading and got dressed reading.

Stupid. Just stupid, because you missed so much if you weren't looking around.

Like this cool car they were coming up on. The windows were black and the body was black and it had a number for a license plate: 010. That was it; no letters. Joey glanced over at his little brother, and sure enough Tony hadn't noticed.

His loss.

The thing looked like one of those police-type jobbies.

As they came up to it, he nabbed his brother's collar and yanked him up short. Tony didn't question the stop—just turned another page. He probably thought they were at a curb.

Joey leaned in a little and tried to see inside, all the while braced for something in a uniform to get out and yell at them for being nosy. When he saw nothing and nothing happened, he cupped his hands and put them against the cold glass—

He jumped back. "I think there's someone in there."

"Is not," Tony said without lifting his head.

"Is too."

"Is not."

"Is too. And how would you know?"

"Is not."

Okay, Tony didn't know what he was talking about and this argument could go on forever. And then he and his little brother would be late for homeroom and he'd get grounded. Again.

But . . .

How coooooooooool if they found a dead body—right in front of the McCready Funeral Home!

Dropping his book bag, Joey moved his brother away from the car by picking him up and relocating his feet. "This is dangerous. I don't want you hurt."

That finally got Tony's eyes out of the book. "Is there really somebody inside?"

"You stay back."

It was the kind of thing his father would have said, and Joey felt all big-man about it—especially as Tony nodded and held his book to his chest. But this was how it was supposed to be. Joey was gonna be thirteen soon, and he was in charge when there was no one else around. And sometimes even when there were other folks in sight.

Recupping his hands, he resumed his position against the glass, and retried to see past the darkened— "It's a pirate!"

"You're lyin'."

"No, I'm not—"

A car slowed to a halt in front of them and a lady put down her window—it was Mrs. Alonzo from across the street. "What are you up to now, boys?"

Like all they did was get up to stuff.

Part of Joey wanted her to keep going and let him run this situation. But the other part wanted to show off. "There's a dead guy in here."

He felt very important as she got all white and nervy-lookin'. Man, if he'd known all this was going to happen, he would have been in more of a hurry leaving the house. This was way better than gym.

Except then Tony had to jump in. "It's a pirate!"

Abruptly, Mrs. Alonzo didn't look so grown-up scared. "A pirate."

His brother was such a pain—and Joey was not about to lose his audience. Pirates were a kid thing. Dead guy in a car? That was all grown-up, and that was where he wanted to be.

"See for yourself," he said.

Mrs. Alonzo pulled her Lexus in front of the black-on-black car and got out, her high heels making pony-clopping sounds on the road. "Okay, enough, boys. Get in and I'll drive you the rest of the way to school. You're going to be late." She held out her phone to Joey. "Call your mother and tell her I'm taking you in. Again."

This did happen a lot. Mrs. Alonzo was a business lady whose office was not far from school, and they were late a lot and she did drive them a lot. But this morning was different.

He crossed his arms over his chest. "You have to look in the window."

"Joey—"

"Please." Another grown-up thing: the please-and-thank-you stuff.

"Fine. But get in my car."

Mrs. Alonzo marched over while grouching something about being a taxi service. And Tony, who always followed the rules, took his book into the front seat of her SUV—except he was still interested in what was happening because he didn't shut the door and *Diary of a Wimpy Kid Dog Days* remained against his chest.

Joey stayed put.

Normally, he would have gotten upset about Tony taking the better seat: older brothers rode in the front; younger babies went in the back. But there were things more important than that right now, so he stayed where he was on the sidewalk, the phone unused in his hand.

He was wondering what he'd seen—

Mrs. Alonzo leaped back so far, she nearly ended up in traffic, a minivan honking its horn as it barely missed her.

She ran over and snatched the phone as well as his arm. "Get in the car, Joey—"

"What is it? Is it a dead guy?" Jeez, what if it was a pirate—holy shit!

Mrs. Alonzo put her phone to her ear as she dragged

him to her Lexus. "Yes, this is an emergency. There's a man in a car in front of the McCready Funeral Home on St. Francis. I don't know if there's something wrong with him, but he's behind the wheel and he doesn't seem to be moving. . . . I have small children with me and I don't want to open the door—right. . . ."

*Small children*. God, he hated that *small-children* stuff. He was the one who'd found the guy, after all. How many grown-ups had tooled by on their way to work and not seen it? Biked by? Run by?

It was *his* dead guy.

"My name is Margarita Alonzo. Yes, I'll stay until the paramedics and police get here."

Okay. This was officially the best morning in the history of his life, Joey thought as he jumped into the backseat—which had the best view, as it turned out.

As Mrs. Alonzo got in and locked all the doors, he imagined the three of them being here until noon, one o'clock. Maybe they'd get a Happy Meal for lunch. He really hoped the police didn't rush—

The bummer of all bummers hit him when he heard Mrs. Alonzo say, "Sarah? I have your boys, and they're okay. But there's a little problem and I need you to come pick them up."

Joey put his head down on his arm.

Knowing his luck, his mother would zoom to the scene and get here before he found out about the dead pirate in the front seat of that car.

Ruined. Just ruined.

And they were probably going to get to school right in time for the assembly.

As Matthias slept behind the wheel of his car, he dreamed of the night Jim Heron had saved his life over and over again. The events that had led up to the bomb and the long, painful trek back to relative health played and replayed in an endless loop through his mind, as if the needle on his old-fashioned mental record player was stuck.

Matthias had lured Jim Heron to that abandoned, dusty hut as a witness because there was nobody else in the XOps community whose word held more weight and credibility. The idea had been for the soldier to leave the body parts in the sand and go home to tell the others there had been a terrible accident: If anyone else had filed a report like that, the assumption would have been that they had done the killing. Not in Jim's case, though—he was a straight shooter in a world full of curves, and he'd never had any problem copping to what he'd done, right or wrong.

Which was proof there was a little bit of good in Matthias, after all—at least he wasn't dumping his suicide on the head of another guy.

And yeah, of course he could have just blown his own head off in a bathroom somewhere, but although he was suicidal, he had his pride. Taking a self-administered lead injection was just too fucking weak—much better to spackle the crap out of a few stone walls and be mourned as the strong fighter he'd always been.

Pride, however, had had its costs: instead of leaving him in the sand, that cocksucker Heron had saved him—and figured out his little secret. The explosive device had been the tip-off. As Matthias had lain there bleeding like a stuck pig, Jim had found remnants of the bomb and recognized them for what they were. Namely, one of their own.

The SOB had taken the fragments, put them in his pocket, and slipped off his belt. Then he'd thrown a tourniquet on Matthias's leg, picked him up, and started hauling ass. He'd been royally pissed off, and his savior routine had clearly been part punishment, part leverage—and all consuming. The bastard had walked and walked and walked . . . until sometime later, Isaac Rothe had showed up among the dunes with a Land Rover.

Jim's demands had come weeks afterward, at a hospital in Germany. By that point, Matthias's head had been nothing but a huge hot-air balloon of agony, and he was having to get used to only one eye working. Heron had sat at the bedside and laid down his terms: Out. Free and clear. Or he took what was left of the bomb and all of the story to the only person who could have done anything about it.

Hello, Mr. President.

Irony of ironies, had it been any other soldier, any other human with a beating heart and a trigger finger, Matthias wouldn't have worried about the threat. But again, Jim Heron—good ol' Zacharias—was one of those motherfuckers people believed in. Bomb fragments could be fabricated; the believability of a worthy guy? Pretty damn indisputable.

And there was no surviving as boss if people didn't think you had the balls for the job anymore.

At that point, Matthias had felt like there was no other choice, and told the man to go along his merry way.

In the aftermath, the suicidal thing had come back and he had considered it seriously. But then his second in command had shown up just in time—sure as if the guy had seen where he was headed.

Very persuasive man, that one. And as it had turned out, Jim had saved his body, but that second in command had somehow brought him back to life.

Although there had been consequences to the renewal: almost immediately, Matthias had opened his eyes—or one eye, as it were—to the mistake of letting Heron go: that soldier was out in the world with too much information, and the exposure wasn't acceptable.

His second in command had agreed, and they had been about to set the wheels in motion for an "accident" when Jim had called looking for information on one Marie-Terese Boudreau. Perfect. Timing. The plan had been to have Jim take out Isaac in exchange for the intel he wanted—and then to murder Jim.

Except someone had gotten to Heron first.

Dead. Jim was dead. Matthias had seen the body with his own eyes. And yet ... somehow he felt as though he'd spoken to the guy. Yes, he had dreamed that he had talked with Jim Heron—

Matthias came awake with his gun in his hand, the safety off the weapon and the muzzle pointed at a white guy in a navy blue uniform—who had, going by the jimmy in his hand, just pried the lock and opened the car door.

The paramedic froze and put his hands up. "I just want to help you, man."

Probably true enough. But damn it to hell, the guy's partner was undoubtedly calling in the police right now, and p.s., doing any kind of face-to-face with a civilian wasn't a bene in Matthias's book.

He lowered his gun. "I'm a federal agent." He put his hand into his coat and decided to flash his FBI credentials— which were legit to a point.

The paramedic leaned in and squinted at the laminated photograph and the bullshit name and the very real crest. "Oh ... sorry, sir. We got a call. . . ."

"It's okay. Just pulled three days straight up at the Canadian border and I'm on my way to Manhattan. I got off the Northway looking for some chow around four a.m., but there was nothing open and I had to get some sleep. You know how that is."

"Oh, I so get that."

Chatter, chatter, chatter ... blah, blah, blah ...

When the police showed up, they ran the ID in their system, and gee frickin' whiz, it checked out. And his story about being on a classified mission and having to pull over from exhaustion was consumed like a Thanksgiving dinner: He went from criminal to celebrity.

Stupid fools.

After he sent them off, he drove away himself and took his phone out. There were a number of voice mails . . . and one high alert.

Well, what do you know . . . looked like Isaac Rothe had turned himself in and his location was the house of his lovely and talented defense attorney. How fucking perfect: Although they could have picked him off standing up in Grier Childe's kitchen if they'd absolutely had to, this was going to make things much less complicated.

Matthias called his number two, and as the phone rang, he thought of how many times he'd had this conversation: Go. Get the bastard. Cap him. Take care of the body.

He'd done it so many times.

As that pain in the left side of his chest fired up again, he ignored the sensation—

"Yeah?" his number two answered.

"Isaac Rothe is ready for you."

There wasn't even a pause. "The Beacon Hill address?"

"Yes. Go there now and get him."

"I'm out of state."

"Well, get 'in state' and get to him. ASAP."

"Roger that. Where do you want him?"

Good question. Isaac wasn't known for great escapes; his reputation was for fast, clean kills in extraordinary circumstances. But you didn't pull off jobs like he had without being highly resourceful.

"Hold him at that house for me," Matthias said abruptly.

As he considered the situation, instinct told him that a change in strategy was appropriate. After all, Grier Childe and her father could use some reining in—and nothing got a civilian's attention more than watching someone get murdered. Good old Albie was proof of that—

For some reason, Jim Heron's voice popped into Matthias's brain. No specific words, just a tone that lingered, a grave, imploring tone that made Matthias feel like he had to stop everything and . . . do what exactly?

"Hello?" his number two demanded, like the guy had either said something that hadn't been responded to or there'd been nothing but silence for a while.

"I don't want you to kill him," Matthias heard himself say.

"Oh, I know. You're going to do that yourself." Satisfaction. Such satisfaction, like that was the plan all along.

For no good reason, Matthias's central processor started to spark and smoke, images flitting in and out of his mind in a mad jumble that made him think of dice rolling across a felt table. And then from out of the chaos, he saw Alistair Childe being held up off a filthy rug by two operatives in black as his son was injected with enough heroin to put an elephant into a perma-nod.

*Danny . . . oh, Danny, my boy . . .* Like that Irish bar song, only not musical at all when a father was hoarsely crying out the words.

"Boss," his number two cut in. "Talk to me. What's going on."

So level-voiced, but it was a false pragmatism. The soldier was no doubt worried that the wheels were falling off again—that just as he had two years ago, he was going to have to drag Matthias into his fighting boots once more.

"Do not kill him," Matthias heard himself repeat. "That's an order."

"I know, so you can do it. He's for you. You *have* to take him."

For a moment, Matthias felt an inescapable, tantalizing draw . . . "No," he blurted, shaking hmself. "No, I don't."

"Yes, you must—"

"Just follow the fucking order without commentary or I'll find someone else who will."

With a curse, he hung up, sent a signal back to Isaac and

then tried to find some solid internal ground to stand on. Shit, all of sudden, he felt like he had two different voices in his head and not only were they pulling him in opposite directions, neither was his own.

Fortunately, the return transmission from Rothe cut into the struggle.

"Matthias," came that old, familiar voice.

"Isaac. How are you."

"Where? When?"

"Always so to the point." Matthias pushed his knee into the bottom of the steering wheel to keep the sedan on the road while he massaged the pain in his left pec. "I'm sending someone for you. So you stay put."

"Unacceptable. I can't be picked up here."

"Dictating terms? I don't think so."

"Grier Childe is not going to be involved in this. I'll turn myself in at midnight tomorrow in a public place."

"And now you want to tell me when? Fuck you, Rothe. If you want her to stay out of it, you'll do what I tell you to. Or do you think I can't get past that fancy security system of hers on any night of my choosing?" Silence. "Surprised that I know about the damn thing? Well, there are other tricks to that house, Isaac. I wonder how many of them *you* know about."

See, this was good. The back and forth was clearing out some of that fuzzy, foggy, waffling shit—and it reminded him of the reason behind Daniel Childe's death: good ol' Albie's flapping gums.

A shot of adrenaline woke him up even further as he wondered just what kind of plans Isaac and the retired captain might have been hatching while he was out cold at the side of the road.

He cleared his throat. "Yeah, you stay tight—and in case you've gotten any bright ideas from that father of hers, let me set you straight. If you do anything to expose me or my organization, I will do things to that woman that she will survive physically and never heal from. And know this: My reach extends beyond my own grave." More silence. "You've met the father—don't deny it. And I'm well aware he's been trying to take notes on XOps for the last decade. No bright ideas, Isaac. For her sake. Or I'll ignore you and come after her. I'll let you live a long life, knowing that you are the reason she's ruined from the inside out—"

"She's not part of this!" Rothe hissed. "She's got nothing to do with me or her goddamn father!"

"Maybe. But shit happens. And I assigned her to you for a good reason—which panned out better than I thought. I never expected the two of you to get so personally involved—or did you think I didn't hear what the pair of you got up to in that guest bedroom of hers last night?" Matthias fought against the pain in his chest, feeling as if he were drowning. "Don't make me hurt her, Isaac. I'm getting tired of all that, I truly am. Stay where you are—I'm sending someone, and you'll know when he gets there. And if you and her and her father are not there when he arrives, I'm going to have him find her, not you. You follow instructions and I'll make sure no one but you gets hurt."

Matthias hit the *end* button and tossed the phone onto the passenger seat.

Wincing, he struggled to keep the car heading straight as the agony behind his ribs swelled to unmanageable levels. Under the onslaught, he briefly thought about driving over to the Caldwell International Airport again, but he decided to keep driving because he needed to get a grip and that was going to take time. And privacy.

Squeezing his left pec, he pulled over and tried to breathe through the pain in his chest. Which didn't really help much . . . to the point where he wondered whether this was it. The Big One. Just like what had killed off his father.

Looking out of the front windshield, he realized he was in front of a church.

For no good reason, he turned off the engine, picked up

his cane and got out. He hadn't been in anything remotely God-like for years and to be limping toward its huge double doors felt ... wrong in a lot of ways. Especially given everything that was waiting for him in Boston. But his number two needed time to get things set and Matthias ... needed this heart attack to either get organized and kick his bucket or shut the fuck up.

Inside was warm and smelled of incense and lemon floor polish. The place was huge, with hundreds and hundreds of pews spanning out in three directions from where the altar was.

Matthias didn't make it all the way to the back. He collapsed in a sit about halfway down the side aisle, all but falling onto the wooden bench.

Moving his cane between his knees he looked up at the crucifix ... and began to cry.

# CHAPTER
## 36

After he cut off the communication with Matthias, Isaac shoved the Life Alert transmitter into his sweatshirt. What he wanted to do was put it on the granite counter and smash it with his fist. Then maybe light the pieces on fire.

Bracing his hands on the kitchen sink, he leaned into his shoulders and stared out at the back garden. Almost eight a.m. and the place was all but pitch-dark because the houses in the neighborhood were packed so closely together. No clue whether Jim's buddies were still back there. No word from Jim.

But Isaac had other problems right now.

Shit. All things considered, the fact that Matthias was savvy enough to be suspicious wasn't a news flash. But the nail-on-the-head component to what was hopefully just speculation put Isaac in a tight one. If he left now, he ran the risk of Grier and her father getting slaughtered. If he stayed . . . they were probably going to be made to watch him die.

Mother. Fucker.

"They got in touch with you."

He looked over his shoulder. Grier was fresh out of her shower, her hair down and drying naturally.

"Isaac." Her face grew tight. "Did they get back to you?"

"No," he said. "Not yet."

To make the lie stick, he pulled out the transmitter and let it dangle, banking on the fact that she wouldn't notice that the light was now off.

"Is that thing working?"

"Yeah." He put it away as she came over. "How's your father?"

"On the phone again in the bathroom." She glanced at the clock. "God, I thought last night would never end."

"I just want Jim to show," he said as she started to make coffee by the sink.

"Do you think . . . he really is dead?"

At this point—maybe. "No."

Sitting down on one of the stools, he watched her pop the top off the Hills Bros can and put the filter into the maw of the machine. As she went through the routine task, the sunlight on her face made him want to weep, she was so beautiful.

On some level, he couldn't believe he'd been with her—and not as in the he-wasn't-worthy shit. Duh, that was self-evident. But all that pounding, hot-and-heavy sex seemed like a dream. She was all cleaned up, smelling like shampoo instead of his sweat, her hair smooth, her face unflushed.

She took his breath away. To him, she was proof positive that life was worth the sacrifices it demanded of people: Just to look at her and be in the same room, to have the memories he had given not just her, but himself . . .

The idea of anything hurting her, ever, was simply unsupportable. And if he was the cause of it?

*I'll let you live a long life, knowing that you are the reason she's ruined from the inside out.*

Not a threat. Not from a guy like Matthias, who didn't draw any distinctions that stopped at the feet of the female sex. And he would hurt her in ways that made that special thing Isaac had shared with her down in the cellar impossible for her to enjoy ever again.

As much as it pained him, he had to be realistic: When he was gone, she would find another lover. Maybe one she'd marry and have kids with and grow old beside. And there would be none of that for her at all unless he stuck around, waited it out . . . and prayed that when Matthias's operative showed up, he was able to kill the fucker and then quickly disappear.

After all, he was a goddamn assassin. It was what he did for a living.

One thing was clear: there was going to be no coming forth with intel anymore. No way. Grier's life was worth more than her respecting him and whatever was set in motion by her father could be undone fast as a phone call after the dust settled—so as far as they were going to know, it was business as usual until Isaac took off.

And as for his ever after? He was going to turn himself in to Matthias and have his reckoning, but it would be on his terms. Grier's pops was on to something with those dossiers, and Jim Heron or one of his boys was just the kind of guy who'd keep a first-person, taped narration of every single murder Isaac had ever done locked in a safe—provided Grier and her father died of natural causes.

After all, he was under the impression that death's door confessions were admissible in court—so as long as Isaac stated that Matthias was going to kill him shortly, he had a whole lot of clout, didn't he—or at least enough to open one fucker of an investigation.

His testimony would be her and her father's life insurance policy.

Across the way, Grier hit the *on* button, and as the machine started hissing it out, she stayed where she was, staring at the thing.

Compelled by something he didn't question, Isaac stood

up and went behind her, putting his chest to her back. Her breath caught as she felt his body, and though she stiffened, she didn't move away.

He reached up and touched the blond waves that fell around her shoulders, running his fingertips over them. Then he swept them slowly to the side, exposing the nape of her neck.

God, he'd made his mind up, hadn't he.

He'd chosen his path.

"Can I kiss you," he said roughly. Because it seemed like the gentlemanly thing to ask first.

Her head dropped. "Please . . ."

He went in for her lovely neck, pressing his lips to her skin. That wasn't nearly enough, but he didn't trust himself to go any further or even put his hands on her waist—if he did, he wasn't letting go until she was under him and he was in her again.

"Grier," he whispered hoarsely.

"Yes . . ."

"I need to tell you something."

"What?"

Sometimes emotions were like a locomotive for words: Once they got a reveal rolling, there was no slowing the thing down, no brakes strong enough to grab onto the tracks of your throat.

"I love you," he said with more breath than syllable.

She heard it, though. Dear God, she heard it, because she inhaled on a hiss.

Grier whipped around so fast, her hair spun out in a halo, and even though his heart was pounding, he didn't look away.

When her mouth opened, he put his finger to her lips and shook his head. "I just needed you to know. Once. I just needed to say it . . . once. I realize I haven't known you long enough or well enough, and I'm very aware that I'm not the man for you . . . but some things need to be said."

What didn't require airtime was the terror inside his skin.

As much as he wanted to do the right thing, his old boss had him by the short hairs: There was no sacrifice too great to ensure Grier's safety. Even Isaac's own salvation. Even Matthias's downfall.

A throat being cleared discreetly had him looking up. In the glass over the sink, he saw her father standing just inside the kitchen—and out of respect for the man's daughter, Isaac stepped back.

"Coffee, Father?" Grier said evenly as she leaned to the side and got two mugs from the cupboard.

"Yes, thank you."

Isaac could feel the guy's eyes going back and forth, but he sure as hell wasn't answering any of those questions.

And neither was Grier, evidently. "Are we all set?" she asked.

Instead of replying, the man cleared his throat again. No doubt because he was choking on all the stay-away-from-hims and the don't-touch-my-daughters.

But he didn't need to worry. He was too late on the latter, but the former . . . was going to be taken care of.

"Father? Are we all set?"

"Everyone will arrive tomorrow morning—"

*"Tomorrow morning?"*

"This is a delicate situation. Excuses had to be made—these men and women can't just duck out for no good reason without questions being raised."

Isaac could feel Grier staring at him like she was looking for some backup on the hell-no front, but as it was, he disagreed with her. Tomorrow morning was just perfect.

He'd be gone by then.


Out at the Framingham Comfort Inn & Suites, Jim woke up in his dimly lit room and felt like he'd been in a car accident. With a semi. And he hadn't had his seat belt on.

He was on the bed he'd been sleeping in and curled on

his side, his busted-up body having carved out a section of the mattress and settled in like a dog waiting to die in the woods. But he was immortal now . . . and what that apparently meant was no matter how much damage was done, he healed from it.

Yeah, except this was no Samantha-the-witch nose-twitch kind of job, where everything was cleaned up on a oner. He felt very human with the aches and pains, with the inhales that made his ribs burn, with the skips of his heart as it beat the same way a drunk walked. But the worst part of it wasn't physical. It was in his head.

That he had left Sissy behind in Devina's realm killed him.

Opening his eyes, he realized it was morning; over the top of Dog's fuzzy head, the alarm glowed with red numbers. 7:52.

Rise and shine, he thought as he gingerly rolled over onto his back. On the other side of him, Adrian was out like a light, the angel breathing deeply, his eyes jogging behind his closed lids.

Given the glower on his face, he clearly wasn't having a good time in dreamland.

God, what a night, Jim thought. After Colin had left him, he'd assumed it was just going to be him and Dog. But then someone had come through the other room, and he'd assumed it was Eddie—the nursey-nurse shit was clearly more up his alley.

But no. Adrian had been the one to come in . . . and stay.

At the moment, Jim didn't have the strength to deal with how any sympathy was going to make him feel, so he carefully pulled a blanket around himself and quietly stood up on legs that were about as strong as pencils. Limping over to the laptop, he was dizzy as all get out, and he just barely made it to the chair in time—although, fuckin' A, that ass-plant hurt like a bitch.

In spite of the fact that he had to piss like a racehorse,

he fired up the Dell and waited impatiently for the Internet browser to get rolling. To pass the time, he took a gander at the ligature marks around his wrists. The pair of them were a pattern of brilliant red, twisted lines that were shiny and raw, and the tangible reminder of where he'd been and what had been done to him tantalized his mind with a field trip into PTSD. Except that was one permission slip he refused to sign.

Dragging himself into focus, he started to type, although because his fingers were numb, it took forever to get to the *Caldwell Courier Journal*'s site and put in a search for Cecilia Barten. . . .

Up came an article from some two weeks prior, and Sissy's picture brought a sheen to his eyes. She was smiling into the camera while standing in the center of a bunch of kids her own age. There was no telling how long it had been between when the photo was snapped and when she'd been taken by Devina—but the fact that she'd had no idea what was around the corner for her made his unreliable heart get even flakier on the job.

Probably good that she hadn't known.

And he was so going to get Devina for this.

The only other article was one that reported she remained missing a week later—and the two together made him realize why his first search of the database had failed. He'd only told the computer to look for murdered or dead blond girls. Not ones who were MIA.

Stupid fucking mistake.

And the details were as she had told him: She was a freshman at Union College in Albany, and home on spring break in Caldwell. The last anyone had seen of her was when she'd left at nine p.m. to go to the local Hannaford for groceries.

No pictures of her parents. He was going to find them, however.

"Did you see her," Adrian said in a voice that was mostly gravel.

"Yeah." Jim stared at the picture of his girl smiling with her friends. Then he blinked and saw that blond hair matted with blood. "How do I get her out of the wall?"

The other angel's exhale was the kind you made when there was no good news to be had. Anywhere. And you were aching from that. "You can't."

"Unacceptable. There has to be a way."

"Not that I've found." There was a curse and then a creaking of the mattress and a variety of cracks, as if Ad was stretching. "I'll be right back."

As heavy footsteps headed for the other bedroom, Jim didn't acknowledge the guy's exit. But when Dog's muzzle nudged against his bare leg, he looked down.

Big brown eyes stared up out of a face of strawlike fur. "Do you know how to get her out? She doesn't belong there. She shouldn't have ended up there."

Jim took the little whimper to mean the animal agreed— and also needed to go out to use the facilities.

"Two secs," Jim said, bracing himself to get to his feet. "I need a shower."

Heaving his deadweight up from the chair, he let the blanket fall from him and went into the modestly sized bathroom. Closing himself in, he flicked on the light, stood over the toilet and wondered whether his cock still worked on any level.

The pink stream he pissed out answered that one. And also suggested that his kidneys had been damaged.

After he was finished, he grunted as he leaned over to hit the flusher and then twisted to the left to turn on the shower. Soap. He needed more soap than the half-used bar that was in there—

Jim froze as he saw himself in the mirror.

Bad. Very bad.

Much worse than he'd thought.

His mouth was purple and swollen from all the shit that had been shoved into it, and his chest and abs were nothing but raw meat. As for his cock . . . The damn thing was hanging off his hips like it had lost the will to live. And he didn't want to know what the backside of him looked like.

*Used and abused* was the term.

And his only thought, his only . . . anything . . . was that he hated that Sissy had seen him like this.

As his stomach flopped around in his pelvic girdle, he remembered the horrified expression on her face as she had looked at him. That poor girl . . . He'd been trained for this shit. He'd been through it before—well, not exactly what Devina had done to him, but he'd certainly been worked over a couple of times with fists and knives. Even a bullet or two. But Sissy . . .

He barely made it back to the toilet in time.

As his body clenched up and nothing but bile came out of his mouth, his eyes watered from the strain.

Damn it, Sissy had seen him like this. Sexually violated, bloody, beaten—

More vomiting.

He wasn't sure exactly when Adrian came in, because round three of heaving hopped up the bunny trail when it dawned on him that he didn't know whether she was safe from what had been done to him. After all, she was captured. She was stuck there in that hellhole. And Devina had plenty of things that were male-like.

"Here," Adrian said, passing over a cold washcloth.

Jim couldn't wipe his face because it hurt too much, so he patted at it, feeling the cool dampness like a balm against his flaming cheeks and burning lips.

Hanging his head, he noticed that he'd left fresh bloodstains on the creamy tile from the wounds that had reopened on his knees.

Yeah, immortal didn't mean embalmed; that was for sure.

Adrian sat down next to him, his face far too pale as he stared across the toilet seat. "You want me to get you into the shower? That's what helps me when she . . ."

As their eyes locked, it was survivor-to-survivor.

"Ah, shit . . ." As Jim spoke, his voice was rough and his throat felt like it had been hit with a plumber's snake. "She saw me like this. Sissy . . . she saw this."

He couldn't believe he said it, but keeping that inside was a no-go.

Unable to retain eye contact, Jim squeezed his lids shut and eased back against the flank of the tub. As the water fell like rain in the shower behind him, and the hard floor bit into his ass, he whispered, "She saw me ruined."

It was the last thing he said before he passed the fuck out.

# CHAPTER
## 37

You wouldn't have thought that a six-thousand-square-foot town house with three floors—four, if you counted the basement where the wine cellar was—could be cramped as a shoe box.

But as the morning dragged on and bloomed into noon, Grier felt like she couldn't get enough air . . . or any alone time with Isaac. Her father was a pacing, eagle-eyed presence who seemed to fill every room, even when he wasn't in it. And Isaac was just as bad, constantly moving around, glancing out windows, going up and back from the front of the house to the kitchen.

By two o'clock, she couldn't stand it any longer and went to organize her bedroom closet. Which was ridiculous, because it was already tidy—although she found a quick cure for that.

After standing in the middle of the room and doing a three-sixty on the rows of clothes hanging by category, she took each and every blouse, skirt, dress, suit, and pair of slacks off the racks and tossed them into a pile on the floor. Ostensibly, she was reordering the various sections. In reality, she was giving herself a mess to clean up so she could enjoy a slice of control.

Hanger by hanger, item by item, she set about righting her wardrobe.

God . . . Isaac.

If she'd heard him right, down in the kitchen, by the coffeemaker . . . he'd said that he loved her.

Come on . . . of course she'd heard him right. And his incredible eyes had confirmed what her ears had struggled to comprehend.

There were a lot of *buts,* however, that the lawyer in her wanted to lay out. The thing was, the woman under the attorney-at-law didn't care about any of that: she felt something equally as strong.

Naturally, logic told her not to trust the emotion in either of their cases, pointing out that it was all a matter of the circumstance, the drama, the tension, the sex—God, the sex. Except her heart had a different theory. She'd felt the spark between them the instant she'd laid eyes on him, and his decision to come forward and do the right thing about his corrupt, dangerous boss . . . well, that was even better than the amazing orgasms.

It made her respect the hell out of him.

As she retrieved one of her black pin-striped suits, she briefly entertained a fantasy where they ended up together on some safe, remote island with nothing but what to have for lunch and dinner to weigh on their minds. The *Gilligan's Island* daydream with all its tropical never-going-to-happens was a nice diversion, but she wasn't fooling herself. Isaac was going to disappear. The government was going to take him and hide him until whatever congressional hearings or judicial procedures rolled out. And if he didn't end up in jail for war atrocities here in the States, he might well get extradited to some foreign hell.

Which was why he'd said what he had. It was his good-bye.

"Wow."

Grier spun on her heels, the suit in her hand flaring out in a circle around her body before settling back down—as if it had momentarily forgotten its reserve, only to regain its composure.

And didn't she know how the damn thing felt.

Isaac cursed himself. "Sorry, I really need to learn how to knock."

Grier eased up a little. "I'm also jumpy as hell."

Cocking his brow, he measured the pile in the middle of the creamy carpet. "Lot of clothes."

"Probably too many. I need to give some to Goodwill."

He came forward and picked up one of her gowns. It was long and black, like all of them, because she wasn't a sparkles or color kind of girl. "Where does this go?"

"Ah . . ." There was only one section with the bar set high enough for full-lengths. So she'd dumped them for nothing but a rehang. "There. In the corner, please."

He carried the evening dress over and set it where it had been. Then he went back for the next one, straightening the padded shoulders on their padded satin seat. Before he put it in place, he surprised her by bending down to put his nose to the neckline.

"This smells like your perfume," he murmured before placing it on the brass rod.

Didn't that just send a shiver through her — in a good way. Unfortunately, the tingle was overridden by everything that was hanging over them. "Have you heard from . . . them?"

"No."

"What are you going to do if they don't get back to you."

"They will."

He didn't say anything further, just picked up a taffeta gown with a velvet bodice and a broad tartan sash. "Christmas dress?"

"Yes."

"It's pretty."

"Thank you. Isaac?" When he looked at her, she said, "I—"

He cut her off. "What's that sound?"

"What sound—"

The suit fell from her hands as she recognized the subtle beeping and she scrambled to take the fob to the security system out of her pocket. Sure enough, a red light was flashing. *"Someone's in the house."*

She cut the noise and started for the phone by the bed, but he caught her arm. "No. No police. We've got enough innocent lives caught up in this already."

His gun came out and so did a tube about as long as her fist. As he screwed the silencer on the end of the muzzle, he looked around and then stalked over to the grated crawl space where the mechanicals of the security system were.

Keeping the weapon in hand, he popped off the metal face. "Get in there. And do not come out until I—"

"I can help—"

The expression on his face made her take a step back: His stare was cold and utterly foreign—like she was looking into frosted glass . . . with no hope of ever seeing what was behind it.

"Get in there, *now*."

Her eyes flicked to the gun and then returned to his harsh and unforgiving face. It was hard to know what was more frightening: the idea that someone was in her house, or the stranger standing in front of her. And then it dawned on her . . .

"Oh, my God, my father!"

"I got him. But I can't be effective if I'm worrying about you." The weapon pointed at the black hole he'd opened up. "Go now."

Putting her faith in him, Grier ducked out of view, crouching down and breathing the musty air of the eaves as Isaac put the grate back in place. There was a shift, *click*, shift, *click* as the thing was locked to the wall, and then through the slats, she watched him leave at a jog, quiet as a passing shadow.

She checked her watch. Listened hard.

Dread squeezed into the tight confines of her hideout with her, taking up more space than she did, blowing up that image of Isaac as a stranger until it was all she could see.

Silence.

More silence.

Which was promptly filled by a raucous paranoia in her head.

Oh, God . . . what if all this was a trap? What if Isaac had been sent for the sole purpose of enticing her father to determine how far he would go to expose the agency?

Except that she'd been the one who suggested it.

Or had he only wanted her to believe that?

His profile had said he'd needed moral imperative, though—unless that was a lie? And thus made him the perfect infiltrator? What if this was only a play to get her father to come forward with the dossiers . . . before they murdered him?

And yet Isaac had put her in here to protect her.

Except she hadn't recognized him when he had—

Dear Lord, the Life Alert—the light had been off, hadn't it. When he'd dangled it in front of her in the kitchen this morning, the light she'd seen before had been off. What did that mean? And come to think of it, the time lag had struck her as bizarre—between when he'd apparently turned himself in until now.

She had to get out of here. Get help.

Grier shuffled around and squeezed behind the stacked components of the security system's nerve center. The hidden staircase that ran down the middle of the house had been part of its original construction, and built because suspicion and mistrust of the British had still been brewing in 1810, some thirty years after the Revolution.

Turned out the house's tricks had uses in the present.

The glow of the security system provided enough illumination for her to find the dust-covered flashlight that hung on a nail at the head of the secret stairs. Clicking on the beam, she padded down the ancient, hand-carved steps, leaving prints behind in the dust. As she went, cobwebs clung to her hair and her shoulders were scraped by the rough mortar between the bricks.

When she got to the first floor, she paused. Naturally, she couldn't hear a damn thing because of the sturdy, thick walls, but her father had added an iron vent that looked like just another part of the HVAC system. Actually, however, it served as a covert surveillance post.

Grier went up a step and bent to the side to get her eyes in line, bracing herself on a pair of bricks that stuck out more than the others.

As she squinted, her vision penetrated the slats and focused on the front hall. If she arched a little more and craned her neck, she could see down toward the kitchen—

Grier dropped the flashlight and clamped her hands over her mouth.

To keep from screaming.

# CHAPTER
## 38

After Isaac made sure Grier was safely out of the way, he padded out into her bedroom and gave a listen. When the lack of footsteps, scrambling, or gunshots gave him no information, he continued out into the hall. Another pause. Should he use the back stairs? The front ones?

Front. More likely that an infiltration would occur from the rear garden. More cover that way.

Shit, he hoped it was Jim Heron, but he didn't think the guy would just bust in. And Grier's father could disarm the system—he'd already proved that. So he obviously hadn't let whoever it was inside.

Goddamn it, if it was Matthias's boy, why hadn't the arrival been announced through the Life Alert? Then again, Isaac wouldn't have let them inside, and they no doubt knew that: Matthias may have demanded that Grier and her father stick around, but Isaac wasn't about to get himself killed in front of them.

She'd never recover from that.

Please, God, he thought. Let her stay where she was.

Back-flatting it against the wall, he went down the stairs, leading with his gun. Sounds . . . where were all the sounds? There was literally nothing moving in the house, and considering that Grier's father had been pacing like a caged lion, the all-quiet was not encouraging.

As soon as the wall broke away and the free-standing banister started, he pulled another swing-and-drop, and deliberately landed hard as a rock on the Oriental in the front hall.

Sometimes noise was a good directive, giving your opponent a target to come running for.

And what do you know. The boom of Isaac's feet hitting the floor drew their visitor out: From down in the kitchen, a man dressed in black stepped into full view.

Matthias's second in command.

And he had Grier's dad up as a human shield.

"Want to trade?" the guy said grimly.

The gun to Childe's head was a nasty-looking auto-loader with a silencer. So not a surprise. It was identical to the one in Isaac's own palm.

Moving slowly, Isaac bent down and put his weapon to the floor. Then he kicked it away. "Let him go. Come and take me."

Childe's eyes went wide, but he held tight. Thank fuck.

Isaac turned to the wall, put his hands up on the plaster, and spread his ankles in a classic apprehension pose. Looking over his shoulder, he said, "I'm ready to go."

The second in command cracked a smile. "Check you out, all compliant and shit. Brings a tear to the eye."

With a slash, the operative lights-outed Grier's father with the butt of the gun, the elder Childe dropping to the ground like a bag of sand. Then it was saunter city as the second in command strolled toward Isaac, that gun trained on him and unwavering.

Just like the man's oddly matte, black eyes.

"Let's do this," Isaac said.

"Where's your other gun. I know you've got one."

"Come and get it."

"You really want to fuck with me?"

Isaac reached in and took out his other weapon. "Where do you want it?"

"Loaded question. On the floor and give it a kick."

As Isaac bent down, so did the other man. And it wasn't until they'd both righted themselves that Isaac realized his first gun, the one with the silencer, had been picked up by a black-gloved hand.

"So yeah," the second in command drawled, "Matthias has enjoyed the little convos you two have been having and he wants me to keep you in holding until he gets here." The shark-eyed bastard drew up close. "But here's the thing, Isaac. There are larger issues at play and this is one situation that your boss is not in charge of."

What was with the "your boss" thing, Isaac wondered.

And then he frowned as he realized that the guy's arm, the one that had been broken just a day and a half ago, seemed to be fully healed.

And that grin was wrong . . . there was something wrong about that grin, too.

"Things are taking a different course," the second in command said. "Surprise."

With that, he put Isaac's gun muzzle to his own chin and pulled the trigger, blowing his head clean off.

# CHAPTER
## 39

J im came out of his coma with the nape of his neck on fire. He had no clue how long he'd been out, but Ad had clearly moved him back to the bed: The softness under his head was definitely a pillow and not the cold, hard tile by the shower.

As he sat up in the darkness, he was shocked: He felt curiously strong, miraculously steady. It was as if whatever state he had been in for ... well, hours, assuming he was reading the clock right ... had rebooted him inside and out.

Which was all good news.

The tightness at the tippy top of his spine, however, was anything but: *Isaac.*

*Isaac was in trouble.*

Swinging his legs off the bed and bolting upright, he felt no dizziness, no nausea, no aches or pains. Except for the ants at the base of his skull, he was not just ready to go, but roaring.

"Adrian!" he called out as he went to his duffel and yanked out a pair of jeans.

Where the hell was Dog?

Through the open connector, he could see that the lights were on in the other room, so the angel had to be in there.

"Adrian!" He went commando and jerked on his pants; then grabbed for a shirt. "We've got to go!"

He snatched his crystal gun and dagger along with his coat. "Yo, Ad—"

Adrian all but skidded into the room with Dog under his arm. "Eddie's in trouble."

Well, didn't that just make that nape of his feel soooo much better. "What?"

Adrian undid Dog's leash and let him scamper over to say hello. "He's not answering his phone. I just called. And called again. And called a third time. Never happens."

"Fuck."

As Ad weaponed up, Jim checked over Dog and put some food down and then he and his wingman—literally—took off. Man, he'd never been so grateful for the blink-and-you'll-miss-it ride of those flapping numbers on their backs: Only minutes later, they were in Beacon Hill.

He and Adrian landed in the walled garden in a shimmering blaze and they kept themselves hidden from prying eyes because it was only four in the afternoon. The house looked fine on the outside and the red glimmering spell was still in place, but his neck was killing him. And where in the hell was Eddie—

"Shit," he spat as he saw the soles of the angel's combat boots sticking out from under a bush.

Jim beat feet over and crouched down. The guy was flat on his ass, looking like he'd played chicken with a bulldozer and lost. "Eddie?"

The grounded angel opened his eyes. "Holy hell ... what ... I don't know what happened. One minute I was up. Next ..."

"You were a welcome mat."

Adrian reached out a hand to help his best friend up. "What the fuck was it?"

"No clue." Eddie slowly got to his feet. Then he looked over at Jim and cringed. "Jesus Christ ..."

Jim frowned and glanced around. "What?"

"Your face . . ."

Okay, maybe he only just felt better. Hopefully the looks part would come later. "You're saying my days as a calendar model are over?"

"Didn't know you were into that." Eddie shook his head. "Listen, Isaac wants to talk to you. ASAP."

Jim glanced at Adrian. "You stay with the welcome mat."

"Like I would be anywhere else?"

Jim jogged over to the house. The back door was wide open, which was another piece of bad news—and shit only got more critical as he went into the kitchen.

God, you never got used to the smell of a mortal gunshot wound: There were different flavors, gut versus chest versus brain, but the palette was everything metallic between the lead of the shot and the copper of the fresh blood.

First body he found was a man he knew: Captain Alistair Childe. The poor guy was lying in the archway that led out into the front hall, having crumpled to the floor in a heap.

Not the source of the blood, though. There was none on the clothes or the tile, and Childe was breathing evenly in spite of the little knockout nap he was having.

Body number two was halfway down to the front door and clearly the source of the smell. . . . Yeah, wow, that bastard was a candidate for a closed coffin if Jim had ever seen one: His face was distorted from the inside out, the bullet having traveled up the meat and bone of his chin and nose before exiting on a throw-open-the-doors-and-sing-like-Ethel-Merman routine at the crown of his skull.

Going by the snake tattoo around the guy's neck, it had to be Matthias's second in command.

And Isaac was standing over the guy with a puss full of what-the-fuck.

Rothe looked up and raised his weaponless hands. "He

did it himself. He fucking did it ... himself. Damn it. . . . How's the father?"

Jim knelt beside the captain to double-check. Yup, Childe had been beaned on the head, likely with the butt of a gun, but he was already starting to moan as if he were coming around.

"He'll be all right." Jim rose up and headed down to Isaac and the other guy. As he got closer, the smell got worse—

He slowed and then stopped altogether. And rubbed his eyes.

A shimmering gray shadow covered the body of Matthias's second in command from head to foot, moving around the arms and legs and blown-off head in the same way Jim's spell shifted and covered the house they were all in. And the blood was all wrong—gray, not brilliant red.

Devina, Jim thought. She was either in the man or had taken him over.

"He just put it under his chin and pulled the trigger." Isaac sank down onto his haunches and nodded to the gun that was in the corpse's right hand. "He used my weapon to do it."

"Get away from the body, Isaac."

"Fuck that, I have to clean it up before—"

Jim wasn't interested in arguing and grabbed hold of the guy, pulling him up and back a couple of feet. "You don't know what it is."

"The hell I don't. He came to pick me up."

Jim glared at Isaac. "Last I heard you were lamming it."

"Change of priorities."

Damn it, get abducted for twelve hours and the world goes to shit: Isaac turning himself in, dead demon in a civilian's front hall, no one making sense anymore.

"I won't let you go back in, Isaac. Or sacrifice yourself to keep someone else alive." Because how much you want to bet that was what was going on here.

"Not your choice. And no offense, but I still can't imagine why you give a shit." The soldier took out one of XOps' transistors, which had this time been disguised as a Life Alert. "Besides, it's moot. I've already resummoned."

That blinking light made Jim want to holler. So he did. "What the *fuck* are you doing? Matthias is going to kill you—"

"So."

A patrician voice interjected. "I thought you were coming forward with information on Matthias."

Jim glanced over his shoulder. Alistair Childe had gotten to his feet and was coming down to them, his hand on the wall like he needed help balancing.

"I thought that was the plan, Isaac. And, Jim, I thought you had died over in Caldwell. Three or four days ago."

Jim and Isaac both hopped on the Total Pass Train and ignored the rhetoricals. Which was easy to do considering how much needed figuring out.

The fact that Matthias's number two had come in and killed himself with Isaac's gun was only surface dressing. The core truth was that Devina was all over this situation. But to what end? If Isaac was the target, why the fuck hadn't she just taken him now while Jim wasn't around?

"Did she—*he* have a clear shot at you?" Jim asked. "At any point?"

"You mean to kill? Hell, yeah—I was up against the wall, palms planted, with my weapons on the floor. That's about as clear as you get."

"This makes no sense." He looked down at the body. "No sense."

"We have to get rid of the body," Isaac said. "Before I go, we have to—"

"I'm not letting you turn yourself in."

"Not your call."

"God damn *it*—"

"My thoughts exactly." Isaac frowned, his narrowed eyes

roving around Jim's puss. "And what the fuck happened to you last night?"

For a split second, Jim strongly considered banging his head against the wall, except that was redundant, given the shape he was in. How the hell was he going to get Isaac out of this mess?

It wasn't like he could come clean and explain what was really doing: *Well, see, I really did die, and Matthias is not the problem. I'm trying to keep you away from a demon who wants your soul. And I don't have a clue what she's playing at here.*

Yeah, that would go over like a lead balloon.

Isaac didn't wait for an answer to the question about Jim's face. Clearly, the guy had been in a brawl with eight hundred bouncers or some shit, and that was not his business. What did have his name written all over it was this operative who'd somehow managed to magically fix his own arm before he killed himself.

Unless . . . twins?

Shit . . . *yes*. That had to be it. And what a tool for Matthias to fuck with people's minds. No wonder he'd picked the SOB to be second in command.

As Jim cursed again and took up wearing a path in the hall's runner, Isaac bent down and quickly unbuttoned the second in command's sleeve. No trace of anything on that forearm in the form of a surgical repair, no evidence the skin or bone had ever been broken.

Twins. Had to be.

With a quick rip, he tore open the black shirt, buttons popping off and bouncing on the floor. The bulletproof vest that was revealed was a surprise. Yeah, they were standard-issue, but why would you bother with one if you were going to turn your skull into a piñata?

Unsure exactly what he was looking for, he stripped the Velcro straps off the vest—

"Holy ... crap ..." He leaned in to make sure he was seeing right.

All down the guy's stomach there were deep scars that formed a pattern, and as Jim took a looksee and started in on another round of cursing, Isaac kept going with a fast pat-down. Cell phone, which he put aside. Wallet with a hundred in cash and no ID. Ammo. Nothing in the boots except socks and soles.

Stepping over the body, he headed for the kitchen to get a trash bin. As he was pulling the thing out of its cabinet and wondering how many arms and legs would fit in it, he heard footsteps behind him. Obviously, the peanut gallery had followed, but come on, people. No more talk; they needed action. Grier was locked in the damn closet upstairs and he had to get the shit cleaned up before he let her out—

"You lied."

Isaac froze and cranked his head around. Grier was standing on the far side of the island with the cellar door just shutting behind her. How in the hell had she ... Crap, there must be a hidden stairwell that linked to the basement. He should have guessed there would be multiple escape routes.

As she stared at him, she was white as Kleenex and shaking in her shoes. "You never intended to come forward. Did you."

He shook his head, not knowing what to say and all too aware of what was in her front hall. This situation was totally out of control. "Grier—"

"You bastard. You lying b—" Abruptly, she focused over his shoulder. "You ..." She pointed at Jim, who'd come to stand in the archway. "You were the one in my room the other night. Weren't you."

An odd expression filtered across Jim's features, kind of a fuck-me, but then he just shrugged and looked at Isaac. "I will not allow you to turn yourself in."

"Your new theme song is getting on my nerves," Isaac bit out as he decided to bag the bin and go unstructured with some of Hefty's best.

Chatter, a lot of chatter from just about everyone—and all of it directed at him. But whatever. Selective deafness was something he had excelled at as a kid, and what do you know, the skill set came back to him without a hint of rust.

Isaac bent down under the sink and prayed that the most logical place for more trash bags was in fact—bingo. He took out two of them along with a broom and dustpan that were not going to survive this particular job.

God, he wished he had a hacksaw. But maybe with some rope, they could fold the bastard up tight and carry him out like a sloppy suitcase.

"Stay with her," he said to her father. "And keep her in here—"

"I saw it happen." As Isaac froze, she glared at him. "I watched him do it."

There was a long, silent pause, as if she had snapped all the chains of the men in the room.

She shook her head. "Why did you even pretend to go along with it, Isaac?"

As she stared at him, the trust was gone from her eyes. And in its place, there was a cold regard that he imagined people in laboratories wore as they watched the results of petri-dish cultures.

There would be no talking to her, no denying the shift he'd made. And maybe that was for the best. They had no business being together anyway—and that was before he layered on his professional pursuit of excellence in the field of deading up people.

Isaac got his Merry Maid on and headed for hall. "I need to move the body."

"Don't you turn away from me," she barked out.

He heard Grier coming behind him as if she had every intention of yelling at him some more, so he stopped short and pivoted around just as he got to the archway. As she pinwheeled to keep from running into his body, he pegged her in the eyes.

"Stay here. You don't want to see—"

"Fuck. You." She shoved past him, marching by until— "Oh ... God ..." She choked off the word, her hand coming up to her mouth.

Bingo, he thought grimly.

Fortunately, her father was on it, going over to her and gently maneuvering her out of eyeshot.

Cursing himself and everything about his life, Isaac continued down the hall, more determined than ever to take care of the problem ... except his urgency took a time-out as he came up to the body.

A cell phone was in the corpse's hand and the thing was sending a message; the little screen on the phone was glowing with a picture of an envelope going into a mailbox over and over again.

Okay. Time to back the bus up, here: Guys who had no frontal lobe geeeenerally speaking didn't reach out and touch something with their T-Mobile.

A little glowing check mark appeared, indicating success.

"Isaac, you're going to need more than a dustpan to handle that."

At the sound of Jim's voice, he looked over his shoulder. And had to blink a couple of times. The man was standing in the dark part of the hall, well away from the light that came through the arches of the study and library ... but he was illuminated, a glow surrounding him from head to foot.

Isaac's heart did a couple of jumping jacks in his chest cavity. Then seemed to take a little breather.

There had been a number of times when he'd been out in the field, in the middle of an assignment, and things had gone tits-up on him: You thought you knew your target's patterns and resources, weaknesses and protective covers, but just as you were about to move on him, the landscape changed sure as if someone dropped a bomb in the middle of the town square of your perfect plan. Weapon malfunctioned. A potential witness fucked your timing up. The target stepped out of range.

What you had to do was a fast recalibration of the situation, and Isaac had always excelled at that. Hell, that video game he'd unwittingly trained himself on had made his mind totally open to the lickety-split.

But this shit was out of his expertise. Big-time.

And that was before Jim took out a long dagger . . . that was made of crystal. "You're going to let me handle this now. Step away from the body, Isaac."

# CHAPTER
## 40

Matthias spent way too much time in the stone embrace of that church. And when he finally forced himself to leave, he assumed he'd been there a good hour or so, but the instant he looked at the sun's position in the sky, he realized he'd wasted all of the morning and most of the afternoon.

Yet he would have stayed longer if he could have.

He was hardly a religious man, but he'd found a shocking and rare peacefulness beneath the stained glass gallery and before the glorious altar. Even now, as his mind told him that it was all bullshit, that the place had been just another building, and that he was so tired you could have put him on a Disney ride and he would have fallen asleep, his heart knew better.

The pain had stopped. Shortly after he'd sat down, the pain in his left arm and chest had disappeared.

"Whatever," he said out loud as he got in his car. "Whatever, whatever . . ."

Getting back in the game was something he felt compelled to do, and there was a pleasurable, needling sting to it, as if he were picking a scab. On some level, he was captivated by what he'd found in the church, but his job, his deeds, his very way of life was a whirlpool that sucked him in and kept him down and he just didn't have the energy to fight it.

Still . . . maybe there was a middle way, he thought, when it came to Isaac Rothe. Maybe he could get the guy to keep working only in a different capacity. The soldier had obviously responded well to the threats against Grier Childe — that could be enough to keep him in line.

Or . . . he could let the guy go.

The instant the thought crossed his mind, some inner part of him slammed it down as if it was an utter blasphemy.

Annoyed with himself and the situation, he started the engine and checked his phone. Nothing from his number two. Where the hell was the bastard?

He sent a text demanding an update and giving his ETA, which would be well after dark at this point. Out of state his ass. That fucker had better be there with Isaac Rothe duct taped to a chair before Matthias rolled up — and God help him if he'd killed Rothe.

As impatience cranked his hands down on the wheel, Matthias eased away from the curb and headed for the highway thanks to the GPS screen on the dash. He'd gone less than a mile before the pain underneath his sternum came back, but it was like a familiar suit of clothes after he'd been trying on someone else's wardrobe: easy and comfortable in a fucked-up kind of way.

His phone went off. Picture message. From his number two.

As he accepted the thing, he was relieved. A little visual confirmation that Isaac was alive and in custody was a good thing —

It was not a picture of Isaac.

It was the remnants of his second in command's face. And that snake tattoo that ran around the man's throat was the only way he was sure who it was.

Underneath the picture: *Come and get me — I.*

Matthias's first and only thought was ... the fucking *nerve*. The goddamn cocksucking *nerve*. What the *hell* was Rothe thinking? And shit, if threats against dear sweet lovely Grier Childe didn't work, Isaac was utterly uncontrollable and therefore he had to be put down.

Raw fury cast aside the last lingering remnants of his time in that church, a wellspring of vengeance letting loose to roar. As it hit him, in the back of his mind, he had a thought that this wasn't him, that the cool, knifelike precision of thought and action that had always been his hallmark would have precluded this white-hot burn. He was, however, incapable of turning away from the need to act — and act personally.

Fuck delegation. ... There were countless operatives he could have called in, but this he would handle himself.

In the same way he'd had to see Jim Heron's body with his own eyes, he was going to go and take down Rothe himself.

The man had to die.

# CHAPTER
# 41

As Grier sat on the couch in the corner of the kitchen, she revisited her choice to go into law instead of medicine and knew she'd made the right decision: She'd never had the stomach to be a doctor.

Her grades and test scores could have gotten her into either graduate school, but the tipping factor had been Gross Human Anatomy, that first-year med-school staple: one look at those muslin-covered dead bodies on all those tables during her pre-admission tour and she'd had to put her head between her knees and try to breathe like she was in yoga class.

And what do you know. The fact that there was someone in an even juicier condition in her front hall was so much worse.

Surprise, surprise.

Another shocker at the moment—not that she needed one—was her father's hand making slow, calming circles on her back. The times he had done something like this were few and far between, as he was not the kind of man who handled shows of emotion well. And yet when she'd really needed it, he'd always been there: her mother's death. Daniel's. That horrible breakup with the guy she'd almost married right out of law school.

This was the father she had known and loved all her life. In spite of the shadows that surrounded him.

"Thank you," she said without looking at him.

He cleared his throat. "I don't believe I deserve that. This all is because of me."

She couldn't argue the point, but she didn't have the strength to condemn him; especially given that terrible ache in his voice.

Now that her rage had passed, she realized that his conscience was going to haunt him to the day he died, and that was the punishment he'd earned and was going to carry out. Plus, he'd already had to bury one child, an imperfect son who he had loved in his own way and had lost in a horrible manner. And although Grier could have spent the rest of her days alienating him and hating him for Daniel's death . . . was that really a burden she wanted to carry around?

She thought of the body in the front hall and how life could be snatched away between one breath and the next.

No, she decided. She would not allow the hurt and anger she felt to cheat her out of what was left of her family. It would take time, but she and her father would rebuild their relationship.

At least that was one thing Isaac had been right and truthful about.

"We can't call the police, can we," she said. Because surely anyone in a uniform who showed up would be hunted as well.

"Isaac and Jim will handle the body. That's what they do."

Grier winced at the idea. "Won't he be missed by someone? Anyone?"

"He doesn't exist. Not really. Whatever family he had thinks he's dead—that's the requirement for men in that branch of XOps."

God, morally, she had twelve kinds of problems not saying something or doing something about the death. But she wasn't going to put her own life at risk for the guy who had been sent to kill Isaac and maybe herself.

Except . . . well, apparently, he'd come to commit suicide with witnesses.

"What are we going to do," she said, talking out loud and not expecting an answer.

And the *we* in that was her and her father. The *we* did not include Isaac.

He'd lied. To her face. He had in fact had contact with those evil people—and meanwhile, she'd been thinking that they'd had a plan. Sure, he hadn't betrayed her father, but that was only a measure of comfort because obviously, he'd decided to turn himself in—or at least appear to. A man like him, who fought like he did and was as comfortable as he was with weapons? It was far more likely that he'd decided to kill whoever took him into custody and bolt out of the country free and clear.

Fine. She was letting him go.

He was nothing but sexual attraction packaged in a ticking box—and that sound was the timer running out on the bomb underneath all the hard-bodied bows and ribbons. As for the I-love-you stuff? The thing with liars was that you believed anything they said to you at your own risk—not just the stuff you knew to be false. She wasn't sure where that "admission" got him, but she knew better than to view it as anything other than more hot air.

Her mind made up, she was too tired to be anything but numb. Well, numb and feeling stupid. But come on, like that "rare combination" of raw and gentle really existed?

"Wait here," her father said.

As he got up, she realized two large men had come into her kitchen. The pair of them were cut from the same mold as Isaac and the very-definitely-not-dead Jim Heron—and the sight of them was yet another reminder of what was going on in the front hall.

Like she needed the help, though?

"We're friends of Jim's," the one with the braid said.

"In here," Heron called out from down the corridor.

As the pair headed for the body along with her father, she got annoyed with herself and pulled up her mental big-girl pants. When she stood up, her head spun, but that whirling-dervish stuff receded as she went over to the coffee machine and went through the motions of making a fresh pot.

Filter. Check.

Water. Check.

Coffee grinds. Check.

Button to *on*. Check.

Normalcy helped stitch her back together a little more tightly, and by the time she had a steaming mug in her palms, she was ready to deal.

Good thing, too. It was time to think about the future ... of what lay beyond this ugly night and these gut-wrenching past three days.

Unfortunately, her mind was like a spectator at a car accident, loitering around the twisted wreckage and the bodies on the pavement, tangling up in memories of her and Isaac together. Eventually, however, she cut that unhealthy focus off, her rational side playing cop and forcing her thoughts to move along, just move along now.

The thing was, Isaac had come into her life for a good reason: Thanks to him, she had finally learned the lesson that Daniel's death had failed to teach her. Bottom line? As much as you wanted someone to change and believed they could, they were in control of their life. Not you. And you could throw yourself against the wall of their choices until you were black-and-blue and dizzy as hell, but unless they decided to take a different road, the outcome wasn't going to be what you wanted.

The realization wasn't going to keep her from helping down at the jail or doing pro bono cases. But it was time to put some limits on how much she had to give ...

and how far she was willing to go. In all her peripatetic, Good Samaritan scramblings, she had been trying to resurrect Daniel—even though talking to his ghost should have been her first clue he wasn't coming back. In discovering the truth about what had happened to him, however, and in trying to find some balance for herself, maybe she could finally put him to rest and move on.

Taking another sip from her mug, she felt a measure of peace in spite of the bizarre circumstances—

Which was when another gunshot went off in the front of the house.

Out in the hall, Jim had just been approaching the body with his crystal knife when he'd felt Eddie and Adrian's presence in the kitchen. God, they'd timed their entrance perfectly. He'd been prepared to act on his own, but backup was never a bad idea.

"I'm in here," he called out.

The pair came right along and neither seemed surprised at what was on the floor.

"Oh, man, Devina's all over that one," Ad muttered as he walked over to the remains.

"What the hell are you doing with that dagger?" Isaac demanded.

Well, matter of fact, he was going to do a quick exorcism. It was the only way to make sure that Devina was out of—

The first clue to the corpse's reanimation was a twitching in the hands. And then in a rush, that godforsaken piece of meat picked itself off the ground and managed to focus the one eyeball that appeared to be working.

And didn't that just remind him of Matthias.

Isaac let out a shout and fired his weapon, but that was like shooting a rubber band at a charging bull: The bull didn't notice and you just lost what had held your newspaper together in a tidy roll.

Jim shoved the soldier out of the way and attacked in a

lunge, his body tackling the zombie into the wall. The moment impact was made, the image of Devina's face overlaid the decimated features of the man whose body she'd taken control of, the morphing reconfiguration smiling in satisfaction at him.

Like she'd won already.

Jim went for the stab in a quick, powerful jab, the crystal knife penetrating between the set of eyes that were corporeal as well as the pair that were metaphysical.

A screeching sound exploded from the zombie and a shaft of black smoke shot up in a vile stench, the dark fog coalescing, and then making a beeline for the front door. At the last second, it flashed under the wooden panels, sure as if it had been sucked out from the other side— and in its absence, the body of Matthias's second in command crashed to the floor like the bag of bones it was, the source of its animation no longer held within the bounds of its flesh.

"Now it's fucking dead," Jim said as he breathed heavily.

In the shocked silence that followed, he looked over his shoulder at Isaac. The guy's eyes could have given truck tires a run for the money in the diameter department, and water was dripping off of him, Adrian and Eddie having emptied the barrels of their crystal guns over his head to protect him.

Good move. Except . . . the evil hadn't even tried to go for the soldier. It had taken off in the opposite direction.

Jim's mental circuits went Las Vegas on him, his instincts screaming that this was wrong. All wrong. Second chance at getting to Isaac . . . and Devina had passed. Again.

Why had—

Like a curtain being wrenched back from a window, the landscape of the game suddenly became clear to him and what he saw rocked him to the core. *Holy fucking shit . . .*

Abruptly unsteady, he threw his hand out and caught himself on the wall.

"You are not the one," he said bleakly to Rothe. "Oh, God save us all, *you're not the one*."

As Grier Childe burst into the archway in from the kitchen, Isaac spoke up. "We're okay. Everyone's okay."

Which was only accurate to a point. Sure, Devina had apparently pulled an Elvis and left the building. And yeah, no one in the group glowed with an unholy shadow and Jim's neck was no longer doing the OMGs. But they were far from hunky-dory.

The urgent question now became . . . who was that demon after? Which soul were they fighting over?

The cell phone, Jim thought.

As all kinds of people started talking and the air filled with voices, he put the noise out of his head and sunk down on his haunches. From beside the now twice-dead body, he picked the phone up off the floor and went into the sent box for texts.

He recognized the last number that had been hit immediately.

Matthias had gotten the picture.

The cold clarity that came upon Jim brought with it a kind of terror: He'd been trying to save the target . . . when all along, he should have been focused on the shooter.

# CHAPTER
## 42

Reflex, not reflection.

That was where Isaac was as he stood in Grier's hall with some kind of solution dripping off his nose and chin.

His brain could have spent a decade or two trying to figure out what the fuck he'd just seen, but that would have required time he didn't have. As much as he didn't understand—and that black hole was on a football-stadium scale—he was going to have to rely on what his eyes had shown him and leave it at that: He had witnessed a dead man get up; he had shot the bastard; and the only thing that had refloored the corpse had been some kind of glass or crystal knife. Then something had left the body and escaped out under the front door.

It was kind of like *s*Killer*z*, when you went into the paranormal-world part of the game. With a flick of the switch, the normal rules went into the shitter and you stepped into an alternate universe where people could disappear right in front of you and vampires lived in the shadows and pale men came after you instead of humans.

Of course, that was role play that you could turn off— and there was no pause button on this sitch. Which was why he wasn't going to waste a lot of energy figuring it all out. Yeah, sure, maybe after this was over he'd ask Jim what the hell had just happened . . . but that was only if there was an "afterward."

With the way things were going, some portion of the people standing in this hall might well be headed for an "afterlife."

"Where did it go?" he asked Jim. "Not that black thing—the picture."

As Jim looked up from the cell phone, the second in command's words came back: *Matthias is not in charge.* So that meant some other mastermind was engineering a certain result by hitting the levers and pulleys of various puppets and scenes.

"Who?" he repeated.

"Matthias got it," Heron said, getting to his feet.

"Is Matthias . . . one of those?" As Isaac pointed to the pop-up corpse, he thought it was just fucking great to be in a situation where there were no terms to describe anything.

"He wasn't when I saw him last night."

Well, maybe that explained why the guy's face had been used as a punching bag. And yup, if both of them lived through this, Jim so had some explaining to do.

"Are you one of them?" Isaac demanded.

Cue the *Jeopardy* theme as Jim looked over at his two buddies and then at Grier and her father. "After a fashion, yes. But we're on the other side."

Isaac shook his head and left all that for later. What was more important was the path that was being constructed by the series of events: "Matthias gets that picture and he'll think I killed . . . him . . . it . . . whatever."

And step two in the extrapolation? Matthias would *really* be gunning for him now.

"Who are you calling?" he asked as Jim put that phone up to his ear like he was making a call.

The guy mouthed, *Matthias* . . . and then the next thing

that came out of his mouth was a curse. "Fucking voice mail."

As the others continued talking, Isaac pulled Heron aside. "I'm 'not the one.' Tell me what it means."

"We don't have that kind of time—"

"We've got a minute and a half. I'll guarantee it."

"And that won't cover anything at all." Jim's eyes bored into Isaac's. "Do you remember what I told you when I first saw you? That I wasn't going to let anything happen to you? I still mean it. But I have to go."

Isaac squeezed the guy's arm, holding him in place. "Where?"

Jim glanced at his buddies. "I've got to get to Matthias. I think she's after him."

Who was she, Isaac wondered. And then it dawned on him.

"You don't have to go anywhere then. You want to see him?" He pulled out that Life Alert and let it dangle off its chain as he pointed to his own chest. "You have your bait right here."

In the end, it turned out Grier needed the suitcase she'd packed.

She was going to her father's to stay out in Lincoln for a couple of days—and Isaac and Jim were remaining behind here in her house to face that man, Matthias. Although it felt odd to be giving her family's home over to relative strangers, the reality was that the place offered ways of exit that would make things safer for the two men.

And regardless of what she thought of them, she wasn't going to be a party to their deaths if there was something she could do about it.

Tragically, there was no more talk about coming forward and her father had called off his contacts. Isaac wasn't going to say a word about anything and her father didn't know enough to do any real damage—so the risks, as balanced against the likely benefits, just couldn't be justified.

Which flat-out sucked. But that was the real world for you.

Staring at her suitcase, she decided leaving here actually had a lot of benefits. She didn't want to stick around during the removal of that body—no need to see that on a good day, much less with the way things had been going. Besides, she just plain needed a break. When this stuff with Isaac had started, it had been so familiar, all the keyed-up exhaustion, the block and tackle of events and crises. But she was tired . . . and determined to stick to her new conviction: Time to pull out, pull away, leave behind.

So she was heading for Lincoln with a heavy heart, but eyes that were wide open.

Grabbing the second season of *Three's Company* from her bookshelf, she unlatched her suitcase to put it in—

Grier stiffened and braced herself.

This time, for once, she knew that Isaac was standing in the doorway to her bedroom—even though he hadn't knocked.

Looking over her shoulder, she saw that his hair was curling up from whatever had been poured over his head and his stare was as intense as ever.

"I came to say good-bye," he murmured quietly, that delicious Southern drawl weaving through the deep, low words. "And to tell you that I'm sorry I lied to you."

As he took a step into her room, she turned back to the suitcase, slid the DVD inside, and shut the lid. "Are you."

"Yes."

She clicked both locks into place. "You know, the part I don't understand is why you bothered. If you never had any intention of going through with it, why did you talk to my father? Or was it to get at him? Figure out how much he knows and then warn your friends?" When he didn't answer, she pivoted around. "Was that it?"

His eyes roamed her face as if he were memorizing it. "I had another reason."

"Hope it was good enough to ruin the trust I had in you."

Isaac nodded slowly. "Yes. It was."

Well, didn't that make her feel used as hell.

Grier grabbed the suitcase's handle and hefted the thing off her bed. "And you did it again."

"Did what?"

"Activated that damn Life Alert. Called that Matthias nightmare to you." She frowned. "I think you've got a death wish. Or some other agenda I can't begin to guess at. But in either event, it's not my business."

Staring up at his hard, beautiful face, she thought, God, this hurts.

"Anyway, good luck," she said, wondering whether, by the end of the night, he was going to be in the condition of that other soldier.

"I meant what I said, Grier. Down in the kitchen."

"Hard to tell what is real and what's a lie, isn't it."

Her heart was breaking even though that made no sense whatsoever, and in the face of the pain, all she wanted was to get away from the man who stood so still and powerful on the far side of her bedroom.

On the far side of her life, actually.

"Good-bye, Isaac Rothe," she murmured, heading for the door.

"Wait."

For a brief moment, some kind of odd, disastrous hope took flight in her chest. The flare didn't last, however. She was done with fantasies and fantastic excitement.

She did, however, let him approach as he held something out to her.

"Jim asked that I give this to you."

Grier took what was in his hand. It was a ring—no, a piercing, a little dark silver circle with a ball into which the free end screwed. She frowned as she looked at the tiny inscription that ran around the inside. It was in a language she wasn't familiar with, but she recognized the PT950 stamp. The hoop was made of platinum.

"It's Adrian's, actually," Isaac murmured. "They're giving it to you and they want you to wear it."

"Why?"

"To keep you safe. So they say."

It was hard to imagine what the thing could do for her, but it did fit on her forefinger, and when Isaac took a deep, relieved breath, she was a little surprised.

"It's just a ring," she said softly.

"I'm not sure anything is a 'just' right now."

She couldn't disagree there. "How are you going to get that body out of here?"

"Move it."

"Well, there you go." She took one last look at him. The idea that he could be dead in a matter of hours was inescapable. And so was the reality that she was probably not going to know what happened to him. Or where he went next if he survived. Or whether he would ever sleep in a safe bed again.

Feeling herself slipping, she hiked up her suitcase, nodded at him and walked out, leaving him behind.

There was no other choice.

She had to take care of herself.

# CHAPTER
## 43

The choice had to be the result of free will.

That was the problem with this whole contest thing: The soul in question had to choose their path of their own free will when they got to their crossroads.

As Devina stepped out of the shower in her suite at the Four Seasons, she thought about how much she hated the freewill bullshit. It was far more efficient for her to take possession and drive the bus, so to speak. The Creator, however, had limited the impact she was allowed to have under the rules.

Jim Heron was the only one who was supposed to set up the souls . . . the only one who was allowed to try to influence the choices made in any fashion.

Fucking Jim Heron.

Fucking *bastard*.

And fuck the Creator, too, for that matter.

She snapped a towel off a brass rod and dried off the beautiful brunette's body, all the while thinking that this was such a better home than that snake-tatted soldier's. But she didn't have time to do the flesh-reunion justice. The final round with the current soul in play was not just approaching—it was here.

Time to close this match down and win it.

After vacating the familiar skin of Matthias's second in command, she had taken to the air and extricated herself from that brick house. The spiteful side of her had wanted to park it inside that female attorney or in her father—just for kicks and giggles and the drama of it all. But with the way things were, she didn't think that was a wise idea: everything was so perfectly arranged, the players' predilections and proclivities ensuring how they would act.

It was the wardrobe equivalent of a perfect outfit.

And she needed to win this one for reasons more than the game: She wanted payback for Jim Heron's performance in her private quarters. And not the one with her minions, the one when the pair of them had been alone.

She'd been utterly unprepared for his attack. Or the fact that he was so clearly much more than just another angel. Adrian or Eddie could not have pulled off something like that. She didn't know anyone who could.

It just made no sense—Jim Heron had been chosen for a defined role and he was supposed to be a lackey who was neither good nor bad. Matter of fact, he'd been agreed upon by both sides because each team thought that he would influence things according to their values and take cues from a prescribed amount of "coaching."

What utter bullshit that had turned out to be.

That first soul they'd battled over? Jim had done everything possible to push the man toward the good—proving that Devina's faith in him had been misplaced. That son of a bitch was a savior in a sinner's clothes, *not* one of her kind. Which was why she was going to have to get even more involved from this point on; there was no one on the field representing her interests, and manipulation of the situation was critical if she was going to prevail in any of these innings.

If she didn't finesse things, she was going to lose after going oh-for-four.

And that was why she'd taken Jim down below to her realm when she had. She'd needed to get him away from Matthias—any contact between those two was a bad idea.

But at least her choice of soul seemed to have been the right one. She'd been nurturing the head of XOps for the last two years and by now, she all but owned him—so when Nigel and she had conferred over the next individual in play, she'd picked Martin O'Shay Thomas, aka Matthias.

Next round was back to Nigel's choice, and undoubtedly he'd pick someone much more difficult for her.

Matthias . . . oh, dearest, corrupt Matthias. One last immoral act and he was hers for eternity—as well as her first win.

All he had to do was take the life of Isaac Rothe and ding-ding-ding! she could do a victory lap on Jim Heron's ass.

Although . . . given what Heron had done to her, she feared he was not just a quarterback in this game, but an entity of another sort. And that was another reason she hadn't stuck around in Beacon Hill. The exchange between her and him down below had drained her, and she wasn't strong enough to face a full-on confrontation with the male so soon.

Especially given that underestimating her nemesis's powers was clearly a mistake.

Wrapping herself up, she looked at the marble counter that ran around the sinks. Part of her therapist's assignment from two weeks before had been to clean out her makeup collection, and she'd complied, throwing away countless Chanel compacts and lipsticks and eye shadows.

Now, as she stared at the emptiness of the space, she panicked at the lack of possessions. One Gucci bag of stuff was all she had. That was it.

With fumbling hands, she grabbed the little tote and tipped it over, black tubes and squares and pots going all over the place. Breathing through her mouth, she set about ordering the dozen or so containers, arranging them by size and shape, not utility.

It wasn't enough. She needed more—

In the dim reaches of her mind, Devina knew she was spiraling, but she couldn't help it. The realization that Jim was far more formidable than she'd thought . . . and that she was in far greater danger of losing than she'd believed . . . rendered her a slave to her inner weakness.

Her therapist maintained that buying more shit or taking more trinkets or ordering and reordering the placement of objects wasn't going to solve anything. But it sure made her feel better in the short run . . .

In the end, she had to all but drag herself out of the bathroom. Time was wasting and she had to make sure that all the little dominoes she'd arranged fell in the right and proper order.

To soothe her OCD, she repeated what her therapist had told her three days ago: *It's not about the things. It's about your place in this world. It's the space you declare as yours emotionally and spiritually.*

Whatever. She had work to do.

And another suit of skin to slipcover herself in.

# CHAPTER
## 44

After the Childes set off in their cars, with Eddie and Adrian surreptitiously on their heels, Jim and Isaac stayed behind in the house of a thousand secret passages — all of which Jim had been shown, thanks to Captain Childe.

In the wake of the departures, the house was dark, inside and out, and he and Isaac stood at the ready.

It was the old times back again, Jim thought.

Especially as he put his phone up to his ear and waited for Matthias to answer the call. Although . . . if it really was back in the day, the bastard would fucking pick up.

At this point, he was desperate for a way to reach the guy before he arrived with all guns blazing —

His former boss's voice shot into his ear. "Isaac."

"No." Jim trod carefully, because God knew there were loose ends hanging all over the place. "Not Isaac."

There was a moment of pause which was filled by a subtle whir in the background. Car? Plane? Hard to be sure, but probably a car.

"Jim? Is that you." The voice was robotic, deader than dead. Obviously, even a hi-how're-ya from the grave wasn't enough to shake the guy, but it seemed in this instance not to be a case of the great mastermind being unflappable. More like the man was numbed out.

Jim carefully chose his words. "I'm more interested in how you are. That and I'd like to talk about the picture you received."

"Do you. Well, I got other things on my mind—like how you are on my phone. You're dead."

"Not really."

"Funny, I had a dream about you. I tried to shoot you and you didn't die."

Shit, straddling the two worlds was complicated. "Yeah, I know."

"Do you."

"I'm calling about your number two. Isaac didn't kill him."

"Oh. Really."

"I did." Liar, liar, pants on fire. Good thing he'd never had a problem with that kind of shit.

"And again, I say to you, I thought you were dead."

"Not that dead."

"Clearly." Long pause. "So if you are alive and well, why'd you go and do that to my number two, Jim?"

"I told you I wouldn't let anyone get near my boy Isaac. In that dream. I know you heard me."

"You saying I should start calling you Lazarus instead of Zacharias?"

"You can call me anything you want."

"Well, whatever the fuck your name is, you just put a bullet in your 'boy's' head. Congratulations. Because Isaac's the one I'm going to settle the debt with—and you know me. I'll do it my own special way."

Shit. Grier Childe. How much you want to bet, Jim thought. "That's not logical."

"It's highly logical. Either Isaac did it and you're covering for him and hoping for leniency. Or you did do it, in which case I actually do have a score to settle with you—

and the way I'm going to take care of that you-owe-me is leaving you with a murder on your conscience. Since you hate collateral damage, it's going to be a real ass slap."

"Rothe helped save you. In that dustbowl you nearly killed yourself in."

Now the guy all but growled: "Don't give me another reason to come after him."

Bingo, Jim thought, tightening his grip on the phone. This was his way in, and more important than a who-shot-the-demon showdown.

"Bitter, Matthias. You sound very bitter. You know, you've changed."

"No, I haven't—"

"Yeah, you have, and you know what? You don't have the heart for this anymore. Not sure that's dawned on you yet. But the old Matthias wouldn't be coming to do this personally. It would be business."

"Who says I'm on my way?"

"I do. You have to be. You don't know this either, but you're being compelled to come here and kill an innocent man." The silence told him that he was on the right motherfucking trail. "You don't understand why you have to do it yourself. You don't understand the way you're thinking right now. And you know you're losing control. You're making choices and doing shit that doesn't make any sense. But I can give you the whys—it's because you're being set up by something you wouldn't believe in if I told you it existed. It hasn't totally taken you over yet, though, so there's still time."

Jim paused and let that intel settle into his ex-boss's brain. What Matthias needed was an exorcism, but that required consent. The goal was to get him to the house and go to work on him . . .

And on that note: "It's that thing you called your second in command. He wasn't what you think he was, Matthias." Digging deeper, he pushed. "When he spoke with you, you felt like he made too much sense, right? He influenced you in subtle ways, steering you, always being there when you needed him. It was barely noticeable at first, and then you trusted him, delegated to him, started grooming him as a successor—"

*"You don't know what the fuck you're talking about."*

"Bull. Shit. I know *precisely* what's doing. You really were going to let Isaac come back to XOps, weren't you. You were going to try to find a way not to kill him. Weren't you. Matthias . . . ? Matthias, answer the goddamned question."

Long pause. Then a soft reply: "Yes. I was."

"And you didn't tell your number two that—because you know that he would have changed your mind."

"He would have been right, though."

"No, he would have been evil. That's what he was. Think about it. Although you tried to get out of XOps, he pulled you back in."

"FYI, you're talking to a sociopath. So I'm in my element."

"Uh-huh. Right. Sociopaths who are about la vida loca don't plant bombs in the sand and step on them. Admit it, you wanted out back then in the desert—and you want out now. *Admit it.*"

For a while, there was nothing more than that whirring in the background. And then Matthias dropped another bomb, so to speak.

"It was Childe's son."

Jim frowned and recoiled a little. "Excuse me?"

"Childe's son . . . was what changed everything. I watch the tape of it . . . of Childe weeping while his son died in front of him. My father would never have done that if I'd been on that couch. More likely he'd have tapped my vein with the needle. I couldn't get that . . . out of my mind. The way that poor bastard looked and what he'd said . . . he'd loved that kid like a father should."

Yeah, whoa . . . on some level it was hard to imagine Matthias had had a parent. Spawned was more like it.

Jim shook his head, feeling bad for the guy for the first time since they'd met all those years ago. "I'm telling you, let Isaac go. Forget the vengeance. Forget XOps. Forget the past. I'll help you disappear and stay safe. Leave it all behind . . . and trust me."

Long pause. Loooooong pause where there was nothing but that white noise of a car in motion.

"You're at a crossroads, Matthias. What you do about Isaac tonight can save you . . . and save him. You have more power than you know. Work with us. Come here and sit down and talk with us."

Probably best to keep the whole slitting him wide with a crystal knife and pulling Devina's pestilence out by the throat thing on the QT for the time being.

Matthias let out a shuddering exhale. "Never pictured you for the 'Kumbaya' type."

"People change, Matthias," Jim said roughly. "People can change. *You* can change."


Standing across the kitchen, Isaac wasn't sure he'd heard right: Matthias had set the bomb that had exploded all over him?

God, he remembered driving that Land Rover through the dunes, back to camp. As soon as Matthias had been unloaded from it, the boys with the bags of blood and the sharpies and the latex gloves had swarmed over him and that was pretty much all Isaac had known.

Bottom line, Heron hadn't said a goddamn thing about the hows or wheres or whys of the explosion, and Isaac hadn't asked. "Need to know" was the rule of thumb in XOps: The boss and an operative show up with one blown into deli meat and the other dragging both their sorry asses through the sand in the middle of the night?

Fine. No biggie. Whatever.

After all, sometimes the information you carried was more dangerous than a loaded gun at your temple.

As Jim abruptly ended the call to the boss, Isaac had a bone to pick with the SOB. "First of all, I don't need you going all martyr on me—so can the 'I shot him' shit. And what the hell? Matthias tried to kill himself?"

"First of all," Jim echoed, "I don't do collateral damage, so you can suck it up on whatever I do to save your ass. Second . . . yes. He did. The device was one of ours, and he knew precisely where to step. He met my eyes as he put his foot down . . . and mouthed something." The guy shook his head. "Not a clue what he'd said. Then boom! Most of the detonator was vaporized. But not all of it. Not all."

Fascinating. "How long until he gets here?"

"I don't know. But he's coming. He has to."

Yeah, as for the stuff about the second in command? That was nothing he wanted to know about, frankly. He had enough intel swelling his skull. The only thing he cared about was getting tonight over with.

"I'm shit-tired of waiting," he muttered.

"Join the club."

On that note, Isaac looked around. The ADT system was off and so was the big boy behind Grier's closet, but all the doors were locked, so chances were good they'd know if someone broke in.

"Listen, I'm going to go upstairs," he said. "Keep an eye out up there."

"Okay." Jim's shrewd eyes refocused on the rear garden like he expected an infiltration at any moment. "I'll cover the back forty."

As Isaac went to mount the rear staircase, he paused and leaned back into the kitchen. Heron was standing in front of the glass, hands on his hips, frown clamped on his brow.

No, the guy wasn't dead. And he honestly didn't seem

bothered by the reality that a bullet could come crashing through all that see-through at any second.

"Jim."

"Yeah." The man looked over.

"What are you? Really."

As silence stretched, the word "angel" winged around in the space between them. Except surely that wasn't possible?

The man shrugged. "I just am."

Roger that, Isaac thought. "Well . . . thank you."

Jim shook his head. "We're not out of the woods yet."

"Regardless. Thank you." Isaac cleared his throat. "Can't say that anyone has ever stuck their neck out for me like this."

Well, that wasn't true, was it. Grier had in her own way. And God, the mere thought of her nearly made his eyes sting.

Heron bowed a little and seemed honestly touched. "You're welcome, my man. Now quit being a sap and guard the third floor."

Isaac had to smile. "I may need a job after this, you know."

A grin appeared, but faded quick. "I'm not sure you want to go through the job-application process for where I'm at. It's rough."

"Been there. Done that."

"Which was what I thought, too."

With that, Isaac hit the stairs.

Yeah, sure, ostensibly he was going to look out from the top floor, but there was another truth to be had, another driver.

When he entered Grier's bedroom, he went straight to her closet and stood over the mess of clothes that remained on the creamy carpet. She'd left the project of rehanging half-done—because, duh, some asshole had gotten capped in her front hall.

But he could take care of the problem.

As he waited to see whether there was going to be a bizarre kind of reunion with Matthias or a shoot-out that left the pair of them dead, he picked up her blouses and skirts and dresses and, one by one, made order from the chaos.

At least he could clean up something for her; God knew, that body was still downstairs, albeit wrapped in plastic like something about to be shipped through a mail-order house.

There would be time to move it later, however.

And no other opportunity to take care of her things.

Besides, the "sap" in him wanted some kind of final contact with her—and the closest he was going to get was handling with care what had once lain against her precious skin.

# CHAPTER
## 45

Grier followed her father's Mercedes out to Lincoln, and when the familiar pylons on either side of the farmhouse's drive appeared, she took the first deep breath since they'd left Beacon Hill. Turning right down the cracked-seashell lane, she pulled up in front of the gray-and-white clapboard and put her Audi in park. Although the heart of downtown Boston was only twenty miles away, it might as well have been two hundred. Everything was quiet as she turned off the engine and stepped out of her car, the clean, crisp air tingling through her nose.

God, how she loved this place, she thought.

The gentle, fading light of the gloaming softened the tree line that ran around the six acres of fields and gardens and bathed the clapboard in a buttery illumination. Before her mother's death, the place had been a retreat for the four of them, a way to get out of the city when they didn't go to the Cape—and Grier had spent a lot of weekends here, running through the meadow and playing around the pond.

After her father became a widower, he had needed a fresh start, and so she'd moved into the town house and he'd come out here permanently.

As her father approached from the garage where he'd docked that huge sedan of his, his loafers crunched over the little shell fragments. When she'd been young, she'd thought that drives like this were covered with a special kind of Rice Krispies. Instead of milk poured into a bowl, all you needed were feet to get the chattering sound going.

He was cautious as he came up to her. "Would you like me to get your things?"

"Yes, thank you."

"And perhaps we should have dinner?"

Even though she wasn't hungry, she nodded. "That would be lovely."

God, they were like people at some cocktail party. Well, a cocktail party that involved dead bodies, guns, and running from killers—fashionably late, in this case, meant you were dead, not just the victim of a hair catastrophe or bad traffic on one-twenty-eight.

Which reminded her . . .

Grier looked around and felt the back of her neck tingle. They were being watched. She could feel it. But she wasn't anxious; she was calmed by whatever it was she sensed.

It was Jim's men, she was willing to bet. She hadn't seen them drive up, but they were here.

After her father got her suitcase out and shut her trunk, she locked the car—and tried not to think about the fact that the man with the eye patch had been inside the damn thing. Frankly, it made her want to sell the Audi, even though it only had thirty thousand miles on it and ran like a top.

"Shall we?" her father asked, indicating the front walk with an elegant hand.

Nodding, she stepped forward and led the way up the brick path to the door. Before opening the way in, her father turned off the security system, which was just like hers, and then unlocked the dead bolts one by one. The moment

408     J. R. Ward

they'd both cleared the jambs, he shut them in, reengaged the system and relocked everything.

No one was going to get at them here: This place made the one in town look like a papier-mâché pup tent when it came to security.

After Daniel's death, this house had been prepared for a siege—something she hadn't understood until now. All the clapboards had been stripped off and microthin fire-retardant panels put in place on the interior and exterior; all the leaded glass had been replaced with bulletproof panes that were an inch thick; the antique doors had been swapped out for ones that had reinforced lead frames; oxygen-monitoring equipment and heavy-duty HVAC systems had been installed; and there were no doubt other improvements that she wasn't aware of.

It had cost more than the house was worth, and at the time Grier had questioned her father's mental health.

Now she was grateful.

As she looked around at the familiar Early American antiques and the wide-plank floors and the atmosphere of casual grace, the evening ahead stretched out into infinity. Which was what happened when all you had before you was a whole lot of wait-and-see: Jim and Isaac would be getting in touch with her father at some point, but there was no telling when. Or what the news would be.

Gruesome. How gruesome was all of this.

God, typically, she thought of death in terms of accidents or disease. Not tonight. Tonight it was all about the violent and the premeditated, and she didn't like this world. It was hard enough to get through the day when only Mother Nature and Murphy's Law were after you.

She had a really bad feeling about all of this.

"Would you like something to eat now?" her father asked. "Or would you prefer to freshen up?"

So strange. Usually when she came into this home, she treated it as her own, going to the refrigerator or the coffeepot or the stove without a thought. It felt odd and uncomfortable to be treated as a guest.

Glancing over her shoulder, she stared at her father, tracing the handsome lines of his face. In the awkward silence of the armored house, it dawned on her how alone they both were. For their sake, they really needed to get back to being family from this place of being foreigners.

"Why don't I make us both some dinner."

Her father's eyes watered a little and he cleared his throat. "That would be lovely. I'll just take this up to your room."

"Thank you."

As he passed by, her father reached out and touched her arm, squeezing it ever so slightly—which was his version of a hug. And she accepted the gesture by placing her palm over his hand. Just as they had always done.

After he went up the front stairs, she headed to the kitchen feeling shaky and off her game . . . but she was up on her feet and moving forward.

Which, at the end of the day, was all you got, wasn't it.

There was just one thing missing . . . and she paused to look over her shoulder again. Then she strode into the kitchen and checked the table in the alcove . . . and the long stretch of counter where the cooktop was . . . and the foot of the back stairs . . .

"Daniel?" she hissed. "Where are you?"

Maybe he didn't want to be in their father's house. But if he could show up at the Four Seasons for a charity benefit and then at an underground fighting ring, he could damn well drag his ass here.

"I need you," she said. "I need to see you. . . ."

She waited. Called his name quietly a couple more times. But it appeared as if only the double ovens and the refrigerator were listening to her.

Oh, for God's sake, she knew her brother had always despised conflict—and that their father had made him jumpy.

But no one had ever seen him except her, so clearly he could pick who he showed himself to.

*"Daniel."*

In a moment of panic, she wondered if he was never coming back. Had there been a good-bye on his part that she hadn't caught?

Again, no response from the appliances.

Figuring she'd have more luck putting them to work, she went over to the icebox and cracked the door, wondering what the hell she could whip up for her and her father.

One thing was for sure: dinner wasn't going to include omelets.

It was going to be a while before she made an omelet again.

As darkness settled in, the headlights of Matthias's unmarked swept over the road ahead. There were other cars traveling along the same asphalt as his, other people behind those wheels, other plans in other heads.

All of it was irrelevant to him, with no more significance than a movie playing on a screen.

No more depth, either.

He had issues. Bad issues. The kind that tied his brain in knots and made that pain he'd been having on his left side fire up to the point that he struggled to keep conscious.

Shit ... Jim Heron knew way too much about what should have been private thoughts and private knowledge. It was as if the man had tuned in to Matthias's inner radio station and heard all his songs and jingles and traffic reports.

And the fucker was right. Matthias's second in command had only truly distinguished himself after Matthias's little "accident" in the desert: In the last two years, that operative had made himself indispensible and, looking over the assignments and situations Matthias had dealt with, the guy had gradually influenced Matthias's decisions until he was all but making them himself.

It had been so subtle. Like someone slowly turning the flame up under a pot of water. His second in command had been the one to change his mind about letting Jim Heron go. And the man had been driving Matthias to kill Isaac. And there had been a hundred more examples—many of which he'd acted on.

He hadn't even noticed it happening.

God, it had started with killing Alistair Childe's son. That had been the first of the bright ideas.

Of course, the logic had been unassailable and Matthias hadn't hesitated to pull the trigger. But when he'd watched the footage of the death, the captain's weeping had touched him. Opened up a door he hadn't even known had been in his hallway.

Matthias had turned the video off and gone to bed. And the next morning he'd woken up and decided enough was enough. Time to leave the party he had started all those years ago—let the guests take over his house and burn it down, fine. But he was done.

Straw. Camel's back.

Focusing on his hands on the car wheel, he realized someone else had been driving him, steering him, dictating his exit ramps and his directional signals. How had it happened?

And why the fuck did Jim Heron know?

As his mind went laundry machine on him and started another spin cycle on the past, he decided all that mental wash and rinse wasn't material. Not tonight. Not on this road. What mattered was not how he'd gotten behind this wheel and found himself on the way to Boston. What mattered was what he did when he got there.

Crossroads was right. He felt it in his bones—the same way he had when he'd prepared that bomb years ago.

The question was, What now? Believe what Jim Heron had said. Or follow through on the anger impulse that was driving him east.

Which destination did he go to.

As he ruminated, it sure as fuck felt like he was choosing between Heaven and Hell.

# CHAPTER
# 46

As Adrian watched over a gray clapboard gentleman's estate from a stand of oaks, he was beginning to feel like a fucking tree himself. Except for that skirmish back in town the night before, he'd spent waaaaaay too much time waiting in the wings over the last two days.

He'd never been a big bencher to begin with, but on a night like tonight, when the action was in town and he and Eddie were stuck out in the sticks babysitting for a couple of grown-ups, he got really damn twitchy. Especially given that the pair he and his buddy were in charge of were locked into a house that made Fort Knox look like a Porta-Potti in the sturdiness department.

Fucking hell. He couldn't believe they had been going after the wrong soul.

All their conclusions had seemed sound, but in fact, the shit was like an algebra equation that had gone awry: looked great on paper, but the answer was incorrect.

And what a squeaker this one had been. It gave him a case of the cold sweats to think they had been so close but so far away at the end of a match.

But the near-miss wasn't the only thing making his balls tight in a bad way. The other half of it was where Jim was at in his aftermath routine: in spite of what Devina had done to him, the guy was making like he was all tight in the membrane . . . and yeah, fine, maybe that was the case right now. Hell, the fact that everything with Isaac and Matthias was coming to a head tonight was probably a good thing, because it gave Jim something to focus on. The only trouble was, as Adrian knew firsthand, this crisis was going to pass and then the guy would be facing a lot of long, quiet hours by himself with nothing but those ugly memories pinging around his skull like stray bullets.

The hardest thing, at least in Ad's opinion, was knowing that it was going to happen again. When the situation called for it, Adrian would go back down there to Devina's Playgirl Mausoleum . . . and so would Jim. Because that was the kind of men they were. And that was the kind of bitch she was.

Next to him, Eddie smothered another sneeze.

"God bless you."

"Fucking lilacs. I'm the only immortal with allergies. I swear."

As the guy glared at the blooming whatever next to his head, Adrian took a deep breath thinking at least his best friend didn't have to go through hell down on that table. Then again, he'd been marked by that demon, which was hardly a lifetime pass to Disneyland.

Ten minutes, three more sneezes, and a whole lot of nothing else later, Adrian took out his cell phone and dialed up Jim. The guy answered on the second ring.

"Tell me," he barked.

"Nada. We've been out here in the lilacs—I guess they're called—staring at Grier eating with her dad. Looks like a pair of pork chops." The exhale that came across the connection was pure frustration. "Nothing on your end, either, I take it."

Man, sometimes bad action was better than this stalled-out, thumb-twiddling shit.

Jim cursed. "I spoke with Matthias about an hour ago,

but I have no idea where he was. Definitely in transit, however."

"I think we should come back in." Adrian frowned and leaned forward in his boots. Inside the rustic kitchen, Grier got up, snagged some dishes out of a cupboard and lifted the glass cover off a cake plate. Looked like a whole lot of chocolate. With white icing.

Fuck it. Maybe they should stay a little longer. Invite themselves in for dessert.

"You hang tight," Jim said. "But maybe I do need to come out there. I'd prefer to keep the showdown well away from the Childes, except I'm not sure Grier won't be the target. At this point, I don't know what Matthias is thinking—I could only get so far with him on the phone before he cut me off."

"Look, all I know is that we want to be where the party is." As Eddie sneezed again, Ad amended that in his head to include where the antihistamines were. "And listen, I've walked around this house. It's secure as a motherfucker. Matthias is the soul in play so wherever he is will be where the action goes down—and he's coming for Isaac."

There was a beat of silence. And then Jim said, "Grier's an innocent soul, though, and an excellent way for Matthias to get revenge—maybe she's the one he's supposed to take out. We just don't fucking know. Which is why I want to give it some more time . . . and then maybe we'll trade places."

"Fine. Wherever you want us, we'll go," Ad heard himself say before hanging up.

Check him out, being all good-little-soldier and shit. And didn't that just suck ass.

"We're staying put," he groused. "For now."

"Hard to know where to position."

"We need more fighters."

"If Isaac lives . . . we could turn him. He's got the stuff."

Adrian glanced over. "Nigel would never give his permission for that." Pause. "Would he?"

"I think he'd dislike losing more, I'll tell you that."

Adrian resumed watching Grier cut two slices and plate them up. He got the impression by the way her lips were moving that she and her father were talking pretty steadily, and he was glad. He didn't know what having a dad was like, but he'd been on the Earth long enough to know that a good one was a great thing.

He cursed as Grier headed for the freezer. "Oh, man. Ice cream, too?"

"How you can have an appetite at a time like this astounds me."

Adrian took a little bow. "I *am* amazing."

"'Freak' is also a word."

On that note, Ad pulled some "Super Freak" out of his vocal cords, doing a fantastic Rick James impression. In the lilac bushes. In . . . where the hell were they? Roosevelt, Massachusetts? Or was it Adams?

Washington?

"By all that is holy," Eddie muttered as he covered his ears, "stop—"

"—in the name of loooooove." Putting his hand out, Ad switched it up and Diana Ross–ed it, shaking his ass. "Be . . . fore. . . . you . . . breaaaaak . . . my—"

Eddie's soft chuckle was what he'd been gunning for, and as soon as he got one, he shut up.

As things grew quiet again, he thought about good old Isaac Rothe. That hardheaded, strong-backed motherfucker might be an excellent addition to the team.

Of course, he'd have to die first.

Or be killed.

Either of which, given how shit was going, could be arranged tonight.

In the farmhouse's kitchen, Grier sat across from her father at a table made of boards taken from an old barn. Between them, there were two small white plates marked up with smudges of chocolate and dessert forks down for a rest at steep angles.

Over the course of the meal, they had spoken of nothing important, just everyday things about work and his garden and her ongoing cases in the penal system. The conversation was so normal ... perhaps deceptively so, but she'd take what they had under the fake-it-till-you-make-it rule.

"Another piece?" she asked, nodding over at the cake stand on the counter.

"No, thank you." Her father dabbed the corners of his mouth with his napkin. "I shouldn't have had the first."

"You look as if you've lost weight. I think you should—"

"I lied about Daniel to keep you safe," he blurted, as if the pressure of holding back had built to an unsustainable level.

She blinked a couple of times. Then reached out and played with her fork, drawing little Xs and Os through the frosting she hadn't eaten, her stomach flip-flopping around the dinner she'd just had.

"I believe you," she said eventually. "It hurts like hell, though. It's like he's just died again."

"I'm so sorry. I can't say that enough."

Her eyes lifted up to his. "It's going to be okay, though. I just need some time. You and I ... we're all we've got left, you know?"

"I know. And that's my fault—"

From out of nowhere light blazed in through the windows, illuminating the alcove and the two of them in a burst of brightness.

Chairs screeched as she and her father burst up and dove for cover behind the solid wall of the den.

Outside on the front lawn, the motion-activated security lights had come on and a man was walking over the cropped grass toward the house. Behind him, in the shadows, a car that she didn't recognize was parked on the gravel drive.

Whoever it was must have come in without headlights

on. And if it were Jim or Isaac or those two men, someone would have called.

"Take this," her father hissed, pressing something heavy and metal into her hand.

A gun.

She accepted the weapon without hesitation and followed him to the front door—which was where their unannounced "guest" appeared to be heading. Where was the sense in that, though? You snuck down the drive without your lights on, but then marched right up to the—

"Oh, thank God," her father muttered.

Grier relaxed as well as she recognized who it was. In the security lights, Jim Heron's big body and hard face were as clear as day, and the fact that he'd ghosted down the lane made sense.

Her first thought was for Isaac, and she searched the pool of illumination for him as her father disarmed the system and opened the door. He wasn't with Jim, though.

Oh, dear Lord . . .

"Everyone's okay," Jim called out across the lawn, as if he'd read her mind. "It's all done."

The relief was so great she excused herself briefly, ducking into the kitchen, putting the gun down, and bracing her arms on the table. From the other room, she heard the deep voices of her father and Heron, but she doubted she would have tracked the conversation if she'd been standing next to them. Isaac was all right. He was okay. He was all right. . . .

It was over. Done with. And now, just as Isaac would be taking off in relative freedom, she could try to move on as well.

Man, she needed a vacation.

Somewhere frivolous and warm, she decided as she went over and picked up the dessert plates. Somewhere with palm trees. Mai tais and umbrellas. Beach. Pool—

*Tick . . . tick . . . whir . . .*

Grier frowned and slowly looked across her shoulder.

Over by the refrigerator, the back door's dead bolt was shifting from right to left at the same time the old-fashioned latch lifted up.

The voices out in the living room went suddenly silent. Too silent.

This was wrong. *All wrong—*

She dropped the plates and lunged for the gun she'd left on the counter—

Grier didn't make it. Something bit into her shoulder blade, and then an electrical charge slammed through her body, throwing her into a backward arch that knocked her off her feet and took her down hard onto the floor.

# CHAPTER
## 47

B ack in Beacon Hill, Isaac walked up the town house's front stairs, paused at the second-floor landing and then kept going to Grier's bedroom. In her private space, he paced around the bed, and felt like he was losing his ever-loving mind.

He checked her alarm clock. Walked to the French doors. Looked out onto the terrace.

Nothing moved outside, and there was no one else in the house but him and Jim.

Time was passing, but nobody was showing, and no matter how many times he went down to Jim and then came back upstairs again, he wasn't able to jump-start the next sequence of events.

It was like a director with no bullhorn and a cast and crew who didn't give a shit what he had to say.

The inescapable fear that drove him was that they were in the wrong place. That he and Jim were cooling their heels out here while the action was happening elsewhere. Like Grier's father's farmhouse.

On a vicious curse, he headed back for the staircase and jogged downward, expecting nothing else along the way or at the bottom other than a short pause in the kitchen and another trip up.

Except . . .

When he came to the landing, the front door down below creaked as if it were being opened. Palming his guns, he was ready to pounce—until he heard Jim's annoyed voice rising up.

"What are you doing here?" Heron demanded.

"You texted us."

Isaac frowned at the sound of the pierced man's voice.

"No, I did not."

"Yeah, you did."

At that moment, the Life Alert went off with a subtle shimmy in Isaac's pocket.

All instincts firing, he ducked quietly into the guest-room he'd stayed in. Holding the transmitter in his palm, he activated the device, and this time there was no delay in response.

Matthias answered right away. "I have your girl at her dear old dad's place. Get out here. You have a half hour."

"If you hurt her—"

"Time's wasting. And it goes without saying that you come alone. Don't keep me waiting, or I'm likely to get bored and have to fill my time. You won't like that, I promise. Be here in thirty."

The light went out, the transmission ending sharply.

When Isaac wheeled around to leave, he jumped back. Jim had somehow made it up the stairs and through the closed door to stand right behind him.

"He has her," Jim said flatly. "Doesn't he."

"I'm going solo or he'll kill her."

Shoving the man out of the way, Isaac jogged downstairs. The body in the front hall had been frisked for weapons before it had been gift wrapped, but car keys were another thing.

Bingo. Front pocket. Ford.

Now to find the bastard's ride.

When Isaac stood up, he realized everything was totally silent and nobody was in the front hall. Glancing around, he had the feeling he was alone in the house even though he hadn't a clue how they'd moved out so fast.

Whatever—fuck it. And fuck them.

Isaac lit for the door—but at the last minute, he pivoted in the archway and went back to the body to strip it some more. Then he shot out into the darkness.

The unmarked that he'd watched from the Pinckney Street house the day before was parked a block up, and the dead guy's key got him in. Engine started just fine and the GPS was functional, so he quickly plugged in the address Grier's father had given them all.

"Bat out of hell" described the trip.

He went flat-out on the Mass Pike, pushing the speed limit until he busted the fucker into pieces. Even still, it felt like he was moving in slow motion—and that got worse when he left the highway and tried to get through some town that was filled with stop signs and curvy roads.

Fortunately, the GPS took him exactly where he needed to go, his destination fronted by a pair of stone markers that sat on either side of a pale, glowing drive.

He canned the headlights and hung a right, downshifting from rush, rush, rush to slow, slow, slow. Cracking his window so he could hear better, he inched along, hating the sound of the tires crunching over a million seashells. The only good news was that the perma-glow of the city didn't exist out here in the semi-sticks, and the moon was covered by clouds. But how much you want to bet they had motion-activated exteriors on the house and/or trees?

Isaac rolled up behind another unmarked that had to be Matthias's car. A K-turn later and he was facing out. Taking the keys with him, he jogged along the fringes of the lawn, his senses alive, his rage an inferno in his blood.

Matthias would die if he laid even a finger on Grier. One hair out of place on that woman and that bastard was going to get slaughtered.

As he approached the house, he searched out the doors. The front was open and he couldn't see the back.

But then what did it matter—he was expected. And on that note, he should just fuck the DL ninja shit and announce himself.

Coming up to the farmhouse's entrance, he kept his guns hidden and his eyes sharp as he curled up a fist and beat at the wooden jamb.

"Matthias," he called out.

As he stepped inside, the resounding silence was more terrifying than any scream or pool of blood. Because God only knew what he was walking into.

Jim had had a plan as he and the angels had flashed to Grier's father's place. He hadn't wanted to leave Isaac on his own back in town, but all they would have done was argue, and God knew the canny bastard could take care of himself.

Bottom line, Devina was playing deadly games, and that was something only Jim could deal with. And having a delay before Isaac arrived might not be a bad thing: If Matthias had done anything to that Grier woman, the soldier was going to be impossible to control.

Yup, as Jim landed and went gunning for the open door of the farmhouse with his wingmen in tow, he was prepared to take care of things.

Nigel, however, derailed him.

The archangel appeared right in his path, and this time he wasn't in his tuxedo or his croquet whites or a nice little dapper-ass seersucker: He was nothing but a glowing form, a wavy silhouette of rippling light.

And he spoke only one word: "No."

As Jim hauled up on his momentum, he would have punched the fucker if there had been anything solid to aim for. "What the fuck is the matter with you!" First the mislead over Isaac and now this?

"The die is cast." Nigel lifted his barely-there hand. "And if you intervene now, you will ultimately lose."

Jim pointed through the open door. "There's a man's soul at risk."

File that under: No, really, you supercilious little prick.

Nigel's voice got dark. "As if I was unaware of that."

"If I can get to Matthias—"

"You had the chance—"

"I didn't know it was him! This is bullshit!"

"That is nothing I can change. But I tell you, let the ending happen—"

"Oh, you can't change anything, but you can get in the way now? Great fucking timing!" Jim was damned well aware that his voice was blaring, but he had no trouble announcing his presence to Devina or anybody else.

"Fuck this, I'm going in—"

On a quick shimmer, Nigel's form blanketed him from head to foot, the illumination acting as a kind of glue that held him in place. And then that English voice was not just in his ear but through his whole brain.

"What is the truer course? The passionate or the rational? Think, Jim. *Think*. If one breaks the rules, a punishment flows. *Think* this through. If one breaks the rules, punishment flows. Think, damn you!"

Rage clouded his mind and shook his body until he thought he would come apart ... but then suddenly, lightning hit marble head and he realized what the archangel was trying to tell him.

If one breaks the rules ... punishment flows.

"That's right, Jim. Take this to its natural conclusion— beyond this night. And know that you shall go farther in this game if you use your head rather than your anger. Please, I implore you, trust in me in this regard."

Easing up his muscles, Jim felt a curious calm overtake him and he turned his head through the molasses Nigel had created.

Looking at Adrian and Eddie as they ran up, he saw that they were every bit as pissed off as he was. Which given what Nigel was saying wasn't a value add.

"Trust me, Jim," Nigel said. "I want to win as badly as you do. I am not without my own burdens of lost loved ones. I too would do aught that it takes to render them a peaceful eternity. Think not that I would e'er steer you upon a wrong course."

Jim shook his head at his boys.

"Let it go," Jim said to them. "We're going to stay on the sidelines. We stay out here."

As his comrades looked at him like he was out of his cocksucking head, he couldn't agree more. It was going to kill him to not go in there, but he got the picture ... and he was ultimately glad the archangel intervened. Thanks to Devina's making fast and loose with the rules, the best shot Matthias had was Jim staying the fuck out of this.

Even though it went against every instinct he had.

After a moment, Nigel slowly extricated himself, and his magical illumination gradually dispersed. In its absence, Jim fell to his knees on the grass, his eyes locked on the open door of the clapboard house as Adrian and Eddie started to go off on him, demanding an explanation for the halt order.

Around the fringes of his mind and emotions, the urge to fly into the path of whatever Devina had engineered still tantalized him.

Especially as he thought of Isaac's woman in the hands of Matthias—

Oh, God ... Rothe was going to be sacrificed, wasn't he.

Jim's hands sought out the earth and he dug into the lawn with his fingers, holding his body in place.

Bowing his head, he prayed that his faith was well placed and good would, eventually, prevail. But the sad fact was, doing the right thing was going to be the death of a man who didn't deserve to die tonight.

# CHAPTER
## 48

Matthias had things with the Childes all tied up well before he expected Isaac to come tooling through the front door.

After he'd stun-gunned her, he'd discovered that picking Grier off the floor and putting her into a chair required more strength than he had—so he left her where she lay, tying her legs and wrists up with some duct tape he found in Alistair's pantry.

And as for her father?

No clue what had made the man open the way in and stand there in a trance, but the distraction and space-cadet routine had been perfectly timed. Matthias had been able to walk up right behind the guy and put a gun to his head.

So yeah, getting him to sit in a chair in the kitchen had been a piece of cake; he'd all but bound his own hands and feet.

Which had been helpful, given that Matthias's chest hurt so badly he could barely breathe.

And now, it was just a case of waiting for Isaac, all three of them together in this house with the door wide open.

There was a groan and then a shift on the floor as Grier

Childe started to come around. She had a moment of confusion, as if trying to figure out why she was lying on the hardwood and why she couldn't open her mouth. And then she jerked in a full-body spasm, her eyes peeling wide and locking on him.

"Wakey-wakey," he said gruffly, giving her a nod as her father started to fight against his bonds and make muffled noises under the duct tape across his mouth.

Matthias leveled his gun muzzle at the guy's head. "Shut it."

There wasn't anyone around to hear, but the distress and the struggle pricked Matthias's nerves. In fact, as he stood between the two, he was far from the calm, master-of-all-he-surveyed guy he'd always been in the past: He was in great pain. He was exhausted. And he felt that what was about to happen next was predestined, but not something he would have chosen.

He was utterly out of control and totally locked in at the same time.

With the eyes of both Childes on him and everyone quiet again, he braced himself against the counter, his creaky body protesting at the shift in position.

"You know what pisses me off about you," he said to Alistair. "I saved the good one." He nodded down at Grier. "I could have left you with that son of yours. But no, I took the broken one—put your dear Danny boy out of his misery and yours."

He could remember being surprised at his own thought process at the time. It was much more characteristic of him to take the one that would have hurt worse, but he'd gone a different way at that crossroads.

Maybe he'd started to change before he'd ordered the death. Who knew.

Who cared.

He was too far down for saving, and his conversation with Jim over the phone had shown him, instead of the possibilities for his redemption, the reality of his condemnation. It was time to end this . . . and go out with a bang.

Only this time, get it right.

At that moment, Isaac Rothe appeared in the archway of the kitchen. His eyes went to Grier first, and not even his stoic self-possession could hide his stark fear.

He loved that woman.

Well, good for him, the poor bastard.

"Welcome to the party," Matthias said numbly, as he brought up his gun and pointed it at her.

"Don't do it," Isaac bit out. "Take me, not her."

Matthias stared at the woman's wide, terrified eyes and the way she seemed to be mouthing something along the lines of, *Oh, God, no . . .*

"I'm really sorry about all this," Matthias said to her. And he meant it. He wasn't sure what was crueler: to kill her in front of Isaac . . . or leave her to survive the man's death—assuming that love of his was reciprocated.

Too bad one of them was going to die now—so that Jim Heron would be forced to come in and shoot Matthias—thus evening their score. The soldier had saved him two years ago against his wishes and now . . . tonight . . . he was going to do what he should have back in the desert.

"Matthias," Isaac said sharply. "I'll put my gun down."

"Don't bother," he murmured, still focused on Grier. "You know, Ms. Childe, he turned himself in to me to save you. Twice. It was all about you."

*"Matthias, look at me."*

But he didn't. Instead, he glanced at Alistair's face and that was what made up his mind.

He shifted the weapon around.

Isaac was ready—and he'd expected nothing less.

Both of them pulled their triggers at the same time.

# CHAPTER
## 49

G rier screamed against the tape that covered her mouth as the gunshots exploded in the kitchen, their echoing blasts making her ears ring and her eyes sting.

She heard two bodies hit the floor, but from her vantage point, she didn't know who had been hurt.

Someone was moaning.

With her heart thundering, she lifted her head and craned her neck. Matthias was no longer in sight—so he must have been hit. . . . She prayed he'd been hit.

Isaac . . .? Her father . . . ?

Caterpillaring along the floorboards, she inched around the island. The first thing she saw was her father upright in the chair. And he was the one moaning as he fought furiously against the tape around his hands and feet.

Where was Isaac?

Ice-cold dread replaced every ounce of blood in her veins, and she knew the answer to the question even before she saw him lying flat on his back just inside the room.

He wasn't moving, his gun lying in his lax, open palm, his eyes staring sightlessly up to the ceiling.

Grier screamed again, her body contracting, her cheek

squeaking on the varnished floor, her whole soul and everything in her mind denying what was inescapable. Flailing around, she inched toward him, hoping to help, struggling to cross the distance—

Suddenly her hands were free.

With all her thrashing, she'd ripped them out of their bindings. Exploding into unexpected coordination, she tore the tape from her mouth and dragged herself with her arms to Isaac.

The bullet had gone right into his heart.

It was such a small hole through the sweatshirt, nothing but a relative pinprick with a sooty stain around the edges. Except it was more than enough to kill him.

"Isaac," she said, touching his cold face. "Oh, God ... don't go...."

His mouth was slightly open, his pupils fixed and dilated, his breathing shallow to the point of nearly stopping.

He had done it all to save her, the change in plans, the turning himself in. After all, that crazed, evil man had had no reason to lie.

"Isaac ... I love you.... I'm sorry ..."

His head slowly turned toward her, his eyes struggling to focus. As he appeared to lock on her face, tears licked over that frosty stare, one escaping out of the corner and rolling down his temple to fall onto the floor.

"I ..."

"I'll call nine-one-one," she said in a rush.

Except as she went to jump up for the phone, he caught her arm in a surprisingly strong grip. "No ..."

"You're dying—"

*"No."* With his free hand, he reached up to the zipper on his sweatshirt. Even though his fingers were trembling, he managed to grasp the toggle and pull it down....

To reveal the bulletproof vest he was wearing.

"Breath ... just ... knocked ... out ... of ... me." With that he took a proper inhale, one that expanded his chest fully and was expelled evenly and cleanly. "Took it off ... dead soldier ..."

Grier blinked. Then shoved his hands out of the way and probed the hole ... where the bullet had been caught and held in the tensile fibers of the Kevlar.

Her body reacted on its own, a bizarre superstrength overtaking her as she yanked him up off the floor and held him to her heart.

"You're a ..." She started to cry properly as horror and terror gave way to sweeping relief. "You're a brilliant man. You're a brilliant ... stupid man ..."

And then his arms were around her and he was, against all odds, holding her back.

All too soon he was separating them, though, and picking up his gun.

"Stay here."

With a grunt, he got up and shuffled around to check on Matthias, and as he went over, she unbound her feet and scrambled to her father.

"Are you okay," she asked as she went to work freeing his arms.

He nodded furiously, his eyes not on her but on Isaac as if he couldn't believe the guy had survived either. And the instant his hands were free, he took over undoing his ankles.

Grier looked around, and then as a precaution in case anyone else showed up or was in the house, she went for the nine-millimeter she'd been given when Jim Heron had appeared.

Assuming that actually had been the man.

Something told her that perhaps what she and her father had seen hadn't really been there at all.

Matthias knew it was a mortal hit and he was glad. Yeah, he'd wanted Jim Heron's gun to do the deed, but Isaac's had worked just fine—and Rothe had been part of the whole survivor problem, hadn't he.

At least he'd gotten even with one of them.

As the arterial tear in his heart started to leak into his chest cavity, breathing became difficult and his blood pressure dropped, his body going numb and cold. Which was nice. No more pain.

Well, not exactly. That stinging, left-sided agony stuck with him ... and it was as he lay dying that he figured out what it was: He'd been wrong. It wasn't his heart preparing for a coronary. It was—shock of all shocks—his conscience. And the way he knew that was because as he thought of the fact that he'd killed a relatively innocent man, in front of a woman who loved him, the pain got exponentially worse.

Wasn't this ironic. Somehow, in the depths of his sin, the sociopath had found his soul.

Too late.

Ah, hell, that was okay, though. He was going to be dead soon, and after that nothing mattered. The white light that had come for him before, when he'd coded on the operating table a couple of times, was going to stick around this time. He didn't think it was Heaven. The shit was probably a figment of some ocular malfunction, just another part of the mechanics of dying—

Isaac appeared in front of him, standing tall and strong, his sweatshirt open to show a bulletproof vest.

When he was certain he was seeing correctly, Matthias started to laugh ... and the pain in his left side abruptly eased.

"Son of a ..." He didn't get out the *bitch* as a round of coughing shook him up.

After it had passed, he could feel blood leaking out of his mouth and down his cheek as his heart started to bang around in his rib cage like an animal thrashing in a cage.

As Isaac got down on his haunches, Matthias thought about that tattoo on the man's back. Grim Reaper, indeed. He wondered if the soldier would go and get another notch tattooed on the bottom.

How much you want to bet it would be the final one, too?

Isaac shook his head and whispered, "I have to let you die. You know that, right."

Matthias nodded. "Thank . . . you . . ."

He lifted his frozen hand and, a moment later, felt it encased in something warm and solid. Isaac's.

So weird how things worked out. Back in that desert, Jim had set out to save him, but here and now, in this kitchen, Isaac was giving him what he'd wanted all along.

Before Matthias closed his eyes for the last time, he looked over at Alistair Childe. His daughter had freed him and he was embracing her, holding her safe, his head down next to hers. As if the man felt the stare that was upon him, he glanced up.

The relief in his face was epic, like he knew Matthias was dying and never coming back—and that even though that wouldn't resurrect the son he had lost, it would protect his and his daughter's future for evermore.

Matthias nodded at the guy and then shut his lids in preparation for the great nothingness that was coming. God, he was hungry for it. His life hadn't been a gift to himself or the world, and he was looking forward to not existing.

As he waited out the stretch of neither here nor there, when he wasn't really alive, but not quite dead, he thought of Alistair the night his son had died.

". . . Dan . . . ny . . . boy . . . my Danny boy . . ."

Matthias frowned and then realized he hadn't just thought the words, but spoken them aloud.

They were the same ones he'd said right before he'd put his foot on that bomb trigger.

At that moment, white light came upon him, a product of the numbness . . . or maybe it had walked through the sensation as if the feeling was a door. Upon its arrival, a great, peaceful calm overtook his mind, body, and soul sure as if he had been wiped clean of all the sins he'd imagined or wrought during his time on Earth.

The illumination was so much more than anything his eyes were doing. It was all he saw, all he knew, all he was.

Heaven did actually exist.

And oh, the lovely nothingness . . . ah, the blissful—

In the corners of his nonvision, a gray fog boiled up, at first appearing as nothing distinct, but then expanding and darkening to a blackness that started to eat at the light.

Matthias fought against the invasion, his instincts telling him that this was not what he wanted—but it wasn't a battle he would win.

The fog became tar, coating him and claiming him, pulling him downward into a spiral that tightened, tightened . . . tightened . . . until he was flushed out into a sea of others.

As he writhed against the choking, cloaking tide, he bumped into flailing bodies.

Trapped in an oily black infinity, he screamed . . . along with the rest of them.

But no one came. No one cared. Nothing happened.

His eternity had finally claimed him and it was never going to let him go.

# CHAPTER
## 50

"He's dead."

As Isaac spoke the words, he rose to his feet and took a deep breath. Across the way, Grier and her father were wrapped tightly around each and he gave himself a moment to appreciate the sight of them alive, and well, and together.

Thank you, God, he thought—in spite of the fact that he wasn't a religious man.

*Thank you, Almighty God.*

"Stay here," he told them before going around and shutting and locking the back door.

It took him ten minutes to search and secure the whole house and the final thing he did was go to the front door and double-check that the dead bolts were properly engaged—

Isaac frowned and looked through a window onto the lawn. There was a small dog out there ... standing on stocky legs, with his head cocked as he stared in at Isaac. Cute little thing ... could use a haircut, but that happened to the best of men and boys and terriers.

Isaac cracked the door and called out, "You live here?"

While that head tilted to the other side, Isaac searched

the front yard and prayed that at any minute Jim Heron would step out of the trees.

Nothing but the dog, however.

"You want to come in?" he said to the animal.

The thing seemed to smile as if it appreciated the kind invitation. But then it turned and trotted off, a slight limp listing him to the right.

Between one blink and the next the thing disappeared.

Theme song of the fucking night, Isaac thought as he shut the door again.

As soon as he walked into the kitchen, Grier broke away from her father and came running at him, hitting his body hard, her arms wrapping around him with vital strength. And with a sigh of gratitude, he held her against him, tucking her head into his chest, feeling her heart beat against his.

"I love you," she said against the bullet proof vest. "I'm sorry. I love you."

Shit, so he'd heard her right when he'd been on the floor.

"I love you, too." Shifting her face up, he kissed her. "Even though I don't deserve you."

"Shut up."

Now she was the one kissing him and he was more than willing to let her—but not for long. All too soon, he was breaking off the contact.

"Listen, I want you and your father to do something for me."

"Anything."

He glanced at the clock. Nine fifty-nine. "Go back to town—somewhere public. One of your private clubs or something. I want you both to be seen tonight, together. Tell people you had dinner or saw a movie. A father-daughter thing."

As her eyes shot to Matthias's body, her father said, "I can help."

"*We* can help," Grier amended.

Isaac stepped back and shook his head. "I'll take care of the bodies. Better that neither of you know where they end up. I'll deal with this—but you have to go now."

The Childes looked like they were in the mood for arguing, but he was having none of that. "Think about it. It's all over. Matthias is dead. So is his second in command. With them gone, XOps will return to what it should be—and be run by the right people. You're out." He nodded at Childe, "I'm out. The slate is wiped clean—provided you let me handle it from here. Let's do this the right way—one last time."

Her father cursed—which was something the man no doubt didn't do very often. And then he said, "He's right. Let me go change."

As her father disappeared, Grier looked at Isaac, her arms slowly crossing around herself, her eyes growing grave. "Is this good-bye for you and me? Tonight? Here and now?"

Isaac went to her and captured her face in his hands, feeling all too vividly the reality he couldn't escape and she wasn't going to be able to live with.

With a pain in his chest that had nothing to do with the bullet, he said one, devastating word: "Yes."

As she sagged, her eyes closing tight, he had to speak the truth: "It's better that way. I'm not your kind of man—even if I don't have to worry about XOps anymore, I'm not what you need."

Her lids flipped open and she glared at him. "How old am I?" she demanded. "Come on, how old. Say it."

"Ah . . . thirty-two."

"And you know what that means, legally? I can drink, I can smoke, I can vote, I can serve in the army, and I can make my own damn decisions. So how about you let me choose what's good for me—and what isn't."

Right. It was so not the time to get turned on. And he really didn't think she'd thought through all the implications of being with a man who had his background.

He stepped back. "Go with your father. Let me clean up here and back in town."

Her eyes held his. "Don't break my heart, Isaac Rothe. Don't you dare break my heart when you know perfectly well you don't have to."

With that, she kissed him and strode out of the kitchen . . . and as he watched her go, he felt pulled between two outcomes: one where he stayed with her and tried to make it work, the other where he left her to stitch up her life and move along.

Overhead, he heard her and her father walk around as they got themselves ready to go out and pretend like they hadn't seen two men get killed in their homes and weren't praying that a soldier who they shouldn't have ever met disappeared the bodies.

Christ, and he even considered being in her life?

Isaac was alone no more than twenty minutes later, the two of them making a hurried departure for the city in Childe's Mercedes.

Before they left, Isaac shook her father's hand, but didn't offer even his palm to Grier—because he didn't trust himself not to kiss her one last time: Looking at her in her black dress, with her hair put together and her makeup on, she was as he had first met her, a beautiful, well-educated woman of privilege with the smartest eyes he'd ever had the privilege of staring into.

"Be safe," he said to her hoarsely. "I'll call you to let you both know when it's okay to come back here."

No tears, no protest on her end. She just nodded once, turned on her heel, and went to her father's car.

As the pair left, he walked to the front door and tracked the sedan's taillights.

He had to wipe his eyes. Twice.

And upon the disappearance of those glowing red beacons, he felt as if he had been left behind. But that was such bullshit, wasn't it. You couldn't be left, if you were the one doing the departure.

Right?

Needing some kind of contact, some sort of hope, he looked around at the treeline on the far side of the rolling lawn again. No sign of Jim or his boys . . . or that dog.

And yet he could have sworn he was being watched. "Jim? You out there, Jim?"

No one replied. Nobody came out of the foliage.

"Jim?"

As he went back inside, he had the strangest feeling he was never going to see Heron again. Which was odd, because Jim had been so fired up to be a savior.

Then again Matthias's body was stiffening on the kitchen floor, which meant Isaac was safe now—so that man's purpose had been served, hadn't it.

Although . . . just to be sure, he was keeping the bulletproof vest on until dawn.

No reason to take being alive for granted.

# CHAPTER
## 51

" **J**im? You out there, Jim?"

As Isaac's eyes searched the trees, Jim stood no more than three feet away from the guy and he wished he could hug the motherfucker. God . . . when those two gunshots had gone off and he'd watched through the kitchen windows as both Matthias and Rothe went down, years had been shaved off his eternal life.

But Isaac had been okay. He'd saved himself with some very clear, defensive thinking. Just as he'd been trained to do.

"Jim?"

And now, as he stared at his fellow soldier, pure, unadulterated elation flooded him. He'd won. *Again*.

Fuck you, Devina, he thought. Fuck *you*.

Isaac was alive and so were Grier and her father. And in spite of getting the soul wrong in the beginning, things had worked out properly—although Nigel's punishment thing had turned out to be a nonissue, hadn't it.

Jim looked over his shoulder at Adrian and Eddie and was surprised to find that they weren't all smiles.

"What's wrong—"

He didn't get a chance to finish the sentence. A mad

swirling rush rose from his feet, twirling around him, rising up to claim his legs and hips and chest. He tried to fight it, but couldn't run from—

His molecules scrambled and scattered until he was a swarm of himself that moved out of the dimensions of time and space, traveling to some unknown destination.

When he coalesced, he knew just where he was ... and the sight of Devina's worktable made his gut sour.

He had not won. Had he.

"No, you did not," she said from behind him.

Turning on his heel, he looked at her as she came in through the archway. She was in her brunette form, all lovely and lush and fake as a Barbie version of herself.

She smiled, her red lips curling off her beautiful white teeth. "Matthias shot Isaac with the intent to kill him. Whether or not there was a death is not the measure. There was *mens rea*—a guilty mind."

Above her head, a black flag hung from the black wall, the first trophy for her.

"You lost, Jim." That smile got even wider as she lifted her arms and indicated her great, viscous prison that rose high above them both. "He's here now, mine forever."

Jim's hands curled into fists. "You cheated."

"Did I."

"You pretended to be me, didn't you. That must have been how Matthias got into the farmhouse. You either made him look like me or you appeared as me."

Her smug satisfaction was all the confirmation he needed.

"Now, now, Jim—I never cheat. So I don't know what you're talking about." Devina strolled over to him, approaching him in a sensuous glide. "Say, would you care to stay awhile? I've got some ideas for how we could spend the time."

When she was right in front of him, her red-tipped nails drifted up his chest and she leaned in. "I love being with you, Jim."

With a hard clap, he captured her wrist and squeezed hard enough to break it. "You must be a glutton for punishment. In case you don't remember, I shattered you last trip through the park."

The bitch had the nerve to pout. "You're hurting me."

He didn't believe that for a second. "And you'll say or do anything."

Now she smiled again. "Too right, Jim, my love. Too right."

He dropped his hold as if she burned him, his stomach clenching up as he recognized the light in her eyes.

"That's right, Jim," she murmured. "I have feelings for you. And that scares you, doesn't it. Afraid you'll reciprocate?"

"Not. At. All."

"Ah, well, we'll have to work on that."

Before he could stop her, she rose up and captured his mouth, kissing him quick and then biting his lower lip hard enough to draw blood.

She stepped back fast, as if she knew she was pushing it. "Bye for now, Jim. But we'll be seeing each other soon. I promise."

With disgust, he wiped his mouth with the back of his hand and spat on her floor. And he was about to cut her down, when he frowned, thinking of what Nigel had said on the lawn.

*Know that you shall go farther in this game if you use your head rather than your anger.*

Now Jim was the one smiling—albeit grimly. There were worse things than having your enemy fall in love with you: As strong as she was, as unpredictable and dangerous as her powers were, that look in her eyes right now, that burning, out-of-control look, was a weapon.

Beating back his own emotions, he found himself reaching down and jacking his cock with his palm.

Devina's reaction was instantaneous and electric. Her hot stare flashed to his hips, her mouth parting like she couldn't catch enough air, her breasts rising over the bodice of her dress.

"You want this?" he asked gruffly.

Like a puppet, she nodded.

"Not good enough," he told her, hating her, hating himself. "Say it, bitch. *Say it.*"

In a hoarse, hungry voice, she breathed, "I *crave* you. . . ."

Jim released the hold on himself, feeling filthy inside and out. But war was ugly, wasn't it, even if you were on the good, moral side.

Means to an end, he thought. His body and her need were means to an end, and he would use them if he had to.

"Good," he growled. "That's good."

With that, he willed his body to rise up from the floor, this time the twisting energy summoned up by him and no one else.

As he levitated higher and higher, Devina reached for him, her face contouring into a kind of painful desire that juiced him up.

And then he wasn't looking at her anymore; he was scanning the walls of her dungeon, searching for the girl he hated leaving behind yet again . . . as well as the boss he had tried to save and failed.

He would be back for the former. But the latter . . . he feared that Matthias had been laid to rest for an eternity, his never-ending suffering having been well-earned.

Jim mourned the loss of the man, however.

He'd wanted to redeem the guy.

Jim came back to consciousness on Captain Alistair Childe's lawn. And as he thought back to his first assignment, it seemed he excelled at coming and going on grass.

Adrian and Eddie were on either side of him, the two angels grave and serious.

"We lost," Jim said. As if they didn't already know.

Adrian put his hand out, and when Jim reached up, the guy helped pull him to his feet. "We lost," Jim muttered again.

Looking over his shoulder, he thought briefly about going into the farmhouse and helping Isaac take care of Matthias's remains, but he decided to stay put. The soldier was going to have a hard enough time making sense of all the things that couldn't be explained—more contact with Jim was just going to give him another thing to get fucked in the head about.

"Caldwell," Jim said to his boys. "We're going back to Caldwell."

"Fair enough," Eddie murmured, like he wasn't surprised in the slightest.

And Jim wasn't going to worry who was next in the game. As he'd learned with this particular assignment, the souls were going to find him. So he might as well follow what the center of his chest was telling him: namely that it was about time for the Barten family to have their daughter's body to bury properly.

Jim was just the angel to make that happen.

Unfurling his great, luminescent wings, he took one last stare through the kitchen windows. Isaac Rothe was working with grim purpose, handling things with the same kind of competence and strength as he always had.

He was going to be fine—provided he was smart enough to hang around with that attorney. God, if you were lucky enough to find love like that? Only a fool would turn that shit down.

Jim took to the night sky as if he'd been born to it, his

wings carrying him through the cool air, the wind hitting his face and fingering through his hair, his team of two right behind him.

Next battle he was going to be quicker on the dime. And he was going to use his new weapon against Devina to its fullest advantage.

Even if it killed him.

# CHAPTER
## 52

*One week later ...*

As Grier got undressed in her closet, she hung her black suit up along with the others and found it impossible not to remember the way everything had been arranged before. Suits had previously been to the left of the door. Now they were straight ahead.

In just her silk blouse and her stockings, she padded around, touching her clothes, wondering which had been rehung that afternoon by her ... and what Isaac had done after she'd left.

Closing her eyes, she wanted to weep but didn't have the energy.

There had been nothing from him since the all-clear that night a week ago—which, incidentally, he'd sent via text instead of doing in person or over the phone.

After that? No calls, no e-mails, no visits.

It was as if he'd never existed.

And he'd left nothing behind. When she'd come back to this house, the business card that Matthias had given her as well as the strips of cloth from the muscle shirt and the file full of dossiers had disappeared. Along with both bodies and the two cars out in Lincoln.

Foolishly, she'd looked for a note, just as she had the first time he'd "left," but there hadn't been one. And sometimes, in the middle of the night when she couldn't sleep, she went searching again, checking her bedside tables and the kitchen counters and even here in the closet.

Nothing.

The only thing she supposed he'd left behind was this closet put back together. But that was hardly something she could keep in her diary and take out from time to time when she was feeling melancholic.

In the intervening seven days, work had kept her going, forcing her to get up in the morning when all she wanted to do was pull the covers over her head and lie in bed all day: Every morning, she'd gotten up and gotten herself dressed and had her coffee and become stuck in traffic on the short drive to the Financial District, where their offices were.

Her father had been great. They'd had dinner together every single night, just as they'd been in the habit of doing before. . . .

The only thing that was even close to a light at the end of the dark tunnel she was in — and it was just a match strike, not a bonfire or anything — was that she'd followed through on the vacation idea. Next week she was going to get on a plane and go to —

Grier froze, a tickle on her neck cutting into the woe-is-me routine. "Daniel?"

When there was no answer, she cursed. In addition to looking for Isaac's nonexistent note, she'd been hoping to see her brother's ghost, but it was as if the two of them had both left her high and dry with no good-bye.

Turning around, she —

"Daniel!" She grabbed her chest. "Christ! And where the hell have you been?"

For once, her brother was not dressed in Ralph Lauren.

He was in a long white robe, looking like he was about to graduate from college or something.

His smile was warm, but sad. "Hey, sis."

"I thought you'd left me." She was about to run forward to hug him when she realized that wasn't going to work—as usual he was mostly air. "Why haven't you—"

"I've come to say good-bye."

"Oh." Her eyes closed of their own volition and she took a deep breath. "I was kind of waiting for this, I guess."

When she reopened her lids, he was right in front of her, and all she could think of was that he looked so healthy. So relaxed. So . . . curiously wise.

"You're ready for this now," he told her. "You're ready to move on."

"Am I." She wasn't so sure. The idea of not seeing him again threw her into a panic.

"Yeah, you are. Besides, it's not a permanent kind of thing. You'll see me again . . . Mom, too. It won't be for a good long while, but you have something to live for now."

"Myself, right. No offense, but I've been doing that for thirty years and it's kind of empty."

Now he grinned and his glowing hand went to hover over her belly. "Not exactly."

As she looked down at herself, she wondered what the good goddamn he was talking about.

"I love you," her brother said. "And you're going to be just fine. I also wanted to tell you that I think I was wrong."

"About what?"

"I thought I was stuck in the in-between because you wouldn't let me go. But that wasn't it. I was the one who couldn't let you go. You're going to be in great hands, though, and everything is going to be all right."

"Daniel, what are you talking about—"

"I'll give Mom your love. And don't worry. I know you love me, too. Say hi to Dad for me sometime if you can. Let

him know that I'm okay and I've forgiven him long ago."
Her brother lifted his ghostly hand. "Bye, Grier. Oh, and
Daniel would be great. You know, if it's a boy?"

Grier recoiled as her brother disappeared into thin air.

In his absence, she stood there, struck stupid, wondering
what in God's name—

Her feet started moving without her giving them an
order, and a split second later, she found herself in the
bathroom. Ripping open the drawer where she kept her
makeup and her . . .

Birth control pills.

With a shaking hand, she picked up the square bubble
pack and started to count.

But it wasn't like she hadn't remembered what she'd
forgotten . . . to take.

The last pill she'd swallowed had been the night before
Isaac had come into her life. And they'd had sex two . . .
maybe two and a half times without protection.

Grier stumbled out of her bathroom and promptly realized she had nowhere to go. Falling onto the foot of her
bed, she sat there in the dimness and stared at the packet
as rain started to fall outside.

Pregnant? Was it possible she was . . . pregnant? Was
she . . .

The knock was so quiet that at first she thought it was
just a function of her heart pounding, but when it came
again, she looked to the French door of the terrace.

On the other side of the glass, a huge shape loomed, and
for a split second she nearly went for the security system
fob. But then she saw there was something other than a gun
in the man's hand.

A rose.

It sure looked like a single rose.

*"Isaac,"* she all but yelled.

Bursting up, she raced for the door and yanked it open.
Her MIA soldier was standing in the drizzle, his hair get-

ting damp, his black muscle shirt leaving his shoulders bare to the droplets.

"Hi," he said in a small voice. Like he was unsure of the reception he was going to get.

Grier tucked the birth control pills behind her back. "Hello . . ."

Her mind whirled into a frenzy as she wondered whether he'd come to tell her that there had been a problem with the cleanup . . . or was he here to warn her that someone else was after them all? But then why would he bring her a—

"It's nothing bad," he said, as if maybe she'd spoken out loud. "I'm just here to give you this." He lifted up the white rose awkwardly. "It's . . . ah, something men do. When they . . . ah . . ."

As his voice seemed to desert him, Grier stared at the perfect petals of the flower and, as she breathed in, she caught the scent—and then she realized she was making him stand out in the rain.

"God, where are my manners—come in," she said. "You're getting wet."

As she stepped back, he hesitated. And then he put the rose between his teeth and bent down to untie the laces of his combat boots.

Grier started laughing.

She couldn't help it and it didn't make any sense, but there was no holding it in. She laughed until she had to back up and sit down on the mattress again. She laughed from joy and confusion and hope. She laughed at everything from the perfect rose to the perfect moment . . . to the perfect timing.

To him being a perfect gentleman—to the point that he didn't want to track in on her bedroom rug.

Her brother was right.

She was going to be okay.

Her soldier was home for good . . . and she was going to be perfectly fine.

\*    \*    \*

Isaac stepped into Grier's room in his stocking feet and he
was careful to shut the door behind himself. Taking the rose
out from between his teeth, he smoothed his hair and beat
back the feeling that he wished he could have shown up in
a tux or something.

But he just wasn't a tuxedo kind of guy.

He approached his woman and got down on his knees
in front of her, watching her laugh, and smiling a little himself. She'd either lost her damn mind or she was glad to see
him—and he hoped like hell it was the latter and didn't
care if it was the former as long as she let him stay.

God, she looked good. With nothing but a black silk
blouse on and a pair of hose, she was the most beautiful
thing he'd ever seen—

As she wiped her eyes, he realized she had something in
her hand and it wasn't some sappy-ass flower. It was a foil
packed of . . . pills?

Grier clearly tweaked to what he'd focused on, because
she stopped laughing and tried to tuck the thing behind
herself.

"Wait," he said, "what is it?"

She took a deep breath, like she was bracing herself.
"Why did you come back?"

"What's up with the pills."

"You first." The look in her eyes was dead serious.
"You . . . go first."

Well, now he felt like a fool, but then again, even though
all was fair in love and war, there was no place for a man's
pride in that mix, was there.

"I came back to stay, if you'll have me. I spent the last
week . . . taking care of things." No reason to elaborate
on that one, and he was relieved when she didn't ask.
"And I had to do some thinking. I want to go legit. As
you've said, you can't change the past, but you can do
something about the future. My time with XOps . . . I'm

going to carry that burden around with me for the rest of my life—but, and I know this is going to sound bad, I'm a murderer with a clear conscience? I don't know if that makes sense . . ."

The thing was, though, that notation in his dossier *Must have moral imperative* hadn't just been window dressing—and that was the only reason why he could live with not sending himself to prison or the electric chair.

He cleared his throat. "I want to go through my trial for the cage fighting—maybe if I agree to cooperate, I can plead out or something. And then I want to get a job. Maybe in security or . . ."

He'd been hoping to join Jim Heron's crew, but then again, with Matthias dead, maybe those three had disbanded—although he was never going to know. If Jim hadn't come to find him by now, he was never going to.

"I think I'm pregnant."

Isaac froze. Then blinked.

Huh, he thought. Going by the ringing in his ears, someone had apparently just clipped him in the back of the head with a two-by-four.

Which would explain not only the noise but the sudden dizziness as well.

"I'm sorry. . . . What did you say?"

She held up the pills. "I forgot to take them. With all the drama, I just . . . didn't do it."

Isaac waited to see if the okay-I've-been-boarded sensation returned, and what do you know, that was a hell-yeah.

The aftermath didn't last, though. A shattering joy beat back the wobbles, and before he knew it, he'd all but jumped on Grier, tackling her onto the mattress in an embrace that brought them bone-to-bone. And promptly *horrified* him.

"Oh, God, did I hurt you?"

"No," she said, smiling and kissing him. "No, I'm fine."

"Are you sure?"

She got an odd, faraway look in her eyes. "Yes, I'm positive. Can we call him Daniel if it's a boy?"

"We can call him anything. Daniel. Fred. Susie would be tough, but I'd deal."

There was no more talking after that. He was too busy undressing her and her him, and then they were naked and—

"*Fuck* . . ." He groaned as he entered her, feeling her tight hold on him and reveling in that warm, slick pressure. "Sorry. . . . I don't mean . . . to curse. . . ."

Oh, the moving, the glorious moving.

Oh, the glorious future.

He was free at last. And thanks to her, he was in out of the rain, literally.

"I love you, Isaac," she breathed against his throat. "But harder . . . I need you to go harder. . . ."

"Yes, ma'am," he growled. "Anything the lady wants."

And then he proceeded to give her everything he had . . . and everything he was and ever would be.

Read on for a sneak peek of

*LOVER UNLEASHED,*

J. R. Ward's next novel in the
#1 *New York Times* bestselling
Black Dagger Brotherhood series,
coming soon from Piatkus

Manny Manello didn't like other people driving his Porsche. In fact, short of his mechanic, no one else ever did.

Tonight, however, Jane Whitcomb was behind the wheel because: One, she was competent and could shift without grinding his transmission into a stump; two, she'd maintained the only way she could take him where they were going was if she were doing the ten-and-two routine; and three, he was still reeling from seeing someone he'd buried pop out of the bushes to hi-how're-ya him.

So many questions. Lot of pissed off, too. And yeah, sure, he was hoping to get to a place of peace and light and sunshine and all that namby-pamby bullshit, but he wasn't holding his breath for it. Which was kind of ironic. How many times had he stared up at his ceiling at night, all nestled in his beddy-bye with some Lagavulin, praying that his former chief of Trauma would come back to him?

Manny glanced over at her profile. Illuminated in the glow of the dash, she was still smart. Still strong.

Still his kind of woman.

But that was never happening now. Aside from the

whole liar-liar-pants-on-fire about her death, there was a gunmetal gray ring on her left hand.

"You got married," he said.

She didn't look at him, just kept driving. "Yes. I did."

The headache that had sprouted the instant she'd stepped out from behind her grave instantly went from grouchy to gruesome, and shadowy memories Loch Ness'd below the surface of his conscious mind, tantalizing him, making him want to work for the full reveal.

He had to cut that cognitive search and rescue off, though, before he popped an aneurism from the strain: As maddening as being lost in his own mind was, he had the sense that he could do permanent damage to himself if he kept struggling.

As he looked out the car window, fluffy pine trees and budding oaks stood tall in the moonlight, the forest that ran around Caldwell's edges growing thicker as they headed north from the city proper and the twin bridges of downtown.

"You died out here," he said grimly. "Or at least pretended you did."

They'd found her Audi in and among the trees on a stretch of road not far from here, the car having careened off the shoulder. No body, though, because of the fire.

Jane cleared her throat. "I feel like all I've got is 'I'm sorry.' And that just sucks."

"Not a party on my end, either."

Silence. Lot of silence. But he wasn't one to keep asking when all he got in return was *I'm sorry*. Besides, he wasn't totally in the dark. He knew she had a patient she wanted him to treat and he knew . . . Well, that was about it, wasn't it.

Eventually, she took a right hand turn off onto . . . a dirt road?

"FYI," he muttered, "this car was built for racetracks, not roughing it."

"This is the only way in."

To where, he wondered. "You're going to owe me for this."

"You're the only one who can save her."

Manny flashed his eyes over. "You didn't say it was a 'her.'"

"Should it matter?"

"Given how much I don't get about all of this, *everything* matters."

A mere ten yards in and they went through the first of countless puddles that were as deep as frickin' lakes, and as the Porsche splashed through, he gritted, "And screw this patient. I want payback for what you're doing to my under carriage."

Jane let out a little laugh, and for some reason, that made the center of his chest ache—but nothing good was going to come from dwelling on the emotional crap. It wasn't like the pair of them had ever been together—yeah, there had been attraction on his part. Big attraction. And, like, one kiss. That was it, however.

And now she was Mrs. Someone Else.

About five minutes later, they came up to a gate that looked like it had been erected during the Punic Wars. The thing was hanging at Alice in Wonderland angles, the chain link rusted to shit and broken in places, the fence that it bisected nothing more than six feet of barbed cattle wire that had seen better days.

Yet the thing opened smoothly. And as they went past it, he saw the first of the video cameras.

While they progressed at a snail's pace, a strange fog rolled in from nowhere in particular, the landscape blurring until he couldn't see more than twelve inches ahead of the car's grille. Christ, it was like they were in a *Scooby-Doo* episode out here.

The next gate was in slightly better condition, and the one after that was even newer, and so was the one after that.

The last gate they came to was spit-and-shine sparkling, and all about the Alcatraz: Fucker reached twenty-five feet off the ground and had High Voltage warnings all over it. And as for the wall it cut into? That shit was nothing for cattle, more like velociraptors, and what do you want to bet that concrete face fronted a solid twelve or twenty-four inches of solid horizontal stone.

Manny swiveled his head around at her as they passed through and began a descent underground into a tunnel that could have had a "Holland" or "Lincoln" sign tacked on it for all its sturdiness and lighting. The farther down they went, the more that big question that had been plaguing him since he'd first seen her loomed: Why fake her death? Why cause the kind of chaos she had in his life and the lives of the other people she'd worked with at St. Francis? She'd never been cruel, never been a liar, and had no financial problems and nothing to run from.

Now he knew without her saying a word:

U.S. government.

This kind of setup, with this sort of security ... hidden on the outskirts of what was a big-enough city, but nothing so huge as New York, L.A. or Chicago? Had to be the government. Who else could afford this?

And who the hell was this women he was treating?

The tunnel terminated in a parking garage that was standard issue with its pylons and little yellow painted spots, and yet as large as it appeared to be, there were just a couple of nondescript vans with darkened windows and a small bus that also had blackouts for glass.

Before she even had his Porsche in park, a steel door was thrown open and—

One look at the huge guy who stepped out and Manny's head exploded, the pain behind his eyes going so intense, he went limp in the bucket seat, his arms falling to the sides, his face twitching from the agony.

Jane said something to him. A door was opened. Then his own was cracked.

The air that hit him smelled dry and vaguely like earth ... but there was something else. Cologne. A very woody spice that was at once expensive and pleasing, but also something he had a curious urge to get away from.

Manny forced his lids to open. His vision was wonky as hell, but it was amazing what you could pull out of your ass if you had to, and as the face in front of him came into focus, he found himself staring up at the goateed mother-fucker who had ...

On a wave of pain, his eyes rolled back into his head and he nearly threw up.

"You've got to release the memories," he heard Jane said.

There was some conversating at that point, his former colleague's voice mixing with the deep tones of that guy with the tattoos at his temple.

"It's killing him—"

"There's too much risk—"

"How the hell is he going to operate like this?"

There was a long silence. And then all of a sudden, the pain lifted as if it were a veil drawn back, and memories flooded his mind.

*Jane's patient. From back at St. Francis. The man with the goatee and ... the six-chambered heart.*

Manny popped open his eyes and lasered in on that cruel face. "I know you."

The guy had shown up in his office and taken the files on that heart of his.

"You get him out of the car," was the only response from Goatee. "I don't trust myself to touch him."

Hell of a welcome wagon.

As Manny's brain struggled to catch up with everything, at least his feet and legs seemed to work just fine. And after Jane helped him to the vertical, he followed her and the goateed hater into a facility that was as nondescript and clean as any hospital: Corridors were uncluttered, lights were paneled fluorescents on the ceiling, everything smelled like Lysol.

There were also the bubbled fixtures of security cameras at regular intervals, like the building was a monster with many eyes.

While they walked along, Manny knew better than to ask any questions. Well, that and he was so screwed in the membrane, he was pretty fucking sure ambulation was the extent of his capabilities at this point.

Doors. They passed many doors. All of which were closed and no doubt locked.

Yeah, this sure as hell put the "undisclosed location" in "National Security," didn't it.

Jane eventually stopped outside a pair of double flappers. She was nervous, and didn't that make him feel like he had a gun to his head: In the OR, in countless trauma messes, she'd always kept her cool. That had been her trademark.

This was personal, he thought. Somehow, whatever was on the other side hit close to home for her.

"I've got good facilities here," she said, "but not everything. No MRI. Just CAT scans. But the OR should be adequate, and not only can I assist, but I've got an excellent nurse."

Manny took a deep breath, reaching down deep, pulling himself together. Whether it was his years of training and experience, or who he was as a man, he ditched all the baggage and the lingering ow-ow-ow in his head and the strangeness of this descent into 007 land, and got with the program.

First thing on the list? Ditch the pissed-off peanut gallery.

He glanced over his shoulder at Goatee. "You need to back off, my man. I want you out in the hall."

The response he got to that news flash was . . . just fangtastic. The bastard bared a pair of shockingly long canines and growled, natch, like a dog.

"Fine," Jane said, getting in between them. "That's fine. Vishous will wait out here."

*Vishous?* Had he heard that right?

Then again this boy's mama sure hit the nail on the head, assuming the little dental show Manny was getting wasn't just a figment of this situation, but the motherfucker's personality.

But whatever. He had a job to do, and maybe the bastard could go chew on a rawhide or something.

Manny pushed into the examination room—

Oh . . . dear God.

Oh . . . Lord above.

The patient on the table was lying still as water and . . . she was probably the most beautiful anything he'd ever seen. Hair was jet-black and braided into a thick rope that hung free next to her head. Skin was a golden brown, as if she were of Italian descent and had recently been in the sun. Eyes . . . Her eyes were like diamonds, which was to say both colorless and brilliant, with nothing but a dark rim around the iris.

"Manny?"

Jane's voice was right behind him, and yet he felt as if she were miles away. In fact, the whole world was somewhere else, nothing existing except for the stare of his patient as she looked up at him from the table.

It finally happened, he thought. All his life he'd wondered why he'd never fallen in love and now he knew the answer to that. He'd been waiting for this moment, this woman, this time.

*This female is mine,* he thought.

"Are you the healer?" she said in a low voice that stopped his heart, her words gorgeously accented, and also a little surprised.

"Yeah." He wrenched off his sport coat and threw it into a corner, not giving a shit where the thing landed. "That's what I'm here to do."

As he approached her, those stunning icy eyes slicked with tears. "My legs . . . They feel as though they are moving, but they do not."

Phantom pain. Not a surprise if she were paralyzed.

Manny stopped next to her and glanced at her body, which was covered with a sheet. She was tall. Had to be at least six feet. And she was built with sleek power.

This was a soldier, he thought, staring at the strength in her upper arms. This was a fighter.

God, the loss of mobility to someone like her took his breath away. Then again, even if you were a couch potato, life in a wheelchair was a bitch and a half.

He reached out and took her hand, and the instant he made contact, his whole body went wakie-wakie on him, as if she were the socket to his inner plug.

"I'm going to take care of you," he told her as he looked her right in the eye. "I want you to trust me."

She swallowed hard as one crystal tear slipped out to trail down her temple. On instinct, he reached forward with his free hand and caught it—

The growl that percolated up from the doorway broke the spell that had bound him and turned him into a kind of prey. And as he glanced over at Goatee, he felt like snarling right back at the sonofabitch. Which of course made no sense.

Still holding his patient's hand, he barked at Jane, "Get that miserable bastard out of my operating room. And I want to see the goddamn scans. *Now.*"

Even if it killed him, he was going to save this woman.

And as Goatee's eyes flashed with pure hatred, he thought, well, shit, it might just come down to that. . . .

# DARK LOVER

In the shadows of the night in Caldwell, New York, there's a deadly turf war going on between vampires and their slayers. There exists a secret band of brothers like no other-six vampire warriors, defenders of their race. Yet none of them relishes killing more than Wrath, the blind leader of the Black Dagger Brotherhood.

The only purebred vampire left on earth, Wrath has a score to settle with the slayers who murdered his parents centuries ago. But, when one of his most trusted fighters is killed – leaving his half-breed daughter unaware of his existence or her fate – Wrath must usher her into the world of the undead – a world beyond her wildest dreams . . .

978-0-7499-3818-5

# LOVER ETERNAL

Within the brotherhood, Rhage is the vampire with the strongest appetites. He's the best fighter, the quickest to act on his impulses, and the most voracious lover – for inside him burns a ferocious curse cast by the Scribe Virgin. Possessed by this dark side, Rhage fears the times when his inner dragon is unleashed, making him a danger to everyone around him.

Mary Luce, a survivor of many hardships, is unwittingly thrown into the vampire world and reliant on Rhage's protection. With a life-threatening curse of her own, Mary is not looking for love. Her faith in miracles was lost years ago. But when Rhage's intense animal attraction turns into something more emotional, he knows that he must make Mary his alone. And while their enemies close in, Mary fights desperately to gain life eternal with the one she loves . . .

978-0-7499-3819-2

# LOVER AWAKENED

In the shadows of the night in New York, a secret band of brothers exists like no other – six vampire warriors, defenders of their race. Of these, Zsadist is the most terrifying member of the Black Dagger Brotherhood.

A former blood slave, the vampire Zsadist still bears the scars from a past filled with suffering and humiliation. Renowned for his unquenchable fury and sinister deeds, he is a savage feared by humans and vampires alike. Anger is his only companion, and terror is his only passion – until he rescues a beautiful aristocrat from the evil Lessening Society.

Bella is instantly entranced by the seething power Zsadist possesses. But even as their  desire for one another begins to overtake them both, Zsadist's thirst for vengeance against Bella's tormentors drives him to the brink of madness. Now, Bella must help her lover overcome the wounds of his tortured past, and find a future with her.

978-0-7499-3823-9

# LOVER REVEALED

In Caldwell, New York, there's a deadly war raging between vampires and their slayers. Now, an ally of the Black Dagger Brotherhood will face the challenge of his life and the evil of the ages.

Butch O'Neal is a fighter by nature. A hard living, ex-homicide cop, he's the only human ever to be allowed in the inner circle of the Black Dagger Brotherhood. And he wants to go even deeper into the vampire world to engage in the turf war with the lessers. He's got nothing to lose. His heart belongs to a female vampire, an aristocratic beauty who's way out of his league. If he can't have her, then at least he can fight side by side with the Brothers.

Fate curses him with the very thing he wants. When Butch sacrifices himself to save a civilian vampire from the slayers, he falls prey to the darkest force in the war. Left for dead, found by a miracle, the Brotherhood calls on Marissa to bring him back, though even her love may not be enough to save him . . .

978-0-7499-3822-2